WOMEN DESTROY FANTASY! SPECIAL ISSUE

ISSUE 58 • OCTOBER 2014
GUEST EDITED BY CAT RAMBO

FANTASY MAGAZINE: Women Destroy Fantasy! Special Issue   Issue 58, October 2014

Publisher: John Joseph Adams   Guest Editor: Cat Rambo

© 2014 *Fantasy Magazine*, a division of *Lightspeed Magazine*.

ISBN: 978-1501017964

Published by *Fantasy Magazine*.   First edition: October 2014

To learn more about *Fantasy Magazine*, please visit: www.Fantasy-Magazine.com. To learn more about the other Destroy projects, visit www.DestroySF.com.

FANTASY

WOMEN DESTROY FANTASY! SPECIAL ISSUE
ISSUE 58, OCTOBER 2014

FROM THE EDITORS

ORIGINAL SHORT FICTION
edited by Cat Rambo

REPRINT SHORT FICTION
edited by Terri Windling

NOVEL EXCERPT
presented by Tor Books

NONFICTION
edited by Wendy N. Wagner

AUTHOR SPOTLIGHTS

edited by Jude Griffin

MISCELLANY

PREFACE

WENDY N. WAGNER

Welcome to issue fifty-eight of *Fantasy Magazine*!

As you may know, *Fantasy Magazine* ran from 2005 until December 2011, at which point it merged with its sister-magazine, *Lightspeed*. Since that time, *Lightspeed* has been doing its best to uphold the fine tradition established by *Fantasy*, and we like to think it has kept the old girl alive by continuing to publish the same kind of quality fiction *Fantasy* fans had come to love and expect.

Over at *Lightspeed* we were excited to publish our special issue, Women Destroy Science Fiction!, in June, but when our Kickstarter's tremendous success unlocked all of our stretch goals—thus offering us the chance to expand the destruction into fantasy and horror—we knew that the Women Destroy Fantasy! special issue had to be a *Fantasy Magazine* special issue.

For some of us, Women Destroy Fantasy! is a kind of homecoming. Guest Editor Cat Rambo served as co-editor of *Fantasy* from 2007-2011, earning a World Fantasy Award nomination in 2012 for her fine work. I myself spent 2011 as Assistant Editor of the magazine.

It is an honor and a delight to bring *Fantasy Magazine* to you in this special celebration of women writing and editing fantasy short fiction. If you enjoy this issue and would like to learn more about Women Destroy Science Fiction!, Women Destroy Horror!, and, of course, Women Destroy Fantasy!, visit our new website devoted to the Destroy projects at DestroySF.com.

Thank you for reading!

—Wendy N. Wagner
Managing Editor

Editorial, October 2014

Women Destroy Fantasy!
Editors

Cat Rambo,
Guest Editor

Here's the thing. All humans live inside a vast structure made of the flow of power and resources. All around us are the things that have grown to shape and express those flows: conventions and laws and manners and pop culture and highbrow art, architecture, religion, literature… even genre fiction. Everything around and within us is shaped by those flows and reflects the strongest or most immediate. And one aspect of being part of such a structure is that one's position makes it very hard to see the big picture.

Try this experiment. Find a very large piece of art, preferably one you can stand (or sit or crouch) inside of and which you do not know well. Go inside it and from that angle, try to figure out how it will appear from a distance and where you fit in it. Have a friend take a picture of you from fifty feet away. Then compare that image with your mental one. How well do they map to each other? You'll find in most cases there are at least a few distortions, sometimes wild or misleading ones.

Up close, you notice the fine details: scaling on a pillar, the tessellated mosaic underfoot, the graffiti someone's added to an inside wall. From afar, you see the whole, the overall shape, the way it looks in silhouette. Two different views of the same thing.

Multiply that by the immeasurable vantage points afforded us by society, along so many axes: race, class, gender, ethnicity, religion, age, body shape, and on and on. One of those splits (from one angle) is male/female. From another vantage point it's more complicated than that, but we'll get to that in a bit.

• • •

I used to teach a class, Introduction to Women's Studies, back in the early '90s at the second oldest women's studies program in the country: Towson State University, Maryland. The class was one of those intro classes that is a prerequisite for other classes in the major, and as it was explained to me by the department head, Elaine Hedges, it was supposed to give students a good background in the subject.

The problem was that Women's Studies is less a body of knowledge than an approach to knowledge, a way of looking at things. I was a grad student at the time at Johns Hopkins, and I'd applied for the Towson position because I'd been one of the first students to come through Notre Dame's Gender Studies Certificate Program. I'd taken some classes at ND for that certificate, but I'd concentrated on theory and linguistics. While I knew enough to convince Towson I'd make a decent lecturer, I wasn't prepared. I knew little history, for one.

Preparing to teach the intro class was therefore a crash course in everything. I read deeply in the history of the women's suffrage movement in America and England, from before Seneca Falls up until the Nineteenth Amendment and beyond. I read economics, art history, psychology, religion, and more, and tried to assemble a class that would help students get enough new perspective that they might better perceive the structure they'd been living in all their lives, the background radiation, so to speak, that had affected, sometimes literally stunted, how they grew.

I taught, according to my roster book, close to four hundred students while at Towson. With some of them, I was successful. They didn't always like what they saw, but they were able to find a second perspective on the world and learn a little more about it in the process. I'm very proud of many of those students. I remember one evening class full of nursing students which was particularly lively: A student in it confided that she'd named her plants after famous suffragists because of the stories about them I'd told in class.

I loved that she'd loved the stories as much as I had. Teaching is a noble mission, one that lets us try to leave the world a little better, a little saner, a little happier than before we came to it. I loved teaching that class because I was helping people to learn how to question, to analyze, to think better. To see the structure around them. And I wanted them to question that structure because I think it is deeply flawed in a way that is responsible for much human suffering and unhappiness.

Sexism in genre literature has been documented to the point where it seems silly to question its existence. But it is important to remember that a) sometimes one is too close to the heart of the matter to see the overall shape of it and b) sometimes people have a psychic investment in that structure. Indeed, that's part of how that structure survives, by selling itself to you in countless ways on a daily basis.

So what a joy to pick through close to 250 stories and cull the best in order to show you what a structure more welcoming of women's voices might produce. And why these stories, out of a batch filled with so many wonderful pieces?

"The Scrimshaw and the Scream" was the first story that I decided on, and I knew that from the moment I first read it. It talks about the perils of denying the call to create—or even the call to be oneself, as becomes evident. Because it's a heavy, sensory-laden piece, I knew it would require some lighter pieces to balance it out.

I wasn't going to buy a fairytale, but I couldn't resist T. Kingfisher's "The Dryad's Shoes," a clever retelling of Cinderella. It was so sweet and whimsical that it seemed a natural antidote to the much darker piece. After that, I added "Drowning in Sky," another dark and heavy historical piece that I loved for its texture. I rounded it all out with a superhero story, "Making the Cut."

I love superhero stories and I'd specifically posted asking for submissions along those lines, so I got a slew of them. Of them all, "Making the Cut" managed to be light while asking interesting questions about superhero stereotypes.

All of these stories are about women making choices, sometimes right, sometimes wrong, always unexpected. Because that is part of what the world is to me: a continuum, a rainbow, a myriad of choices, rather than the traditional binary that is such an integral part of the structure we inhabit, one that too often both assumes and imposes a monolithic culture on us, one that defines "normal" along strict and limiting lines. As I mentioned earlier, it isn't just about male vs. female but of several different gender identities. A multiple-choice answer, rather than yes/no.

So here you have four stories in which women destroy fantasy, or rather fantasy as it has been shaped in the past. They use fantasy to entertain and to question and to provide a new vista on some pieces of the tradition. They do it beautifully, with stories that will stay with you long after you've finished reading them. They do it with stories that will make you see things in new ways.

And isn't that why we read fantasy in the first place?

• • •

TERRI WINDLING,
REPRINT EDITOR

That women should be writing fantasy seems to me an entirely unremarkable proposition. Women have been a driving force in the fantasy field from its earliest beginnings in tales told by the fireside straight through to the emergence of the fantastic as a distinct literary genre. There are so many important women writers in our field that the hardest part of choosing reprints for this issue was being limited to just four of them. Where on earth does one even start? With the French salon writers of the seventeenth and eighteenth centuries? With the German Romantics one hundred years later? Or perhaps in the 1920s and '30s, with the likes of Hope Mirrlees, Sylvia Townsend Warner, and C.L. Moore? Or with Joanna Russ and the feminist writers of the 1960s and '70s? The mind boggles.

In the end, I chose reprints from the 1980s onward… for that's when the genre coalesced into the fantasy field as we know it today, and as a result, these stories aren't yet as dated as some of the earlier masterworks. Each reprint comes from a writer who has pushed at the boundaries of the genre over many years, and each covers a different part of the terrain: high fantasy (Bull), historical fantasy (Sherman), contemporary fantasy (Emshwiller) and fantasy with diverse mythic/folkloric roots (Hopkinson). Most importantly, each tale subverts the expectations of fantasy, and of "women's writing," in delightfully sly and skillful ways.

Back in the early '80s, when I was starting out, there was a widely circulated complaint that "green girls from Vassar" were ruining the SF/fantasy field—a complaint, I should explain, that was prompted by the sudden influx of women editors and writers into what had been (with a few sterling exceptions) a largely male preserve. Thirty years later, the barriers women face are less overt—but, alas, not gone altogether. I long for the day when we no longer need "women only" issues like this one to draw attention to women's work… but until that day, I feel much the same as Winifred Holtby, writing back in 1922:

"I am a feminist," she said, *"because I dislike everything that feminism implies. I desire an end to the whole business, the demands for equality, the suggestion of sex warfare, the very name feminist. I want to be about the work in which my real interests lie, the writing of novels and so forth. But while inequality exists, while injustice is done and opportunity denied to the great majority of women, I shall have to be a feminist. And I shan't be happy till I get… a society in which there is no respect of persons, either male or female, but a supreme regard for the importance of the human being."*

Indeed.

• • •

WENDY N. WAGNER,
NONFICTION EDITOR/MANAGING EDITOR

Writing about fantasy is hard: It's a hugely broad genre with nebulous boundaries, and any time you make one claim, some work rises up to contradict what you said. Well, writing about women in fantasy is twice as hard. Women writers and illustrators have played incredible roles in our field, but they have also been overshadowed and underrepresented. I'm thrilled with the essays and interviews in this issue. I asked our nonfiction writers for work that would inspire and encourage the women who read and create fantasy; I wanted to look at the history of women working in the field and to shine a light on the work that is shaping the future of the genre. I think our writers succeeded.

We need special issues like this because fantasy is a genre that tends to destroy women—or if not destroy, then de-story. Our tits and asses get to appear on book covers and movie posters, while our names fall off the recommended reading lists. Women have been writing tales of the fantastic for centuries. Women have been painting and designing the images of the genre as long as there has been paint (in fact, an article in the October 2013 issue of *National Geographic* pointed out that close to three-quarters of the handprints in the Lascaux cave paintings belonged to women).

This is just an introduction to the fantastic work of women. Get out there and experience the destruction!

THE SCRIMSHAW
AND THE SCREAM

KATE HALL

Art by K.A. King

The morning after she lost her art, Felicity sat at her speckled mirror, inspecting the glossy, gray-white feathers covering her cheeks and forehead.

She grasped one and plucked, winced as the barbed shaft ripped free, a tiny blood-jewel welling up in its place. The scream, living in her chest so long she could almost ignore it, turned a somersault behind her lungs. She swallowed, twirled the feather between thumb and forefinger, watched greasy greens and blues flicker along the white.

Not only was she turning into a bird, she was turning into a seagull. A dirty, loud seagull. Felicity opened the bottom drawer of her vanity, pulling up short with the feather hovering over the opening. Emptiness hit her like a physical blow, knocking the breath out of her.

Her whole world had been in this drawer until yesterday: her awl, her ivory, her half-finished scrimshaws. Now ribbons, combs and an elaborate silver hand mirror Mother gave her as a betrothal gift littered the polished wood. Felicity scraped her nails along the bottom panel until they caught in a seam. She pulled, and part of the drawer's underside gave way. Nestled in the gap sat her little treasure box, the only thing Mother hadn't taken. Felicity laid the feather next to it and slammed the drawer closed.

A rap at the door jerked her to her feet and she smoothed her hands down her front as Mother swept into the room.

"Of all the days to laze about—Felicity!" Mother's mouth dropped into a horrified 'o' and she grabbed the bedpost for support. "What have you done?" Her hands flew to her own face, pocked with silver scars. Felicity drew herself straight, swallowed the furious words clanging behind her teeth.

"I didn't do it," she said instead. "I just woke up and . . ."

"You did something. You must have." Mother gestured to her face. "How could you disappoint me like this? And after such wonderful news last night. Do you want me to be ashamed?"

"No."

"Then what did you do?" Felicity shook her head and Mother's eyes narrowed. "Lying won't help, my dear. Don't forget what happened to the von Moren girl. Do you want to shame me like she shamed her mother? Tell me what you've done!"

Felicity turned her hands out, but white down tufted between her fingers, so she curled them again. "Nothing. I retired early last night and never left my room, you know that." A fierce ache curled behind her breastbone and she pressed her fist against it, felt it hammer against the skin. Mother grabbed her chin, fingers slipping over the feathers, and grimaced, turning Felicity's head left and right.

"Filthy." She pulled a handkerchief from inside her sleeve and wiped her hand. "It was those hideous carvings, wasn't it? If I find that you've been scraping about with those vulgar bones again—"

"You threw them out before the party." Felicity glanced towards the vanity drawer, pulled her gaze away again. "You threw them all away."

Mother's lips pursed. She twirled her finger. "Let me see you."

Felicity turned an obedient circle. Mother sighed.

"With long sleeves we should be able to hide the worst of them. We have to pluck your face, though. Sit."

"But Mother—"

"Sit!"

Felicity sank back onto the stool, fingers knotted in her lap as Mother tilted her face up, angling it this way and that with frowns creasing her face. She grasped a feather under Felicity's left eye, and hot pain flared as it ripped free. Felicity jerked back. "That hurts!"

"Hold still." Mother seized her chin again, grabbed another feather, the barb buried behind Felicity's ear, and yanked. Tears stung Felicity's eyes and she swallowed another protest.

"You will not disappoint me"—three more feathers fell to the floor, and Mother wiped her hand—"by mooning over those silly"—another feather—"vulgar"—another—"toys!" Felicity could feel blood trickling over her cheeks and down her neck. The holes left by the barbs burned.

"Our only grace," Mother continued, "is that there aren't too many on your face yet. Be dressed and downstairs in an hour; Ernest called on the house this morning to take a walk with you."

She nodded and Mother wiped her hand again, sighed, and left. Felicity turned to her mirror, stiff and breathless, and blinked at her reflection. A pale face stared back, freckled with red like a pox. She opened the drawer and retrieved her treasure box, egg-shaped and small enough to fit in her palm. The rusting hinge squeaked as she pried open the lid, and she pulled out her last scrimshaw.

A year ago, she had bargained for a handful of bone pieces and an old awl from a sailor, in exchange for a length of satin ribbon for his sweetheart. Now only this remained: a piece small and rough, the beginnings of a bird with a bit of rope clenched in its beak etched into the ivory. Her hand ached to hold the awl again, to make the delicate, meticulous strokes from which a beautiful picture could emerge. Her head throbbed at the memory of the loss. *Unfair it was mine it was beautiful not vulgar.* Her hand closed over the scrimshaw, and her fingers itched as feathers rubbed between them.

The scream had done it, surely. It poisoned her, turned her insides ugly. She glanced down at her arms, layered with soft down. She grabbed a handful. Pulled.

• • •

"You are looking very fine today, Felicity," Ernest said, tucking her hand into his elbow. His watery blue eyes peered at her, skittering over the pale pink wounds on her face as if they weren't there, as if they didn't mirror the ones on his own.

"Thank you," Felicity said.

"Did you enjoy our betrothal dinner last night?"

No. "Yes."

He steered them toward the harbor, and Felicity dragged her feet as much as she dared. Wheeling over snapping lines and luffing sails, the seagulls spun and looped, shrieking and hollering, fighting with each other for fish, for space, for the merry hell of it.

"Filthy things, aren't they?" She startled at the sound of his voice, saw him looking up toward the gulls, nose wrinkled with disdain. Sweat trickled down the feathers on the back of her neck, hidden under a stiff lace collar, and she resisted the urge to touch them.

"Yes." She gripped her parasol until her fingers ached.

They stopped at the edge of the harbor, where clean cobbles gave way to mud and filth. Ernest's voice droned in her ear, but it faded as she took in the graceful curves of a small sloop, a brigantine's tall masts. The full harbor teemed with gleaming wood and crisp sails. Her nose stung with the tang of brine and pitch and she filled her lungs, trying to hold it inside.

Two sailors strolled by, one turning a smoothed piece of ivory over and over in his hands. Their faces, sweat-streaked and leathery, had only a few telltale scars. The seafarers never had as many feathers. Perhaps the ocean protected them.

Ernest guided her out of their path. The sailors nodded, and Ernest nodded in return. "Fine work, sailor."

"Thankee, sir. For my sweetheart, this is." The sailor held it out for Ernest to inspect, and she tried to stare without looking. From the ivory emerged the beginnings of a mermaid, all sensuous curves and come-hither smile. Ernest made a sound of approval and the sailors walked on. He pulled on her hand and she took a few hurried half-steps to catch up.

"Something very romantic about a sailor's art," he said. "What did you think of it, my dear?"

She wanted to chase the sailor down, rip it out of his hands, add frothing waves and steep cliffs to the mermaid's empty world. She shrugged and Ernest patted her hand.

"You're right, forgive me. I forget sometimes that the unrefined arts are inappropriate." He flushed and patted her hand again. Felicity placed one foot in front of the other, toes pointing ahead even as every instinct begged her to go back.

They walked a few feet more before Ernest stopped again. Another artist? She followed his gaze and saw not a sailor, but a woman.

She stood in a canary yellow gown, without a parasol, her sun-weathered skin chestnut-colored under a white shawl slung over her elbows like an afterthought. She wore no head covering and black hair, loose-pinned, fell in luxurious, sweaty ringlets around her smooth, unmarked face. The sailor said something and she laughed, head back and teeth gleaming. Felicity's face burned and she angled her parasol lower.

"Has she no shame at all?" Ernest asked, voice hushed. His hand on her arm dampened with sweat, and his fingers trembled. Felicity shook her head, glanced at the woman again. The scabs on her face stung and feathers itched under her gloves, under her dress. She wanted to run. She wanted to throw her parasol at the smiling, shining woman who would have disappointed Mother, but whose face bore no scars. Bile rose in her throat, threatened to choke her.

"She isn't a lady," she said. "My mother will be unhappy if she hears we were watching her."

Ernest shook himself, steadied his hold on her once more. "Of course." He looked down at her and under his bowler hat, she could see a small, brown feather, poking through his hair. "You look quite pale. Let's go back and get you a drink."

He turned her away from the harbor, and glanced over his shoulder until the woman disappeared from view.

They returned home, where Felicity declined the drink, said a short lie-down before dinner would restore her, and hurried upstairs. In her room, she ripped the drawers out of her vanity, spilling their contents on the floor. Balling her fists and taking a deep breath, she knelt and sorted the shiny baubles, ribbon scraps, and sewing pins. She picked up Mother's hand mirror and turned the glass toward her, running one finger over her cheeks. Soon, the marks would pale, look almost normal again. No one would remark on them, just as she didn't remark on theirs, and life would go on.

Maybe she would get lucky and the change would stop here. Maybe she wouldn't turn out like Claudette von Moren.

She pawed through the rest of her contents, found the scrimshaw in its box, and turned it over between her fingers. The scream thundered in her chest, and she placed the scrimshaw on the vanity, pulled her gloves off. Then she plucked handfuls of feathers out of the backs of her hands, between her fingers, up her arms like a butcher plucking a hen.

She would show that bare-headed hussy at the harbor. She would show Mother. She pulled harder, and her shaking, bloody fingers made the feathers slippery and hard to grip.

The whispers said that Claudette had turned into a nightingale for not listening to her parents, and that she sang and sang until she fell over, stiff-legged and open-beaked. That was what happened to people who didn't behave as they should.

"But I do behave as I should," she told her reflection, throwing sodden red clumps onto the vanity. "I don't deserve to turn into a filthy gull. Let it stop here, like it does with everyone else. It stops when people are good, and I'm good."

Not the point, the scream said. *Good was never the point.*

"Be quiet," she said.

• • •

She woke before dawn with more feathers, grey and black-tipped, longer, prickling down her back. Her arms looked scrawny, and her mouth felt stiff, lips waxy and jaundiced.

She spent two hours plucking the feathers, and then peeled the hard layers off her mouth, leaving her teeth stained scarlet. She washed and dressed, and went out into the early lavender morning.

The von Moren house stood at the far end of the green at the center of the neighborhood. Once it had been the epicenter of social events, windows aglow until late in the night. Now it hunkered between its neighbors, heavy shades drawn. Felicity strode over the grass, plucking bits of down that poked through her sleeves. Other people strolled by or read on the benches, faces scabbed and scarred, a few stray feathers clinging to chins and temples. One old man sat regarding a fountain, his hands, withered talons, curled in his lap. A little girl, no more than twelve, sat near her mother, playing with a doll. Red flecks dotted her throat like an elaborate necklace.

Felicity walked faster. She thought of Claudette von Moren, who had opened her first season alongside Felicity. Claudette, who had played the pianoforte like an angel, and for hours at a time, the wildest and most beautiful music anyone had ever heard. Felicity mounted the steps of the house, and dropped the tarnished knocker with an echoing *thud*. A tired butler answered, gave her a strange look, and saw her into the parlor where she used to spend countless autumn evenings, listening to Claudette play or whispering over cards. Now sheets covered the couches and mirrors, and dust motes twirled in the air, settling on the wood tables and sideboard. Claudette's pianoforte sat in the corner, lid closed. Felicity ran a hand over the dull wood, leaving long streaks behind.

I have a scream inside me, Claudette had confided to her the day before she changed. She had peered at Felicity over the rim of her teacup, fresh scabs marring her white forehead, her brilliant green eyes muted and tear-filled. Feathers had poked through her sleeves, feathers that hadn't started growing until her parents barred her from her instrument. *It's gotten so loud, I'm afraid I'll explode. It wants me to play again. I want to play again.*

"Can I help you?" Mrs. von Moren stood in the parlor door, small and bent under her black dress. Russet down grew in clusters over her face, and bright red feathers poked through her unkempt hair and under her sleeves.

"Tell me what she did wrong," Felicity blurted. "I don't want to turn into a bird."

Mrs. von Moren's eyes dimmed. She gripped the lintel with crooked, white fingers. "She disobeyed."

"How? She played so beautifully—"

"It wasn't beautiful." The hand tightened and her mouth tightened with it. "Her music was too intense for a young lady. She wouldn't stop, so we took the pianoforte away." Her bony shoulders lifted, dropped, defeated. "She… she left us two weeks later."

"But did she play again?" Pain warmed her thumb where she tore at the nail, and Felicity jerked her hand back to her side. "Did she play before she… left?"

Mrs. von Moren shook her head, and covered her mouth with one twisted hand. Felicity leaned on the pianoforte for support. Claudette hadn't disobeyed, however she might have wanted to. And still, she had changed.

Felicity half-ran home, skirts tangling around her legs, hurried up the stairs and knocked on Mother's door, knocked and knocked and almost hit the maid on the brow when the door swung open. She pushed past the girl, dismissing her with a wave, and dropped on her knees before Mother, breathless and gasping.

"What am I doing wrong? I've done everything everyone has asked of me, haven't I? I don't listen to my scream. Why am I still changing?" She lifted her face, her hair sticking to her cheeks. Mother pushed it back into its pins.

"Your scream?"

"That's what Claudette called it," she said, voice small. "It wanted her to play, even though her parents didn't want her to. You have one too, don't you?"

Mother nodded, face solemn. "I did."

"How did you stop it?"

Mother sighed. "I stopped listening to it," she said. "I focused on being a good mother, a good wife, until it went away. Oh, at first the change seemed even faster, but it slowed with my effort. It will go away, my darling, if you try hard enough."

"But I have!"

Mother tapped her on the nose. "Then why are you still changing?"

Back in her room, she dug up the scrimshaw and held it in her palm.

Before the betrothal party, Mother had taken all of them away, and Felicity had cried and promised never to engage in such a crude, violent art again. Ladies painted pretty watercolors and wielded sewing needles; they didn't wrestle animal bone and scratch it with sharp awls. But she had saved just one, this one, small enough to hide in her hand as Mother stormed around the room and shouted.

She hadn't ignored her scream. And now this had happened.

Felicity took the piece to the harbor, secreted inside her glove, its warm weight against her hand as she scurried down the boulevard. Silence met her at the shipyards; few people worked on a Sunday. She threaded her way through crates and pallets stacked high with sacks and barrels. She reached the water's edge and pulled off her glove, held the scrimshaw up. Sunlight gleamed through the tiny hole she had once painstakingly bored through the ivory. She stretched her arm out over the dark water.

"What happened to you?"

Felicity jumped, feet slipping on the rotted wood. A long-fingered hand clamped down on her upper arm, pulled her away from the water, and the smell of tropical fruit and vanilla suffused the air, warm and velvety. When Felicity regained her footing she saw the woman, arms crossed and a look of frank curiosity on her face. She wore sky blue today, her head still uncovered, her skin even more golden up close.

"You're turning into a bird." Her deep voice tolled like a bell. "What happened?"

Acid surged into her mouth and Felicity clapped a hand over it. The woman stepped closer; Felicity stepped back. The woman reached out again, warm hand on Felicity's elbow to steady her, keep her from falling into the harbor. The heady perfume made Felicity's mouth water and she swallowed the burning away.

"You're all like this here." The woman shook her head. "What is this place, that it turns broken people into birds?"

"We aren't broken," Felicity said through her fingers. "I listened to my scream. If I get rid of this"—she held up the scrimshaw—"I'll be fine."

The grip on her elbow tightened and the woman pried the scrimshaw out of Felicity's hand. Sunshine limned the etchings in gold.

"But this isn't bad," the woman said. "It's beautiful."

"If you don't try hard enough, you turn into a bird." Felicity's words ran together and she snatched the scrimshaw back. "I was wrong to keep it, I should have thrown it out with the rest." She gulped for air and tried to pull away, but the woman held on. Dark eyes raked over her wounds, the straggling feathers she hadn't been able to remove, the look like hot needles. The woman dropped Felicity's elbow and stepped back, taking the delicious scents with her, leaving nothing but salt and wood in her wake.

"You think if you silence yourself, the changes stop?" She raised an eyebrow, and Felicity bristled as her voice acquired a mocking lilt. "It would seem most of you have stopped listening, and I still see feathers everywhere."

"You don't know what you're talking about," Felicity snapped. "You're not from here."

"No," the woman agreed. "I am not." She ran a finger down the side of

Felicity's face, leaving a warm, tingling trail. "Hold onto your art," she said, serious now. "Hold it tightly. Your forced goodness isn't saving any of you, but your art might."

Heat flushed through Felicity's body, making her limbs burn and her vision blur. The scream sang, *she's right she's right she's right*, until it drowned out all her other thoughts and Felicity inched away, shaking her head.

A flash of black at the far end of the harbor froze her where she stood. Ernest picked his way through the maze, eyes scanning the harbor.

He would see her. He would see her with this strange woman and be disappointed, so disappointed. He wouldn't want to marry her anymore. He would tell Mother and Mother would be disappointed. She had to throw away the scrimshaw and leave, quickly. She could feel more feathers growing, longer and faster. Her fingers stiffened, numb, and the scrimshaw slipped through them. She locked eyes with the woman, then gathered her skirts, turned and ran.

Not until late that night did she allow herself to believe Ernest hadn't seen her at the harbor. She had gotten rid of the scrimshaw bird, and now the change would stop. She stood naked before her mirror and pulled feathers out one by one. Relief, comforting as a warm bath, suffused her with every patch of flesh the feathers revealed. She wouldn't be the filthy, loud seagull, but Felicity the girl, who made people proud. She smiled at her reflection. For the first time in years, the scream didn't respond.

• • •

For the next two weeks, she threw herself into planning her wedding. She visited the dressmaker with Mother, touched silks and velvet, and stood before a full-length mirror in her tight corset as a seamstress took her measurements and murmured what beautiful posture she had. Mother's proud smile over her shoulder as she stood, arms outstretched like an elegant doll, brimmed her with relief.

The scream said nothing. The feathers still grew, but fewer and further between. Mother assured her that this might persist, but the worst had passed. She soothed Felicity's face with cool compresses and a gentle kiss on her brow.

Only once, as she walked past the harbor, she felt the familiar ache in her chest, the buzz in her head. She avoided the harbor after that, and worked even harder to fill the ship-shaped hole its absence left in her day. But time always found her empty-handed after a while, and she passed it sitting in the drawing room window, staring in the direction of the distant masts.

She had just settled on the window seat when Ernest arrived, flushed and disheveled. He declined a chair, and paced back and forth in front of the fireplace. Wrinkles curled his clothes, and mud caked the bottom of his trousers, streaked his shoes. Short brown feathers stubbled his jaw and the sides of his face. He stopped, mopped his brow.

"I'm sorry," he said, "but I must break off our betrothal."

For a moment, it felt as if the floor fell away, leaving her unmoored and breathless. Inside her, the scream stirred.

"What do you mean?"

"I mean I—we—I made a mistake." He paced again, four steps left, turn, four steps right, turn. "I have great affection for you, please don't doubt that. You are a charming woman and very attractive."

"Then what's the matter?" The scream climbed her ribs like a ladder, heading toward her throat.

"I'm in love." Ernest dropped onto an ottoman, head hanging. He appeared stunned by the declaration, rubbing his neck with one shaking hand. "It's horrible, like my body and mind are no longer mine."

Did the window seat roll like a ship's deck? No, only Felicity, weaving in her seat. He saw her after all, that day at the harbor. She had disappointed him but he wanted to be gallant, place the blame on himself. She steadied herself. "Is this because you saw me at the harbor? I haven't been there since, I swear. You'll have no cause to be ashamed of me—"

"Harbor? What—no, Felicity, listen." He stood, sat, stood again, sat and grabbed her hand between both of his. "You are sweet, very sweet, and very good. But… this woman, she's intoxicating." He sucked in a breath and shook his head, eyes distant and fevered. "She's like nothing I've ever seen before. Please don't think you did something. You did nothing."

He stood, mopped his face again, and nodded to her. His hand rested on the doorknob, and he looked desperate to escape. "I'm sorry. I'll show myself out. Please don't think too ill of me, if you can."

She remained on the seat even after the heavy front door closed, the weight of his words pressing down on her. *You did nothing.* Her wedding dress, half-finished, wouldn't be worn. *You did nothing.* Mother would be heartbroken, so disappointed in the daughter who let a fine husband slip through her fingers. *You did nothing.* Hadn't she ignored her scream until it went silent? Hadn't she tried enough? *You did nothing.*

"What else was I supposed to do?" Her voice bounced around the drawing room, rough-edged and ugly. Her whole body prickled, invisible insects crawling over her skin. She lurched to her feet, raced from the drawing room and up the stairs. In the safety of her room, she approached the mirror and swallowed a wail.

Feathers grew, fast, thick and silver-white over every inch of available skin. They popped out like spring seedlings, unfurling and blanketing her. Her mouth and nose puckered, and the skin around them tightened like she had been burned by a hot iron. She tried to touch it, but her fingers found only long feathers and soft down. She scrabbled at the feathers on her arms, trying again and again to pull them out, but her hands wouldn't grasp. They teemed, too many, and her fingers disappeared. She tried to tear them out with her shrinking teeth, but they slid through. Her face and hair vanished as if under snow.

Tears blurred her vision as she sank onto her stool, only to leap forward when she noticed her eyes. Her eyes, the pupils widening, eyelashes falling out, her eyes were turning yellow.

Yellow, like the strange woman's dress.

• • •

She didn't grab her parasol, or her gloves. She just ran, down the stairs, out the door, and down the street, feathers rustling in the afternoon breeze. Her feet felt too small in her shoes and she stumbled, tripped, landing on the hard cobbles and tearing the grey silk, scraping her hands and knees. She clambered back to her feet, kicked off the shoes, kept going. A red ache sang behind her eyes, inside her nose and throat, under her tongue and deep in her chest. She dashed across the harbor, dodging unaware sailors and merchants left and right, searching, searching for the telltale glimpse of dark hair and bright color.

She found them in the purple shadow of a full-rigged tall ship, Ernest's face beseeching, the woman's apologetic and remote. She played with a pendant around her neck and her yellow dress blazed in the gloom. Felicity ran toward them both and the woman's eyes widened.

She would open her mouth, unleash the scream. They had been wrong, they had all been wrong, it had tried to protect them, not change them. Not listening to it had sparked the change, and letting it howl inside only made the change faster. She would shout at Ernest, didn't he see that his new love had woken his up, and that stifling it propelled him closer to animal than man? Her shouts would bounce off the tall ship's hull, echoing and sending the words skyward. The scream would stretch, cramped from so many years trapped, and soar through the air, whoop and twirl, while she raved on the ground.

And then, breath and voice ragged, she would tell the woman, the strange woman, who hadn't turned into a bird, to run.

"You were right. You were right the whole time. Claudette lost her music. I lost my art. Run away before you lose yourself and change too."

And then, spent, she would collapse in a flurry of molting feathers, chest heaving and whole body aching, but lighter than she had ever been before.

• • •

She would have said those things, had she a voice. But she didn't.

The scream ripped out of her lungs but her tongue, hard and pointed, clicked inside her beak and her voice wouldn't, couldn't form words. She plummeted in a tangle of wings and garments, skidded along the cobbles, and thrashed inside a monstrous whale-boned cage. She screeched, tiny lungs pressing against her feathered breast, but no words came.

Hands plunged through the suffocating silk folds, grabbed her around the neck, under her gnarled, webbed feet, and lifted her as though she weighed nothing. A pair of wide eyes regarded her, a red mouth drawn into a grim, sad line. The woman cradled Felicity in her wide, long-fingered hands. Next to her, Ernest's eyes darted to and fro, looking everywhere but at the pile of discarded garments.

"I think we should be away," he said, fidgeting with his walking stick. The woman turned, Felicity still in hand, and her body vibrated with her voice.

"You saw nothing?" Incredulity laced her words. Ernest looked first at her face, then at Felicity. He shook his head.

"No. No. There is nothing to see. Drop that thing, you don't know how filthy those creatures are."

The woman drew back, her warm hand pressing Felicity into the soft wool shawl. "A woman turned into a bird right in front of you, and yet you see nothing?"

The brown feathers stood out on Ernest's pale face and he swallowed. "Nothing." His voice quavered.

"I see," the woman said, voice clipped. "Good day, sir." She spun on her heel, and colors whipped a frenzied dance around Felicity. Her wings strained against their confines, desperate to take her high, away, far away from the noise, the horror of people stepping around her unnoticed clothes. The woman bore her through the crowds, and when Felicity cocked her eye upwards, she could only see the lifted chin, the regal slope of a neck. Men parted ways and the woman strode through them, looking neither left nor right. They stared, but their gazes skittered over Felicity, not seeing her. They saw a seagull.

Felicity fluffed her feathers and cried out again, tried to call for Ernest, Mother, tried to call out her own name. A seagull's raucous shouts left her mouth, each one more frustrated than the last.

The woman stopped at the edge of the pier, and Felicity felt herself lowered onto a splintered dock pole. She fluttered her wings and wobbled, webbed feet dancing back and forth to gain purchase. The woman crouched over her, sticky tears coating her tanned cheeks. A familiar scrimshaw swung from her neck by a leather thong: a bird, with rope in its beak. Whose was it?

"I heard you," the woman said, stroking Felicity's feathers. "I won't lose myself. I'm so sorry. I heard you."

The scream died, taking Felicity with it.

The seagull shivered, ruffled its feathers. The woman's mouth kept moving, kept making sounds, but the seagull's eye drew to the water's silver sheen, the sparkle of scales flashing beneath. Hunger filled the emptiness inside it, and the seagull spread its wings, dropped off the pier, and looped over the water, its loud voice joining the shrieks of a hundred others.

～

Kate Hall is a speculative fiction writer and graduate of the 2013 Odyssey Writing Workshop. Her fiction has appeared in *Penumbra eMagazine*, and *Inscription*. Growing up, she lived in Ohio, St. John's Newfoundland, Chicago, and Amsterdam: all places which informed her writing. She now lives in Minneapolis with her husband, a horde of pets named after various deities, cupboards full of tea, and a great many books (because there is no such thing as too many books. Or too much tea).

MAKING THE CUT

H.E. ROULO

I got lost flying over South Asia. Pilots could check their instruments; I didn't even have a *plane*. Sighing, I banked my body to catch a glimpse of the land below, and zeroed in on the village I'd left so quickly this morning.

Hovering, I yanked on a blue shalwar kameez, which felt like a pair of oversized pajamas compared to my usual trim bodysuit. I swooped a scarf around my head, fussing with the folds. Even when battling criminals, I took pride in my appearance. I was a role model. And shapeshifters wore faces the way other people chose outfits. A bad picture in the papers meant I hadn't given my appearance enough thought. But if these clothes could mollify local religious views, then it exceeded my mere superpowers, because I must see Aisha.

I sank through night shadows to the road. Their store stood boarded up for the night. In the upstairs living quarters, regular breathing indicated the rest of the family slept. Rumors maintained Aisha lived a solitary life within her family's home. More importantly, she possessed superpowers.

I tried the back door, unsurprised to find it locked. Focusing, I thinned my substance and slipped between door and jamb. The top half of my body made it through but from the ribcage down I remained standing outside. Perhaps my unborn baby couldn't shapeshift, or perhaps my body needed to keep the organs and muscles supporting the baby undisturbed, but I couldn't sculpt my midsection anymore. Holding my breath, since my lungs remained compressed between wall and door, I slid my finger into the inner knob like a key. The lock clicked open. I slipped inside and gasped myself back into normal human dimensions.

In a narrow chamber, like a hallway, a woman draped in a black burka sat on a stool. Before her lay mounds of colored fabric on a workbench made from a pair of two-by-fours pressed against the wall beneath a small window.

She ran her finger along a strip of rust-colored fabric. Bare from nail to knuckle, the rest of her hid within cloth that ran from a small cap on top of her head to her hips. Another all-encompassing layer flowed to her ankles. As her finger lifted, shining black beads settled into place. The woman, who must be Aisha, lifted the reddish fabric and shook it. Beads dangled in tiny arcs from the shawl. She made a sound of satisfaction.

"Pretty," I said.

Aisha turned on her stool and pulled her hands beneath the weight of black fabric.

"I thought you might return." She straightened the burka's edge, as if indicating she'd worn it inside the house in preparation for my arrival.

Since translating languages was another of my many kickass powers, I understood her.

"I didn't mean to upset your family." I said

When I'd dropped onto the street this morning, Aisha's people had scolded me. *Me*, a superhero! I pinched the shoulder of my shalwar kameez to show I'd covered up.

I said, "I needed to see you."

"I do not speak with anyone but my family."

"I know, but—"

"They only wish to protect me," Aisha interrupted, but her voice was soft. A gleam hinted at eyes hidden within the burka's eyehole. "I… I have your trading card. You are Vixen."

She slid off her stool and bent beneath the edge of the table, rustling through a roll of bedding.

I did a double-take toward my chest, checking for the emblem on my bodysuit before I remembered it was covered in layers of blue fabric. I puffed my cheeks out with disgust.

I'm too paranoid I'll forget which identity I'm wearing.

I flipped flowing red hair over my shoulder and laughed, giving the little chest shake I'd practiced in the mirror, like Vixen always did.

Aisha spread the cards along the edge of her workbench. She pointed at candid shots of each superhero. As she slid a finger over muscled bodies covered in skin-tight outfits, she quoted their powers. Each familiar face added a weight of empty sadness inside me. At the end of the row, she'd unknowingly placed my favorite shot of my husband. My heart ached.

And I didn't need to see pictures of myself. I'd chosen each curve and dimple with excruciating care.

Clearing my throat, I covered the cards with my forearm to interrupt Aisha's recitation of catch phrases.

"We'd like you to join our ranks. You'll use your powers to make the world better."

She laughed violently. I stepped back, nonplussed. I'd saved people in dire situations, even visited Camp 14 in North Korea where children lived their entire lives imprisoned, but her laugh was the most hopeless I'd ever heard.

Aisha slapped my hand aside. "You see these girls? They are all alike—perfect. They fly. They have round eyes, straight hair, and clear skin. I am not one of them."

My breath whooshed out as if punched from my body. I pressed between Aisha and the cards, afraid they'd reveal my secrets. But no one looked beyond the costumes. My breathing calmed, though my teeth chattered. My secret identity would stay hidden, even with the truth laid out like this.

"You don't need to look like this to be a hero. It is your strength we need."

"I have no strength," Aisha sounded bewildered. "I cut cloth and string beads."

"Oh, no!" I didn't want to frighten her with my enthusiasm, but she had it wrong. "That's all you see yourself able to do! Women who develop powers aren't stepping forward and that must change. There are so many opportunities for—"

"Not for me."

"But—"

"I will live my life in this room, dependent on others. It is all I have left."

I rolled my eyes. Arguments rushed to my tongue, overriding caution. I had plenty to say about the obligations of power.

Aisha touched my elbow. Beneath the burka's folded edge her golden wrist trembled.

My anger evaporated. "I don't understand."

Squaring herself, Aisha lifted her burka. Half her face looked boiled and put on wet. Strangely pale skin oozed smoothly, the result of burns and scarring. I struggled for a blank expression.

Rather than look at me, Aisha folded her burka and set it beside her. "When I was fifteen my cousin asked to marry me. My father refused him, because I was too young. But when I went to get water a few days later, two of my cousins splashed my face with acid, and blinded me in one eye." She angled her face so the dead white eye could not be missed. "Perhaps I would be cast as a supervillain. Never a hero.

"Despite my disgrace, my father gave up his practice and moved us. My parents let me live here. Without someone to take care of me, I would starve and not be able to feed myself even by selling my body. Who wants a woman with a face like this? When they took my beauty, they took my heart and my voice."

I blinked back tears, sick. Such injustice should make me angry, not teary. The situation sounded unreal except her scarred visage gazed at me from a pace away. Worse than the violence to her face was what her words said about her inner workings.

"It isn't your fault. You are not *gone* because of what was done to you." I tried to imagine why, hidden in her parents' house, she'd bartered trinkets to neighborhood children for copies of superhero trading cards.

Her healthy skin flushed. "You are a superhero. Can you make me beautiful again?"

Of course. I, who could change even the curve of my eyelashes. Injustice silenced me. I shook my head.

A tear trickled from Aisha's brown eye. She pulled her burka back into place and retreated to scraps of fabric and cheap beading, slumping on the stool.

I never expected this. I'd caused this woman more suffering. As a superhero, it went against everything I fought for. I'd never questioned why Aisha hid. Even if I had, I'd never have conceived of something so awful.

"Please leave."

I hesitated.

"Do my wishes mean nothing, just because you are stronger than me?" Sensing my resistance, she added, "Can you remember what it is to be powerless?"

Apologizing, I slipped from the room. The doorknob to the back door of the mud room rattled in my sweaty grip. Locked, of course. Aisha couldn't leave, not that she would allow herself to want to.

Cursing in English, I thinned a finger to make a key and slipped out the door, struggling to hold myself together. The headscarf snarled around my shoulders like a deadly snake. I shook free and stomped it flat on the doorstep. The shalwar kameez tore beneath my clutching fingers, leaving me free. Quivering, I shot into the welcoming sky. There had to be help somewhere else.

And I believed it, as long as I ignored the weight in my belly that said I'd be back.

• • •

The small village hadn't changed over the last four months. Dogs barked. Someone spoke on a cell phone a few streets over. The moon wasn't out, and alleys hung with shadows. The pregnancy had progressed so far I could no longer shape-change from neck to knees. Fortunately, I could still fly.

I eased to the window above Aisha's workbench and tapped a pane. Swirling color signaled movement behind the warped glass. Since I knew she couldn't open the back door, I slipped to the front of the building and peered around the corner wearing Vixen's face, even if I couldn't wear her body. Unlike last visit, I was thankful for the excuse to dress in layers of fabric instead of my bodysuit.

Aisha waved me in, looking fearful. "Why have you come back? My family will hear!"

Keeping to the shadows, I drifted after her. I'd spent months searching for help but found only three other Supers. One had been a baby, one senile, and the last wasn't trustworthy. He'd had such a criminal mind I couldn't bring myself to train him. I pressed a thumb against the bridge of my nose, wondering if he'd join the ranks of supervillains.

A pang shot through my abdomen, compressing muscles and stealing breath. I'd hoped my uneven contractions would slow or stop; each pain heightened my urgency.

Aisha gravitated to the stool in her narrow workroom, but I lingered outside the doorway. Strips of fabric hung from every surface, embroidered and beaded in a cheerful burst of energy reminiscent of a circus tent. I pressed a hand to the doorframe, belly outside her view, panting for breath.

"Have you reconsidered?"

Aisha pulled off her burka, reminding us both of the savage scars on the left side of her face. "There is no such thing as a half-blind superhero."

"This is my fault," I admitted.

My teeth started to chatter, the way they had the moment Aisha pointed to the girls on the cards, but I hadn't confessed my mistakes. I had let her down, and it was time to face up to it. "Do you still have those cards?"

Aisha dragged herself off the stool, pulling forth the cards. Seeing she hadn't thrown them out, as I'd feared, buoyed my spirit.

I waddled into the room. When she spied my stomach, Aisha muffled a gasp.

I took the cards and stacked the men, leaving the women lined up. "It is my fault you don't see yourself in them. Look—you still have one good eye and that's all anyone needs to see what I've done."

She watched me, not the cards, sensing my distress.

I placed my hand over each card, covering masks and colored outfits to reveal facial features that were just variations on a theme, shuffled like a child's three-piece flip book of separate mouths, eyes, and noses.

Aisha straightened, gulping. "They're all you."

"I was wrong to choose to be tall, and white, and young. Even I'm not what I tried to be, it just seemed more heroic. I'm sorry I bought into that. I'm not that ideal either. I'm like her, Quijin." My blunt nail pointed to the first superhero. Short and Asian, though from the very beginning I'd enhanced my bust and added big round eyes.

"She punishes the wicked." Aisha recited. "She is the Chinese unicorn."

"All me." I pointed from one to the next. "But I need help. I was able to split myself, for short times. I'd limit myself to a few powers and give myself another name and shape. I let the world think there were many superwomen when there was only me. The guys formed the League, but they've left on a mission while I hold down the fort. I can't do it by myself anymore."

Aisha shook her head. "My powers are small, like me."

"You haven't tried to be big! You cut without scissors, make holes without needles, string wire and bend them closed with your mind. Can you weld them shut? You have many gifts."

"I'm not a superhero."

"None of us are, until we choose to be. Women with powers are out there but they've kept quiet. I wanted the world to think there were more of us. But if I made other women think they can't be superheroes because they must fly like I do, or look like I tried to look… then I'm part of a grave injustice… and. . . ."

I hissed, muscles involuntarily clenching. "Can we talk about this another time? I'm here because *I* need your help. It's time to deliver this baby and I'm scared."

A labor pang rippled through my lower half, not ending like the others but increasing in waves. "The father was a Super, too, but from another world. He says we'll have a son. I don't know what kind of baby it'll be—or if it'll even be human, but I want him and he probably can't get out of me… I just don't expect it to be a normal birth!" I gritted my teeth over a scream and gripped the workbench.

Aisha shied away. "You should go to a hospital!"

"I did. They couldn't see or hear through me… They were useless!"

The workbench splintered beneath my grip. Trading cards tipped off the shattered tabletop and fluttered to the ground.

Aisha dragged her pallet into the open and helped me onto it. "I'll get my father."

"No!" I gripped her arm, careful not to rip it from her socket.

"He is a doctor." Aisha pulled away.

I panted, imagining delivering my baby inside this small hallway. For weeks, vivid dreams of alien births and demon spawn had scared me awake, praying they were imagination and not intuition.

The older man who returned with Aisha moved me into a seated position and his daughter supported my back. He checked my progress and urged me to push. The baby didn't budge. Despite being a shapeshifter, I was no longer stretchy on the inside. Quite the reverse, I was rigid.

I might not make it. Always invulnerable to outside threats, I found the thought shocking.

"If the baby survives and I don't, you must protect him until his dad returns,"

I said.

"I?" Her hand fluttered to the left side of her face, which even now, she kept turned away from me.

"Aisha, what happened to the men who attacked you?" During our meeting, I'd felt ignorant. But since then I'd done my research. I already knew the answer. "Please, just answer."

"My father was the doctor in the village, and important. He insisted they be arrested. They were found guilty."

"And sentenced to have acid put in their eyes. To suffer as you did." I concentrated on my breathing, trying to hold the pain back long enough to hear Aisha's answer.

"But when the day came, I stopped it, because no one should suffer as I did."

Another pang rose by degrees. I gritted my teeth, turning my prepared speech into just a few guttural words. "You were always a hero." Then the scream took over.

Time passed in a horrible stream of rising and falling agony.

Aisha's father said, "I fear the baby is too large. There is no progress."

Aisha held my hand. "He will cut the baby out."

I suffered too much to argue with any plan that might end my pain. "He can try."

The doctor brought out a kit of shiny instruments. He angled a blade toward my beached-whale, bared stomach. Social conventions, whatever they might have been, no longer applied and my shalwar kameez resided somewhere around my armpits.

Aisha's sweaty face nestled beside mine as she eased me back. Her cheek pressed mine. She'd apparently forgotten about her scars as she helped.

Lying flat, I turned my head away from the blade hovering over my belly. Trading cards scattered on the floor seemed to mock me with the perfect forms I'd created. Worse, they highlighted the sad reality of life as a woman that not even a superhero could escape—biology. Whether cancer, a splash of acid, or a difficult birth, bodies could derail the most carefully laid plans. But I was more than a physical body, powers, or a womanly shape. I claimed to have courage, when things were going my way. Now I had to prove it.

Metal clattered as Aisha's father dropped a bent tool and reached into his bag for another blade. I exhaled my fears, and watched the last scalpel twist uselessly against the steep curve of my abdomen.

I licked my dry lips. "Aisha must do it."

Aisha blanched. Her cloudy eye flickered in time with her good one, as if seeking a path of escape.

Her father lifted the bent blade but didn't offer it to his daughter. He studied her. "I remember how we worried after the attack. We gathered everything sharp while you were in the hospital and kept them from you."

"You would not even give me a needle so I might embroider."

They shared a long look. He opened his hand, urging her to take the bent scalpel. It slid into her shaking grip.

Aisha fingered the blade. "You were right to do it. I would have harmed myself. But my powers developed so I might work with fabric again, contribute to our shop, and lessen the burden of my presence."

She grimaced at the dull blade and said to her father, "This will not work any better for me than for you. Perhaps if I were to think of her as fabric? Can I part her and sew her as if she were cloth?"

Their discussion fragmented as another pang swept through me. "… have never tried anything but cloth… what if she comes apart, but my power is not to bring her together?… skin is nothing like beads and embroidery… kill her and blame yourself? Better to do nothing and let nature take its course… Inshallah."

The heaviness of my child pressed my hips painfully into the thin mat. My muscles clenched once more in pointless effort to push. The child would not budge. "Save him."

Aisha moved from my sight. Warm hands slid over the taut skin of my swollen stomach. My belly parted like the papery skin of a lychee fruit. Searing pain jolted through me and I screamed.

Aisha gagged. The girl's father worked quickly, then instructed her to seal the layers.

At the thin cry, my body relaxed of its own accord, as if whatever came next no longer mattered. Aisha smoothed a hand along my stomach. Pain dissolved. I sagged with relief. Across the room, Aisha's father worked over the baby, cooing.

"It's done." Aisha sounded amazed.

"*You* did it," I said.

Aisha's father wrapped the baby in blankets and handed the large infant to me, grinning. "A boy."

Smiling, I heaved onto my side, too tired to do more than cuddle my son. My eyes wanted to drift shut, but I resisted the urge. "Aisha, thank you. Without you—"

Once again the girl cut me off, as had happened so often before, and my heart sank until her words registered. "I'll do it. Teach me to use all my gifts. You have given me back what I had lost."

"I did?" I smiled in muzzy wonder. "Your heart and your voice?"

"My worth."

You never lost that, Aisha. You only thought you did.

But that argument could wait. I would rest, and when I woke in the morning I would train my maternity leave replacement.

~

H.E. Roulo is a Pacific Northwest author of fantasy, science fiction, and horror. Her stories have appeared in over a dozen magazines, anthologies, and podcasts. In 2009 her science fiction podcast novel *Fractured Horizon* was a Parsec Award Finalist and she received the Wicked Women Writers award from HorrorAddicts.net. Recent publications include *Nature* and *InfectiveInk*. The first book in her *Apocalypse Masters* series will be available in 2015. Find out more @hroulo, facebook.com/heroulo, or heroulo.com.

THE DRYAD'S SHOE

T. KINGFISHER

Art by Tara Larsen Chang

Author's Note: Tufted titmice are exclusively North American birds. The geography of Hannah's country is of questionable archetype.

Once upon a time, in a land near and far away, there was a girl whose mother died when she was young.

Her mother had been merry and loving and devoted, but these things were no proof against fever. She died and was buried in a grave at the edge of the forest, past the garden gate.

In the way of young children, the girl (who was named Hannah) mourned for her mother and then forgot her. She visited the grave dutifully with her father, but her attention strayed more and more often to the garden fence, to the tall poles of beans and the thin green tentacles of the onions.

She loved the garden, which her mother had tended, and which was now under the care of an old man from the village. He showed her how to chit out fat nasturtium seeds and the importance of soaking peas before planting, how to prepare a bed with well-rotted leaves and break up the soil so that the plants could slip their slender roots inside it. He showed her how to keep a hive of bees without being stung too often—for a beehive was, in that time, considered a vital part of any garden—and when she *did* get stung, the gardener put dock leaves on it and patted her shoulder until the sniffles went away.

It was perhaps not a normal occupation for a young lady of moderate birth, but Hannah's father had little to say about it. He had little to say about anything since his wife had died. Hannah was ten years old before she realized that her friend's name was not simply "the Gardener," because her father never spoke to him.

The garden kept them well fed and Hannah was very proud on the days when the cook used *her* beets and *her* beans and *her* cucumbers to feed the household.

On her eleventh birthday, a bird flew down and landed atop a beanpole in front of her. The bird was gray above and white below, with a fine dark eye, no different than the other birds that flocked to the garden in the morning.

"Woe!" cried the bird. "Woe, child, what a state you've come to!"

Your mother's dead,
Your hands are dirty,
Your father's away—

Hannah picked up a clod of dirt and tossed it underhand at the bird, who dove out of the way.

It eyed her balefully, then settled back atop the beanpole, smoothing down its feathers.

"That wasn't very nice," said the bird.

"You started it," said Hannah. "It's not very polite to go around reminding people that their mothers are dead. And my hands are dirty because I've been thinning carrots, thank you *very* much."

The bird had the grace to look ashamed of itself. "It's the magic," it said. "It, um, comes over you. No offense was intended."

Hannah dusted off her hands. "I thought you might be magic," she said, "because you're talking, and birds don't, generally. But then I thought maybe you were a parrot, and I've heard that parrots can talk."

"I'm not a parrot," sighed the bird. "Don't I wish! Parrots are gloriously colored and they live halfway to forever. No, I'm only an enchanted titmouse, I'm afraid."

"I'm sure you're as good as any parrot," said Hannah, who was basically tenderhearted toward animals when they weren't insulting her.

The titmouse preened a little. "Well," he said (Hannah was nearly sure that it was a he) "I *have* been enchanted. It's a great honor, if you're a bird."

"Who enchanted you?"

The titmouse stood on one foot and waved his other one toward the garden gate. "A mother's love," he said. "Also the tree just behind the grave, which is inhabited by a particularly sentimental dryad."

"Can you get seeds from a dryad tree?" asked Hannah, with professional interest.

"No," said the titmouse shortly. "They get very annoyed if you ask. It's very personal for them."

"Oh, well." Hannah sat down on the edge of one of the beds. "What's it like to be enchanted?"

"It's marvelous," said the titmouse. "You're very focused all the time when you're a bird, you know. Here's a seed, there's a seed, this is my seed, give me back my seed." He fluffed up his feathers. "But when you're enchanted, all of a sudden you can see everything. Hello, independent cognition! It's a transcendent experience. Pity it doesn't last long."

Hannah had understood perhaps one word in three of that, but said politely, "It doesn't last?"

"No," said the bird sadly. "Only until my message is delivered. Would you mind? It's very important to the dryad."

"All right," said Hannah. "But no more making fun of my hands or talking about my mother."

"Mmm," said the bird.

"And no poetry!"

The bird lowered his crest a little. "Fine…fine…"

He gazed at the sky. Hannah went back to thinning carrots.

"All right," said the bird finally. "How's this? Your father's about to bring home a new wife."

"Yes?"

The titmouse paused, nonplussed. "You don't seem bothered."

"Well, it's not like *I* have to marry her. And the cook says it's about time he remarried and it does nobody good to keep moping about."

"Mmm," said the bird again. "You may find, I expect, that it's a little more tricky than that. Humans stay in the nest an awfully long time. But anyway. New wife, woe is you—she'll be unkind and treat you poorly."

Hannah scowled. "I'll put nettles in her bed."

"I can see," said the bird gravely, "that you are not without defenses. But should she treat you too abominably, you must go to the tree that grows behind your mother's grave and shed three tears and say—oh, this bit's poetry."

Hannah sighed. "All right, if you must."

The titmouse fluffed out his breast and sang:

O chestnut tree, chestnut tree
Shake down what I need to me.

Hannah gazed fixedly at the carrot seedlings.

"Dryads," said the titmouse apologetically. "They mean well, the poor dears, but they think if it's got a rhyme, it's high art."

"Well," said Hannah. "Thank you for the warning. I guess that will come in handy…"

"Glad to help," said the bird. "I'm sure we'll speak again. In factttcch *tchhh tchhirp!*"

He spread his wings, chirped again, like an ordinary bird, and flew away.

Hannah finished with the carrots and went to go ask the cook what the word *transcendent* meant.

• • •

Hannah's father did indeed come home with a new wife, and the new wife came with a pair of stepsisters, and things did not go as well as they could.

We will gloss over the various indignities, some of which are inevitable when households merge, some of which were particularly awful to this situation. Hannah's stepmother was tall and lean and beautiful and her daughters were tending in that direction. Hannah, who was short and sturdy from double-digging beds with shovels that were too large for her, was given a brief stare and dismissed out of hand.

"Poor thing!" said her stepmother. "Something should be done about the dirt under her nails, I suppose, but I am far too shattered from the move to take it in hand. I suppose she is not educated? No, of course not."

"I help out in the garden," said Hannah.

"Yes, I can tell by the dirt on your knees. Well, I suppose it keeps you out of trouble… "

Hannah went out into the garden, feeling very strange and rather as if she should be angry. It is not much use being angry when you are eleven years old, because a grown-up will always explain to you why you are wrong to feel that way and very likely you will have to apologize to someone for it, so Hannah sat on the edge of the raised bed and drummed her heels and thought fixedly about when the next sowing of beets would have to be planted.

After awhile, she scrubbed at her cheeks and went to go and plant them.

The next few years went along in that vein, more or less. Her stepmother did not wish to be bothered with her and her stepsisters did not understand gardening and Hannah did not understand embroidery or boys and so they had very little to talk about.

Her stepmother instituted a "no filthy nails at the table" policy, which meant that Hannah ate in the kitchen. It started as an act of rebellion against pumice stones and nail clippers, but eventually it just became the way things were. Hannah found it much more restful.

There was talk of sending Hannah to finishing school, but nothing came of it. The joy of getting rid of her was outweighed, to her stepmother's mind, by the exorbitant expense. So long as Hannah stayed out in the garden and made herself scarce, there was a minimum of trouble.

"It ain't right," muttered the cook. "She treats that girl like a serf."

The Gardener shrugged. "We're serfs," he said. "We do well enough."

"Yes, but she's not. Her father owns the house free and clear, not the Duke."

The Gardener was slow to reply, not because he was stupid but because he had come to a point where he considered his words very carefully.

After a time he said, "There are worse things. She's warm and fed. No one beats her."

"She should have pretty dresses," said the Cook, annoyed. "Like the other two do. Not go around like a servant."

The Gardener smiled. "Oh, sure, sure," he said. "Nothing wrong with pretty dresses. Do you think she could keep them out of the vegetable garden?"

The Cook scowled. Hannah's abuse of clothing was no secret. The laundry maids had to use their harshest soap on the knees of her trousers. What Hannah might do to muslin was not to be contemplated.

If anyone had asked Hannah herself, she would have shrugged. She had no particular interest in her stepmother or her stepsisters. The older stepsister was rude, the younger one kind, in a vague, hen-witted way, and obsessed with clothing. Neither understood about plants or dirt or bees, and were therefore, to Hannah's way of thinking, people of no particular consequence.

Hannah did not have any difficulty interacting with people; she just had little interest in doing so. She went to the village school long enough to learn to read, but never particularly embraced it, except insomuch as there were herbals and almanacs to be read. People in books tended to do very dramatic (or very holy) things and none of them, while trampling their enemies or falling in love or being overcome on the road to Damascus, ever stopped to notice what was growing along the sides of the road.

There had been an incident with the priest and the parable of the fig tree. Hannah had opinions about people who did not understand when figs were ripe, even if those people were divine. She was brought home in disgrace and her stepmother spent several days having vapors about the difficulties of an impious child.

In this not entirely satisfactory fashion, they bumped along, until Hannah was seventeen and the Duke threw an extraordinary ball for his son.

• • •

"We are going to the ball!' said Hannah's older stepsister when Hannah came in with an armload of vegetable marrows.

"Good for you," said Hannah, dropping her armload on the Cook's table.

"You should come too," said the younger stepsister. "All the girls will be there. Everyone is wearing their very best dresses."

The older one snorted. "Fancy Hannah being there!"

"I hear the Duke has an orangery," said Hannah thoughtfully. She had never seen an orangery, although she'd heard of them. They were frightfully expensive and required a great deal of glass.

"An orangery," agreed the younger, knowing that Hannah was fond of plants. She chewed on her lower lip, clearly wracking her brain. "And vast formal gardens with a hedge maze. And—oh, all manner of things! The centerpieces are supposed to be as large as wagon wheels, with so many flowers!"

"What would she wear?" demanded the eldest.

"Oh!" The younger stepsister considered. "We'd have to make her something. We could take in the hem on my green dress, perhaps—"

Hannah had not the least interest in floral centerpieces and only a vague professional curiosity about hedge mazes. She had less than no interest in hems and green dresses. But her stepsister meant well. She patted the other girl's arm and went back outside.

She also had no interest in the ball. Balls sounded deathly dull. It might have been a good excuse to enter the Duke's manor house, however, and perhaps there would have been tours of the orangery.

"But really," she said aloud, scowling in the direction of the beans, "it's probably not worth having to go to a ball. And she's right—what *would* I wear?"

"Ahem," said the tufted titmouse.

Hannah raised her eyebrows.

She was a good bit taller now than she had been at eleven, and so she and the bird were nearly at eye-level.

It looked like the same bird. Did they live that long?

Perhaps the magic ones did.

"I'm just saying," said the bird, "you haven't asked for anything. Not once."

"I did too," said Hannah. "I went and asked for a packet of nasturtium seeds. And received *nothing*, might I add."

The bird sighed. "Dryads do not deliver the seeds of *annuals*," it said, with a good bit of contempt. "Anyway, you're not supposed to ask for anything. You're supposed to take what you're given."

"I would have, if she'd given me nasturtium seeds."

The titmouse rubbed a wing over its face.

"Just try it," it said. "Tomorrow night, when your sisters are gone to the ball."

"All right," said Hannah. "If it gets me a look at that orangery, I'll try it."

The titmouse turned its head from side to side, in order to give her the full effect of its disapproving stare. "An orangery."

"I want to see how it's done," said Hannah. "Oh, I can't build one, I know—I haven't the money for glass. Still, one might make do."

"You haven't got *any* money, have you?" said the titmouse.

"Yes, I do. I raise queen bees and sell them off. And I've been selling honey. The Gardener would normally take it but he hates going to the market. So I sell the honey for him and we split the money."

"Shouldn't the honey go to the house?" asked the titmouse.

Hannah shrugged. "It's not like we don't have plenty. And we're the ones who take care of the bees. "

"You're embezzling honey from your father," said the titmouse. "*Lovely.*"

Hannah had no idea what that word meant. "Um. Maybe? They're *my* queens, anyhow."

The titmouse clamped its beak shut and gazed at the sky in silence.

"Look, Silas at the market gives me a dollar per jar. And I get five dollars for a queen." Hannah was feeling a bit defensive about the matter.

"What do you *do* with that money?" asked the titmouse.

"Well, I buy seeds sometimes. Mostly I save it, though. It's all in a tin. I won't tell you where."

"Sound fiscal policy," said the titmouse wearily. "All right. Tomorrow night, don't forget."

"I won't," said Hannah, and the bird flew away.

• • •

It was a long morning. There was a great deal of uninteresting fretting about dresses. Hannah escaped into the garden as quickly as possible and set about thinning the carrots.

Even so, she caught occasional snippets through the windows—"Now remember, my dears, eye contact. You must make it boldly, but when he sees you, look down and blush. No, dear, that's a flush, it's not the same thing…"

And, a few minutes later, when the carrots were thinned, "*Positively no drinking. Not even ratafia.* Unless the Duke's son offers it to you, in which case you will allow yourself to be led by him. It is *vital* that you not become intoxicated."

Hannah moved on to the beets, thinking that it was all very stupid. It was hardly even worth planting beets, come to that, since it was starting to get hot and they were likely to bolt, but there was a wall of the house that got afternoon shade . . .

She lugged the watering can over to the shaded bed and encountered the Gardener.

"Going to the ball?" he asked.

"I doubt it," she said. "Though I hear the Duke has an orangery."

The Gardener snorted. "Lot of nonsense," he said. "You grow plants when *they* want to grow, not when you want them to."

"*You* use cold frames," said Hannah.

"Don't get smart," said the Gardener. Then he cracked a rare smile. "Ah, fine. I'd not have an orangery if you paid me—too many fiddly bits. But a little glasshouse for extending the season—well, perhaps."

Hannah grinned and went to plant beets.

Just before the supper hour, there was a great commotion and Hannah's stepmother and stepsisters poured out of the house in a froth of lace and seed-pearls. They climbed into a carriage (Hannah was secretly amazed that they could all fit) and drove off toward the Duke's manor.

"And not a word to her!" Cook groused to the Gardener. "Not a word! Her blood's as good as theirs."

The Gardener shrugged. "She's good with bees," he said. "Be a shame to waste her on a Duke."

The Cook stared at him as if he had lost his mind, but Hannah, who was pulling her gloves off, out of the Cook's sight, heard the praise and was warmed by it.

She ate her dinner quickly and went back into the garden. The back gate was overgrown, the hinges red with rust. She climbed over it instead of trying to open it, and landed with a thump in front of her mother's grave.

"Right," she said. "I'm here."

Nothing happened.

The wind sighed in the chestnut's branches. Hannah wiped her palms on her trousers.

Nothing continued to happen.

It occurred to her that she was standing on her mother's grave. That was awkward, but flinching away seemed even more awkward, so she had no idea what to do. She gazed up at the sky and said "Um."

The titmouse landed on a branch and looked at her. "You have to say the words," it said.

Hannah sighed. "Do I have to?"

"Yes."

"They're silly words."

The tree gave a long, disapproving groan, as if the branches were moving in a high gale. The titmouse fixed a warning glare on her.

Hannah took a deep breath and recited:

O chestnut tree, chestnut tree
Shake down what I need to me.

The leaves rustled.

Other than that, Hannah didn't see much difference.

"Um," she said after a moment. "Am I supposed to close my eyes, or do I go back inside and my problems are fixed, or…?"

The titmouse pointed one small gray foot over her shoulder.

Hannah turned.

Draped across the fence, looking absurdly out of place, lay a ball gown. It had enormous skirts that twinkled in the evening light. The sleeves were the color of a new leaf in springtime and belled out in enormous slashing ribbons.

"Good lord!" said Hannah, quite astonished.

"Now you can go to the ball!" crowed the titmouse.

"Um," said Hannah. "Y-e-e-e-s. That is a thing I can do. I suppose."

She glanced over her shoulder at the tree and the grave.

The bird beamed as encouragingly as something with a small, immobile beak can beam.

"Right," said Hannah. She gathered up the dress. There were gloves and shoes as well, and a neat black domino mask to hide her face. Her fingers slithered over the fabric, feeling the calluses on her fingertips snag at every thread. She winced. "Okay. Yes."

She slung the dress over her shoulder, climbed over the gate again, and went into the house.

The chestnut tree and the bird sat together in the growing dark.

"She'll be fine," said the bird. "I'm sure of it."

• • •

Late that night, the stepsisters returned. They were tired and downtrodden, and the youngest was carrying her shoes.

"A lady doesn't go barefoot," her mother said reprovingly.

"A lady doesn't have blisters the size of grapes then."

"Who was that girl?" asked the oldest, annoyed. "The one who came in late? The Duke's son didn't so much as glance at the rest of us after she showed up."

"I don't know," said her mother. "No better than she should be, I imagine!"

"I wish I had a dress like that," said the youngest wistfully. "No wonder he danced with her. I'd have danced with her too, in a dress like that."

The bird was asleep with its head tucked under its wing, but the tree jostled the branch and woke it up.

"Eh? What?"

It cocked its head, listening. "Oh. I see. Good for her, then. All as it should be."

The tree creaked.

"I imagine there'll be another ball soon," said the bird. "And another gown. Was she supposed to bring that one back?"

Creaaaaak…

"Hmm."

• • •

The next morning was bright and glorious. Hannah slept late and came out to weed the turnips with her eyes dark and thoughtful.

"Well?" said the titmouse, lighting onto a rain gauge.

"It's a magnificent orangery," said Hannah. "They're heating it under the floors, that's the trick. The fire isn't allowed to go out. You'd need three or four servants to keep it all going, though." She sighed, gazing over the garden. "Not really practical in my situation."

"Bother the orangery!" said the bird. "What about the Duke's son?"

"What about him?"

"You danced with him all night, didn't you?"

"I did nothing of the sort!" said Hannah.

The titmouse blinked.

"But… a girl showed up late in a beautiful dress… " it said slowly. "And the Duke's son danced with her all night… "

"Good for her," said Hannah. "There were dozens of beautiful dresses there, I expect. Hope it was the servant girl, though."

"The servant girl?"

"Sure." Hannah straightened from her weeding. "The one I traded the dress to for a key to the orangery."

The titmouse shot a nervous glance over its shoulder at the chestnut tree.

"Come over by the beehives," it said, "and tell me what you did."

"Not much to tell," said Hannah, following the bird obediently. The buzz of the hive made a gentle background to her words. "I met up with a servant girl over by the gardens. She was dead keen to go to the ball, and I had a magic dress, so I gave it to her. Fit like a glove, might I add—though she had to pad the toes on the shoes, they're a little too large. In return, she smuggled me into the orangery." She rubbed the back of her neck. "I hope it was her."

"Why didn't *you* go to the ball?" squawked the bird. "That was the *point!*"

Hannah rolled her eyes. "Don't be ridiculous. What would I do at a ball? A bunch of people standing around being snippy at each other and not talking about anything of any purpose. I caught a bit of it from the servants as I was passing through the manor. No *thank* you."

"There's dancing, though!"

"I don't dance," said Hannah shortly. "Dancing's not a thing you just pick up in a garden."

The titmouse paused. "Um… " It shifted from foot to foot. "You could sway gracefully? Like a tree?"

"No," said Hannah. "Just… *no*. That is not how dancing works."

"But you're supposed to charm the Duke's son!" said the bird, hopping up and down in its agitation.

"I don't see how. Unless he likes bees."

She picked up her hoe again. "Anyway, the orangery design did give me a few thoughts. If what the plants want is warm *roots*, we're doing this all wrong. I have to experiment with some seed trays on top of the bread ovens."

The bird gaped after her as she left.

After a moment it said, almost to itself, "I don't dare tell the dryad. Chirrrp!"

• • •

In the way of all good stories, there was another ball announced within the week. "So soon!" said Hannah's stepmother. "I cannot get dresses fitted so quickly! Still—this is your chance to charm him again, my dears."

"No strange girl is getting in my way!" vowed the eldest.

"I still wish I had that dress… " said the youngest wistfully. "Even just long enough to see how they sewed the sleeves. And my blisters haven't healed yet."

Hannah heard all of this because she was in the kitchen, checking her seed tray. The seeds atop the oven had sprouted twice as fast as the ones outside. "Warm dirt," she muttered. "How do I keep the dirt warm?" She fisted her hands in her hair, not caring that there was earth on them.

The titmouse was on her the moment she stepped outdoors. "Another ball," it said. "Here's your chance. You can go and charm the prince—"

"Duke's son."

"Yes, him. You can charm him with your—um—graceful swaying—"

Hannah heaved a sigh. "You're talking an awful lot for a temporarily enchanted bird."

"It's because I'm supposed to get you to the ball. I'm your fairy godbird. Apparently. Anyway, I'm getting used to it. Now, go to the tree after your sisters leave for the ball… "

Hannah sighed again. "I don't have the least interest in the Duke's son, you know."

"I'm sure when your eyes meet, it'll be magic."

"I doubt it."

The bird thought for a moment. "If you marry him, you'll inherit an orangery."

This gave Hannah pause. Her finger drifted to her lower lip. "Hmm… that's a thought… "

"And someone else can do the weeding for you," said the titmouse.

Hannah frowned. "Will they? But how will I know if they can be trusted? You have to be very careful with the ones with taproots, you know. And bindweed. You leave even a shred of bindweed in the ground and it's all over." She put her hands on her hips. "And come to think of it, are Duke's son's wives even allowed to garden? Don't they make you wear white gloves and do deportment or something?"

The titmouse was forced to admit its ignorance of the doings of nobility. "I don't know."

"I shall check," said Hannah forthrightly. "The servants will know. I'll ask that nice servant girl about it tonight."

"You will?" asked the bird.

"Yes. She's bound to talk to me. I'll give her another dress."

• • •

The dress this time was the color of a summer sky and the mask was dusted with tiny crystals. The titmouse kept its grave reservations to itself. The dryad creaked approval as Hannah picked the bodice off the fence and went into the house.

The stepsisters returned an hour after they left. Their mother had a grim set to her lips.

"Where is she *getting* those dresses?" demanded the eldest.

"I wish I knew," said the youngest. "I don't even want to wear it. I haven't the hips for the one she wore tonight. I just want to see how they fitted it together." She chewed on her lip.

Hannah returned an hour later, carrying a sack. She dropped it in the shed and went inside, then returned a few minutes later carrying a lamp.

The titmouse, resigned to its duty, landed in front of the shed and squeezed in through a knothole.

Hannah bent over the potting bench, spilling out her sack. It contained dozens of little lengths of stem, some with bits of dirt at the bottom, some severed with a sharp knife.

"Dare I ask?' said the titmouse.

"Cuttings," said Hannah. She pulled out jars. "Willow water, willow water... ah, there we go!"

"Cuttings," said the bird. "I might have known."

"I think I can get most of these to root," said Hannah. "The servant girl's mother is an assistant gardener. She let me have free run of the gardens. Had to do it by moonlight, so some of these aren't as clean as I'd like."

The bird's beak gaped in distress.

"*And* she gave me some nasturtium seeds," added Hannah.

"And the Duke's son?" the bird asked wearily.

"Useless," said Hannah. "I asked. Apparently if you're a Duchess, you don't garden. You sit around and tell other people to garden for you. What's the good of that?"

"Some people might like it."

"If other people are doing the gardening, it's not your garden. And they expect you to have heirs and such."

"That's the general way of things, yes."

"Not gonna happen," said Hannah, dunking a stem in water infused with willow chips. "And *don't* tell me I'll change my mind when I'm older."

"Wouldn't dream of it," said the titmouse. It devoted a few minutes to settling the feathers on one wing. "Well. This is a fine mess."

Hannah shrugged. "The servant girl's happy. Her name's Kara, by the way. She knows how to dance, too. Apparently they practice in the servant's hall. And she has quite good manners, which I don't, and she's soppy about the Duke's son. Let *her* marry him."

The bird was silent for a few minutes.

Hannah carefully shook out her seeds into various jars, and labeled them in her rough, scrawling hand.

"There's going to be a third dress," said the titmouse finally. "Dryads like things that come in threes."

"Poison ivy comes in threes."

"Magic's similar. You don't notice you've run into it, and then it itches you for weeks."

"Well, I don't have to go," said Hannah. "I've seen the orangery and I've got all the cuttings I'll ever need. And Kara's got two dresses. She can wear the first one again."

"You'll have to take the dress, though," warned the titmouse. "The dryad will get very upset otherwise."

"She's a tree," said Hannah. "What's she going to do, drop nuts on me?"

"For my sake?" asked the bird. "It's her magic in my head, you know."

"Oh!" Hannah looked contrite. "I'm sorry, bird, I didn't know. Of course I'll take the dress. I don't want her to take it out on you."

"She probably should," said the bird mournfully. "I've made a hash of things."

"No," said Hannah. "You've been very helpful. I've been glad to talk to you."

She held out her hand, and after a moment, the titmouse jumped onto her thumb. Its tiny feet scratched at her skin, and it seemed to weigh nothing at all.

• • •

The titmouse was an excellent prophet. Three days passed, and then another ball was announced. Hannah's stepmother threw her hands in the air in despair.

"No," said the youngest stepsister, with rare stubbornness. "I'm not going. My feet are completely raw. And he's only going to look at that one girl anyway."

"She can't possibly have a new dress this time," said Hannah's stepmother.

"Then there's even less reason to go," said the youngest, and locked herself in her room.

She stayed there for three hours, until Hannah tapped on her door. "Psst! Anabel!"

"Hannah?" She opened the door a crack. "Are they gone?"

"Long gone," said Hannah cheerfully, "and I've got something you might like to see. Open the door, will you?"

Anabel opened the door, and there was her stepsister, with her arms full of fabric.

The youngest stepsister let out a long breath. "That's a dress like that girl wore! But—but that's not—you're not—" She looked up, her eyes suddenly wide. "But you're not her! She's got totally different colored hair—"

"Ugh, no," said Hannah. "What would I do at a ball? But I've been supplying the dresses. It's—well, it's complicated. But I thought you might want to look at this one."

They laid the dress out on the bed. Hannah fidgeted while Anabel went over the seams, inch by inch, making appreciative noises, like "Will you look at what they did here?" and "Goodness, that's very clever. I wouldn't have thought to do that... "

"All wasted on me, I'm afraid," said Hannah cheerfully. "Anyway, keep it hidden, will you? If your mother finds out, there'll be questions, and I'll deny everything."

Anabel nodded. "I will," she said, sounding much less vague. "I can make a pattern from this, I bet. Thank you, Hannah!"

And she flung her arms around her stepsister, heedless of the dirt on Hannah's knees.

"You're welcome," said Hannah. "What are sisters for, after all?"

• • •

Long after midnight, Hannah's stepmother came home with her oldest daughter. Her eyes were bright—not with triumph, but with gossip.

"You will not believe what happened!" she crowed when Anabel came down to meet them. "It was—oh my, what a thing! You missed it!"

Anabel put the kettle on. Hannah came from her small room by the back door. Hannah's stepmother was in far too good a humor to protest. A story like this needed to be shared with as many people as possible. She would have rousted the neighbors if it hadn't been nearly dawn.

"The girl came back," said Hannah's stepmother. "In the same dress she wore the first time—"

Hannah's younger stepsister handed her a mug of tea, and they shared a secret smile.

"Not that the Duke's son noticed," grumbled the older stepsister. "Boys never notice clothes unless your neckline is halfway to your waist."

"Don't be vulgar, dear," said her mother. "But yes, she was wearing the first dress. And they danced and then at midnight there was an unmasking—you know how it is with these costume balls, everybody knows who everybody is, but you have to do the unmasking—"

"And she's been slipping out beforehand, apparently, so she never did unmask—"

"But this time the Duke's son was watching her like a hawk, and she had to actually run away—"

"—but she left a shoe! A shoe on the ground!" finished the older stepsister triumphantly.

"And he's snatched it up and is guarding it like it was the crown jewels," said her mother. She grinned wickedly. "Never realized he was quite so into shoes, but the way he was caressing it—well, you wonder a bit."

"What do you wonder about?" asked Hannah, who had been silent up until now.

There was a pause. The atmosphere in the kitchen, which had been cozy, started to cool—but her stepmother thawed, mellowed by the hot tea and the gossip. "Feet," she said bluntly. "Some men like a lady's feet. More than the rest of the lady. Fancy shoes are as good as ball gowns to them."

Hannah blinked. Then she thought of her own large, stomping, mud-caked boots and relaxed. Surely there was no chance of such boots becoming objects of desire.

"Then I never had the least chance," said Anabel, sounding decidedly cheerful. "A man who is into feet is *not* going to be interested in my blisters."

Hannah took her cup of tea back to her room. She hoped Kara was all right. Of course the shoe would have come off—it was too large for her. Probably the cotton had come loose. Oh, dear.

She fell asleep wondering what the Duke's son was planning to do with the dryad's shoe.

• • •

Not long after breakfast, the question was answered. It was market day, and Hannah was delivering honey to Silas, when there was a commotion in the middle of the square.

"Hear ye, hear ye!" called a man in the Duke's livery. "Hear ye! By order of the Duke, all young ladies are ordered to gather at their homes, to await the Duke's pleasure!"

Heads snapped up all over the market. Silas muttered something about *droit de seigneur* and reached under his bench for a cudgel.

"We're not going back to those days!" cried the cheesemonger, who had three daughters.

"And the Duke couldn't get it up anyway!" shouted the herb-wife. "Although if he wants to try some of my teas—"

"No!" said the herald. "No, you didn't let me finish! It's not like that! Nobody's droiting anybody's seigneur! And he doesn't need any tea!"

"Guaranteed to put fire back in an old man's belly!" cried the herb-wife, sensing a marketing opportunity.

"The Duke's son is seeking a mysterious woman!"

"I've got three," said the cheesemonger, suddenly interested.

"A *specific* mysterious woman!"

"Nuts."

"All girls of marriageable age in the village are required to present their left foot to try on a shoe!"

There was dead silence in the market.

Silas leaned over and murmured, "I always thought there was something a little peculiar about the Duke's son…"

"I'm sure he's very nice," said Hannah weakly, and slipped away.

Word spread quickly through the village. It was garbled at first, but the details rapidly filtered out. The Duke's son was coming. He had a shoe. Everyone had to try it on. The girl whose foot fit the shoe was the one whom he would marry.

"Oh, hell," said Hannah, staring down at her mud-caked boots. She wiggled her toes grimly.

The shoe was going to fit. The shoe was *made* to fit. That meant she was going to marry a Duke's son, and that meant no more gardening and no more beekeeping and instead graceful swaying and the producing of heirs—

"No," said Hannah furiously. The bees swarmed around her, buzzing like a tiny army. "No. Bird! *Bird!*"

"Eh?" The tufted titmouse landed on the fence. "What?"

"The Duke's son is coming," said Hannah grimly. "With a shoe to try on. You have to go get Kara. She has to be here to try it on."

The titmouse opened its beak to argue.

Hannah leaned in close. Her large human eyes met the titmouse's own small, dark ones.

She glared.

"Right-o," said the bird. "The dryad won't like it—"

"I'll take an axe to the dryad if I have to marry a Duke."

"Kara, you say?" The bird saluted and winged away over the garden.

Hannah exhaled through her nose and settled in to wait.

• • •

The shoe, when finally presented at Hannah's household, was much the worse for wear.

It had stains on it. One embroidered rose flapped forlornly. It had been tried on several dozen times and was looking stretched and shapeless.

It was still far too small for Anabel, who took one look at it and began laughing. "Oh, no," she said. "I'd have to hack my toes off. Will you look at these blisters?"

She wiggled her bare toes. The Duke's herald averted his eyes. Hannah's stepmother put her hand on Anabel's shoulder and murmured, "Not in front of the Duke's son, dear."

Hannah lurked behind the shed, watching the road for Kara.

"She has to get here on time," muttered Hannah. "She *has* to. I *won't* marry him."

The oldest stepsister tried on the shoe to no avail. The embroidered rose dangled by a single thread.

"Sorry to have bothered you," said the herald, turning away.

"Hang on," said Anabel. "There's still Hannah."

"Hannah was not the mysterious girl," said her mother blightingly.

"She might be." Anabel set her jaw stubbornly. "She ought to get to try, anyway."

Her intentions were good, but Hannah could have stuffed her headfirst into a beehive when the whole Ducal procession proceeded into the garden.

"Not there!" she cried, jerking her eyes from the road. "Don't step there! That's where the poppies are sown, and you can't compress the soil, or—oh, *bother.*"

"It's 'Oh bother, *your lordship,*'" said the herald.

His lordship stepped off the poppies and looked contrite.

"If you could just try on this shoe," said the herald, looking at Hannah's muddy boots with contempt. "Then we'll get out of your flowerbeds."

"I'd rather not," said Hannah, eyeing the shoe. "It looks...used."

"Duke's orders," said the herald crisply.

Hannah sat down and began unlacing her boot as slowly as possible. Where *was* that titmouse?

She pulled the boot off. The Duke's son was chased by a bee and began waving his hands frantically.

"You'll only get stung if you do that," said Hannah, much annoyed. She would not marry him, that was all there was to it. She spread her toes in an effort to make her foot seem wider.

The herald extended the shoe.

Her toes slid inside. She flexed her foot, hard, and said "Look, it doesn't fit at all. Much too...err..."

There was a chirp and a whisper of wings on her shoulder.

The garden gate slammed open.

"Wait!" cried Kara. "Let me try that shoe!"

All eyes turned to her. Hannah took advantage of the pause to yank her foot out of the shoe and cram it back into her boot.

The Duke's son's head jerked up.

"That voice," he said. "*I know that voice!*"

He snatched the shoe away from the herald and dropped to his knees, heedless of the mud. "Kara? Is it you?"

"It is!" she said, and stuck her foot in the shoe.

It was much too big and hung like a rag around her foot. The Duke's son stared at it in dismay.

"It got stretched out," said Hannah hurriedly. "Because my feet are so big. Tore the stitches, I imagine. Or the seams, or whatever they are. It's definitely her. Ask her a question only she would know."

"What did I say to you, during the first dance?" asked the Duke's son.

Kara leaned forward and whispered something into his ear.

The Duke's son's face lit up and he flung the shoe aside.

A moment later, he had swept the servant girl up in his arms and was striding toward the gate, while she laughed aloud in delight. The herald squawked and ran after them.

Hannah let out a long sigh of relief.

"Could've been you," said the titmouse on her shoulder.

"God forbid," said Hannah. "All I want is my own garden and my own bees. And perhaps to work out a cheaper method of under-floor heating."

"I expect you may get that," said the titmouse. "At least the bit with your own garden. Providing dresses like that—well, you're practically her fairy godmother. I should expect a reward will find its way here eventually. Particularly if a small enchanted bird were to show up and sing about the benefits of gratitude."

Hannah grinned.

"Perhaps Anabel and I can set up together. She can sew dresses and I'll keep bees. There are worse fates."

"The dryad won't be happy," warned the bird.

"Sod the dryad." She thought for a minute. "What about you, though? Aren't you supposed to go back to being a regular bird?"

The bird shrugged. "Didn't get you married. I may be stuck like this for awhile, or until the dryad gets distracted."

"You don't sound too bothered."

"Once you get in the habit of thinking, it's hard to stop. Perhaps you could throw me a worm now and again."

"I'd be glad to," said Hannah, and the titmouse rubbed its small white cheek against her round pink one.

"That's all right, then," said the bird, and it was.

∼

T. Kingfisher is the pen-name for Hugo-Award winning author and illustrator Ursula Vernon. Under her real name, she writes books for kids. As Ms. Kingfisher, she is the author of *Nine Goblins* and *Toad Words and Other Stories.* Both of her live in North Carolina and blog at redwombatstudio.com

Drowning in Sky

Julia August

Ann tracked the seabed rising for days, or hours, or minutes that felt like months, before the jolt of the ship knocking against the harbour wall jarred her eyes open. Water sloshed in the hollows of the hold. The salted ribs of the ship were singing, as were the tin ingots stacked twenty deep at her back. Under the nasal whine of wood and metal Ann heard the slow, deep hum of earth and stone.

She didn't need the sailors to tell her they had arrived. She flattened her shoulders against the ingots and took a breath. Then another. Her lap was full of dust. The limestone slab that had weighed down Ann's knees at the start of the voyage was only a pebble. Ann rolled it between her palms. She could hear Tethys scratching at the wooden walls.

If she got up, she could get out. She could bury herself in the earth, her hands and her head and her humming ears, and she could damp down her hair with dirt and never, ever go to sea again. Tethys had promised, she told herself. Ann had walked up and down the distant shore, and Tethys had crept over the sand on a skim of foam, and Tethys had *promised*.

The trapdoor opened. Ann crushed the pebble between the heels of her hands and experienced a flush of clearheaded energy. Tethys broke all Her promises. But not this one.

The sky opened up endlessly above the deck and Ann could have drowned in it. It was cold and grey and specked with stinging rain, and Ann, glancing around, saw the horizon merge seamlessly into a froth of cloud.

She clutched at the mast. A colossal Tethys reared up against the tidal sky, holding the whole harbour under Her bronze trident. The seahorse grasped in the Sea-Cat's other hand seemed to be struggling to escape.

"Khelikë," the captain said behind Ann. "Good? You can travel by road to Tharnos."

At Tharnos, the magistrates had refused entry to all ships sailing from Vitulia because of the plague. Ann nodded. As far as she was concerned, the only reason to prefer Tharnos to Khelikë had been the extra week it had taken to get here.

"Simo has your belongings," the captain said. "Where will you go?"

The ground sang out when Ann stepped onto it. Rich river clay, she thought, and clashing voices of disharmonious marl. Already Ann's clarity was clouding. She could feel fault lines, she could taste young growth and silt . . .

The sailor shouldered her bags expectantly. Unseeing, Ann plunged into Khelikë.

• • •

It must have been a festival day. There was music, the jarring sort made by real instruments, and blossoms everywhere, and wine running dark down sanguinary streets. That was real, as were the trees and painted temples. Even now, Ann could see unmoving things. It was only people who flickered past like mist, seen and forgotten in the same breath.

It gave Khelikë a delirious edge that told Ann she should find something to eat. She had been living off limestone for weeks and this flood of sensation was more than the first flush of relief at returning to land. She needed sleep too. It was a long time since she had been a stranger in a strange city. She needed to see things clearly again.

A sycamore leaned over a damp piazza. Ann stopped beneath it, hearing the sap rising from the roots, or her heart thumping in her chest. She should have made the sailors set her down on a beach somewhere. She should have walked to Khelikë. She should have filled herself with earth before she dealt with people.

Great terracotta jars stood open on the steps of a nearby temple. When Ann concentrated, she could see men ladling water and wine from the jars into what must be cheap cups, since fragments of smashed pottery bloomed into concentric circles across the piazza.

"Is the Day of the Opening of the Jars," said Simo, whose Vitulian was rather better than Ann's Dorikan. "For the Feast of the New Wine. You want?"

A woman who had been sitting on the steps stood up. She was staring at Ann.

She was real. She was as real as the tree and the wine jars and the temple. Ann could see every inch of her clearly, from her sandals to her gold-flecked Dorikan cloak to her perfect cheekbones. Her hair's spun gold dazzled Ann's eyes.

She looked angry. She came quickly across the piazza, her feet striking sparks. She was already speaking, but since she was speaking in Dorikan Ann understood very little. Something about mothers and protectors.

"Simo," she said. "What does she want?"

Simo spat. "Says the archons will protect her if the mothers sent you. She's Phaiakian, mistress."

"What does that mean?"

The woman said something to Simo, who spat again and replied with a spiky mouthful of Dorikan. The woman drew back in surprise.

Simo grinned at Ann. "I tell her you Vitulian," he said. "She thinks you come from Phaiakia, like her."

"Why?"

The woman plucked a hair from Ann's gown. "But you're so fair," she said in Vitulian, and smiled suddenly. "Come. I was wrong. I should have known from your dress. Forgive me." She took Ann's wrist familiarly, twitching her cloak to show off its golden border. Ann felt a flush of warmth, not unlike the clarity that came from consumed stone. "Come and drink to the Wine-God with me. My name is Arakhnë."

She led Ann towards the temple and the wine jars. "'Spider'?" Ann said.

Arakhnë laughed. "Very good!" she said. "You know some Dorikan then. But after the weaver, not the spider, you know the story." She placed a cup of well-watered wine in Ann's hands. It tasted of sunlight and baked clay. "Tell me, darling, who are you? We hear bad things from Vitulia. The archons say we should close the gates to travellers from the west. You arrived just in time. Are you flying from the plague or the barbarians?"

"Both."

"Has your city fallen? I am very sorry." Arakhnë put her hand on Ann's shoulder. "Where are you from?"

"Florens."

Arakhnë went still.

"Tell me," she said, as if from a distance. "They say it was in Florens that the dead first began to get up. Is that true?"

"Yes."

"I know a mother when I see one. Are you the lady Anna, who was the duke's prisoner?"

Ann swallowed another sunny mouthful. It helped a bit. She could almost see the edges of things. "Yes," she said.

"Darling, you must come home with me," Arakhnë said, and clasped Ann's hands warmly around the wine cup. Her smile was wide enough to fall into. "I wish you had come to my door. I would have offered you whatever you needed without any of these silly questions. I owe all I have to Dios Xenios, Dios the Hospitable you would say. Let no one say we don't know how to welcome strangers in Khelikë."

• • •

Simo dumped Ann's bags in Arakhnë's patterned courtyard. The mosaic was mostly flesh and froth, twisted up with Dorikan phrases Ann could not make out. There was an altar splashed with wine and spring flowers.

"I go now?" Simo said, looking around.

"Yes. Thank you."

"Phaiakian women are all witches. I know a good inn."

"This is fine."

There was a room and there was a table and there was bread and salted sardines. Arakhnë poured Ann wine herself.

"It is the Feast of New Wine," she said, leaning on the table as a maid would never have done. She had shed her cloak and flashed tawny skin down the open side of her purple Dorikan dress. "For three days, I serve my slaves. You do not do this in Vitulia?"

The wheat had grown in foreign soil. Flavour flooded Ann's mouth: acres and golden acres of fields, the sky alternating blue and rain-washed. She broke off another piece and dipped it in olive oil. She could taste flecks of stone from when the flour had been ground, which had probably happened in Khelikë. The oil was certainly from somewhere nearby.

Arakhnë was smiling. "Eat!" she said. "I go to promise my maid her freedom if she will only draw you a bath."

She would have washed Ann's hair, but Ann said, "No," and Arakhnë went away. Ann's mouth was full of wheat and olives. She washed her arms and her face and sat breathing steam until the flavours faded. Sleep, she thought. She needed sleep now.

It was harder to get up than she expected. Her clothes were nowhere to be seen. She stumbled out wrapped in a towel, her hair dripping down her neck, and found Arakhnë coming up from the courtyard with her arms full of cloth.

"Darling!" Arakhnë said, hurrying up the steps. "You Vitulians wear so many things. Look, I have a good Dorikan peplos for you." It was scarlet and shot through with silk. Two bronze pins rattled together in a brown felt slipper. "I wove it myself. Come and see how it suits you."

She held back a curtain. Ann walked through into a wall of gold and stopped still, dazzled. Light flickered over the walls, over the table, over the spreading bed.

Slowly her eyes cleared. Her bags lay underneath the window. The shutters were open and the golden tapestries whispered against the walls.

Arakhnë set down the slippers. "Come," she said, urging Ann towards the bed. She shook out the peplos, which looked like a tablecloth, and held it up against Ann as if to check the richness of the colour. "Hold it there, darling," she said, digging her thumbs under Ann's collarbone. "Just like that."

Ann lifted her hands unthinkingly and felt the towel fall. The salt breeze caught the water trickling down her spine.

She couldn't move. She felt first cold and then hot, a slow warmth radiating outwards from her parted lips and her navel, tingling to the pit of her stomach as the scarlet cloth brushed against her breasts. The pomegranates woven into its border glittered. She couldn't feel herself breathing.

Arakhnë touched Ann's cheek and bent her bright head, and even her eyelashes shone. Her mouth was soft. The shape of her body pressed against Ann through the cloth. She slid her palms down Ann's naked back, then under the cloth, her hair spilling, shimmering, over her shoulders.

The bed hit Ann's legs. She tumbled backwards as slowly as a feather, her eyes filling up with gold.

• • •

She dreamed of Tethys.

She dreamed she was standing on the beach, any beach, and Tethys lay there like a great cat with Her paws folded under Her, drowning the stars in Her midnight eyes.

Dread knotted Ann's stomach. "You *promised*," she said.

Ann, child, said the Sea-Cat. **How do you find Khelikë?**

A thought flashed its fins, then darted away. It was impossible to catch it beneath the liquid weight of the Sea-Cat's gaze. "Welcoming."

Take My advice, child. Ask your hostess about Nikë Apteros.

"Why?"

I have a kindness for those who shake the earth when they walk, the Sea-Cat said. **For am I not the Mother of Earthquakes?**

• • •

There was a terracotta lamp, and in the lamplight Arakhnë crouched against the wall, her hand raised to shield her face. She looked amazed. Ghostly images of Tethys and the midnight beach were collapsing into shadow.

The scarlet cloth was twisted up around Ann's legs. She began to sit up.

"Anna!" Arakhnë said, turning towards her. "Did you see that?"

"Yes. It's nothing."

"But what *was* it?"

"Sometimes I dream like that." It was hard not to see two of everything, except for Arakhnë, whom Ann could still see clearly. A few more good meals should bring the world back into focus. Ann's bags lay open at Arakhnë's feet. "What are you doing?"

Arakhnë looked momentarily blank. The lamp gave her feet a golden glow.

"I was thirsty," she said, picking up the lamp from the floor. She set it down on the table and filled a two-handled silver cup, which she brought back to the bed.

"Here," she said, sitting beside Ann and holding up the cup. "Drink."

The wine was strong. "This is the old wine," Arakhnë said, sniffing it appreciatively. "I save it for my guests." She sipped, smiled, set the cup down. Her peplos was pinned at the shoulders; she slid out one long bronze pin, letting the cloth slip down just enough to reveal the swell of her breast. "You must not dream, darling. It displeases me."

She straddled Ann's thighs. Ann felt the breath rise out of her as Arakhnë pushed her back into the pillows.

• • •

Arakhnë's voice drifted down:

"You are so fair, darling." She was stroking Ann's hair. "Only the oldest mothers are so fair. And you are so young." Her fingertips brushed Ann's lips. "And your dreams... I never knew there were such women among the barbarians."

Ann opened her eyes and found even Arakhnë was blurring, her hair falling in a shimmering silken curtain around Ann's head. Her knees pressed Ann's hips. The gold flickering behind Arakhnë, above her, in every strip of cloth covering every wall and surface, merged dizzyingly in the dying lamplight. It made Ann's head spin.

She floated upwards into Arakhnë's honey-coloured gaze. "What can you do?"

"Darling?"

"You must have... some sort of talent. What is it?"

Arakhnë's lashes flickered. "I'll tell you," she said, her voice dropping to a purr. She crooked her arm around Ann's head, piling up her hair on the pillow. She was still wearing most of her peplos and the rub of silk and wool between their bodies was more intimate than skin. "I'll tell you when you ask me again. But ask me something else first."

Sleep lapped Ann like the sea. "Who are the mothers?"

"Ah, them! They are the great women of Phaiakia, darling. My city, the city I come from. The most northern of all the Ten Cities. I left the mothers behind long ago."

"Why did you think they sent me?"

"There was a misunderstanding. I went to Pallatinë first. It is our daughter-city. When I was not welcome there, I came here. It was all a long time ago." She had the skin and smile of a young woman; but then, so did Ann. "Tell me, Anna, how did you leave Florens?"

Ann closed her eyes. She didn't want to remember Florens now.

"It fell," she said. "I walked away."

"The duke died, did he not?"

"Yes."

"And you were revenged?"

Ann didn't want to remember Pietro either. "You're a weaver?"

Arakhnë laughed. "I am a woman," she said. "I weave. Do you not in Vitulia? In Phaiakia, even the mothers weave. Especially the mothers. Phaiakia is not the city of Pallas for nothing. But not for money, darling. Do you know the word 'hetaira'?"

"No."

"It means something like 'companion' in your language, I think. I have many friends. You must meet them. I know the archons will want to meet you."

"I don't want to. Who is Nikë Apteros?"

Some of the elasticity went out of Arakhnë's smile.

"Ah," she said. "You mean our Wingless Victory."

"Do I?"

"She was commissioned for the new temple last year. The archons wanted her carved without wings so she could never fly away."

"Is she a god? They don't usually like that sort of idea."

Arakhnë was almost frowning.

"There have been signs," she admitted. "They say pillars of flame have been seen in the countryside. And all the rats ran away towards Kynestris. But it may just be talk." She leaned over the bed. "Let's finish this wine, darling. You won't dream at all after drinking this."

• • •

It was midday and the sun flashed over the shining tapestries. A dull ache gnawed at the back of Ann's skull. She lay feeling slightly sick and slightly dizzy and mostly exhausted, until a savoury wisp of scent prompted her to feel hungry as well.

With some effort, she sat up. The roar of light that flooded her head almost flung her onto her back; she set her feet on the floor and waited for it to subside.

The wine jar had been refilled. There was food on the table and Ann, working methodically through dried figs and bread, tasted stony soil and barley roasted before it was ground. Her faintness was passing. She looked for water and found none, then for her Vitulian clothes, which were gone too. Not even a shift remained in her bags. Her money was still there, as was the only notebook she had brought with her. She had left so much behind in Florens.

She recovered the scarlet peplos from the bed and tried to remember how

Arakhnë wore hers. The top of the cloth doubled down over the breasts, she thought, and then it was wrapped lengthways around the body. She struggled to pin it up over her shoulders. She felt naked. Even fastened with a girdle, the dress was flimsy and insecure.

But she would look less foreign. Looking foreign only made people bother her. She put on the slippers and left the room.

As soon as she went out, she felt better. The house had a loggia above an inner court like Ann's house in Florens, although the windows, of course, were not barred and there were no inaccessible rooms set aside for servants and guards. Down in the courtyard, a great many people seemed to be coming and going. Arakhnë sat by a table laden with wine and cakes, the fanciest of Ann's three gowns lying over her lap.

She jumped up when she saw Ann, her eyes widening. "Anna, darling!" she exclaimed. "If I'd known you were awake, I would have come to help you dress."

"This is wrong?"

"No—no, you look very fine. You are a beautiful woman, darling." She twitched the peplos over Ann's shoulders, unpinning and repinning with busy fingers, and kissed Ann's cheek. "Did you eat? Have a cake. Come and walk with me in the garden."

It was a second courtyard planted with grass and climbing roses. The buds already nodded among the thorns. Arakhnë glanced around with pleasure. "They have no idea of gardens here," she told Ann. "In Pallatinë, every great house has a garden. They learned that from Khivrenté, which is a great empire beyond the desert." She must have caught Ann's interest. "You know of Khivrenté?"

"My grandfather told me stories. I wanted to go there one day."

"And then the wicked duke imprisoned you. I see." She pressed Ann's hand. "Darling, you must forgive me for stealing your clothes away. I thought you would want me to wash them. And I wanted to see what Vitulian cloth is like. It is very lovely. But do you not weave even a little true-silk into it?"

"I don't know. I didn't make it. What's true-silk?"

Arakhnë seemed taken aback. "But how did you—when your dreams appeared last night, how did that happen?"

Ann shrugged. Standing in Arakhnë's garden, as small as it was and however shallow the soil, made her feel like a depression in wet sand, filling up effortlessly with energy.

She looked around for a rosebud. It opened under her fingers, spreading its damp pink petals to the sun. "Like that," she said.

Arakhnë's mouth fell open.

"Come and sit down with me," she said, faintly. She drew Ann down to the grass. "Do you not weave at all? Or spin?"

"No."

"You are a remarkable woman. You must have made that duke sorry he ever saw you."

The last time Ann had seen Pietro, he had been dying in the rain. She had been trying to forget that moment for months. It still surfaced too often in the depths of the night: his curls, his clothes, his laboured breathing. How, even at the end, he had struggled to smile.

A heavy lassitude crept over Ann. Arakhnë's voice seemed to come from very far away: "What happened?"

Ann closed her eyes.

"He loved me," she said. "What happened to the first Arakhnë, the weaver?"

"Ah, her. There are two stories. I like the tale they tell in Pallatinë better, but the mothers are very strict in Phaiakia, much stricter than in Pallatinë. Arakhnë was a poor girl who thought she could weave better than Pallas. Well, there was a competition and Arakhnë lost, of course, and she was so upset she hanged herself from her own loom. Then Pallas felt sorry for the girl, so she turned her into a spider. It seemed like a kindness to a goddess, you know?"

"It's not your real name, is it?"

"No, no. I left that behind in Phaiakia." She knotted a filament of gold around Ann's wrist and kissed Ann's palm. Ann's eyes clouded over. "Your hair is so fine, Anna. What would happen if I cut it for you?"

"Nothing. Why?"

"It doesn't matter. It was just a thought. You look tired. Sleep."

• • •

In the dark, she woke to find Arakhnë bending over her. "Get up, darling!" Arakhnë said. There was wine on her breath and she wore a great deal of jewellery. Pipes and stringed instruments jangled below. "Two of the archons are here. They want to meet you."

Ann's head was too heavy for her shoulders. "No."

"Come on, Anna, darling, just for me." She had a fresh peplos over her arm. This one was blue. "It won't take long, I promise. And you must want supper."

She poured wine before she dressed Ann and drank most of it too. "You're going to be so beautiful," she said, fastening a heavy collar set with carnelian around Ann's neck. She gathered Ann's hair up, knotting and twisting. "You look so slim, darling. But you're so heavy."

"I turned my bones to stone. I didn't know what I was doing."

Arakhnë's breath caught. "I should paint your face," she muttered. "But there isn't enough light. No. You look lovely as you are." She took Ann's hand, then peered with sudden concern at Ann's bare wrist. "Where did it go?"

"What?"

"Just sit down, darling. Just give me a moment." She disappeared, reappearing a few minutes later with a length of gold thread wrapped around her fingers. "For good luck," she said, tying it around Ann's wrist. "Come."

Ann followed her through a golden blur. She could hardly remember where she was any more, let alone what she was doing, or where to put her feet.

The noise was unbearable. It was a party and it was happening in a room painted to look like a lagoon, the walls awash with sand and sea shells. There were considerably more than two men there. They lay on couches, talking and drinking and picking at dishes on low tables. Three pretty musicians played by the door.

"Sit here, darling," Arakhnë said, leading Ann to a couch. Ann sat down. "What can I get you? Wine? Food?"

Ann stared at her. Arakhnë she could see, but the other faces merged and blurred, voices coalescing into a deafening hum. The painted waves on the walls seemed to tower higher. Arakhnë ran a finger along Ann's collarbone, and licked her fingertip, and faintness roared in Ann's ears. Her face was hot. Everything felt unreal.

She tried to find her way through the fog while the conversation swam around her. Sharp Dorikan words flashed backwards and forwards and Arakhnë, halfway down another cup of wine, gestured with both hands, and Ann thought it might all be a dream. She might really be asleep still in Arakhnë's bed. Out of the flood of sound, with perfect clarity, a man said, *How did he imprison her?* and Ann stood up.

"I want to go," she said. Something cut into her wrist; she snapped it, discarding it unthinkingly. Arakhnë stared up at her with round eyes and a round, startled mouth. "Now."

Arakhnë jumped up.

"Of course, darling, if that's what you want," she said, so fast she tripped over her words. She took a lamp from one of the tables. "Why don't we go out to the garden? You remember, it's quiet, you like it there."

The sounds of the dinner party could still be heard in the garden. It was cool, though, and dark, and Ann's head began to clear. She filled her throat with the freshness of grass and rose leaves. Salt flew like snow in the sea breeze.

Arakhnë set down the lamp on a chair. "There, darling. Better?"

"Yes."

"I am glad." She took Ann's hands, kissing each of Ann's palms in turn. "You are so lovely, Anna. Will you make another rose bloom for me? I think it would look very well in your hair."

It opened with a burst of scent that flooded the garden. "Beautiful," Arakhnë said. There was a tremor in her voice. "I would never have thought it possible. But you can do impossible things, I know." She took a breath. "They say those who die of the plague in Vitulia get up again. That it began in Florens, where the duke kept a witch chained up in a tower. That now the dead walk the fields and the cities. That they can fight, or be herded like cattle. Is that true?"

"Yes."

"Did you do it?"

"Yes."

"Show me," Arakhnë said. "Look, show me with this."

It was a magpie. It had been killed recently, so recently that its feathers had not begun to loosen and it smelt of meat rather than corruption. Ann turned it over in her hands. There were still mites under the feathers. The wings splayed out, white and black, and the sad, shrivelled feet curled against her fingers.

The stench of Florens, at the end, rose up in her memory like an angry ghost. It had been early summer and the greasy heat mingling with rot had shimmered in the air. Ann had walked through it blindly and breathed it in and used it to make the dead things get up as she passed by. Just like opening rosebuds. But rosebuds were as fresh as any other green thing, whereas death tasted of decaying meat. One or two would not have been so bad. In Florens, the dead had numbered in the tens of thousands. Swimming in power, Ann had raised them all, and then struggled not to drown.

They had rotted. On their feet, and all through the city.

Revulsion surged in Ann's throat. She cast the bird away compulsively, her skin crawling. It spread its wings and disappeared into the dark.

Arakhnë sank to her knees.

"You are truly remarkable, Anna," she said in a low tone. "You make me think of the saying that only a god or a beast can live outside society. You can restore life to the dead. What do you need city walls for? Are you a god?"

"It's not life. It's just—movement."

"Is there a difference? You can do such things. And yet that terrible duke held you in chains. I don't understand. How could *anyone* imprison you?"

Pietro might have got up from his chair. But Ann had burnt his body instead. She wanted to think of him when she had first met him, as he had been through the long, comfortable years she had lived in his house, in his city, but it was the dying Pietro she remembered instead, the man she had gone to save from the mob, the Pietro who had clung to her and told her to burn him and let him go.

Just movement. "He didn't."

"What do you mean?"

"He didn't imprison me. He loved me. Of course he couldn't have kept me there if I didn't want to stay."

Arakhnë's eyes were very wide. "Could anyone?"

"No. I don't think so."

Arakhnë got up slowly.

"Come to bed," she said. "I'm sorry. I should never have woken you."

• • •

The dead magpie scraped its beak against the open shutters. Ann observed it through a soporific haze. The feathers that should be white shone bright as brass, and even the magpie's black tail had a metallic tinge. A silk braid an inch wide glowed around each of Ann's wrists. Through the window, Ann saw only yellow sky.

She was halfway through a yawn that was taking months when Arakhnë burst in. "You're awake!" Arakhnë said, or seemed to say, since her voice sounded distorted, like someone speaking through water. A cup shook in her hands, three quarters full of wine she had probably been drinking already. "Anna, I have to tell you something. But maybe you should drink this first."

It was the old vintage. Arakhnë watched her drink with reddened eyes. "Why don't we go down to the garden?" she said. "Come on. Get up. You like my garden. It might be better there."

The golden air was as heavy as water. It thickened as Ann descended, her head swimming, until she found herself in a garden where she struggled to breathe and all the leaves were gold. The magpie peered down at them from the roof. Arakhnë seemed not to see it. "Anna," she said, pressing Ann's hands. "Sit, darling. I'm sorry. I'm so sorry. I wish this hadn't happened. I want you to know that. I want your forgiveness."

"For what?"

Arakhnë closed her honey-coloured eyes. It looked as if she had been crying.

"Darling," she said. "You never asked me again. Ask me now."

It took Ann a moment, or possibly an hour, to realise what she meant. "Your talent," she said. Her foot was numb; she shifted position. "It must be… something to do with cloth. True-silk. What is that?"

Arakhnë's laughter frayed in the middle. "Oh, darling," she said. "It's our secret. The secret of the women of Phaiakia. You don't know how much people will pay for just a skein of it. Yes. You're right. I spin true-silk."

"What does it do?"

"That depends on the woman, darling. We all spin different threads."

Ann's wrists burned. "It makes it hard to think," she said.

She stripped off first one silk band, then the other. Most of the pressure weighing down on her lifted abruptly. The edges of things were still gilded, but then the gleaming borders of Ann's peplos must be shot through with true-silk too.

She tossed the bands to the magpie, which swooped out of the garden with a triumphant squawk. Arakhnë's eyes filmed over with tears.

"No," Ann said. She thrust her fingers into the grass, seeking the shallow layer of earth and pebbles between the roots. In a moment, she would be able to think clearly. "It's more than that. What is it?"

Arakhnë kissed her fingertips and pressed them to Ann's cheek.

"It's useful to be loved," she said simply. "For a stranger in a strange city. I *am* sorry."

The discarded wrist-bands were pure silk, but the peplos was mostly wool. Ann turned up her hem to the light, looking for colours and patterns. Cloth was not something she had thought about much before. She regretted that suddenly. Now she knew what to look for, she could feel the heat flickering along the golden border. "It's very good. How do you do it?"

"Darling?"

"True-silk." She glanced up and found Arakhnë looking at her with a peculiar expression. The sweep of Arakhnë's hair shone in the sun. "Oh!" Ann said. "It's your hair. You spin it from your hair. Don't you?"

Arakhnë opened her mouth, then sat looking bewildered. "Aren't you cross?"

"I never heard about this before. Will you teach me how to spin?"

"There's something else," Arakhnë said. "When my hair turned gold instead of white, the mothers knew. You spin your colour into the silk, we say. But I... I found how to replenish it. I killed my husband, Anna. I never wanted to get old. And outside Phaiakia, no one knows you can drink the life from your lovers." She spread her hands helplessly. "Forgive me."

Ann, who had already known it, drew in a burning breath. She thought of her occasional faintness, especially in Arakhnë's bed.

"Don't do it again," she said. "I wouldn't like it."

"I know, darling. I'm sorry." Arakhnë's eyes welled up. "I thought you could stay here. I thought you could do such things for us. For Khelikë. We have enemies. And you have such power... but Anna, darling, you frighten me. You frighten the archons. You can do such things, and how could anyone stop you? You broke every spell I laid on you. You can bring back the dead. We thought your duke had kept you in Florens, and if he could then it must be possible, but it wasn't true. He didn't. We can't control you. What if you raised an army here?"

"I don't want to. Why would I?"

Arakhnë rubbed her wet eyes. "That's what I said, darling, but the archons insisted. You have to understand, I only live here. I'm not a citizen. I don't have a citizen's rights."

"So?"

Arakhnë leaned forwards and pinched Ann's ankle.

"Did you feel that?" she said. "When the cold reaches your heart, it's the end."

Ann thrust her arms into the earth up to her elbows. She was very much awake suddenly and seeing more clearly than she had for weeks. *Hemlock*, she thought.

In a moment, she would be furious. Numbness tickled her knees and ran its cold fingers up her inside thigh. Below the earth, the volatile Dorikan marl-stone, shoving and shrugging, sang its cracked song. She reached down to it.

"I am so sorry," Arakhnë was saying. "It was in the wine. I thought it might not be so bad to die in a garden. Forgive me."

The rosebuds crumbled, then the glossy leaves. Remotely, Ann was aware of the grass collapsing into dust around her. Energy filled her from mouth to stomach, from her crackling hair to her bloodless toes. Sensation flooded back into her legs. She rolled her head on her shoulders, feeling the fault lines dance deep in the earth.

She got up. Arakhnë rocked back, pressing both hands to her drowned mouth.

Ann's head was humming. "Tell me," she said, "what happened to the second Arakhnë, the one you liked better? Did she win her contest?" Arakhnë seemed unable to speak. Ann brought down her heel on a fault line, hard. The ground jumped. "*Tell me.*"

"She was cheated," Arakhnë whispered. "She showed Pallas to herself. She wove all the evil things the gods ever did to mortals and Pallas destroyed her cloth and cursed her to weave forever. Please, Anna. Please. I never wanted this."

Ann kicked another fault line. This time, the whole house shook.

"You can die in a garden," she said and walked out.

• • •

Khelikë groaned as Ann walked through the sinking streets. The paving stones bucked and the houses creaked and juddered, people running in confusion through a hail of roof tiles. With every fresh tremor, another section of the city sank. Ann was aware the instant the sea swept over the harbour walls.

She went on in a cold fury. She could see exactly how she had been used now. She might have undone it, but there was no way to lay the fractured marl to rest and anyway her toes still tickled from the aftereffects of Arakhnë's poison. The dead magpie flew ahead, wearing Arakhnë's golden bands around its feathered neck.

At the piazza, the great jars had been flung down from the temple steps and lay in pieces on the ground. The wine bled into the waves already lapping at Ann's calves. Under the sycamore tree sat the Sea-Cat. **Ann, child**, She said. **I knew I should never be disappointed in you**.

She looked practically human. Ann was too angry to be afraid. "You promised me safe passage," she said. "You never said You wanted the city! Well, You can have Khelikë. You can have the people. Your Victory can *swim* free. But You can't have me."

The water was rising fast. Tethys laughed, showing all Her teeth.

I would not keep you, She said. **Go**.

~

Julia August is fascinated by drowned cities and the ancient world. Her short fiction has appeared in *Lackington's*, *SQ Mag*, and *Cabinet des Fées*. She is @JAugust7 on Twitter and j-august on Tumblr.

MISS CARSTAIRS
AND THE MERMAN

DELIA SHERMAN

Art by Sandra Buskirk

The night Miss Carstairs first saw the merman, there was a great storm along the Massachusetts coast. Down in the harbor town, old men sat in taverns drinking hot rum and cocking their ears at the wind whining and whistling in the chimneys. A proper nor'easter, they said, a real widow-maker, and huddled closer to the acrid fires while the storm ripped shingles from roofs and flung small boats against the piers, leaping across the dunes to set the tall white house on the bluffs above the town surging and creaking like a great ship.

In that house, Miss Carstairs sat by the uncurtained window of her study, peering through a long telescope. Her square hands steady upon the barrel, she watched the lightning dazzle on the water and the wind-blown sand and rain scour her garden. She saw a capsized dinghy scud past her beach in kinetoscopic bursts, and a gull beaten across the dunes. She saw a long, dark, seal-sleek figure cast upon the rocky beach, flounder for a moment in the retreating surf, and then lie still.

The shallow tidal pool where the figure lay was, Miss Carstairs calculated, not more than two hundred yards from her aerie. Putting aside the telescope, she reached for the bell pull.

The peculiarities of both ocean storms and seals had been familiar to Miss Carstairs since earliest childhood. Whenever she could slip away from her nurse, she would explore the beach or the salt marshes behind her father's house, returning from these expeditions disheveled: her pinafore pockets stuffed with shells, her stockings torn and sodden, her whole small person reeking, her mother used to say, like the flats at low tide. On these occasions, Mrs. Carstairs would scold her daughter and send her supperless to bed. But her father usually contrived to slip into her room—bearing a bit of cranberry bread, perhaps—and would read to her from Linnaeus or Hans Andersen's fairy tales or Lyell's *Natural History*.

Mr. Carstairs, himself an amateur ichthyologist, delighted in his daughter's intelligence. He kept the crabs and mussels she collected in the stone pond he had built in the conservatory for his exotic oriental fish. For her fifteenth birthday, he presented her with a copy of Charles Darwin's *The Origin of Species*. He would not hear of her attending the village school with the children of the local fishermen, but taught her mathematics and Latin and logic himself, telling her mother that he would have no prissy governess stuffing the head of his little scientist with a load of womanish nonsense.

By the time Mr. Carstairs died, his daughter had turned up her hair and let down her skirts, but she still loved to tramp all day along the beaches. In hopes of turning her daughter's mind to more important matters, her mother drained the pond in the conservatory and lectured her daily on the joys of the married state. Miss Carstairs was sorry about the pond, but she knew she had only to endure and eventually, she would be able to please herself. For five years, endure she did, saying, "Yes, Mama" and "No, Mama" until the day when Mrs. Carstairs followed her husband to the grave, a disappointed woman.

On her return from her mother's funeral, Miss Carstairs promptly ordered a proper collecting case, a set of scalpels, and an anatomy text from Codman and Shurtleff in Boston. From then on, she lived very much alone, despising the merchants' and fish-brokers' wives who formed the society of the town. They, in turn, despised her. It was a crying and a shame, they whispered over cups of Indian tea, that the finest house in town be wasted on a woman who would all too obviously never marry, being not only homely as a haddock, but a bluestocking as well.

A bluestocking Miss Carstairs may have been, but her looks were more primate than piscine. She had a broad, low brow, a long jaw, and her Scottish father's high, flat cheekbones. Over the years, sun and wind and cold had creased and tanned her skin, and her thin hair was as silver-gray as the weathered shingles on the buildings along the wharf. She was tall and sturdy and fit as a man from long tramps in the marshes. She was patient, as a scientist must be, and had taught herself classification and embryology and enough about conventional scientific practices to write articles acceptable to *The American Naturalist* and the Boston Society of Natural History. By the time she was forty-nine, "E. Monroe Carstairs" had earned the reputation of being very sound on the *Mollusca* of the New England coast.

In the course of preparing these articles, Miss Carstairs had collected hundreds of specimens, and little jars containing pickled *Cephalopoda* and *Gastropoda* lined her study shelves in grim profusion. But she had living barnacles and sea slugs as well, housed in the conservatory pool, where they kept company with lobsters and crabs and feathery sea worms in a kind of miniature ocean. In shape the pond was a wide oval, built up at the sides with a mortared stone coping, nestled in an Eden of Boston ferns and sweet-smelling mint geraniums. Miss Carstairs had fitted it out with a series of pumps and filters to bring seawater up from the bay and keep it clean and fresh.

She was very proud of it, and of the collection of marine life it housed. Stocking it with healthy specimens was the chief pleasure of her life. Summer and winter she spent much of her time out stalking the tidal flats after a neap tide or exploring the small brackish pools of the salt marshes. But nothing was as productive of unusual specimens as a roaring gale, which, in beating the ocean to a froth, swept up rare fauna from its very floor.

As Miss Carstairs stood now with her hand upon the bell pull, her wide experience of such storms told her that she must either bring in the seal immediately, or watch it wash away with the tide. She pulled sharply, and when the maid Sarah sleepily answered it, ordered her to rouse Stephen and John without delay and have them meet her in the kitchen passage. "Tell them to bring the lantern, and the stretcher we used for the shark last spring," she said. "And bring me my sou'wester and my boots."

Soon two oil-clothed men, yawning behind their hands, awaited Miss Carstairs in the dark kitchen. They were proud of the forthright eccentricity of their mistress, who kept lobsters in a fancy pool instead of eating them, and traipsed manfully over the mud flats in all weather. If Miss Carstairs wanted to go out into the worst nor'easter in ten years to collect some rare grampus or other, they were perfectly willing to go with her. Besides, she paid them well.

Miss Carstairs leading the way with the lantern, the little company groped its way down the slippery wooden stairs to the beach. The lantern illuminated glimpses of scattered flotsam: gouts of seaweed and beached fish, broken seagulls and strange shells. But Miss Carstairs, untempted, ran straight before the wind to the tidal pool where lay her quarry.

Whatever the creature was, it was not a seal. The dim yellow lantern gave only the most imperfect outline of its shape, but Miss Carstairs could see that it was more slender than a seal, and lacked a pelt. Its front flippers were peculiarly long and flexible, and it seemed to have a crest of bony spines down its back. There was something familiar about its shape, about the configuration of its upper body and head.

Miss Carstairs was just bending to take a closer look when Stephen's impatient "Well, Miss?" drew her guiltily upright. The wind was picking up; it was more than time to be getting back to the house. She stood out of the way while the men unfolded a bundle of canvas and sticks into a stretcher like a sailor's hammock suspended between two long poles. They bundled their find into this contrivance and, in case it might still be alive, covered it with a blanket soaked in seawater. Clumsily, because of the wind and the swaying weight of their burden, the men crossed the beach and labored up the wooden stairs, wound through the garden and up two shallow stone steps to a large glass conservatory built daringly onto the sea side of the house.

When Miss Carstairs opened the door, the wind extinguished most of the gaslights Sarah had thoughtfully lit in the conservatory. So it was in a poor half-light that the men hoisted their burden to the edge of the pool and tipped the creature out onto the long boulder that had once served as a sunning place for Mr. Carstairs's terrapins. The lax body rolled heavily onto the rock; Miss Carstairs eyed it doubtfully while the men panted and wiped at their streaming faces.

"I don't think we should submerge it entirely," she said. "If it's still alive, being out of the water a little longer shouldn't hurt it, and if it is not, I don't want the lobsters getting it before I do."

The men went off to their beds, and Miss Carstairs stood for some while, biting thoughtfully at her forefinger as she contemplated her new specimen. Spiky and naked, it did not look like anything she had ever seen or read about in Allen, Grey, or von Haast. She dismissed the temptation to turn up the gas and examine it more closely with the reflection that the night was far advanced and she herself wet and tired. The specimen would still be there in the morning, and she in a better state to attend to it. But when she ascended the stairs, her footsteps led her not to her bedroom but to her study, where she spent the rest of the night in restless perusal of True's *Catalogue of Aquatic Mammals*.

At six o'clock, Miss Carstairs rang for Sarah to bring her rolls and coffee. By 6:30 she had eaten, bathed, and dressed herself, and was on her way to the conservatory. Her find lay as she had left it, half in and half out of the water. By the light of day, she could see that its muscular tail grew into a powerful torso, scaleless and furless and furnished with what looked like arms, jointed like a human's and roped with long, smooth muscles under a protective layer of fat. Its head was spherical, and flanked by a pair of ears shaped and webbed like fins.

At first, Miss Carstairs refused to believe the evidence of her eyes. Perhaps, she thought, she was overtired from reading all night. The creature, whatever it was, would soon yield its secrets to her scalpel and prove to be nothing more wonderful than a deformed porpoise or a freak manatee.

She took its head in her hands. Its skin was cool and pliant and slimy, very unpleasant to touch, as though a fish had sloughed its scales but not its protective mucus. She lifted its thick, lashless lids to reveal pearly eyes, rolled upward. She had never touched nor seen the like. A new species, perhaps? A new genus?

With a rising excitement, Miss Carstairs palpated its skull, which was hairless and smooth except for the spiny ridge bisecting it, and fingered the slight protrusion between its eyes and lipless mouth. The protrusion was both fleshy and cartilaginous, like a human nose, and as Miss Carstairs acknowledged the similarity, the specimen's features resolved into an unmistakably anthropoid arrangement of eyes, nose, mouth, and chin. The creature was, in fact, neither deformed nor freakish but, in its own way, harmonious. A certain engraving in a long-forgotten book of fairy tales came to her mind, of a wistful child with a human body and a fish's tail.

Miss Carstairs plumped heavily into her wicker chair. Here, lying on a rock in her father's goldfish pond, was a species never examined by Mr. Darwin or classified by Linnaeus. Here was a biological anomaly, a scientific impossibility. Here, in short, was a mermaid, and she, Edith Carstairs, had collected it.

Shyly, almost reverently, Miss Carstairs approached the creature anew. She turned the lax head toward her, then prodded at its wide, lipless mouth to get a look at its teeth. A faint, cool air fanned her fingers, and she snatched them back as though the creature had bitten her. Could it be alive? Miss Carstairs laid her hand flat against its chest and felt nothing; hesitated, laid her ear where her hand had been, and heard a faint thumping, slower than a human heartbeat.

In terror lest the creature awake before she could examine it properly, Miss Carstairs snatched up her calipers and her sketchbook and began to make detailed notes of its anatomy. She measured its cranium, which she found to be as commodious as most men's, and traced its webbed, four-fingered hands. She sketched it full-length from all angles, then made piecemeal studies of its head and finny ears, its curiously muscled torso and its horny claws. From the absence of external genitalia and the sleek roundness of its limbs and body, she thought her specimen to be female, even though it lacked the melon breasts and streaming golden hair of legend. But breasts and streaming hair would drag terribly, Miss Carstairs thought: a real mermaid would be better off without them. By the same token, a real merman would be better off without the drag of external genitals. On the question of the creature's sex, Miss Carstairs decided to reserve judgment.

Promptly at one o'clock, Sarah brought her luncheon—a cutlet and a glass of barley water—and still the creature lay unconscious. Miss Carstairs swallowed the cutlet hastily between taking wax impressions of its claws and scraping slime from its skin to examine under her microscope. She drew a small measure of its thin scarlet blood and poked curiously at the complexity of tissue fringing the apparent opening of its ears, which had no parallel in any lunged aquatic animal she knew. It might, she thought, be gills.

By seven o'clock, Miss Carstairs had abandoned hope. She leaned over her mermaid, pinched the verdigris forearm between her nails, and looked closely at the face for some sign of pain. The wide mouth remained slack; the webbed ears lay flat and unmoving against the skull. It must be dead after all. It seemed that she would have to content herself with dissecting the creature's cadaver, and now was not too early to begin. So she laid out her scalpels and her bone saw and rang for the men to hoist the specimen out of the pool and onto the potting table.

"Carefully, carefully, now." Miss Carstairs hovered anxiously as Stephen and John struggled with the slippery bulk and sighed as it slipped out of their hands. As it landed belly-down across the stone coping, the creature gave a great huff and twitched as though it had been electrified. Then it flopped backward, twisted eel-quick under the water, and peered up at Miss Carstairs from the bottom of the pool, fanning its webbed ears and gaping.

The men fled, stumbling and slipping in their haste.

Fairly trembling with excitement, Miss Carstairs leaned over the water and stared at her acquisition. The mer-creature, mouthing the water, stared back. The tissue in front of its ears fluttered rhythmically, and Miss Carstairs knew a moment of pure scientific gratification. Her hypothesis was proved correct; it did indeed have gills as well as lungs.

The mer undulated gently from crest to tail-tip, then darted from one extremity of the pool to the other, sending water slopping into Miss Carstairs's lap. She recoiled, shook out her skirts, and looked up to see the mer peering over the coping, its eyes deep-set, milk-blue, and as intelligently mournful as a whipped dog's.

Miss Carstairs grinned, then hastily schooled her lips into a solemn line. Had not Mr. Darwin suggested that to most lower animals, a smile is a sign of challenge? If the creature was the oceanic ape it appeared to be, then might it not, as apes do, find her involuntary smile as terrifying as a shark's grinning maw? Was a mer a mammal at all, or was it an amphibian? Did it properly belong to a genus, or was it, like the platypus, *sui generis*? She resolved to reread Mr. Gunther's *The Study of Fishes* and J.E. Grey on seals.

While Miss Carstairs was pondering its origins, the mer seemed to be pondering Miss Carstairs. It held her eyes steadily with its pearly gaze, and Miss Carstairs began to fancy that she heard—no, it was rather that she sensed—a reverberant, rhythmic hushing like a swift tide withdrawing over the sand of a sea cave.

The light shimmered before her eyes. She shook her head and recalled that she had not eaten since lunch. A glance at the watch pinned to her breast told her that it was now past nine o'clock. Little wonder she was giddy, what with having had no sleep the night before and working over the mer-creature all day. Her eyes turned again to her specimen. She had intended ringing for fish and feeding it from her own hand, but now thought she would retire to her own belated supper and leave its feeding to the servants.

• • •

The next morning, much refreshed by her slumbers, Miss Carstairs returned to the conservatory armored with a bibbed denim apron and rubber boots. The mer was sitting perched on the highest point of the rock with its long fish's tail curled around it, looking out over the rose beds to the sea.

It never moved when Miss Carstairs entered the conservatory, but gazed steadily out at the bright vista of water and rocky beach. It sat extremely upright, as if disdaining the unaccustomed weight of gravity on its spine, and its spiky crest was fully erect. One clawed hand maintained its balance on the rock; the other was poised on what Miss Carstairs was obliged to call its thigh. The wide flukes of its yellow-bronze tail draped behind and around it like a train and trailed on one side down to the water. This attitude was to become exceedingly familiar to Miss Carstairs in the weeks that followed; but on this first morning, it struck her as being at once human and alien, pathetic and comic, like a trousered chimpanzee riding a bicycle in a circus.

Having already sketched it from all angles, what Miss Carstairs chiefly wanted was for the mer to *do* something. Now that it was awake, she was hesitant to touch it, for its naked skin and high forehead made it look oddly human and its attitude forbade familiarity. Would it hear her, she wondered, if she tried to get its attention? Or were those earlike fans merely appendages to its gills?

Standing near the edge of the pool, Miss Carstairs clapped her hands sharply. One fluke stirred in the water, but that might have been coincidence. She cleared her throat. Nothing. She climbed upon a low stool, stood squarely in the creature's field of vision, and said quite firmly, "How d'ye do?" Again, nothing, if she excepted an infinitesimal shivering of its skin that she might have imagined. "Boo!" cried Miss Carstairs then, waving her arms in the air and feeling more than a little foolish. "Boo! Boo!"

Without haste, the mer brought its eyes to her face and seemed to study her with a grave, incurious attention. Miss Carstairs climbed down and clasped her hands behind her back. Now that she had its attention, what would she do with it?

Conquering a most unscientific shrinking, Miss Carstairs unclasped her hands and reached one of them out to the creature, palm upward, as if it had been a strange dog. The mer immediately dropped from its upright seat to a sprawling crouch, and to Miss Carstairs's horrified fascination, the movement released from a pouch beneath its belly a boneless, fleshy ocher member that could only be its—unmistakably male—genitalia.

Miss Carstairs hid her confusion in a Boston fern, praying that the merman would withdraw his nakedness, or at least hide it in the water. But when she turned back, he was still stretched at full length along the stone, his outsized privates boldly—Miss Carstairs could only think defiantly—displayed.

He was smiling.

There was nothing pleasant, welcoming, friendly, or even tangentially human about the merman's smile. His gaping mouth was full of needle teeth. Behind them, his gorge was pale rose and palpitating. He had no tongue.

Although she might be fifty years old and a virgin, Miss Carstairs was no delicate maiden lady. Before she was a spinster or even a woman, she was a naturalist, and she immediately forgot the merman's formidable sexual display in wonder at his formidable dentition. Orally, at least, the merman was all fish. His grin displayed to advantage the tooth plate lining his lower jaw, the respiratory lamellae flanking his pharynx, the inner gill septa. Miss Carstairs seized her notebook, licked the point of her pencil, and began to sketch diligently. Once she glanced up to verify the double row of teeth in the lower jaw. The merman was still grinning at her. A moment later she looked again; he had disappeared. Hurriedly, Miss Carstairs laid aside her book and searched the pool. Yes, there he was at the deep end, belly-down against the pebbled bottom.

Miss Carstairs seated herself upon the coping to think. Had the merman acted from instinct or intelligence? If he had noted her shock at the sight of his genitals, then his flourishing them might be interpreted as a deliberate attempt to discomfit her. On the other hand, the entire display could have been a simple example of instinctive aggression, like a male mandrill presenting his crimson posterior to an intruder.

Miss Carstairs mounted to her study and picked up her pen to record her observations. As she inscribed the incident, she became increasingly convinced that the merman's action must be the result of deliberate intention. No predator—and the merman's teeth left no doubt that he was a predator—would instinctively bare rather than protect the most vulnerable portion of his anatomy. He must, therefore, have exposed himself in a gesture of defiance and contempt. But such a line of reasoning, however theoretically sound, did not go far in proving that her merman was capable of reasoned behavior. She must find a way to test his intelligence empirically.

Miss Carstairs looked blindly out over the autumn-bright ocean glittering below her. The duke of Argyll had written that Man was unique among animals in being a tool-user. Yet Mr. Darwin had argued persuasively that chimpanzees and orangutans commonly use sticks and stones to open hard nuts or knock down fruit. Surely no animal lower than an ape would think to procure his food using anything beyond his own well-adapted natural equipment.

Since he was immured in a kind of free-swimming larder, Miss Carstairs could not count upon the merman's being hungry enough to spring her trap for the bait alone. The test must engage his interest as well. Trap: now there was an idea. What if she were to use one of the patent wire rattraps stacked in the garden shed? She could put a fish in a rattrap—a live fish, she thought, would prove more attractive than a dressed one—and offer the merman an array of tools with which to open it—a crowbar, perhaps a pair of wire snips. Yes, thought Miss Carstairs, she would put the fish in a rattrap and throw it into the pool to see what the merman would make of it.

Next morning the merman had resumed his station on the rock looking, if anything, more woebegone than he had the day before. Somewhat nervously, Miss Carstairs entered the conservatory carrying a bucket of water with a live mackerel in it. She was followed by Stephen, who was laden with the rattrap, a crowbar, a pair of wire snips, and a small hacksaw. With his help, Miss Carstairs introduced the mackerel into the trap and lowered it into the deep end of the pool. Then she dismissed Stephen, positioned herself in the wicker chair, pulled *Descent of Man* from her pocket, and pretended to read.

The tableau held for a quarter of an hour or so. Miss Carstairs sat, the merman sat, the rattrap with its mackerel rested on the bottom of the pool, and the tools lay on the coping as on a workbench, with the handles neatly turned toward their projected user. Finally, Miss Carstairs slapped over the page and humphed disgustedly; the merman slithered off the rock into the pool.

A great rolling and slopping of briny water ensued. When the tumult ceased, the merman's head popped up, grinning ferociously. He was clearly incensed, and although his attitude was comic, Miss Carstairs was not tempted to laugh.

With an audible snap, the merman shut his gaping mouth, lifted the rattrap onto the rock, hauled himself up beside it, and carefully examined the tools set out before him. The wire snips he passed over without hesitation. The hacksaw he felt with one finger, which he hastily withdrew when he caught it upon the ragged teeth; Miss Carstairs was interested to observe that he carried the injured member to his mouth to suck just as a man or a monkey would. Then he grasped the crowbar and brought it whistling down upon the trap, distorting it enough for him to see that one end was not made all of a piece with the rest. He steadied the trap with one hand and, thrusting the crowbar through the flap, pried it free with a single mighty heave. Swiftly, he reached inside and grabbed the wildly flapping mackerel.

For a time the merman held the fish before him as if debating what to do with it. He looked from the fish to Miss Carstairs and from Miss Carstairs to the fish, and she heard a sound like a sigh, accompanied by a slight fluttering of his gill flaps. This sigh, combined with his habitual expression of settled melancholy, made his attitude so like that of an elderly gentleman confronted with unfamiliar provender that Miss Carstairs smiled a little in spite of herself. The merman stiffened and gazed at her intently. A long moment passed, and Miss Carstairs heard—or thought she heard—a noise of water rushing over sand; saw—or thought she saw—a glimmer as of sun filtered through clear water.

Now, Miss Carstairs was not a woman given either to the vapors or to lurid imaginings. Thunderstorms that set more delicate nerves quivering merely stimulated her; bones and entrails left her unmoved. Furthermore, she was never ill and had never been subject to sick headaches. So, when her head began to throb and her eyes to dazzle with sourceless pinwheels of light, Miss Carstairs simply closed her eyes to discover whether the effect would disappear. The sound of rushing waters receded; the throb subsided to a dull ache. She opened her eyes to the merman's pearly stare, and sound and pain and glitter returned.

At this point she thought it would be only sensible to avert her eyes. But being sensible would not teach her why the merman sought to mesmerize her or why his stare caused her head to ache so. Deliberately, she abandoned herself to his gaze.

All at once, Miss Carstairs found herself at sea. Chilly green-gray depths extended above and below her, fishy shadows darted past the edges of her vision. She was swimming in a strong and unfamiliar current. The ocean around her tasted of storm and rocks and fear. She knew beyond doubt that she was being swept ever closer to a strange shore, and although she was strong, she was afraid. Her tail scraped sand; the current crossed with windblown waves and conspired to toss her ashore. Bruised, torn, gasping for breath in the thin air, Miss Carstairs fainted.

She came to herself some little time later, her eyes throbbing viciously and her ears ringing. The merman was nowhere to be seen. Slowly, Miss Carstairs dragged herself to her chair and rang for Sarah. She would need tea, perhaps even a small brandy, before she could think of mounting the stairs. She felt slightly seasick.

Sarah exclaimed in shock at her mistress's appearance. "I've had a bit of a turn," said Miss Carstairs shortly. "No doubt I stayed up too late last night reading. If you would bring me some brandy and turn down my bed, I think I should like to lie down. No,"—in answer to Sarah's inquiring look—""you must not call Dr. Bland. I have a slight headache; that is all."

Some little time later, Miss Carstairs lay in her darkened bedroom with a handkerchief soaked in eau de cologne pressed to her aching forehead. She did not know whether to exult or to despair. If her recent vision had been caused by the feverish overexcitement of an unbridled imagination, she feared that excessive study, coupled with spinsterhood, had finally driven her mad as her mother had always warned her it would.

But if the vision had been caused by the merman's deliberate attempt to "speak" to her, she had made a discovery of considerable scientific importance.

Miss Carstairs stirred impatiently against her pillows. Suppose, for the sake of argument, that the experience was genuine. That would suggest that somewhere in the unexplored deeps of the ocean was a race of mermen who could cast images, emotion, even sounds, from mind to mind. Fantastic as the thing sounded, it could be so. In the first edition of the *Origin*, Mr. Darwin had written that over the ages a bear might develop baleen and flippers, evolving finally into a kind of furry whale, if living upon plankton had become necessary to the species' survival. The general mechanism of evolution might, given the right circumstances, produce anthropoid creatures adapted for life in the sea. Why should not some ambitious prehistoric fish develop arms and a large, complex brain, or some island-dwelling ape take to the sea and evolve gills and a tail?

Evolution could also account for a telepathic method of communication, just as it accounted for a verbal one. To Miss Carstairs's mind, the greater mystery was how she could have received and understood a psychic message. Presumably, some highly evolved organ or cerebral fold peculiar to mermen transmitted their thoughts; how could she, poor clawless, gill-less, forked creature that she was, share such an organ?

An exquisitely stabbing pain caused Miss Carstairs to clutch the handkerchief to her brow. She must rest, she thought. So she measured herself a small dose of laudanum, swallowed it, and slept.

Next morning, armed with smelling salts and a pair of smoked glasses that had belonged to her mother, Miss Carstairs approached the conservatory in no very confident mood. Her brain felt sore and bruised, almost stiff, like a long-immobilized limb that had been suddenly and violently exercised. Hesitantly, she peered through the French doors; the merman was back on his rock, staring out to sea. Determined that she would not allow him to overcome her with visions, she averted her gaze, then marched across the conservatory, seated herself, and perched the smoked glasses on her nose before daring to look up.

Whether it was the smoked glasses or Miss Carstairs's inward shrinking that weakened the effect of the merman's stare, this second communion was less intimate than the first. Miss Carstairs saw a coral reef and jewel-like fish darting and hovering over the sea floor like images painted on thin silk, accompanied by a distant chorus of squeaks, whistles, and random grunts. She did not, however, feel the press of the ocean upon her or any emotion other than her own curiosity and wonder.

"Is that your home?" she asked absurdly, and the images stopped. The merman's face did not, apparently could not, change its expression, but he advanced his sloping chin and fluttered his webbed fingers helplessly in front of his chest. "You're puzzled," said Miss Carstairs softly. "I don't wonder. But if you're as intelligent as I hope, you will deduce that I am trying to speak to you in my way as you are trying to speak to me in yours."

This speech was answered by a pause, then a strong burst of images: a long-faced grouper goggling through huge, smoky eyes; a merman neatly skewered on a harpoon; clouds of dark blood drifting down a swift current. Gasping in pain, Miss Carstairs reeled as she sat and, knocking off the useless smoked spectacles, pressed her hands to her eyes. The pain subsided to a dull ache.

"I see that I shall have to find a way of talking to you," she said aloud. Fluttering claws signed the merman's incomprehension. "When you shout at me, it is painful." Her eye caught the hacksaw still lying by the pool. She retrieved it, offered it to the merman blade-first. He recoiled and sucked his finger reminiscently. Miss Carstairs touched her own finger to the blade, tore the skin, then gasped as she had when he had "shouted" at her and, clutching her bleeding finger dramatically, closed her eyes and lay back in her chair.

A moment passed. Miss Carstairs sat slowly upright as a sign that the performance was over. The merman covered his face with his fingers, webs spread wide to veil his eyes.

It was clearly a gesture of submission and apology, and Miss Carstairs was oddly moved by it. Cautiously, she leaned over the coping, and grasped him lightly by the wrist. He stiffened, but did not pull away. "I accept your apology, merman," she said, keeping her face as impassive as his. "I think we've had enough for one day. Tomorrow we'll talk again."

• • •

Over the course of the next few weeks, Miss Carstairs learned to communicate with her merman by working out a series of dumb shows signifying various simple commands: "Too loud!" and "Yes" and "No." For more complex communications, she spoke to him as he spoke to her: by means of images.

The first day, she showed him an engraving of the Sirens that she had found in an illustrated edition of *The Odyssey*. It showed three fishtailed women, rather heavy about the breasts and belly, disposed gracefully on a rocky outcropping, combing their long falls of hair. The merman studied this engraving attentively. Then he fluttered his claws and sighed.

"I don't blame you," said Miss Carstairs. "They look too stupid to sit on the rocks and sing at the same time, much less swim." She laid aside *The Odyssey* and took up a tinted engraving of a parrotfish. The merman advanced his head and sniffed, then snatched the sheet from Miss Carstairs's fingers and turned it this way and that. Catching her eyes, he sent her a vision of that same fish, shining vermilion and electric blue through clear tropical waters, its hard beak patiently scraping polyps out of coral dotted with the waving fronds of sea worms. Suddenly one of the coral's thornier parasites revealed itself as a merman's hand by grabbing the parrotfish and sweeping it into the predator's jaws. "Oh," said Miss Carstairs involuntarily as she became aware of an exciting, coppery smell and an altogether unfamiliar taste in her mouth. "Oh my."

She closed her eyes and the vision dispersed. Her mouth watering slightly and her hands trembling, she picked up her pen to describe the experience. Something of her confusion must have communicated itself to the merman, for when she next sought his eyes, he gave her a gossamer vision of a school of tiny fish flashing brilliant fins. Over time, she came to recognize that this image served him for a smile, and that other seemingly random pictures signified other common emotions: sunlight through clear water was laughter; a moray eel, heavy, hideous, and sharply toothed, was grief.

Autumn wore on to winter, and Miss Carstairs became increasingly adept at eliciting and reading the merman's images. Every morning she would go to the conservatory bearing engravings or sepia photographs and, with their help, wrestle some part of the merman's knowledge from him. Every afternoon, weather permitting, she would pace the marshes or the beach, sorting and digesting. Then, after an early dinner, she would settle herself at her desk and work on "A Preliminary Study of the Species *Homo Oceanus Telepathicans*, With Some Observations on His Society."

This document, which she was confidant would assure E. Monroe Carstairs a chapter of his own in the annals of marine biology, began with a detailed description of the merman and the little she had been able to learn about his anatomy. The next section dealt with his psychic abilities; the next was headed "Communication and Society":

As we have seen (Miss Carstairs wrote), quite a sophisticated level of communication can be achieved by an intelligent merman. Concrete as they necessarily are, his visions can, when properly read and interpreted, convey abstract ideas of some subtlety. But they can convey them only to one other mer. Chemical exudations (*vide supra*) signal only the simplest mer emotions: distress, lust, fear, anger, avoidance; booms and whistles attract a companion's attention or guide cooperative hunting maneuvers. All fine shades of meaning, all philosophy, all poetry, can pass from one mer to another only by direct and lengthy mutual gazing.

This fact, coupled with an instinctive preference for solitude similar to that of the harlequin bass (*S. tigrinus*) and the reef shark (*C. melanopterus*), has prevented *H. oceanus* from evolving anything that *H. sapiens* would recognize as a civilized society. From the time they can safely fend for themselves at about the age of six, mer-children desert their parents to swim and hunt alone, often faring from one ocean to another in their wanderings. When one of these mer-children meets with another of approximately its own age, it will generally pair with that mer-child, whether it be of the same or of the opposite sex. Such a pairing, which seems to be instinctive, is the merman's only means of social intercourse. It may last from a season or two to several years, but a couple with an infant commonly stays together until the child is ready to swim free. Legends exist of couples who swam faithfully together for decades, but as a rule, the enforced and extreme intimacy of telepathic communication comes to wear more and more heavily on one or both members of a pair until they are forced to part. Each mer then swims alone for whatever period of time fate and preference may dictate, until he meets with another receptive mer, when the cycle begins again.

Because of this peculiar behavioral pattern, the mer-folk can have no government, no religion, no community; in short, no possibility of developing a civilization even as primitive as that of a tribe of savages. Some legends they do have (*vide* Appendix A), some image-poems of transcendent beauty remembered and transmitted from pair to pair over the ages. But any new discovery made by a merman or a merwoman swimming alone may all too easily die with its maker or become garbled in transmission between pair and pair. For, except within the pair-bond, the mer's instinct for cooperation is not strong.

• • •

The more she learned about the customs of the mer-folk, the more conscious Miss Carstairs became of how fortunate she was that the merman had consented to speak to her at all. Mermen swimming solitary were a cantankerous lot, as likely to attack a chance-met pair or single mer as to flee it.

Though Miss Carstairs realized that the merman must look upon her as his companion for the duration of his cycle of sociability, she did not fully understand the implications such a companionship had for him. When she thought of his feelings at all, she imagined that he viewed her with the same benevolent curiosity with which she viewed him, never considering that their relationship might seem different from his side of the equation.

The crisis came in early December, when Miss Carstairs determined that it was time to tackle the subject of mer reproductive biology. She knew that an examination of the rituals of courtship and mating was central to the study of any new species, and no scientist, however embarrassing he might find the subject, was justified in shirking it. So Miss Carstairs gathered together her family album and a porcelain baby doll exhumed from a trunk in the attic, and used them, along with an anatomy text, to give the merman a basic lesson in human reproduction.

At first, it seemed to Miss Carstairs that the merman was being particularly inattentive. But close observation having taught her to recognize his moods, she realized at length that his tapping fingers, gently twitching crest, and reluctance to meet her eyes, all signaled acute embarrassment.

Miss Carstairs found this most interesting. She tapped on his wrist to get his attention, then shook her head and briefly covered her eyes. "I'm sorry," she told him, then held out a sepia photograph of herself as a stout and solemn infant propped between her frowning parents on a horsehair sofa. "But you must tell me what I want to know."

In response, the merman erected his crest, gaped fiercely, then dove into the deepest cranny of the pool, where he wantonly dismembered Miss Carstairs's largest lobster. In disgust, she threw the baby doll into the pool after him and stalked from the room. She was furious. Without this section, her article must remain unfinished, and she was anxious to send it off. After having exposed himself on the occasion of their first meeting, after having allowed her to rummage almost at will through his memories and his mind, why would he so suddenly turn coy?

All that afternoon, Miss Carstairs pondered the merman's reaction to her question, and by evening had concluded that mer-folk had some incomprehensible taboo concerning the facts of reproduction. Perhaps reflection would show him that there was no shame in revealing them to her, who could have only an objective and scientific interest in them. It never occurred to her that it might bewilder or upset the merman to speak of mating to a female to whom he was bonded, but with whom he could never hope to mate.

The next morning, Miss Carstairs entered the conservatory to see the merman sitting on his rock, his face turned sternly from the ocean and towards the door. Clearly, he was waiting for her, and when she took her seat and lifted her eyes to his, she felt absurdly like a girl caught out in some childish peccadillo and called into her mother's sitting room to be chastised.

Without preamble, the merman sent a series of images breaking over her. Two mer—one male, one female—swam together, hunted, coupled. Soon they parted, one to the warm coral reefs, the other to arctic seas. The merwoman swam, hunted, explored. A time passed: not long, although Miss Carstairs could not have told how she knew. The merwoman met a merwoman, drove her away, met a merman, flung herself upon him amorously. This exchange was more complex than the earlier couplings; the merman resisted and fled when it was accomplished.

The merman began to eat prodigiously. He sought a companion and came upon a merman, with whom he mated, and who hunted for him when he could no longer easily hunt for himself. As the merman became heavier, he seemed to become greedier, stuffing his pouch with slivers of fish as if to hoard them. *How ridiculous*, thought Miss Carstairs. Then, all at once, the scales covering the pouch gave a writhing heave and a tiny crested head popped out. Tiny gills fluttered; tiny arms worked their way out of their confinement. Claiming its wandering gaze with iridescent eyes, the merman's companion coaxed the infant from its living cradle and took it tenderly into his arms.

• • •

Three days later, Miss Carstairs sent John to the village to mail the completed manuscript of her article, and then she put it out of her mind as firmly as she could. Brooding, she told herself, would not speed it any faster to the editor's desk or influence him to look more kindly upon it once it got there. In the meanwhile, she must not waste time. There was much more the merman could tell her, much more for her to learn. Her stacks of notes and manuscript pages grew higher.

In late January, "Preliminary Study of the Species *Homo Oceanus Telepathicans*" was returned with a polite letter of thanks. As always, the editor of *The American Naturalist* admired Mr. Carstairs's graceful prose style and clear exposition, but feared that this particular essay was more a work of imagination than of scientific observation. Perhaps it could find a more appropriate place in a literary journal.

Miss Carstairs tore the note into small pieces. Then she went down to the conservatory. The merman met her eyes when she entered, recoiled, and grinned angrily at her; Miss Carstairs grinned angrily back. She felt that her humiliation was his fault, that he had misled or lied to her. She wanted to dissect his brain and send it pickled to the editor of *The American Naturalist*; she wanted him to know exactly what had happened and how he had been the cause of it all. But since she had no way to tell him this, Miss Carstairs fled the house for the windy marshes, where she squelched through the matted beach grass until she was exhausted. Humanity had always bored her and now scholarship had betrayed her. She had nothing else.

Standing ankle-deep in a brackish pool, Miss Carstairs looked back across the marshes to her house. The sun rode low in a mackerel sky; its light danced on the calm water around her and glanced off the conservatory glazing. The merman would be sitting on his rock like the Little Mermaid in the tale her father had read her, gazing out over the ocean he could not reach. She had a sudden vision of a group of learned men standing around him, shaking their heads, stroking their whiskers, and debating whether or not this so-called merman had an immortal soul. Perhaps it was just as well the editor of *The American Naturalist* had rejected the article. Miss Carstairs could imagine sharing her knowledge of the merman with the world, but she could not share the merman himself. He had become necessary to her, her one comfort and her sole companion.

Next morning she was back in the conservatory, and on each morning succeeding. Day after day she gazed through the merman's eyes as if he were a living bathysphere, watching damselfish and barracuda stitch silver through the greenish antlers of elkhorn coral, observing the languorous unfurling of the manta ray's wings and the pale groping fingers of hungry anemones. As she opened herself to the merman's visions, Miss Carstairs began not only to see and hear, but also to feel, to smell, even to taste, the merman's homesick memories. She became familiar with the complex symphony of the ocean, the screeching scrape of parrotfish beaks over coral, the tiny, amatory grunts of frillfins. In the shape of palpable odors present everywhere in the water, she learned the distinct tastes of fear, of love, of blood, of anger. Sometimes, after a day of vicarious exploration, she would lie in her bed at night and weep for the thinness of the air around her, the silent flatness of terrestrial night.

The snow fell without Miss Carstairs's noticing, melted and turned to rain, which froze again, then warmed and gentled toward spring. In her abandoned study, the ink dried in the well and the books and papers lay strewn around the desk like old wrecks. Swimming with the merman in the open sea, Miss Carstairs despised the land. When she walked abroad, she avoided the marshes and clambered over the weed-slick rocks to the end of the spit, where she would stand shivering in the wind and spray, staring into the waves breaking at her feet. Most days, however, she spent in the conservatory, gazing hungrily into the merman's pearly eyes.

The merman's visions were becoming delirious with the need for freedom as, in his own way, he pleaded with Miss Carstairs to release him. He showed her mermen caught in fishermen's nets, torn beyond recognition by their struggles to escape the ropes. He showed her companions turning on each other, mate devouring mate when the social cycle of one had outlasted the patience of the other. Blinded by her own hunger, Miss Carstairs viewed these horrific images simply as dramatic incidents in his submarine narrative, like sharks feeding or grouper nibbling at the eyes of drowned sailors.

When at last the merman took to sulking under the rock, Miss Carstairs sat in her wicker chair like a squid lurking among the coral, waiting patiently for him to emerge. She knew the pond was small; she sensed that the ocean's limitless freedom was more real to him when he shared his memories of it. She reasoned that no matter how distasteful the process had become, he must eventually rise and feed her the visions she craved. If, from time to time, she imagined that he might end her tyranny by tearing out her throat, she dismissed the fear. Was he not wholly in her power? When she knew the ocean as well as he, when she could name each fish with its own song, then she would let him swim free.

• • •

One spring morning, Miss Carstairs came down to the conservatory to find the rock empty. At first she thought the merman was hiding; only when she moved toward the pool did she notice that the floor of the conservatory was awash with water and the door was ajar. Against all odds, her merman had found a way to escape her.

Miss Carstairs groped for her wicker chair and sat, bereaved and betrayed as she had not been since her father's death. Her eye fell on the open door; she saw blood and water smeared over the steps. Rising hurriedly, she followed the trail through the garden to where the merman lay unconscious at the head of the beach stairs. With anxious, delicate fingers, she caressed his mouth and chest to feel the thin breath coming from his lips and the faint rhythmic beat under his ribs. His tail was scored and tattered where the gravel garden path had torn away the scales.

Somewhere in her soul, Miss Carstairs felt dismay and tenderness and horror. But in the forefront of her brain, she was conscious only of anger. She had fed him, she thought; she had befriended him; she had opened her mind to his visions. How dare he abandon her? Grasping him by the shoulders, she shook him violently. "Wake up and look at me!" she shouted.

Obediently, the merman opened his opalescent eyes and conjured a vision: the face of a middle-aged human woman. It was a simian face, slope-jawed and snub-nosed, wrinkled and brown.

The ape-woman opened her mouth, showing large, flat teeth. Grimacing fearfully, she stooped toward Miss Carstairs and seized her shoulders with stubby fingers that stung and burned her like anemones. Harsh noises scraped over Miss Carstairs's ears, bearing with them the taint of hunger and need and envy as sweat bears the taint of fear. Miss Carstairs tore herself from the ape-woman's poisonous grasp and covered her face with her hands.

A claw gripped her wrist, shook it to get her attention. Reluctantly, Miss Carstairs removed her hands and saw the merman, immovably melancholy, peering up at her. How could he bear to look at her? she wondered miserably. He shook his head, a gesture he had learned from her, and answered her with a kind of child's sketch: an angular impression of a woman's face, inhumanly beautiful in its severity. Expressions of curiosity, wonder, joy, discovery darted across the woman's features like a swarm of minnows, and she tasted as strongly of solitude as a free-swimming mer.

Through her grief and remorse, Miss Carstairs recognized the justice of each of these portraits. "Beast and angel," she murmured, remembering old lessons, and again the merman nodded. "No, I'm not a mer, am I, however much I have longed for the sea. And it isn't you I want, but what you know, what you have seen."

The merman showed her a coral reef, bright and various, which seemed to grow as she watched, becoming more complex, more brilliant with each addition; then an image of herself standing knee-deep in the sea, watching the merman swim away from her. She smelled of acceptance, resignation, inwardness—the taste of a mer parting from a loved companion.

Wearily, Miss Carstairs rubbed her forehead, which throbbed with multiplying thoughts. Her notebooks, her scholarship, her long-neglected study, all called to her through the merman's vision. At the same time, she noted that he was responding directly to her. Had she suddenly learned to speak visions? Had he learned to see words? Beyond these thoughts, Miss Carstairs was conscious of the fierce warmth of the spring sun, the rich smell of the damp soil, and the faint green rustle of growing leaves. She didn't know if they were the merman's perceptions or her own.

Miss Carstairs pulled herself heavily to her feet and brushed down her skirts with a shaking hand. "It's high time for you to be off," she said. "I'll just ring for Stephen and John to fetch the sling." Unconsciously, she sought the savor of disapproval and rum that was John's signal odor; it lingered near the kitchen door. At the same time, she had a clear vision of Stephen, wrapped in a disreputable jacket, plodding with bucket and fishing pole across the garden to the seawall. She saw him from above, as she had seen him from her bedroom window early that morning. So it was her vision, not the merman's. The scientist in her noted the fact, and also that the throbbing in her head had settled down to a gentle pulse, discernible, like the beating of her heart, only if she concentrated on it.

A laughing school of fish flashed through the ordered currents of her thoughts, and Miss Carstairs understood that the merman found her new consciousness amusing. Then a searing sense of heat and a tight, itching pain under her skin sent her running into the house shouting for John. When he appeared—from the kitchen, she noted—she said, "Get a bucket and a blanket and wet down the merman. You'll find him in the garden, near the sundial. Then bring the stretcher." He gaped at her uncomprehendingly. "Hurry!" she snapped, and strode off toward the seawall in search of Stephen.

Following his scent, she found him hunched over his fishing pole and his pipe. He tasted of wet wool, tobacco, and solitude. "Stephen, I have learned everything from the merman that he is able to tell me. I have decided to release him."

Stephen began to pull in his line. "Yes, Miss," he said. "About time."

• • •

The tide was going out, and the men had to carry their burden far past the tidal pool where the merman had first washed ashore. It was heavy going, for the wet sand was soft and the merman was heavy. When they came to water at last, Miss Carstairs stood by as they released the merman into the shallows, then waded out up to her knees to stand beside him. The sun splintered the water into blinding prisms; she turned her eyes inshore, away from the glare. Behind her, Stephen and John were trudging back toward the beach, the conservatory glittering above them like a crystal jewel box. Sharp tastes of old seaweed and salt-crusted rocks stung her nose. Squinting down, Miss Carstairs saw the merman floating quietly against the pull of the sea, one webbed hand grasping the sodden fabric of her skirt. His crest was erect, his mouth a little open. Miss Carstairs read joy in his pearly eyes, and something like regret.

"I shall not forget what you have shown me," she said, although she knew the words to be superfluous. Mentally, she called up the ape-woman and the scientist and fused them into a composite portrait of a human woman, beast and angel, heart and mind, need and reason; and she offered that portrait to the merman as a gift, an explanation, a farewell. Then he was gone, and Miss Carstairs began to wade back to shore.

$\sim$

Delia Sherman's most recent short stories have appeared in the young adult anthology *Steampunk!* and in Ellen Datlow's *Naked City*. Her novels for younger readers are *Changeling*, *The Magic Mirror of the Mermaid Queen*, and *The Freedom Maze*, a time-travel historical about ante-bellum Louisiana which recently won the Andre Norton Award. When she's not writing, she's teaching, editing, knitting, and cooking. She loves to travel, but when not on the road, she lives in a rambling apartment in New York City with partner Ellen Kushner and far too many pieces of paper.

SILVER OR GOLD

EMMA BULL

Moon Very Thin sat on the raised hearth—the only place in the center room out of the way—with her chin on her knuckles. She would have liked to be doing something more, but the things she thought of were futile, and most were undignified. She watched Alder Owl crisscross the slate floor and pop in and out of the stillroom and the pantry and the laundry. Alder Owl's hands were full of things on every crossing: clean clothes, a cheese, dried yellow dock and feverfew, a tinderbox, a wool mantle. She was frowning faintly all over her round pink face, and Moon knew that she was reviewing lists in her head.

"You can't pack all that," said Moon.

"You couldn't," said Alder Owl. "But I've had fifty years more practice. Now remember to cure the squash before you bring them in, or there'll be nothing to eat."

"You told me," Moon sighed. She shifted a little to let the fire roast a slightly different part of her back. "If I forget it, I can look it up. It's awfully silly for you to set out now. We could have snow next week."

"If we did, then I'd walk through it. But we won't. Not for another month." Alder Owl wrapped three little stoneware jars in flannel and tucked them in her wicker pack.

Moon opened her mouth, and the thing she'd been busy not saying for three days hopped out. "He's been missing since before Midsummer. Why do you have to go now? Why do you have to go at all?"

At that, Alder Owl straightened up and regarded her sternly. "I have responsibilities. You ought to know that."

"But why should they have anything to do with him?"

"He is the prince of the Kingdom of Hark End."

Moon stood up. She was taller than Alder.

Alder Owl had a great many wrinkles, which deepened all over her face

84

when she was about to smile. They deepened now. "First, youngest sons have never been known to quest in packs. Second, all the witches worth their salt and stone have tried to find him, in whatever way suits them best. All of them but me. I held back because I wanted to be sure you could manage without me."

Moon Very Thin stood still for a moment, taking that in. Then she sat back down with a thump and laced her fingers around her knees. "Oh," she said, halfway between a gasp and a laugh. "Unfair, unfair. To get at me through my pride!"

"Yes, my weed, and there's such a lot of it. I have to go, you know. Don't make it harder for me."

"I wish I could do something to help," said Moon after a moment.

"I expect you to do all your work around here, and all of mine besides. Isn't that enough?" Alder Owl smoothed the flap down over the pack and snugged the drawstring tight.

"You know it's not. Couldn't I go with you?"

Alder Owl pulled a stool from under the table with her foot and sat on it, her hands over her knees. "When I travel in my spirit," she said, "to ask a favor of Grandmother, you can't go with me."

"Of course not. Then who'd play the drum, to guide you back?"

Alder Owl beamed. "Clever weed. Open that cupboard over the mantel-shelf and bring me what you find there."

What Moon found was a drum. It was nothing like the broad, flat, cowhide journey-drum, whose speech echoed in her bones and was like a breathing heartbeat under her fingers, whose voice could be heard in the land where there was no voice. This drum was an upright cylinder no bigger than a quart jar. Its body was made of some white wood, and the skins of its two heads were fine-grained and tufted with soft white hair around the lashings. There was a loop of hide to hold it with, and a drumstick with a leather beater tucked through that.

Moon shook her head. "This wouldn't be loud enough to bring you home from the pump, let alone from—where are you going?"

"Wherever I have to. Bring it to me."

Moon brought her the drum, and Alder Owl held it up by the loop of hide and struck it, once. The sound it made was a sharp, ringing tok, like a woodpecker's blow.

Alder Owl said, "The wood is from an ash tree planted at the hour of my birth. The skins are from a ewe born on the same day. I raised the ewe and watered the tree, and on my sixteenth birthday, I asked them for their lives, and they gave them gladly. No matter how far I go, the drum will reach me. When I cannot hear it, it will cease to sound.

"Tomorrow at dawn, I'll leave," Alder Owl continued. "Tomorrow at sunset, as the last rind of the sun burns out behind the line of the Wantnot Hills, and at every sunset after, beat the drum once, as I just did."

Moon was a little shaken by the solemnity of it all. But she gathered her wits at last and repeated, "At sunset each day. Once. I'll remember."

"Hmph. Well." Alder Owl lifted her shoulders, as if solemnity was a shawl she could shrug away. "Tomorrow always comes early. Time to put the fire to bed."

"I'll get the garden things," Moon said. She tossed her cloak on and went out the stillroom door into the night.

Her namesake was up and waxing. Alder Owl would have good light, if she needed to travel by night. But it would be cold traveling; frost dusted the leaves and vines and flagstone paths like talcum. Moon shivered and sighed. "What's the point of having an able-bodied young apprentice, if you're not going to put all that ableness to use?" she muttered to shifting air. The cold carried all her S's off into the dark.

She pinched a bloom from the yellow chrysanthemum, and a stalk of mer-ry-man's wort from its sheltered bed. When she came back into the house she found that Alder Owl had already fed the fire and settled the logs with the poker, and fetched a bowl of water. Moon dropped the flowers into it.

"Comforter, guard against the winter dark," Alder Owl said to the fire, as always, as if she were addressing an old friend. She stirred the water with her fingers as she spoke. "Helpmeet, nourisher of flesh and heart, bide and watch, and let no errant spark leap up until the sun should take thy part."

Firelight brushed across the seamed landscape of Alder Owl's face, flashed yellow in her sharp, dark eyes, turned the white in her hair to ivory. Tomorrow night, Moon thought, she won't be here. Just me. She could believe it only with the front of her mind where all untested things were kept. The rest of her, mind and lungs and soles of feet, denied it.

Alder Owl flicked the water from her hand onto the hearth, and the line of drops steamed. Then she handed the bowl to Moon, and Moon fed the flowers to the fire.

After a respectful silence, Moon said, "It's water." It was the continuation of an old argument. "And the logs were trees that grew out of the earth and fed on water, and the fire itself feeds on those and air. That's all four elements. You can't separate them."

"It's the hour for fire, and it's fire that we honor. At the appropriate hours we honor the other three, and if you say things like that in public, no educated person in the village will speak to you." Alder Owl took the bowl out of Moon's hands and gathered her fingers in a strong, wet clasp. "My weed, my stalk of yarrow. You're not a child anymore. When I leave, you'll be a grown woman, in others' eyes if not your own. What people hear from a child's mouth as foolishness becomes something else on the lips of a woman grown: sacrilege, or spite, or madness. Work the work as you see fit, but keep your mouth closed around your notions, and keep fire out of water and earth out of air."

"But—"

"Empty the bowl now, and get on to bed."

Moon went into the garden again and flung the water out of the bowl—southward, because it was consecrated to fire. Then she stood a little while in the cold, with a terrible hard feeling in her chest that was beyond sadness, beyond tears. She drew in great breaths to freeze it, and exhaled hard to force the fragments out. But it was immune to cold or wind.

"I'd like to be a woman," she whispered. "But I'd rather be a child with you here, than a woman with you gone." The sound of the words, the knowledge that they were true, did what the cold couldn't. The terrible feeling cracked, melted, and poured out of her in painful tears. Slowly the comforting order around her, the beds and borders Alder Owl had made, stopped the flow of them, and the kind cold air wiped them off her face.

At dawn, when the light of sunrise lay tangled in the treetops, Alder Owl settled her pack on her back and went out by the front door. Moon went with her as far as the gate at the bottom of the yard. In the uncertain misty land of dawn, Alder Owl was a solid, certain figure, cloaked in shabby purple wool, her silver and black hair tucked under a drunken-brimmed green hat.

"I don't think you should wear the hat," Moon said, past the tightness in her throat. "You look like an eggplant."

"I like it. I'm an old woman. I can wear what I please."

She was going. What did one say, except "Goodbye," which wasn't at all what Moon wanted? "When will you come back?"

"When I've found him. Or when I know he can't be found."

"You always tell me not to try to prove negatives."

"There are ways," Alder Owl replied, with a sideways look.

Moon Very Thin shivered in the weak sun. Alder Owl squinted up at her, pinched her chin lightly. Then she closed the gate behind her and walked down the hill. Moon watched her—green and purple, silly and strong—until the trees hid her from sight.

She cured the squash before she put them in the cellar. She honored the elements, each at its own hour. She made cheese and wine, and put up the last of the herbs, and beat the rugs, and waxed all the floors against the coming winter muck. She mended the thatch and the fence, pruned the apple trees and turned the garden beds, taking comfort from maintaining the order that Alder Owl had established.

Moon took over other established things, too. By the time the first snow fell, her neighbors had begun to bring their aches and pains to her, to fetch her when a child was feverish, to call her in to set a dog's broken leg or stitch up a horse's gashed flank. They asked about the best day to sign a contract, and whether there was a charm to keep nightshade out of the hay field. In return, they brought her mistletoe and willow bark, a sack of rye flour, a tub of butter.

She didn't mind the work. She'd been brought up for it; it seemed as natural as getting out of bed in the morning. But she found she minded the payment. When the nearest neighbor's boy, Fell, trotted up to the gate on his donkey with the flour sack riding pillion, and thanked her, and gave it to her, she almost thrust it back at him. Alder Owl had given her the skill, and had left her there to serve them. The payment should be Alder Owl's. But there was no saying which would appear first, Alder Owl or the bottom of the sack.

"You look funny," Fell said.

"You look worse," Moon replied, because she'd taught him to climb trees and to fish, and had thus earned the privilege. "Do you know those things made out of wood or bone, with a row of little spines set close together? They call them 'combs.'"

"Hah, hah." He pointed to the flour. "I hope you make it all into cakes and get fat." He grinned and loped back down the path to the donkey. They kicked up snow as they climbed the hill, and he waved at the crest.

She felt better. Alder Owl would never have had that conversation.

Every evening at sunset, Moon took the little drum out of the cupboard over the mantel. She looked at it, and touched it, and thought of her teacher. She tried to imagine her well and warm and safe, with a hot meal before her and pleasant company near. At last, when the rim of the sun blinked out behind the far line of hills, she swung the beater against the fine skin head, and the drum sounded its woodpecker knock.

Each time Moon wondered: Could Alder Owl really hear it? And if she could, what if Moon were to beat it again? If she beat it three times, would Alder Owl think something was wrong, and return home?

Nothing was wrong. Moon put the drum away until the next sunset.

The Long Night came, and she visited all her neighbors, as they visited her. She brought them fir boughs tied with bittersweet, and honey candy, and said the blessing-charm on their doorsteps. She watched the landscape thaw and freeze, thaw and freeze. Candle-day came, and she went to the village, which was sopping and giddy with a spell of warmer weather, to watch the lighting of the new year's lamps from the flame of the old. It could be, said the villagers, that no one would ever find the prince. It could be that the King of Stones had taken him beneath the earth, and that he would lie there without breath, in silence, forever. And had she had any word of Alder Owl, and hadn't it been a long time that she'd been gone?

Yes, said Moon, it had been a long time.

The garden began to stir, almost invisibly, like a cat thinking of breakfast in its sleep. The sound of water running was everywhere, though the snow seemed undisturbed by the ice as thick as ever. Suddenly, as if nature had thrown wide a gate, it was spring, and Moon was run off her legs with work. Lambing set her to wearing muddy paths in the hills between the cottage and the farmsteads all around. The mares began to foal, too. She thanked wisdom that women and men, at least, had no season.

She had been with Tansy Broadwater's bay thoroughbred since late morning. The foal had been turned in the womb and tied in his cord, and Moon was nearly paralyzed thinking of the worth of the two of them, and their lives in her hands. She was bloody to the elbows and hoarse with chanting, but at last she and Tansy regarded each other triumphantly across the withers of a nursing colt.

"Come up to the house for a pot of hot tea," Tansy said as Moon rinsed soap off her hands and arms. "You won't want to start out through the woods now until moonrise, anyway."

Moon lifted her eyes, shocked, to the open barn door. The sun wore the Wantnot Hills like a girdle.

"I have to go," she said. "I'm sorry. I'll be all right." She headed for the trail at a run.

Stones rolled under her boots, and half-thawed ice lay slick as butter in the shadows. It was nearly night already, under the trees. She plunged down the hill and up the next one, and down again, slithering, on all fours sometimes. She could feel her bones inside her brittle as fire-blasted wood, her ankles fragile and waiting for a wrench. She was afraid to look at the sun again.

The gate—the gate at the bottom of the path was under her hands. She sobbed in relief. So close... She raced up through the garden, the cold air like fire in her lungs. She struggled frantically with the front door, until she remembered it was barred inside, that she'd left through the stillroom. She banged through the stillroom door and made the contents of the shelves ring and rattle. To the hearth, and wrench the cupboard door open . . .

The drum was in her hands, and through the window the sun's rind showed, thin as thread, on the hills. She was in time. As the horizon closed like a snake's eyelid over the disk of the sun, Moon struck the drum.

There was no sound at all.

Moon stared at the drum, the beater, her two hands. She had missed, she must have. She brought the beater to the head again. She might as well have hit wool against wool. There was no woodpecker knock, no sharp clear call. She had felt skin and beater meet, she had seen them. What had she done wrong?

Slowly Alder Owl's words came back to her. *When I cannot hear it, it will cease to sound.* Moon had always thought the drum would be hard to hear. But never silent. *Tell me if you can't hear this,* she thought wildly. Something else they'd said as she left, about proving negatives—that there were ways to prove the prince couldn't be found.

If he were dead, for example. If he were only bones under the earth.

And Alder Owl, beyond the drum's reach, might have followed him even to that, under the dominion of the King of Stones.

She thought about pounding the drum; she could see herself doing it in her mind, hammering at it until it sounded or broke. She imagined weeping, too; she could cry and scream and break things, and collapse at last exhausted and miserable.

What she did was to sit where she was at the table, the drum on her knees, watching the dark seep in and fill the room around her. Sorrow and despair rose and fell inside her in a slow rhythm, like the shortening and lengthening of days. When her misery peaked, she would almost weep, almost shriek, almost throw the drum from her. Then it would begin to wane, and she would think, No, I can bear it, until it turned to waxing once again.

She would do nothing, she resolved, until she could think of something useful to do. She would wait until the spiders spun her white with cobwebs, if she had to. But she would do something better than crying, better than breaking things.

The hide lashing of Alder Owl's drum bit into her clenched fingers. In the weak light of the sinking fire, the wood and leather were only a pale mass in her lap. How could Alder Owl's magic have dwindled away to this—a drum with no voice? What voice could reach her now?

And Moon answered herself, wonderingly: Grandmother.

She couldn't. She had never gone to speak with Grandmother herself. And how could she travel there, with no one to beat the drum for her when she was gone? She might be lost forever, wandering through the tangled roots of Grandmother's trees.

Yet she stood and walked, stiff-jointed, to the stillroom. She gathered up charcoal and dried myrtle and cedar. She poured apple wine into a wooden cup, and dropped in a seed from a sky's-trumpet vine. It was a familiar set of motions. She had done them for Alder Owl. She took down the black-fleeced sheepskin from the wall by the front door, laid it out on the floor, and set the wine and incense by it, wine to the east, charcoal to the south. Another trip, to fetch salt and the little bone-handled knife—earth to the north, the little conical pile of salt, and the knife west, for air. (Salt came from the sea, too, said her rebellious mind, and the knife's metal was mined from earth and tempered with fire and water. But she was afraid of heresy now, afraid to doubt the knowledge she must trust with the weight of lives. She did as she'd been taught.)

At last she took the big drum, the journey-drum, out of its wicker case and set it on the sheepskin. The drum would help her partway on her travels. But when she crossed the border, she would have to leave body, fingers, drum all at the crossing, and the drum would fall silent. She needed so little: just a tap, tap, tap. Well, her heart would have to do.

Moon dropped cross-legged on the sheepskin. Right-handed she took up the knife and drew lightly on the floor around herself as if she were a compass. She passed the knife to her left hand behind her back, smoothly, and the knife point never left the slate. That had been hard once, learning to take the knife as Alder Owl passed it to her. She drew the circle again with a pinch of salt dropped from each hand, and with cedar and myrtle smoking and snapping on their charcoal bed. Finally she drew the circle with wine shaken from her fingers, and drank off the rest. Then she took up the drum.

She tried to hear the rhythm of her breathing, of her heart, the rhythm that was always inside her. Only when she felt sure of it did she begin to let her fingers move with it, to tap the drum. It shuddered under her fingers, lowing out notes. When her hands were certain on the drum head, she closed her eyes.

A tree. That was the beginning of the journey, Moon knew; she was to begin at the end of a branch of the great tree. But what kind of tree? Was it night, or day? Should she imagine herself as a bird or a bug, or as herself? And how could she think of all that and play the drum, too?

Her neck was stiff, and one of her feet was going to sleep. You think too much, she scolded herself. Alder Owl had never had such trouble. Alder Owl had also never suggested that there was such a thing as too much thinking. More of it, she'd said, would fix most of the world's problems.

Well, she'd feel free to think, then. She settled into the drumbeat, imagined it wrapped around her like a featherbed.

—A tree too big to ever see all at once, one of a forest of trees like it. A tree with a crown of leaves as wide as a clear night sky on a hilltop. Night time, then. It was an oak, she decided, but green out of season. She envisioned the silver-green leathery leaves around her, and the rough black bark starry with dew in the moonlight. The light came from the end of the branch. Cradled in leaves there was a pared white-silver crescent, a new moon cut free from the shadow of the old. It gave her light to travel by.

The rough highroad of bark grew broader as she neared the trunk. She imagined birds stirring in their sleep and the quick, querulous chirk of a squirrel woken in its nest. The wind breathed in and out across the vault of leaves and made them twinkle. Moon heard her steps on the wood, even and measured: the voice of the drum.

Down the trunk, down toward the tangle of roots, the knotted mirror-image of the branches above. The trunks of other trees were all around her, and the twining branches shuttered the moonlight. It was harder going, shouldering against the life of the tree that always moved upward. Her heartbeat was a thin, regular bumping in her ears.

It was too dark to tell which way was down, too dark to tell anything. Moon didn't know if she'd reached the roots or not. She wanted to cry out, to call for Grandmother, but she'd left her body behind, and her tongue in it.

A little light appeared before her, and grew slowly. There were patterns in it, colors, shapes—she could make out the gate at the bottom of the garden, and the path that led into the woods. On the path—was it the familiar one? It was bordered now with sage—she saw a figure made of the flutter of old black cloth and untidy streamers of white hair, walking away from her. A stranger, Moon thought; she tried to catch up, but didn't seem to move at all. At the first fringes of the trees the figure turned, lifted one hand, and beckoned. Then it disappeared under the roof of the woods.

Moon's spirit, like a startled bird, burst into motion, upward. Her eyes opened on the center room of the cottage. She was standing unsteadily on the sheepskin, the journey drum at her feet. Her heart clattered under her ribs like a stick dragged across the pickets of a fence, and she felt sore and prickly and feverish. She took a step backward, overbalanced, and sat down.

"Well," she said, and the sound of her voice made her jump. She licked her dry lips and added, "That's not at all how it's supposed to be done."

Trembling, she picked up the tools and put them away, washed out the wooden bowl. She'd gathered up the sheepskin and had turned to hang it on the wall when her voice surprised her again. "But it worked," she said. She stood very still, hugging the fleece against her. "It worked, didn't it?" She'd traveled and asked, and been answered, and if neither had been in form as she understood them, still they were question and answer and all that she needed. Moon hurried to put the sheepskin away. There were suddenly a lot of things to do.

The next morning she filled her pack with food and clothing, tinderbox and medicines, and put the little ash drum, Alder Owl's drum, on top of it all. She put on her stoutest boots and her felted wool cloak. She smothered the fire on the hearth, fastened all the shutters, and left a note for Tansy Broadwater, asking her to look after the house.

At last she shouldered her pack and tramped down the path, through the gate, down the hill, and into the woods.

Moon had traveled before, with Alder Owl. She knew how to find her way, and how to build a good fire and cook over it; she'd slept in the open and stayed at inns and farmhouses. Those things were the same alone. She had no reason to feel strange, but she did. She felt like an imposter, and expected every chance-met traveler to ask if she was old enough to be on the road by herself.

She thought she'd been lonely at the cottage; she thought she'd learned the size and shape of loneliness. Now she knew she'd only explored a corner of it. Walking gave her room to think, and sights to see: fern shoots rolling up out of the mushy soil, yellow cups of wild crocuses caught by the sun, the courting of ravens. But it was no use pointing and crying, "Look!," because the only eyes there had already seen. Her isolation made everything seem not quite real. It was harder each night to light a fire, and she had steadily less interest in food. But each night at sunset, she beat Alder Owl's drum. Each night it was silent, and she sat in the aftermath of that silence, bereft all over again.

She walked for six days through villages and forest and farmland. The weather had stayed dry and clear and unspringlike for five of them, but on the sixth she tramped through a rising chill wind under a lowering sky. The road was wider now, and smooth, and she had more company on it: Carts and wagons, riders, other walkers went to and fro past her. At noon she stopped at an inn, larger and busier than any she'd yet seen.

The boy who set tea down in front of her had a mop of blond hair over a cheerful, harried face. "The cold pie's good," he said before she could ask. "It's rabbit and mushroom. Otherwise, there's squash soup. But don't ask for ham—I think it's off a boar that wasn't cut right. It's awful."

Moon didn't know whether to laugh or gape. "The pie, then, please. I don't mean to sound like a fool, but where am I?"

"Little Hark," he replied. "But don't let that raise your hopes. Great Hark is a week away to the west, on foot. You bound for it?"

"I don't know. I suppose I am. I'm looking for someone."

"In Great Hark? Huh. Well, you can find an ant in an anthill, too, if you're not particular which one."

"It's that big?" Moon asked.

He nodded sympathetically. "Unless you're looking for the king or the queen."

"No. A woman—oldish, with hair a little more white than black, and a round pink face. Shorter than I am. Plump." It was hard to describe Alder Owl; she was too familiar. "She would have had an eggplant-colored cloak. She's a witch."

The boy's face changed slowly. "Is she the bossy-for-your-own-good sort? With a wicker pack? Treats spots on your face with witch hazel and horseradish?"

"That sounds like her... What else do you use for spots?"

"I don't know, but the horseradish works pretty well. She stopped here, if that's her. It was months ago, though."

"Yes," said Moon. "It was."

"She was headed for Great Hark, so you're on the right road. Good luck on it."

When he came back with the rabbit pie, he said, "You'll come to Burnton High Plain next—that's a two-day walk. After that you'll be done with the grasslands pretty quick. Then you'll be lucky if you see the sun 'til you're within holler of Great Hark."

Moon swallowed a little too much pie at once. "I will? Why?"

"Well, you'll be in the Seawood, won't you?"

"Will I?"

"You don't know much geography," he said sadly.

"I know I've never heard that the Seawood was so thick the sun wouldn't shine in it. Have you ever been there?"

"No. But everyone who has says it's true. And being here, I get to hear what travelers tell."

Moon opened her mouth to say that she'd heard more nonsense told in the common rooms of inns than the wide world had space for, when a woman's voice trumpeted from the kitchen. "Starling! Do you work here, or are you taking a room tonight?"

The blond boy grinned. "Good luck, anyway," he said to Moon, and loped back to the kitchen.

Moon ate her lunch and paid for it with a coin stamped with the prince's face. She scowled at it when she set it on the table. It's all your fault, she told it. Then she hoisted her pack and headed for the door.

"It's started to drip," the blond boy called after her. "It'll be pouring rain on you in an hour."

"I'll get wet, then," she said. "But thanks anyway."

The trail was cold, but at least she was on it. The news drove her forward.

The boy was right about the weather. The rain was carried on gusts from every direction, that found their way under her cloak and inside her hood and in every seam of her boots. By the time she'd doggedly climbed the ridge above Little Hark, she was wet and cold all through, and dreaming of tight roofs, large fires, and clean, dry nightgowns. The view from the top of the trail scattered her visions.

She'd expected another valley. This was not a bowl, but a plate, full of long, sand-colored undulating grass, and she stood at the rim of it. Moon squinted through the rain ahead and to either side, looking for a far edge, but the grass went on out of sight, unbroken by anything but the small rises and falls of the land. She suspected that clear weather wouldn't have shown her the end of it, either.

That evening she made camp in the midst of the ocean of grass, since there wasn't anyplace else. There was no firewood. She'd thought of that before she walked down into the plain, but all the wood she could have gathered to take with her was soaked. So she propped up a lean-to of oiled canvas against the worst of the rain, gathered a pile of the shining-wet grass, and set to work. She kept an eye on the sun as well; at the right moment she took up Alder Owl's drum and played it, huddling under the canvas to keep it from the wet. It had nothing to say.

In half an hour she had a fat braided wreath of straw. She laid it in a circle of bare ground she'd cleared, and got from her pack her tinderbox and three apples, wrinkled and sweet with winter storage. They were the last food she had from home.

"All is taken from thee," Moon said, setting the apples inside the straw wreath and laying more wet grass over them in a little cone. "I have taken food and footing, breath and warming, balm for thirsting. This I will exchange thee, with my love and honor, if thou'lt give again thy succor." With that, she struck a spark in the cone of grass.

For a moment, she thought the exchange was not accepted. She'd asked all the elements, instead of only fire, and fire had taken offense. Then a little blue flame licked along a stalk, and a second. In a few minutes she was nursing a tiny, comforting blaze, contained by the wreath of straw and fueled all night with Alder Owl's apples.

She sat for a long time, hunched under the oiled canvas lean-to, wrapped in her cloak with the little fire between her feet. She was going to Great Hark, because she thought that Alder Owl would have done so. But she might not have. Alder Owl might have gone south from here, into Cystegond. Or north, into the cold upthrust fangs of the Bones of Earth. She could have gone any-where, and Moon wouldn't know. She'd asked—but she hadn't insisted she be told or taken along, hadn't tried to follow.

"What am I doing here?" Moon whispered. There was no answer except the constant rushing sound of the grass in the wind, saying hush, hush, hush. Eventually she was warm enough to sleep.

The next morning the sun came back, watery and tentative. By its light she got her first real look at the great ocean of golden-brown she was shouldering through. Behind her she saw the ridge beyond which Little Hark lay. Ahead of her there was nothing but grass.

It was a long day, with only that to look at. So she made herself look for more. She saw the new green shoots of grass at the feet of the old stalks, their leaves still rolled tight around one another like the embrace of lovers. A thistle spread its rosette of fierce leaves to claim the soil, but hadn't yet grown tall. And she saw the prints of horses' hooves, and dung, and once a wide, beaten-down swath across her path like the bed of a creek cut in grass, the earth muddy and chopped with hoofprints. As she walked, the sun climbed the sky and steamed the rain out of her cloak.

By evening she reached the town of Burnton High Plain. Yes, the landlord at the hostelry told her, another day's walk would bring her under the branches of the Seawood. Then she should go carefully, because it was full of robbers and ghosts and wild animals.

"Well," Moon said, "Robbers wouldn't take the trouble to stop me, and I don't think I've any quarrel with the dead. So I'll concentrate on the wild animals. But thank you very much for the warning."

"Not a good place, the Seawood," the landlord added.

Moon thought that people who lived in the middle of an eternity of grass probably would be afraid of a forest. But she only said, "I'm searching for someone who might have passed this way months ago. Her name is Alder Owl, and she was going to look for the prince."

After Moon described her, the landlord pursed his lips. "That's familiar. I think she might have come through, heading west. But as you say, it was months, and I don't think I've seen her since."

I've never heard so much discouraging encouragement, Moon thought drearily, and turned to her dinner.

The next afternoon she reached the Seawood. Everything changed: the smells, the color of the light, the temperature of the air. In spite of the landlord's warning, Moon couldn't quite deny the lift of her heart, the feeling of glad relief. The secretive scent of pine loam rose around her as she walked, and the dark boughs were full of the commotion of birds. She heard water nearby; she followed the sound to a running beck and the spring that fed it. The water was cold and crisply acidic from the pines; she filled her bottle at it and washed her face.

She stood a moment longer by the water. Then she hunched the pack off her back and dug inside it until she found the little linen bag that held her valuables. She shook out a silver shawl pin in the shape of a leaping frog. She'd worn it on festival days, with her green scarf. It was a present from Alder Owl—but then, everything was. She dropped it into the spring.

Was that right? Yes, the frog was water's beast, never mind that it breathed air half the time. And silver was water's metal, even though it was mined from the earth and shaped with fire, and turned black as quickly in water as in air. How could magic be based on understanding the true nature of things if it ignored so much?

A bubble rose to the surface and broke loudly, and Moon laughed. "You're welcome, and same to you," she said, and set off again.

The Seawood gave her a century's worth of fallen needles, flat and dry, to bed down on, and plenty of dry wood for her fire. It was cold under its roof of boughs, but there were remedies for cold. She kept her fire well built up, for that, and against any meat-eaters too weak from winter to seek out the horses of Burnton High Plain.

Another day's travel, and another. If she were to climb one of the tallest pines to its top, would the Seawood look like the plain of grass: undulating, almost endless? On the third day, when the few blades of sun that reached the forest floor were slanting and long, a wind rose. Moon listened to the old trunks above her creaking, the boughs swishing like brooms in angry hands, and decided to make camp.

In the Seawood the last edge of sunset was never visible. By then, beneath the trees, it was dark. So Moon built her fire and set water to boil before she took Alder Owl's drum from her pack.

The trees roared above, but at their feet Moon felt only a furious breeze. She hunched her cloak around her and struck the drum.

It made no noise; but from above she heard a clap and thunder of sound, and felt a rush of air across her face. She leaped backward. The drum slid from her hands.

A pale shape sat on a low branch beyond her fire. The light fell irregularly on its huge yellow eyes, the high tufts that crowned its head, its pale breast. An owl.

"Oo," it said, louder than the hammering wind. "Oo-whoot."

Watching it all the while, Moon leaned forward, reaching for the drum.

The owl bated thunderously and stretched its beak wide. "Oo-wheed," it cried at her. "Yarrooh. Yarrooh."

Moon's blood fell cold from under her face. The owl stooped off its branch quick and straight as a dropped stone. Its talons closed on the lashings of the drum. The great wings beat once, twice, and the bird was gone into the rushing dark.

Moon fell to her knees, gasping for breath. The voice of the owl was still caught in her ears, echoing, echoing another voice. Weed. Yarrow. Yarrow.

Tears poured burning down her face. "Oh, my weed, my stalk of yarrow," she repeated, whispering. "Come back!" she screamed into the night. She got no answer but the wind. She pressed her empty hands to her face and cried herself to sleep.

With morning, the Seawood crowded around her as it had before, full of singing birds and softness, traitorous and unashamed. In one thing, at least, its spirit marched with hers. The light under the trees was gray, and she heard the patter of rain in the branches above. Moon stirred the cold ashes of her fire and waited for her heart to thaw. She would go on to Great Hark, and beyond if she had to. There might yet be some hope. And if there wasn't, there might at least be a reckoning.

All day the path led downward, and she walked until her thighs burned and her stomach gnawed itself from hunger. The rain came down harder, showering her ignominiously when the wind shook the branches. She meant to leave the Seawood before she slept again, if it meant walking all night. But the trees began to thin around her late in the day, and shortly after she saw a bare rise ahead of her. She mounted it and looked down.

The valley was full of low mist, eddying slowly in the rain. Rising out of it was the largest town Moon had ever seen. It was walled in stone and gated with oak and iron, and roofed in prosperous slate and tile. Pennons flew from every wall tower, their colors darkened with rain and stolen away by the gray light. At the heart of the town was a tall, white, red-roofed building, cornered with round towers like the wall.

The boy was right about this, too. She could never find news of one person in such a place, unless that person was the king or the queen. Moon drooped under a fresh lashing of rain.

But why not? Alder Owl had set off to find the prince. Why wouldn't she have gone to the palace and stated her business, and searched on from there? And why shouldn't Moon do the same?

She flapped a sheet of water off her cloak and plunged down the trail. She had another hour's walk before she would reach the gates, and she wanted to be inside by sundown.

The wall loomed over her at last, oppressively high, dark, and shining with rain. She found the huge double gates open, and the press of wagons and horses and pedestrians in and out of them daunting. No one seemed to take any notice when she joined the stream and passed through, and though she looked and looked, she couldn't see anyone who appeared to be any more official than anyone else. Everyone, in fact, looked busy and important. So this is city life, Moon thought, and stepped out of the flow of traffic for a better look around.

Without her bird's eye view, she knew she wouldn't find the palace except by chance. So she asked directions of a woman and a man unloading a cart full of baled hay.

They looked at her and blinked, as if they were too weary to think; they were at least as wet as Moon was, and seemed to have less hope of finding what they were looking for. Their expressions of surprise were so similar that

Moon wondered if they were blood relations, and indeed, their eyes were much alike, green-gray as sage. The man wore a dusty brown jacket work through at one elbow; the woman had a long, tattered black shawl pulled up over her white hair.

"Round the wall that way," said the man at last, "until you come to a broad street all laid with brick. Follow that uphill until you see it."

"Thank you." Moon eyed the hay cart, which was nearly full. Work was ointment for the heart. Alder Owl had said so. "Would you like some help? I could get in the cart and throw bales down."

"Oh, no," said the woman. "It's all right."

Moon shook her head. "You sound like my neighbors. With them, it would be fifteen minutes before we argued each other to a standstill. I'm going to start throwing hay instead." At that, she scrambled into the cart and hoisted a bale. When she turned to pass it on to the man and woman, she found them looking at each other, before the man came to take the hay from her.

It was hot, wet, prickly work, but it didn't take long. When the cart was empty, they exchanged thanks and Moon set off again for the palace. On the way, she watched the sun's eye close behind the line of the hills.

The brick-paved street ran in long curves like an old riverbed. She couldn't see the palace until she'd tramped up the last turning and found the high white walls before her, and another gate. This one was carved and painted with a flock of rising birds, and closed.

Two men stood at the gate, one on each side. They were young and tall and broad-shouldered, and Moon recognized them as being of a type that made village girls stammer. They stood very straight, and wore green capes and coats with what Moon thought was an excessive quantity of gold trim. She stepped up to the nearest.

"Pardon me," she said, "I'd like to speak to the king and queen."

The guard blinked even more thoroughly than the couple with the hay cart had. With good reason, Moon realized; now she was not only travel-stained and sodden, but dusted with hay as well. She sighed, which seemed to increase the young man's confusion.

"I'll start nearer the beginning," she told him. "I came looking for my teacher, who set off at the end of last autumn to look for the prince. Do you remember a witch, named Alder Owl, from a village two weeks east of here? I think she might have come to the palace to see the king and queen about it."

The guard smiled. Moon thought she wouldn't feel too scornful of a girl who stammered in his presence. "I suppose I could have a message taken to Their Majesties," he said at last. "Someone in the palace may have met your teacher. Hi, Rush!" he called to the guard on the other side of the gate. "This woman is looking for her teacher, a witch who set out to find the prince. Who would she ask, then?"

Rush sauntered over, his cape swinging. He raised his eyebrows at Moon. "Every witch in Hark End has gone hunting the prince at one time or another. How would anyone remember one out of the lot?"

Moon drew herself up very straight, and found she was nearly as tall as he was. She raised only one eyebrow, which she'd always found effective with Fell. "I'm sorry your memory isn't all you might like it to be. Would it help if I pointed out that this witch remains unaccounted for?"

"There aren't any of those. They all came back, cap in hand and dung on their shoes, saying, 'Beg pardon, Lord,' and 'Perishing sorry, Lady.' You could buy and sell the gaggle of them with the brass on my scabbard."

"You," Moon told him sternly, "are of very little use."

"More use than anyone who's sought him so far. If they'd only set my unit to it… "

She looked into his hard young face. "You loved him, didn't you?"

His mouth pinched closed, and the hurt in his eyes made him seem for a moment as young as Fell. It held a glass up to her own pain. "Everyone did. He was—is the land's own heart."

"My teacher is like that to me. Please, may I speak with someone?"

The polite guard was looking from one to the other of them, alarmed. Rush turned to him and frowned. "Take her to—merry heavens, I don't know. Try the steward. He fancies he knows everything."

And so the Gate of Birds opened to Moon Very Thin. She followed the polite guard across a paved courtyard held in the wide, high arms of the palace, colonnaded all around and carved with the likenesses of animals and flowers. On every column a torch burned in its iron bracket, hissing in the rain, and lit the courtyard like a stage. It was very beautiful, if a little grim.

The guard waved her through a small iron-clad door into a neat parlor. A fire was lit in the brick hearth and showed her the rugs and hangings, the paneled walls blackened with age. The guard tugged an embroidered pull near the door and turned to her.

"I should get back to the gate. Just tell the steward, Lord Leyan, what you know about your teacher. If there's help for you here, he'll see that you get it."

When he'd gone, she gathered her damp cloak about her and wondered if she ought to sit. Then she heard footsteps, and a door she hadn't noticed opened in the paneling.

A very tall, straight-backed man came through it. His hair was white and thick and brushed his shoulders, where it met a velvet coat faced in crewelled satin. He didn't seem to find the sight of her startling, which Moon took as a good sign.

"How may I help you?" he asked.

"Lord Leyan?"

He nodded.

"My name is Moon Very Thin. I've come from the east in search of my teacher, the witch Alder Owl, who set out last autumn to find the prince. I think now… I won't find her. But I have to try." To her horror, she felt tears rising in her eyes.

Lord Leyan crossed the room in a long stride and grasped her hands. "My dear, don't cry. I remember your teacher. She was an alarming woman, but that gave us all hope. She has not returned to you, either, then?"

Moon swallowed and shook her head.

"You've traveled a long way. You shall have a bath and a meal and a change of clothes, and I will see if anyone can tell you more about your teacher."

Before Moon was quite certain how it had been managed, she was standing in a handsome dark room with a velvet-hung bed and a fire bigger than the one in the parlor, and a woman with a red face and fly-away hair was pouring cans of water into a bathtub shaped and painted like a swan.

"That's the silliest thing I've ever seen," said Moon in wonder.

The red-faced woman grinned suddenly. "You know, it is. And it may be the lords and ladies think so, too, and are afraid to say."

"One of them must have paid for it once."

"That's so. Well, no one's born with taste. Have your bath, and I'll bring you a change of clothes in a little."

"You needn't do that. I have clean ones in my pack."

"Yes, but have they got lace on them, and a 'broidery flower for every seam? If not, you'd best let me bring these, for word is you eat with the King and Queen."

"I do?" Moon blurted, horrified. "Why?"

"Lord Leyan went to them, and they said send you in. Don't pop your eyes at me, there's no help for it."

Moon scrubbed until she was pink all over, and smelling of violet soap. She washed her hair three times, and trimmed her short nails, and looked in despair at her reflection in the mirror. She didn't think she'd put anyone off dinner, but there was no question that the only thing that stood there was Moon Very Thin, tall and brown and forthright.

"Here, now," said the red-faced woman at the door. "I thought this would look nice, and you wouldn't even quite feel a fool in it. What do you say?"

Draped over her arms she had a plain, high-necked dress of amber linen, and an overgown of russet velvet. The hem and deep collar were embroidered in gold with the platter-heads of yarrow flowers. Moon stared at that, and looked quickly up at the red-faced woman. There was nothing out of the way in her expression.

"It's—it's fine. It's rather much, but…"

"But it's the least much that's still enough for dining in the hall. Let's get you dressed."

The woman helped her into it, pulling swaths of lavender-scented fabric over her head. Then she combed out Moon's hair, braided it, and fastened it with a gold pin.

"Good," the red-faced woman said. "You look like you, but dressed up, which is as it should be. I'll show you to the hall."

Moon took a last look at her reflection. She didn't think she looked at all like herself. Dazed, she followed her guide out of the room.

She knew when they'd almost reached their destination. A fragrance rolled out of the hall that reminded Moon she'd missed three meals. At the door, the red-faced woman stopped her.

"You'll do, I think. Still—tell no lies, though you may be told them. Look anyone in the eye, though they might want it otherwise. And take everything offered you with your right hand. It can't hurt." With that the red-faced woman turned and disappeared down the maze of the corridor.

Moon straightened her shoulders and, her stomach pinched with hunger and nerves, stepped into the hall.

She gaped. She couldn't help it, though she'd promised herself she wouldn't. The hall was as high as two rooms, and long and broad as a field of wheat. It had two yawning fireplaces big enough to tether an ox in. Banners hung from every beam, sewn over with beasts and birds and things she couldn't name. There weren't enough candles in all Hark End to light it top to bottom, nor enough wood in the Seawood to heat it, so like the great courtyard it was beautiful and grim.

The tables were set in a U, the high table between the two arms. To her dazzled eye, it seemed every place was taken. It was bad enough to dine with the king and queen. Why hadn't she realized that it would be the court as well?

At the high table, the king rose smiling. "Our guest!" he called. "Come, there's a place for you beside my lady and me."

Moon felt her face burning as she walked to the high table. The court watched her go; but there were no whispers, no hands raised to shield moving lips. She was grateful, but it was odd.

Her chair was indeed set beside those of the king and queen. The king was white haired and broad shouldered, with an open, smiling face and big hands. The queen's hair was white and gold, and her eyes were wide and gray as storms.

She smiled, too, but as if the gesture were a sorrow she was loath to share.

"Lord Leyan told us your story," said the queen. "I remember your teacher. Had you been with her long?"

"All my life," Moon replied.

"Then you are a witch as well?" the king asked.

"I don't know. I've been taught by a witch, and learned witches' knowledge. But she taught me gardening and carpentry, too."

"You hope to find her?"

Moon looked at him, and weighed the question seriously for the first time since the Seawood. "I hope I may learn she's been transformed, and that I can change her back. But I think I met her, last night in the wood, and I find it's hard to hope."

"But you want to go on?" the queen pressed her. "What will you do?"

"The only thing I can think of to do is what she set out for: I mean to find your son."

Moon couldn't think why the queen would pale at that.

"Oh, my dear, don't," the king said. "Our son is lost, your teacher is lost— what profit can there be in throwing yourself after them? Rest here, then go home and live. Our son is gone."

It was a fine, rich hall, and he was a fair, kingly man. But it was all dimmed, as if a layer of soot lay over the palace and its occupants.

"What did he look like, the prince?"

The king frowned. It was the queen who drew a locket out of the bodice of her gown, lifted its chain over her head and passed it to Moon. It held, not the costly miniature she'd expected, but a sketch in soft pencil, swiftly done. It was the first informal thing she could recall seeing in the palace.

"He wouldn't sit still to be painted," the queen said wistfully. "One of his friends likes to draw. He gave me that after… after my son was gone."

He had been reading, perhaps, when his friend snatched that quiet moment to catch his likeness. The high forehead was propped on a long-fingered hand; the eyes were directed downward, and the eyelids hid them. The nose was straight, and the mouth was long and grave. The hair was barely suggested; light or dark, it fell unruly around the supporting hand. Even setting aside the kindly eye of friendship that informed the pencil, Moon gave all the village girls leave to be silly over this one. She closed the locket and gave it back.

"You can't know what's happened to him. How can you let him go, without knowing?"

"There are many things in the world I will never know," the king said sharply.

"I met a man at the gate who still mourns the prince. He called him the heart of the land. Nothing can live without its heart."

The queen drew a breath and turned her face to her plate, but said nothing.

"Enough," said the king. "If you must search, then you must. But I'll have peace at my table. Here, child, will you pledge it with me?"

Over Moon's right hand, lying on the white cloth, he laid his own, and held his wine cup out to her.

She sat frozen, staring at the chased silver and her own reflection in it. Then she raised her eyes to his and said, "No."

There was a shattering quiet in the hall.

"You will not drink?"

"I will not… pledge you peace. There isn't any here, however much anyone may try to hide it. I'm sorry." That, she knew when she'd said it, was true. "Excuse me," she added, and drew her hand out from under the king's, which was large, but soft. "I'm going to bed. I mean to leave early tomorrow."

She rose and walked back down the length of the room, lapped in a different kind of silence.

A servant found her in the corridor and led her to her chamber. There she found her old clothes clean and dry and folded, the fire tended, the bed turned down. The red-faced woman wasn't there. She took off her finery, laid it out smooth on a chair, and put her old nightgown on.

The pin was in her hand, and she was reaching to set it down, when she saw what it was. A little leaping frog. But now it was gold.

It was hers. The kicking legs and goggle eyes, every irregularity—it was her pin. She dashed to the door and flung it open. "Hello?" she called. "Oh, bother!" She stepped back into the room and searched, and finally found the bell pull disguised as a bit of tapestry.

After a few minutes, a girl with black hair and bright eyes came to the door. "Yes, ma'am?"

"The woman who helped me, who drew my bath and brought me clothes. Is she still here?"

The girl looked distressed. "I'm sorry, ma'am. I don't know who waited on you. What did she look like?"

"About my height. With a red face and wild, wispy hair."

The girl stared, and said, "Ma'am—are you sure? That doesn't sound like anyone here."

Moon dropped heavily into the nearest chair. "Why am I not surprised? Thank you very much. I didn't mean to disturb you."

The girl nodded and closed the door behind her. Moon put out the candles, climbed into bed, and lay awake for an uncommonly long time.

In a gray, wet dawn, she dressed and shouldered her pack and by the simple expedient of going down every time she came to a staircase, found a door that led outside. It was a little postern, opening on a kitchen garden and a wash yard fenced in stone. At the side of the path, a man squatted by a wooden hand cart, mending a wheel.

"Here, missy!" he called out, his voice like a spade thrust into gravel. "Hold this axle up, won't you?"

Moon sighed. She wanted to go. She wanted to be moving, because moving would be almost like getting something done. And she wanted to be out of this beautiful place that had lost its heart. She stepped over a spreading clump of rhubarb, knelt, and hoisted the axle.

Whatever had damaged the wheel had made the axle split; the long splinter of wood bit into Moon's right hand. She cried out and snatched that hand away. Blood ran out of the cut on her palm and fell among the rhubarb stems, a few drops. Then it ceased to flow.

Moon looked up, frightened, to the man with the wheel.

It was the man from the hay wagon, white-haired, his eyes as green and gray as sage. He had a ruddy, somber face. Red-faced, like the woman who'd—

The woman who'd helped her last night had been the one from the hay cart. Why hadn't she seen it? But she remembered it now, and the woman's green eyes, and even a fragment of hay caught in the wild hair. Moon sprang up.

The old man caught her hand. "Rhubarb purges, and rhubarb means advice. Turn you back around. Your business is in there." He pointed a red, rough finger at the palace, at the top of the near corner tower. Then he stood, dusted off his trousers, strolled down the path and was gone.

Moon opened her mouth, which she hadn't been able to do until then. She could still feel his hand, warm and calloused. She looked down. In the palm he'd held was a sprig of hyssop and a wisp of broom, and a spiraling stem of convolvulus.

Moon bolted back through the postern door and up the first twisting flight of stairs she found, until she ran out of steps. Then she cast furiously about. Which way was that wretched tower? She got her bearings by looking out the corridor windows. It would be that door, she thought. She tried it; it resisted.

He could have kept his posy and given me a key, she thought furiously. Then: But he did.

She plucked up the convolvulus, poked it into the keyhole, and said, "Turn away, turn astray, backwards from the turn of day. What iron turned to lock away, herb will turn the other way." Metal grated against metal, and the latch yielded under her hand.

A young man's room, frozen in time. A jerkin of quilted, painted leather dropped on a chair; a case of books, their bindings standing in bright ranks; a wooden flute and a pair of leather gloves lying on an inlaid cedar chest; an unmade bed, the coverlet slid sideways and half pooled on the floor.

More, a room frozen in a tableau of atrocity and accusation. For Moon could feel it, the thing that had been done here, that was still being done because the room had sat undisturbed. Nightshade and thornapple, skullcap, henbane, and fern grown bleached and stunted under stone. Moon recognized their scents and their twisted strength around her, the power of the work they'd made and the shame that kept them secret.

There was a dust of crushed leaf and flower over the door lintel, on the sill of every window, lined like seams in the folds of the bed hangings. Her fingers clenched on the herbs in her hand as rage sprouted up in her and spread.

With broom and hyssop she dashed the dust from the lintel, the windows, the hangings. "Merry or doleful, the last or the first," she chanted as she swung her weapons, spitting each word in fury, "fly and be hunted, or stay and be cursed!"

"What are you doing?" said a voice from the door, and Moon spun and raised her posy like a dagger.

The king stood there, his coat awry, his hair uncombed. His face was white as a corpse's, and his eyes were wide as a man's who sees the gallows, and knows the noose is his.

"You did this," Moon breathed; and louder, "You gave him to the King of Stones with your own hand."

"I had to," he whispered. "He made a beggar of me. My son was the forfeit."

"You locked him under the earth. And let my teacher go to her... to her death to pay your forfeit."

"It was his life or mine!"

"Does your lady wife know what you did?"

"His lady wife helped him to do it," said the queen, stepping forward from the shadows of the hall. She stood tall and her face was quiet, as if she welcomed the noose. "Because he was her love and the other, only her son. Because she feared to lose a queen's power. Because she was a fool, and weak. Then she kept the secret, because her heart was black and broken, and she thought no worse could be done than had been done already."

Moon turned to the king. "Tell me," she commanded.

"I was hunting alone," said the king in a trembling voice. "I roused a boar. I... had a young man's pride and an old man's arm, and the boar was too much for me. I lay bleeding and in pain, and the sight nearly gone from my eyes, when I heard footsteps. I called out for help.

"'You are dying,' he told me, and I denied it, weeping. 'I don't want to die,' I said, over and over. I promised him anything, if he would save my life." The king's voice failed, and stopped.

"Where?" said Moon. "Where did this happen?"

"In the wood under Elder Scarp. Near the waterfall that feeds the stream called the Laughing Girl."

"Point me the way," she ordered.

The sky was hazed white, and the air was hot and still. Moon dashed sweat from her forehead as she walked. She could have demanded a horse, but she had walked the rest of the journey, and this seemed such a little way compared to that. She hoped it would be cooler under the trees.

It wasn't, and the gnats were worse around her face, and the biting flies. Moon swung at them steadily as she clambered over the stones. It seemed a long time before she heard the waterfall, then saw it. She cast about for the clearing, and wondered, were there many? Or only one, and it so small that she could walk past it and never know? The falling water thrummed steadily, like a drum, like a heartbeat.

In a shaft of sun, she saw a bit of creamy white—a flower head, round and flat as a platter, dwarfed with early blooming. She looked up and found that she stood on the edge of a clearing, and was not alone.

He wore armor, dull gray plates worked with fantastic embossing, trimmed in glossy black. He had a gray cloak fastened over that, thrown back off his shoulders, but with the hood up and pulled well forward. Moon could see nothing of his face.

"In the common way of things," he said, in a quiet, carrying voice, "I seek out those I wish to see. I am not used to uninvited guests."

The armor was made of slate and obsidian, because he was the King of Stones.

She couldn't speak. She could command the king of Hark End, but this was a king whose rule did not light on him by an accident of blood or by the acclaim of any mortal thing. This was an embodied power, a still force of awe and terror.

"I've come for a man and his soul," she whispered. "They were wrongly taken."

"I take nothing wrongly. Are you sure?"

She felt heat in her face, then cold at the thought of what she'd said: that she'd accused him. "No," she admitted, the word cracking with her fear. "But that they were wrongly given, I know. He was not theirs to give."

"You speak of the prince of Hark End. They were his parents. Would you let anyone say you could not give away what you had made?"

Moon's lips parted on a word; then she stared in horror. Her mind churned over the logic, followed his question back to its root.

He spoke her thoughts aloud. "You have attended at the death of a child, stilled in the womb to save the mother's life. How is this different?"

"It is different!" she cried. "He was a grown man, and what he was was shaped by what he did, what he chose."

"He had his mother's laugh, his grandfather's nose. His father taught him to ride. What part of him was not made by someone else? Tell me, and we will see if I should give that part back."

Moon clutched her fingers over her lips, as if by that she could force herself to think it all through before she spoke. "His father taught him to ride," she repeated. "If the horse refuses to cross a ford, what makes the father use his spurs, and the son dismount and lead it? He has his mother's laugh—but what makes her laugh at one thing, and him at another?"

"What, indeed?" asked the King of Stones. "Well, for argument's sake I'll say his mind is in doubt, and his heart. What of his body?"

"Bodies grow with eating and exercise," Moon replied. This was ground she felt sure of. "Do you think the king and the queen did those for him?"

The King of Stones threw back his cowled head and laughed, a cold ringing sound. It restored Moon to sensible terror. She stepped back, and found herself against a tree trunk.

"And his soul?" said the King of Stones at last.

"That didn't belong to his mother and father," Moon said, barely audible even to her own ears. "If it belonged to anyone but himself, I think you did not win it from Her."

Silence lay for long moments in the clearing. Then he said, "I am well tutored. Yet there was a bargain made, and a work done, and both sides knew what they pledged and what it meant. Under law, the contract was kept."

"That's not true. Out of fear the king promised you anything, but he never meant the life of his son!"

"Then he could have refused me that, and died. He said 'Anything,' and meant it, unto the life of his son, his wife, and all his kingdom."

He had fought her to a standstill with words. But, words used up and useless, she still felt a core of anger in her for what had been done, outrage against a thing she knew, beyond words, was wrong.

So she said aloud, "It's wrong. It was a contract that was wrong to make, let alone to keep. I know it."

"What is it," said the King of Stones, "that says so?"

"My judgment says so. My head." Moon swallowed. "My heart."

"Ah. What do I know of your judgment? Is it good?"

She scrubbed her fingers over her face. He had spoken lightly, but Moon knew the question wasn't light at all. She had to speak the truth; she had to decide what the truth was. "It's not perfect," she answered reluctantly. "But yes, I think it's as good as most people's."

"Do you trust it enough to allow it to be tested?"

Moon lifted her head and stared at him in alarm. "What?"

"I will test your judgment. If I find it good, I will let you free the prince of Hark End. If not, I will keep him, and you will take your anger, your outrage, and the knowledge of your failure home to nurture like children all the rest of your life."

"Is that prophecy?" Moon asked hoarsely.

"You may prove it so, if you like. Will you take my test?"

She drew a great, trembling breath. "Yes."

"Come closer, then." With that, he pushed back his hood.

There was no stone helm beneath, or monster head. There was a white-skinned man's face, all bone and sinew and no softness, and long black hair rucked from the hood. The sockets of his eyes were shadowed black, though the light that fell in the clearing should have lit all of his face. Moon looked at him and was more frightened than she would have been by any deformity, for she knew then that none of this—armor, face, eyes—had anything to do with his true shape.

"Before we begin," he said in that soft, cool voice. "There is yet a life you have not asked me for, one I thought you'd beg of me first of all."

Moon's heart plunged, and she closed her eyes. "Alder Owl."

"You cannot win her back. There was no treachery there. She, at least, I took fairly, for she greeted me by name and said I was well met."

"No!" Moon cried.

"She was sick beyond curing, even when she left you. But she asked me to give her wings for one night, so that you would know. I granted it gladly."

She thought she had cried all she could for Alder Owl. But this was the last death, the death of her little foolish hope, and she mourned that and Alder Owl at once with falling, silent tears.

"My test for you, then." He stretched out his hands, his mailed fingers curled over whatever lay in each palm. "You have only to choose," he said. He opened his fingers to reveal two rings, one silver, one gold.

She looked from the rings to his face again, and her expression must have told him something.

"You are a witch," said the King of Stones, gently mocking. "You read symbols and make them, and craft them into nets to catch truth in. This is the meat of your training, to read the true nature of a thing. Here are symbols—choose between them. Pick the truer. Pick the better."

He pressed forward first one hand, then the other. "Silver, or gold? Left or right? Night or day, moon—" she heard him mock her again, "—or sun, water or fire, waning or waxing, female or male. Have I forgotten any?"

Moon wiped the tears from her cheeks and frowned down at the rings. They were plain, polished circles of metal, not really meant for finger rings at all.

Circles, complete in themselves, unmarred by scratch or tarnish.

Silver, or gold. Mined from the earth, forged in fire, cooled in water, pierced with air. Gold was rarer, silver was harder, but both were pure metals. Should she choose rareness? Hardness? The lighter color? But the flash of either was bright. The color of the moon? But she'd seen the moon, low in the sky, yellow as a peach. And the light from the moon was reflected light from the sun, whose color was yellow although in the sky it was burning white, and whose metal was gold. There was nothing to choose between them.

The blood rushed into her face, and the gauntleted hands and their two rings swam in her vision. It was true. She'd always thought so.

Her eyes sprang up to the face of the King of Stones. "It's a false choice. They're equal."

As she said the words, her heart gave a single terrified leap. She was wrong. She was defeated, and a fool. The King of Stones' fingers closed again over the rings.

"Down that trail to a granite stone, and then between two hazel trees," he said. "You'll find him there."

She was alone in the clearing.

Moon stumbled down the trail, dazed with relief and the release of tension. She found the stone, and the two young hazel trees, slender and leafed out in fragile green, and passed between them.

She plunged immediately into full sunlight and strangeness. Another clearing, carpeted with deep grass and the stars of spring flowers, surrounded by blossoming trees—but trees in blossom didn't also stand heavy with fruit, like a vain child wearing all its trinkets at once. She saw apples, cherries, and pears under their drifts of pale blossom, ripe and without blemish. At the other side of the clearing there was a shelf of stone thrust up out of the grass. On it, as if sleeping, lay a young man, exquisitely dressed.

Golden hair, she thought. That's why it was drawn in so lightly. Like amber, or honey. The fair face was very like the sketch she remembered, as was the scholar's hand palm up on the stone beside it. She stepped forward.

Beside the stone, the black branches of a tree lifted, moved away from their neighbors, and the trunk—not a tree. A stag stepped into the clearing, scattering the apple blossoms with the great span of his antlers. He was black as charcoal, and his antler points were shining black, twelve of them or more. His eyes were large and red.

He snorted and lowered his head, so that she saw him through a forest of polished black dagger points. He tore at the turf with one cloven foot.

I passed his test! she cried to herself. Hadn't she won? Why this? You'll find him there, the King of Stones had said. Then her anger sprang up as she remembered what else he'd said: I will let you free the prince of Hark End.

What under the wide sky was she supposed to do? Strike the stag dead with her bare hand? Frighten it away with a frown? Turn it into—

She gave a little cry at the thought, and the stag was startled into charging. She leaped behind the slender trunk of a cherry tree. Cloth tore as the stag yanked free of her cloak.

The figure on the shelf of stone hadn't moved. She watched it, knowing her eyes ought to be on the stag, watching for the rise and fall of breath. "Oh, what a stupid trick!" she said to the air, and shouted at the stag, "Flower and leaf and stalk to thee, I conjure back what ought to be. Human frame and human mind banish those of hart or hind." Which, when she thought about it, was a silly thing to say, since it certainly wasn't a hind.

He lay prone in the grass, naked, honey hair every which way. His eyes were closed, but his brows pinched together, as if he was fighting his way back from sleep. One sunbrowned long hand curled and straightened. His eyes snapped open, focused on nothing; the fingers curled again; and finally he looked at them, as if he had to force himself to do it, afraid of what he might see. Moon heard the sharp drawing of his breath. On the shelf of stone there was nothing at all.

A movement across the clearing caught Moon's eye and she looked up. Among the trees stood the King of Stones in his gray armor. Sunshine glinted off it and into his unsmiling face, and pierced the shadows of his eye sockets. His eyes, she saw, were green as sage.

The prince had levered himself up onto his elbows. Moon saw the tremors in his arms and across his back. She swept her torn cloak from her shoulders and draped it over him. "Can you speak?" she asked him. She glanced up again. There was no one in the clearing but the two of them.

"I don't—yes," he said, like a whispering crow, and laughed thinly. He held out one spread and shaking hand. "Tell me. You don't see a hoof, do you?"

"No, but you used to have four of them. You're not nearly so impressive in this shape."

He laughed again, from closer to his chest this time. "You haven't seen me hung all over with satin and beads like a dancing elephant."

"Well, thank goodness for that. Can you stand up? Lean on me if you want to, but we should be gone from here."

He clutched her shoulder—the long scholar's fingers were very strong—and struggled to his feet, then drew her cloak more tightly around himself. "Which way?"

Passage through the woods was hard for her, because she knew how hard it was for him, barefoot, disoriented, yanked out of place and time. After one especially hard stumble, he sagged against a tree. "I hope this passes. I can see flashes of this wood in my memory, but as if my eyes were off on either side of my head."

"Memory fades," she said. "Don't worry."

He looked up at her quickly, pain in his face. "Does it?" He shook his head. "I'm sorry—did you tell me your name?"

"No. It's Moon Very Thin."

He asked gravely, "Are you waxing or waning?"

"It depends from moment to moment."

"That makes sense. Will you call me Robin?"

"If you want me to."

"I do, please. I find I'm awfully taken with having a name again."

At last the trees opened out, and in a fold of the green hillside they found a farmstead. A man stood in the farmhouse door watching them come. When they were close enough to make out his balding head and wool coat, he stirred from the door; took three faltering steps into his garden; and shouted and ran toward them. A tall, round woman appeared at the door, twisting her apron. Then she, too, began to run.

The man stopped just short of them, open-mouthed, his face a study in hope, and fear that hope will be yanked away. "Your Highness?"

Robin nodded.

The round woman had come up beside the man. Tears coursed down her face. She said calmly, "Teazle, don't keep 'em standing in the yard. Look like they've been dragged backwards through the blackthorn, both of them, and probably hungry as cats." But she stepped forward and touched one tentative hand to the prince's cheek. "You're back," she whispered.

"I'm back."

They were fed hugely, and Robin was decently clothed in linen and leather belonging to Teazle's eldest son. "We should be going," the prince said at last, regretfully.

"Of course," Teazle agreed. "Oh, they'll be that glad to see you at the palace."

Moon saw the shadow of pain pass quickly over Robin's face again.

They tramped through the new ferns, the setting sun at their backs. "I'd as soon . . ." Robin faltered and began again. "I'd as soon not reach the palace tonight. Do you mind?"

Moon searched his face. "Would you rather be alone?"

"No! I've been alone for—how long? A year? That's enough. Unless you don't want to stay out overnight."

"It would be silly to stop now, just when I'm getting good at it," Moon said cheerfully.

They made camp under the lee of a hill near a creek, as the sky darkened and the stars came out like frost. They didn't need to cook, but Moon built a fire anyway. She was aware of his gaze; she knew when he was watching, and wondered that she felt it so. When it was full dark, and Robin lay staring into the flames, Moon said, "You know, then?"

"How I was . . .? Yes. Just before... there was a moment when I knew what had been done, and who'd done it." He laced his brown fingers over his mouth and was silent for a while; then he said, "Would it be better if I didn't go back?"

"You'd do that?"

"If it would be better."

"What would you do instead?"

He sighed. "Go off somewhere and grow apples."

"Well, it wouldn't be better," Moon said desperately. "You have to go back. I don't know what you'll find when you get there, though. I called down curse and banishment on your mother and father, and I don't really know what they'll do about it."

He looked up, the fire bright in his eyes. "You did that? To the king and queen of Hark End?"

"Do you think they didn't deserve it?"

"I wish they didn't deserve it." He closed his eyes and dropped his chin onto his folded hands.

"I think you are the heart of the land," Moon said in surprise.

His eyes flew open again. "Who said that?"

"A guard at the front palace gate. He'll probably fall on his knees when he sees you."

"Great grief and ashes," said the prince. "Maybe I can sneak in the back way."

They parted the next day in sight of the walls of Great Hark. "You can't leave me to do this alone," Robin protested.

"How would I help? I know less about it than you do, even if you are a year out of date."

"A lot happens in a year," he said softly.

"And a lot doesn't. You'll be all right. Remember that everyone loves you and needs you. Think about them and you won't worry about you."

"Are you speaking from experience?"

"A little." Moon swallowed the lump in her throat. "But I'm a country witch and my place is in the country. Two weeks to the east by foot, just across the Blacksmith River. If you ever make a King's Progress, stop by for tea."

She turned and strode away before he could say or do anything silly, or she could.

Moon wondered, in the next weeks, how the journey could have seemed so strange. If the Seawood was full of ghosts, none of them belonged to her. The plain of grass was impressive, but just grass, and hot work to cross. In Little Hark she stopped for the night, and the blond boy remembered her.

"Did you find your teacher?" he asked.

"No. She died. But I needed to know that. It wasn't for nothing."

He already knew the prince had come back; everyone knew it, as if the knowledge had blown across the kingdom like milkweed fluff. She didn't mention it.

She came home and began to set things to rights. It didn't take long. The garden wouldn't be much this year, but it would be sufficient; it was full of volunteers from last year's fallen seed. She threw herself into work; it was balm for the heart. She kept her mind on her neighbors' needs, to keep it off her own. And now she knew that her theory was right, that earth and air and fire and water were all a part of each other, all connected, like silver and gold. Like joy and pain.

"You're grown," Tansy Broadwater said to her, but speculatively, as if she meant something other than height, that might not be an unalloyed joy.

The year climbed to Midsummer and sumptuous life. Moon went to the village for the Midsummer's Eve dance and watched the horseplay for an hour before she found herself tramping back up the hill. She felt remarkably old. On Midsummer's Day she put on her apron and went out to dig the weeds from between the flagstones.

She felt the rhythm in the earth before she heard it. Hoofbeats, coming up the hill. She got to her feet.

The horse was chestnut and the rider was honey-haired. He drew rein at the gate and slipped down from the saddle, and looked at her with a question in his eyes.

She found her voice. "King's Progress?"

"Not a bit." He sounded just as she'd remembered, whenever she hadn't had the sense to make enough noise to drown the memory out. "May I have some tea anyway?"

Her hands were cold, and knotted in her apron. "Mint?"

"That would be nice." He tethered his horse to the fence and came in through the gate.

"How have things turned out?" She breathed deeply and cursed her mouth for being so dry.

"Badly, in the part that couldn't help but be. My parents chose exile. I miss them—or I miss them as they were once. Everything else is doing pretty well. It's always been a nice, sensible kingdom." Now that he was closer, Moon could see his throat move when he swallowed, see his thumb turn and turn at a ring on his middle finger.

"Moon," he said suddenly, softly, as if it were the first word he'd spoken. He plucked something out of the inside of his doublet and held it out to her. "This is for you." He added quickly, in a lighter tone, "You'd be amazed how hard it is to find when you want it. I thought I'd better pick it while I could and give it to you pressed and dried, or I'd be here empty-handed after all."

She stared at the straight green stem, the cluster of inky-blue flowers still full of color, the sweet ghost of vanilla scent. Her fingers closed hard on her apron. "It's heliotrope," she managed to say.

"Yes, I know."

"Do… do you know what it means?"

"Yes."

"It means 'devotion.'"

"I know," Robin said. He looked into her eyes, as he had since he'd said her name, but something faltered slightly in his face. "A little pressed and dried, but yours, if you'll have it."

"I'm a country witch," Moon said with more force than she'd planned. "I don't mean to stop being one."

Robin smiled a little, an odd sad smile. "I didn't say you ought to. But the flower is yours whether you want it or not. And I wish you'd take it, because my arm's getting tired."

"Oh!" Moon flung her hands out of her apron. "Oh! Isn't there a plant in this whole wretched garden that means 'I love you, too?' Bother!"

She hurtled into his arms, and he closed them tight around her.

Once upon a time there ruled in the Kingdom of Hark End a king who was young and fair, good and wise, and responsible for the breeding of no fewer than six new varieties of apple. Once upon the same time there was a queen in Hark End who understood the riddle of the rings of silver and gold: that all things are joined together without beginning or end, and that there can be no understanding until all things divided are joined. They didn't live happily ever after, for nothing lives forever; but they lived as long as was right, then passed together into the land where trees bear blossom and fruit both at once, and where the flowers of spring never fade.

~

Emma Bull's novel *War for the Oaks* is one of the pioneering works of urban fantasy. Her post-apocalyptic science fiction novel *Bone Dance* was nominated for the Hugo, Nebula, and World Fantasy Awards. She sang in the rock-funk band Cats Laughing, and both sang and played guitar in the folk duo The Flash Girls. She is Executive Producer and one of the writers for *Shadow Unit*, a web-based fiction series. Emma currently lives in Minneapolis, Minnesota.

THE ABOMINABLE CHILD'S TALE

CAROL EMSHWILLER

Did Mother say to always go down?

But maybe she said always go up.

Did she say follow streams, and then rivers? First paths and then a road? And then a road all covered with hard stuff? Did she say there'd be a town if you go far enough?

Or did she say, whatever you do, don't follow roads? Stay away from towns?

She always did say, "You're not lost." She always said, "You're my forest girl. You know which way is up." She didn't mean I know up from down, she meant I always know where I am or that I can find out where I am if I'm not sure.

But Mother didn't come back. Even though she's a forest girl, too. She had her best little bow, her sling shot, and her knife.

I waited and waited. I made marmot soup all by myself. It turned out really good so I was especially sorry she wasn't here. I barred the door, but I listened for her. I studied my subtraction and then I read a history lesson. I didn't sleep very well. I'm used to having her, nice and warm, beside me.

Did she say, "If I don't come back after three days, leave?" Or did she only say that when I was little and not that much of a forest girl like I am now? Way back then I would have needed somebody to help me.

She *did* say that I never listen and that I never pay attention, and I guess this proves it.

But what if she comes back and I'm not here? What if she's tired? I could help. I could pump up the shower.

Except what if she doesn't come back?

I was always asking if we couldn't go where there were people, and she was always saying, "It's safer here." And I'd say, "What about the mountain lions?" And she'd say, "Even so, it's much safer up here—for us."

She said not to let anybody see us, but she didn't say why.

She did say people are always shooting things before they even know what they are.

What if I'm some sort of a creature that *should* be shot? Eaten, too?

Or is *she*? We don't look much alike. Maybe *she's* the odd one.

I asked her about all that once but she wouldn't talk about it.

Now and then, in summer, when there are people camping all the way up here, we go yet higher and hide out until they're gone. Mother always said, "Let's *us* go on a camping trip, too," but she couldn't fool me with that. I knew she wanted to keep us secret, but I played along. I never said I didn't want to go. If we were in trouble some way I wanted us to stay out of it.

I know a lot more than she thinks I do.

• • •

I wander all over trying to see what happened to her. I see where she crossed the stream and started down to the muddy pond, but then I lose track. I check the pond, but she never got there. There's a fish on the line. I bring it home for supper.

The thing is, do I want to spend my life here alone? Waiting? Does Mother even want me to? I can come back after I see what's beyond the paths. Mother said two-story houses and even three-story. Also I'd really, really like to see a paved road—once in my life anyway.

I wait the three days, looking for her all that time, then I leave. I take Mother's treasure. She had this little leather book. Even when we just went up to hide, she took that with her and kept it dry.

There are lots of books here—actually twelve—but I don't take any except the one Mother always wrote in and locked shut.

I stop at the look-over and think to go back, just in case she came home exactly when I left, but I did leave a note. Actually two notes, one on the door and one inside. The one inside I shaped like a heart. It was on the paper we made out of stems. I don't need to tell her where I'm headed. She'll see that. I'm leaving a lot of clues all along the way.

• • •

It turns out exactly like Mother said it would: A river and then a bigger river and a path and then a road, and after that the wonderful, wonderful paved road. Pretty soon I see, in the distance, a town. Even from here I can tell some of the houses are tall.

I wait till dark. I'm not sure what's wrong with me but it's a town with plenty of bushes around. I don't think it'll be hard to hide. I never had a good look at those people that come in the summer. Mother tried to get me away as fast as she could. I've only seen them from a distance. Besides, they were all covered up with clothes, sunglasses, and hats.

We have those.

I want to see what they're like so I can see what might be wrong with me. Though maybe Mother did something really, really bad a long time ago and had to hide out in the mountains. They couldn't put me in prison for something she did, could they?

• • •

I wait till dark and then I creep into town. Everything is closed up. Hardly any lights on. (I know all about electricity, though I've never seen it till now.) I wait till everything except the street lights are out. I wait for them to go out, too, but they don't.

I wander back yards. I try to see into windows, but I waited too long for those street lights to go out. Every house is dark, except now and then an upstairs window.

In one yard I hide behind laundry where somebody's mother forgot to bring it in at dark. Mother sometimes did that, too, but I didn't. She had a lot on her mind. She was always worried.

I just about give up—everybody seems to be in bed—but then I see somebody sneaking out a window, trying to be quiet. It's that very yard where the laundry is still out.

I hide behind the sheets, but so does whoever crawled out the window. We bump right into each other. We both gasp. I can see on that one's face that it's going to yell but I'm about to, too, and then we both cover our mouths with our hands, as if we both don't want to attract attention. Then we stare.

If this one is how I'm supposed to be then I'm all wrong. This one looks like Mother, not like me. I have way too much hair. All over. Are they all like this? But I've suspected something was wrong with me for a long time, else why did Mother act as she did, always keeping us away from everybody?

I can't tell if it's a boy or a girl. I'm not used to how they look here or how they dress. Then I see it's got to be a girl. She's wearing this lacy kind of top. I never had anything like that but Mother did. This one seems to be just my size. At least my size is right.

She's like Mother, no hair anywhere except a lot on her head. Mother always said it was a disadvantage, not having hair all over. And it was. She was always cold. But I'd rather be like everybody else.

So we're standing there with our hands over our mouths staring at each other.

Then she says, "Can you talk?"

And I say, "Of course. Why not?"

What an odd question. What does she think I am? Except I *am* all wrong. I was afraid of that. But we're exactly the same height, and both of us is skinny. I'm wearing shorts and a T-shirt. She wearing shorts, too, and this fancy blouse. And I see now she has the beginnings of breasts just like I do. Hairiness looks to be our only difference. I don't have that much on my face—thank goodness. I guess.

"Am I all wrong?"

It's the question I've been wanting to ask just about all my life but didn't know it till right now.

I can tell from the way she says, "Well…" that I am and that she wants to be nice about it.

She says, "Come."

Way back at the end of her yard, there's a funny little house that we have to lean over to go in. It has two tiny rooms that you couldn't lie down straight out in unless you put your feet though the door into the other room. It has a little table and chairs, too small for any regular sized person. Are there people I never knew about?

The girl lights a candle and we squinch into the little chairs next to the little table.

Even in this light I can see her eyes are blue just like mine. We're an awful lot the same.

"Dad was going to take this house down, but I said, not yet."

She has a dad!

"So what about you? What are you, anyway?"

I can't answer. I feel like crying. I have to say, "I don't know."

"We could look you up on line. There's a lot of choices, Yeti, Abominable Snowman, Sasquatch, Bigfoot… "

She knows more about me than I do.

"I suppose abominable."

"I don't think so. You're too nice looking. Are you crying?"

I thought I was holding it back but that makes me feel worse than ever. I really do start to cry. Mother would be saying, "Where's my forest girl?"

"That's all right, go ahead and cry. I'll make you tea, and there's cookies, too. I don't have a stove in here, Dad wouldn't let me, this is just sun tea, but it's good. I know I'm too old to have a playhouse like this, but I want it, anyway. It comes in handy, like right now."

The tea is nothing like anything I've had before even though we have lots of teas up there. And the cookies are like nothing I ever had either. I say, "I never had these."

"Oatmeal with raisins. Mom thinks they're good for you. She's a great believer in oatmeal."

I guess her mother is right. I feel better after the tea and a couple of cookies.

But I'm thinking maybe she has a bad mother. I've heard of that. After all, she sneaked out the window.

"Were you escaping? I thought maybe your mother was mean and you were running away."

"Oh no, my folks are fine. I sneak out lots of times when there's a moon like this. I'm fourteen. I'm old enough to be on my own."

"I'm fourteen, too, and I *am* on my own, but I don't want to be."

"I don't know what Mother would do about you, though. Call the police… or the doctor. Or maybe the zoo."

"Am I all wrong?"

"You're probably some sort of mutation."

How can she be so sure of herself all the time? But she does seem to know a lot.

"I don't want to be put in the zoo."

"That wouldn't be so bad. I wouldn't mind at all if it were me. I'd come visit you. But I don't even know your name. Mine is Molly. I picked it out myself two years ago when I started Junior High."

"You named yourself?"

"Lots of people do. You could, too. But do you have one?"

"Of course I do. I'm not…"

But maybe I am—sort of animal. "Mother calls me Binny. It's short for Sabine."

"Sabine!"

She looks impressed.

"Don't change it!"

• • •

We both get tired at the same time. Molly goes back in through her window and brings me a pillow and a blanket. Tells me to keep quiet and she'll bring me breakfast after her parents go to work. She says, "Not to worry. Nobody… *Nobody* would dare go in my playhouse unless invited."

It feels good to stretch out all the way through the two rooms after hunching over all that time. And I've never had such a soft pillow before.

• • •

I wake at dawn, as I usually do. Things are pretty much quiet all over the whole town. I hunch myself around the little house. I didn't get a good look at it last night in the candle light. There's a mirror. I see me. Actually Molly and I look kind of alike. Our eyes are blue. Our hair is tawny.

Hair!

On a shelf I find a doll… a very worn out doll (not hairy), and a worn out (hairy) dog doll beside it.

• • •

The town starts waking up. Doors slam. Cars drive by but out along the front of the houses, way across the lawn from me. I saw those last night. Some even came right close to me while I was waiting for it to get dark. Trucks, too. I saw everything Mother talked about and drew pictures of. I even went up to a car and looked in. I saw the steering wheel and the pedals. I can't wait till I get to ride in one. Maybe Molly can get me a ride. A truck would be even more fun than a car, the bigger the better. I'll ask her.

I wait and wait for Molly to bring breakfast. Finally she does. Stuff I never had before. Toast and sausages. Actually, enough for both of us. She wants to eat with me. First thing she says is, "I hate eggs."

I've had eggs lots of times and I like them but I don't say it.

"I have to go to school. Whatever you do, don't leave here in the daytime. I'll take you out tonight. We have to figure what to do about you."

I say okay, but I'm not sure I'm going to stay shut up here all day.

"When do you get back?"

She looks at her watch. (I know what that is, too.) She doesn't notice I don't have one.

She says, "Three-thirty, thereabouts."

• • •

Pretty soon everything gets very quiet. All the cars and all the children are gone. I'm tired of hunching over; I'm not going to stay in here, but I'm a little scared about just walking right out. Then I think about Molly's back window. I cross the lawn (by now the laundry's brought in) and climb in Molly's window.

Here's a nice place! Pale yellow walls, an all-white, really, really soft bed (I try it), a not-so-worn-out stuffed dog on the pillows (even fuzzier than the one in the little house), and a wonderful lot of books. Must be twenty or so on a nice little shelf. I recognize school work things. There's a notebook exactly like Mother has for me.

Time goes faster than I thought it would. I spend a lot of it looking at the books, but then I get hungry. I find the kitchen. The refrigerator! In there it's like winter. I eat a lot of things that I don't know what they are. I've heard of cheese. Besides, I can read the labels: cold cuts, cheddar, cottage cheese…

I taste everything. There's radishes. I'm glad Mother saw to it that I knew about these things. I think she was homesick for all this so she talked about it. Actually she talked about a lot more than I wanted to hear—then, anyway. Talk about not listening! It's a wonder I even remember radishes.

I wander around the whole house. Turns out they have lots of books. And all over the place. I start reading several of them, one after the other, bits and pieces of all sorts of things. Magazines, too. I've been missing a lot. Mother knew it. She tried to make it up to me. When I see all this I realize how hard she worked at it. I start feeling tearful. I wonder where she is and if she's all right.

Their clocks already say after two. I think I'd better go back into that little house.

I bring some books and magazines, but I don't read them. I start thinking about dads. I know enough to know I must have had one. I haven't thought much about it. I thought the way Mother and I lived was the usual way. Like bear cubs and fawns, always a mother and a child or two. And here's a dad living right with them. Out of the little windows, I saw whole families leaving all together. The dads were living right there with everybody.

There's a lot Mother told me, but a lot she didn't. I'd ask her, Where is my dad? Who was he? And, especially, how hairy?

I must have fallen asleep by mistake because Molly wakes me.

"Come quick," she says, "before my parents come home. We'll look you up on the web. If Mother comes in... she always knocks first... you just scoot under the bed."

"Scoot?"

So then I get my first lesson in computer stuff. We look all over the place, but not a one looks at all like me. They're all chunky and have terrible faces.

Molly says, "You're much nicer looking than any of these. I like your hair color. There's a lot of gold in it."

I'm glad she said that, but it worries me that one of these might be my dad. How could Mother have even gotten close to somebody like that? I hope at least he was a nice person... *if* I can think of him as a person.

I ask Molly, "You have a dad. What's that like?"

"Oh, he's okay. He thinks I'm a kid, though. I'll be forty-five before he'll think I'm grown up. Don't you have your dad? Well, you don't or you'd already know what he looks like."

I'm thinking, looks aren't everything. Molly's father might not be so handsome either. But that's too much to hope for. And, anyway, why would I hope for that? That isn't nice.

Then I remember about cars and trucks. I ask Molly if she can take me for a ride in a truck.

"Truck! Of course not. We don't have a truck. But I could take you in our car—after everybody's gone to bed. I don't have a license, but I do know how to drive. Dad already taught me. You're not supposed to drive until you're sixteen. I don't know why they make you wait so long."

I go to the little house before her mother comes back. Molly loads me up with cookies and milk (I never had milk before) just in case she has a hard time bringing me a supper.

"Don't light the candle until all our lights are out here in the house."

• • •

Finally she comes to get me.

She brings me a big floppy hat, one of her father's white shirts, pants, socks and sandals. The sandals are terribly uncomfortable.

She says, "I guess you really are a Bigfoot."

I must look hurt because right away she says, "Sorry, that was supposed to be a joke. Not a very kind one. Look." She puts her foot next to mine. "We're almost the same size." Then, "You don't have to wear the sandals. I don't suppose anybody will see your feet, anyway."

She tells me to button up the shirt and raise the collar to cover my neck as much as I can.

If I need all these clothes and to button up just to go for a ride in a car, I guess I really am entirely wrong.

• • •

Even just getting in the car is exciting.

Then it jerks forward.

"Sorry. I haven't driven very much. But this will be good practice. Better put on your seatbelt."

We drive, and it's wonderful. We go out in the country so we can go fast. She says in town we can only go twenty five. We open the windows and get the breeze.

She says, "I'll go even faster if you stop saying 'thank you' all the time."

I stop and she does.

She turns on the radio, which is another new thing—not that I haven't heard all about it. She pushes buttons to get the right music. She says, "Dad has it on news all the time." I wouldn't have minded hearing news.

We start around a curve and all of a sudden we're in the ditch. Then bouncing up and down, and then upside down.

We're not hurt, but the front doors won't open. Molly finally gets a back door open and we crawl out.

She doesn't look like Molly anymore. She looks scared and like she doesn't know what to do.

She says, "I don't even have my cell phone."

It's still the middle of the night. There's not a light in sight. She starts to cry. I feel like I'm the strongest one now. I say, "Come on. Let's start back to town."

"I wish I hadn't gone so fast. We wouldn't be so far away if I hadn't done seventy. Daddy's going to kill me."

"Your dad will kill you?"

"No, silly, of course not. Don't you know anything?"

Getting angry at me makes her feel better. She starts walking down the road in the dark and trips and falls flat. And then she's crying again.

My eyes must be better than hers. I can see a little bit. There's the sliver of a moon. I say, "We'll be all right. Hang on to me."

Pretty soon it starts getting light and we see a farm house and head for that.

"I'll go in and telephone Dad. You have to hide. Don't let anybody see you."

The more she says things like that, the more I worry about myself.

"What will Daddy do? And we don't even have a car now. And what will we do with *you*?"

"I don't want to be put in the zoo."

"Look, there's a barn. Go hide there, while I go in."

In the barn there's stalls, mostly empty but there are two horses at the back. There's a ladder up to a loft full of hay. That's where I'll go, but I've never seen horses—except in picture books. I check on them first. I worry they might kick or bite, but they come right up to me to see who I am, friendly as can be. It makes me feel better, stroking something big and warm. Then I go up and lie down in the hay.

It takes so long for Molly to come back I think maybe she's just left me here. I'm too shaken up to sleep. I go down again and talk to the horses. I get right in with them. I call one Spotty and the other Brownie.

Finally Molly comes.

"I couldn't get away from the people here. They're too nice. They were going to drive me home since they had to go to town anyway, but I said I needed to call Daddy. They went off to town. I know their kid. He's a couple of grades ahead of me in school. He's still here. He takes the school bus. Daddy's renting a car. He'll be here as soon as he can, but it'll take a while. I didn't tell him about you. What'll we do about you?"

I don't say anything. What do I know?

But suddenly here's the boy. First he says, "What are you doing out here?" And then he sees me and gasps.

I'm still dressed, head to toe... to almost toe, but even so I'm too much for him.

"What *are* you?"

I say, "Bigfoot."

Right away he looks at my feet. Then he laughs. And we all laugh.

He says, "I don't believe in you."

I say, "Nobody does."

And we laugh all the more.

He decides not to go to school—after all, Molly isn't going either—and invites us in for breakfast.

He keeps staring at me as he cooks us pancakes. And he keeps spilling things.

He says, "You're a nice color," and, "I didn't think a Bigfoot would be so attractive," and, "You have nice eyes," until I'm a little worried. Though he could be trying to make me feel good about myself. I suppose I should appreciate it.

He says, "I don't think you should go back with Molly. I think you should stay here where you have a nice barn to hide in."

Molly looks relieved.

I'd really rather be back in her little playhouse, but I don't know how we can get me there.

Then he says, "We could go horseback riding," and I think, maybe it wouldn't be so bad here. I'm learning so many new things. Including rolling over in a car. Horses would be nice.

Molly's father comes by in a rented car. He barely stops, honks, opens the door and yells. I guess he's really angry. She looks at us, scared, then rushes out. There's no way I could have gone with her even if I'd wanted to.

• • •

The boy's name is Buck. He changed his name, too. I didn't know everybody could do that. He used to be Judson. He says, "Judd isn't so bad, but I like Buck better."

He goes to put on his riding clothes. He has the whole outfit, cowboy hat and boots and all. I've seen pictures. I think he's trying to impress me. And maybe himself. He does look as if he likes himself a lot in these clothes.

He brings a bag of stuff for a picnic and we go out and saddle up. First he has to brush the horses so there's no dust and stuff under the saddle. He shows me how, and I help.

I feel funny, getting up on something I just talked to and petted, but he doesn't seem to mind.

Buck heads us up into the hills and pretty soon we're in the trees. He makes us canter even though he can see I'm bouncing and hurting. Trotting isn't much better. He doesn't say a word about what to do. It looks as if he likes to see me not knowing how to do it. He's got this funny little smile all the time.

He's laughing at me.

We get to a nice shady spot and get off and tie up. He spreads out a blanket, he says, for our picnic.

He takes off half his fancy cowboy outfit. And then he takes off even more. Is this what people do?

But I start to know what this is all about. I remember things Mother warned me could happen. I wasn't listening but some of it must have gotten through.

He's a lot taller than I am and stronger, too. He tears Molly's father's shirt practically in two. I have to really fight and I'm losing.

Finally I grab a stone and knock him away.

He says, "What difference does it make? You're just an animal. Why should you care?"

"I'm not an animal, or if I am, I'm only half. My mother was your kind."

He comes after me again but I run… uphill. I'm thinking of getting back to our cabin and maybe finding out what happened to Mother.

I'm way faster than he is. I guess from all my hiking around the mountains. Pretty soon he gives up. I see him from way above, put on his costume, mount up and ride away, leading the other horse.

I sit down and catch my breath. I feel like crying, but I'm angry, too. Molly didn't think I was an animal. Or am I? I wish I was back with her.

I'm glad that, up in the mountains, it's always just mothers and children off by themselves. I was thinking I wanted to meet my father some day, but now I'm not sure. And he'd be more of an animal than I am. Though if Mother liked him he couldn't be that bad. Or maybe she didn't like him. Maybe she couldn't fight him off.

And then I think how Mother's little book is in the pocket of my shorts back in the little house. I have to get back there.

I walked there once before, I guess I can walk there again. I'm going to stay in the foothills and walk mostly at night. I'm pretty well covered up with Molly's dad's shirt even though it's torn and has lost some buttons, and the slacks are OK. I don't have the hat anymore.

I wonder what Molly is expecting to do about me. She might try to come and get me. For sure not driving a car. I wonder what she'll do when she finds out I'm gone. I wonder if she knows about how Buck is. Except maybe he's only that way with somebody who's an animal.

I'm too impatient to wait for dark. I start heading back towards the town, but I keep well away from any roads or houses. I suppose it's pretty far considering how fast Molly was driving. I don't even know the name of the town, but it has a special smell. I'd recognize it right away.

Later, when I come to a river and a nice pile of brush next to it, and berries,

I decide to rest there until dark.

Except I can't rest. I'm too angry and upset. I need to talk to Molly. I keep on across the rocky foothills.

• • •

I should have stayed and rested.

At first I think they're wolves, but then I see it's a pack of all sorts of dogs. I climb a juniper. They're making a terrible racket.

Practically right away, here comes a man with a rifle. He shoots towards the dogs and they run off. Then he comes to see what they've treed. He stares. Walks all around the tree to look at me from every angle. The shirt and slacks don't hide that much. My Bigfoot-big-bare-fuzzy-feet are just above his head.

He isn't dressed like Buck, though he is wearing a cowboy hat. He has a bushy mustache that's mostly gray. He's a lot older than Buck. I don't know if that's good or bad. He might, all the quicker, take off his clothes and grab me. Is he going to climb the tree and pull me down and then try to do what Buck tried?

"Can you talk?"

Why does everybody ask me that? Do I look so animal? I guess I do.

"Of course I can."

And I climb a little higher.

"Don't be scared. I won't hurt you. I won't. I promise. Are you hungry?"

Yeah, lure the animal down with a little bite of food.

He sits under the tree and takes off his hat. He's got a *very* high forehead. I've seen pictures of that. That's being bald. Maybe when I'm older I could get bald all over.

He takes out an apple and a sandwich and begins to eat. He's in no hurry. As he eats, he keeps looking up at me and shaking his head, as if, like Buck, he doesn't believe in me.

"I've heard tell of your kind, but I've never seen one. Where did you come from, anyway?"

I don't know what to say.

"Do you have a name?"

What does he think I am? Well, I know what he thinks.

"Of course I do."

"Mine's Hiram. People call me Hi."

"Mine's Sabine."

"I never knew a Sabine. Is that from your people?"

"My people?"

"Your kind of... Whatever you . . ."

I never thought about being "a kind." Was he going to say, your kind of animal?

For a minute we just look out at the view of the fields far below us with the sprinkling of black cows, both of us as if embarrassed. Then he says, "You might as well come down. You'll have to one of these days. It might as well be now as later. When I leave those dogs might come back. You can have half my sandwich and this apple."

He's right, I might as well come down, so I do.

I take the sandwich and sit a couple of yards away. I hope I'm not eating like an animal or sitting like an animal. I sit as he's sitting. I'm hungry, but I slow down. I try to keep the torn shirt shut as best I can.

He leaves his clothes on all that time and afterwards we just sit quietly. I'm thinking maybe I should ask about men taking their clothes off, but then I think I'd better not. Even if he is a man, maybe he can help me get back to the town.

He keeps looking me up and down. He just can't stop. Then he says, "Sorry, I shouldn't stare. I'd like to take a picture of you. Of course nobody will believe it. They'll think I made it up on the computer."

"Can you drive a car? I'm trying to get back to the town. I'll let you take my picture if you help me get back. It would have to be at night. And I only need to go to the edge. And if you could lend me a hat, I'd try to get it back to you."

• • •

He takes me down to his house. I won't go in. I don't care if he thinks I'm a scared animal, I just won't, and I *am* a scared animal. He gets his camera and takes a lot of pictures, all different views. I'm worried about it because Molly said I should hide and this sure isn't hiding, but this is the only way I know of to get back to her. If he's going to bother helping me, I have to do something for him.

Then we wait till the middle of the night. I apologize for keeping him up.

He never once takes his clothes off. Maybe all men don't do that. I'll have to ask Molly. She said everything is on the computer. If she doesn't know, we can look it up.

He makes me supper. A kind of stew with everything in it. He says it's called slumgullion. He says it's a kind of a guy thing. He serves it outside on his picnic table so I won't need to go in. I'm beginning to think I shouldn't be so scared. I wonder if my father is as nice.

He sits down to eat across from me.

"You've had a bad experience, haven't you. Or are you just scared of all of us?"

"I like Molly. That's where I want to get back to. But I had a bad experience with Buck. He took his clothes off and grabbed me."

Then I tell him all about Molly and the car rolling over and about Buck. I tell him, "You don't seem like him."

"I'm not. And when any man takes his clothes off, you take care. I have a daughter about your age. I live by myself, except my daughter comes here for the summer. If I show those pictures I took of you around, you're in trouble. Everybody will be after you. They'll chase you wherever you try to hide. You ought to go back up into the hills and let yourself be a legend like the rest of your people are. I'll hang on to these pictures until you get well away."

"But I don't know my people. I've never met my father. My mother's one of your kind. Molly wanted to shave me all over with her dad's electric razor. Do you think that would work?"

"Not a good idea. You'd prickle. Nobody could get near you. Here, feel my cheeks. I haven't shaved since yesterday."

I reach across the table and feel them.

"You sure you don't want me to take you up into the mountains far as I can drive and drop you off? I'll give you a knapsack and water bottle and food for a couple of days. That would be best for you."

"I'd like to see Molly first. Besides, I left Mother's book there."

He gets me a shirt of his that isn't torn. It's dark green. Better for hiding in than this white one.

We spend time looking up at the stars. He knows the names of everything up there. I tell him my mother did, too. Then we have coffee, though he doesn't let me have much. He says if I'm not used to it, it'll make me jittery. And then we go—in his rickety old truck. He gives me a stained old cowboy hat. He says it may not look so good but it's beaver so it's waterproof.

He drops me off at the edge of town like I want him to. I think I can smell my way back to Molly's house, but not if I'm in the truck.

When he lets me off he says, "You know I'll not use those photos. Better you folks stay a myth. And you better hurry back in the hills. That's where you belong."

I'm glad I met him after Buck. I was ready to never get near a man again.

• • •

It doesn't take me long to find Molly's place. I kept pretty good track of where I was. I always know where I am when there are trees and rocks, but I knew I'd have trouble finding my way with all these streets and houses.

I go right back to the playhouse and settle in to get some sleep for what there is left of the night. The pillow and blanket aren't there anymore, but I take the old dog doll for a pillow. Hi's shirt will keep me warm.

But first I find my shorts just where I hid them and Mother's book is still in the pocket.

I want to let Molly know I'm here, but I don't want to wake her up in the middle of the night. But then I oversleep. Everybody in the house has gone off just like before. I wonder if Molly tried to find me at Buck's and if Buck tried... that with her? But I suppose not. I'm the one who doesn't count. But I don't see what difference it makes. Animal or not, I shouldn't have to get forced into doing something I don't want to. Hi didn't think so, either.

So then I have to wait around for Molly to come back. I sneak in and get myself some food. I snoop around again. I wish I knew how to use the computer. I don't dare try without Molly. She said you could learn about everything there.

I grab some books and go back. I start reading and don't even notice when Molly comes home. When I realize she must be back, I go look in her window. There she is, on the bed with a magazine. I tap on the window. She gives a shriek when she sees me. It's good nobody else is home. She opens the window and hugs me. She climbs out and we go back to the playhouse.

She says, "I was so worried, and I didn't know how to come and get you back, and Daddy won't let me go *anywhere* now that I ruined our car. I'm going to have to stay home for months and I have to do chores to help pay for the new car." She starts to cry.

I don't know what to do. Mother would have held me, but that's different. At least I think it is. Finally I reach out and pat her shoulder. That seems to be all right. She does stop.

I ask, "Is it all my fault? You were driving for me."

"Of course not. I know it's my fault. I don't even have a license. Daddy says I have to take the consequences."

"Can I help?"

"I don't know. Maybe keep me company now that I have to stay home every single night there is."

"I'll do it. Besides, I want to learn more things on the computer. About men." Then I tell her what Buck tried to do.

She gets really mad and tells me not every boy would be that way, and she is never going to speak to him again, and she's going to tell all her friends to watch out for him.

"Yes, but I'm an animal."

"You're a girl. Anybody with any sense can see that."

"Thank you."

"I like your looks."

I feel like crying, too, but one of us in tears at a time is enough.

"Actually, in your own way, you're quite decent looking."

In my way.

"Maybe there's some kind of medicine you can take that would make all your hair fall out. I'll bet there is. These days there's something for everything. I'll go online and look it up."

I don't trust Molly anymore. She doesn't know as much as she thinks she does. I don't want to take some pill that will make my hair fall out.

I don't tell her, but, even though I owe it to her, I'm not sure I want to stay here much longer. Maybe just look up some more things on the computer. Get her to print some pictures of my possible fathers. I don't belong down here. Hi said so, too. And I miss the mountains. Mother said I was made for them. I was always warm enough up there, even my feet. Mother's feet were always cold. What if she's back there by now? Though I know I shouldn't get my hopes up.

• • •

Next day Molly pretends to go to school and then comes home. She's going to go back to school for her dad to pick her up. I guess her dad can't keep tabs on her all the time.

(Here I am wishing I could go to school and she can and doesn't do it.)

So we print out all the pictures of Sasquatch, and Yeti, and Bigfoot. None of them look very nice. I like having their pictures, though. I fold them up and button them in the pocket of the shirt Hi gave me.

• • •

The next day Molly does go to school. She says she can't afford to miss too much. She's not doing very well in French (French! I wonder if I could ever get to take that) and math. She says her dad is already angry enough without her failing two subjects. So I have the whole place to myself again.

I go to the house and bring back food and books but then I think I should be reading that little book of Mother's. Maybe I can find out why she went with such an odd… creature. I almost thought "person" but I'm not sure if either my father or I can be called a person.

I pry open the lock on Mother's little leather book and there, right on the first page in big letters, she'd written:

A TALE OF TRUE LOVE ! ! !

And underneath that:

Except at first I didn't know it.

I shouldn't have been climbing alone in such a dangerous place, but I like being on the cliffs by myself. I was having an exciting time on a dangerous little trail. I remember falling...

... and then, there I was, looking up into big brown eyes. The creature—Mother calls him a creature, too—was mopping my forehead with a cool cloth. He was grunting little sad grunts. As if he was sorry for me. The way he looked—completely hairy—I never expected him to be able to speak, but when he saw my eyes were open, he said, "I thought maybe you were dead."

I tried to get up, but I hurt all over.

"Lie still," the creature said. And then brought me water in a folding cup, held my head so I could drink.

I had broken my leg and my arm but I didn't know that then.

He whistled a kind of complicated bird song and right after that another one just like him came. They've got a whistling language. Lots of it exactly like real bird songs. I love that. I never mastered it though. They use our language, too.

The other one wore a fisherman's vest full of pockets. He had soft vine like ropes. They tied my arm and leg to pieces of wood to keep them from moving. They put me in a kind of hammock, and took me to their hidden village. Movable village. They hardly spend two nights in a row in the same place.

Then there's a break and the start of a new page.

Dear Sabine,

So this is for me. I'm *supposed* to read it.

As you see, that's what I wrote shortly after the accident, and then such a lot happened that I stopped writing. Actually for years. It was partly because I had to take care of you. But now it's because of you that I'm writing again. I want you to know about us, Growen and me. It was Growen's brother, Greener, who helped Growen rescue me. All the others were against it. They thought helping me was dangerous. I must have lain unconscious for most of the day before they finally decided to help. If not for Growen, they never would have. I think Growen fell in love right then, but it took me a little longer.

You know, Binny, they're beautiful. Not like any of the pictures people make of them. You must NOT think they're like those. And you should know how beautiful you are, too.

Am I really?

At first I couldn't tell them apart. I mean Growen and Greener, or any of them for that matter. Well, I could tell the men from the women. Then I saw that Growen looked at me in a different way. Hopeful. I almost wrote yearning, but it wasn't that because he always looked sure of himself. As if what he wanted would come true, it was just a matter of when. As if he knew I'd soon see how worthy he was.

Binny, I hope you're a grown up as you read this and have fallen in love, too, so you understand.

Should I stop reading and keep this until I'm older? Besides, I haven't even met anybody to be in love with. Or maybe I can read it twice, now, and then again later.

Of course I didn't fall in love right away. Everybody and everything was too odd, but when you're hurting and are treated with kindness, it makes all the difference. Growen was so concerned and helpful and kept looking at me with such admiration.

Except for Growen and Greener, none of the others liked me. They built our cabin and sent me and Growen down from their cliffs and caves and nests.

I don't know what they'd do about you now. You're so much more them than me. I hope they find you, though as long as I'm around they don't want either of us. I'm a danger. Everything is a danger to them and I suppose they're right. They can't have been kept secret all this time without taking great care.

I hope nothing I do reveals them. Can you imagine, all of them shut up in the zoo? Or tourists swarming all over taking their picture? Or yours? Be careful !!!!! Don't ever, ever, ever go down where it's so hard to hide!!!!!!!!!!!!!!!!

Oh, my God. What have I done!

I didn't realize how important it is for me to be a secret. Me just being down here is a danger to all of them . . .. I should say, all of *us*. And now Hi and Buck and Molly know about me. Hi said he wouldn't show the pictures but I'll bet Buck will tell about me. He can't prove it, though. At least I hope not.

And all of a sudden I want to find my kind so much I can't stand to sit here one minute more. I have to get back. But I already roamed all over the place and none of them came to me and I never saw a single sign of them.

Though there are several more pages in the book, Mother only wrote a phrase here and there as if she was going to go back and fill them in. One just has: *Today Growen died.* Maybe she felt too sad to go on except with these little notes.

• • •

I put on my shorts and T-shirt, and on top of that Hi's green shirt, and then his wonderful waterproof hat. I don't take anything of Molly's, not even cookies. Except I wonder if she'd mind if I took her social studies book. I like the idea of all these different kinds and colors of people even though nobody in it has hair all over. Besides, I don't think Molly cares anything about social studies.

It doesn't fit in Hi's big pockets, though Mother's book does. I'll have to carry it separately. I'll pick up one of those plastic bags that keep blowing around everywhere.

I feel bad that I'm not going to say goodbye. Molly got in a lot of trouble because of me. I ought to stay and help, but I'm not going to.

I'm going to find my people if it takes falling off a cliff and lying there with a broken leg.

But what if I don't belong with them either? What if I don't belong anywhere?

• • •

I follow the signs I left for Mother so she could follow me. I find my way back to our cabin, no problem. There's quite a bit of snow. It's getting too cold for most of the regular people to be in the mountains. I only have to avoid a few.

I get excited when I get close. Maybe Mother is waiting for me.

The cabin door is open. She must be there.

But then I get worried. Maybe somebody broke in. Maybe somebody like Buck, not like Hi.

I back away and hide.

And then a beautiful creature comes out, looks up and sniffs. He probably can smell even better than I can. I'll bet he knows I'm hiding here.

He's a tawny golden color—all over. He has a wide forehead, a lion-like look. No wonder Mother fell in love. His face is bare, like mine. I can't believe how beautiful he is and I'm pretty much just exactly like him.

He's wearing a fisherman's vest with all the pockets bulging. And he has a belt with all sorts of things hanging from it.

"Sabine? Binny?"

He knows me. Do I dare show myself?

His voice is deep and kind of whispery—breathy.

"I'm your uncle, Greener. Come on out."

I don't.

"Your mother… I'm sorry. She… We found her not far from Rock Creek. Come on out. Let me tell you face to face."

So it's true. What I suspected. But I can't come out.

He sits down and turns away so his back is towards my hiding place. A broad, strong, golden back.

"I've come to take you home. You'll like it. Your Aunt Sabby is there. You're named for her, you know."

I can't come out.

"We have a pet fox. We've got jays that eat out of your hand."

I can't.

"I'm sorry I didn't get here soon enough—before you went down. I hope you didn't have a bad time there."

I don't come.

"Come on out. I'll teach you how to hide. I'll teach you how to sneak away without making a sound. I'll teach you our whistle language. Come on. I'll take you home."

I'm glad I have Hi's big black hat. I pull it low over my eyes and I come.

~

Carol Emshwiller grew up in Michigan and in France. She lives in New York City in the winter and in Bishop, CA in the summer. She's been doing only short stories lately. A new one will appear in *Asimov's* soon. She's wondering if she's too old to start a novel but if a good idea came along she might do it anyway. PS Publishing is publishing two of her short story collections in a single volume (sort like an Ace Double), with her anti-war stories on one side and other stories on the other. Learn more at sfwa.org/members/Emshwiller.

THE GLASS BOTTLE TRICK

NALO HOPKINSON

Art by Ashley Stewart

The air was full of storms, but they refused to break. In the wicker rocking chair on the front verandah, Beatrice flexed her bare feet against the wooden slat floor, rocking slowly back and forth. Another sweltering rainy season afternoon. The arid heat felt as though all the oxygen had boiled out of the parched air to hang as looming rainclouds, waiting.

Oh, but she loved it like this. The hotter the day, the slower she would move, basking. She stretched her arms and legs out to better feel the luxuriant warmth, then guiltily sat up straight again. Samuel would scold if he ever saw her slouching like that. Stuffy Sammy. She smiled fondly, admiring the lacy patterns the sunlight threw on the floor as it filtered through the white gingerbread fretwork that trimmed the roof of their house.

"Anything more today, Mistress Powell? I finish doing the dishes." Gloria had come out of the house and was standing in front of her, wiping her chapped hands on her apron.

Beatrice felt the shyness come over her as it always did when she thought of giving the older woman orders. Gloria was older than Beatrice's mother. "Ah… no, I think that's everything, Gloria . . ."

Gloria quirked an eyebrow, crinkling her face like running a fork through molasses.

Beatrice gave an abortive, shamefaced "huh" of a laugh. Gloria had known from the start, she'd had so many babies of her own. She'd been mad to run to Samuel with the news from since. But yesterday, Beatrice had already decided to tell Samuel. Well, almost decided. She felt irritated, like a child whose tricks have been found out. She swallowed the feeling. "I think you right, Gloria," she said, fighting for some dignity before the older woman. "Maybe… maybe I cook him a special meal, feed him up nice, then tell him."

"Well, I say is time and past time you make him know. A pickney is a blessing to a family."

"For true," Beatrice agreed, making her voice sound as certain as she could.

"Later, then, Mistress Powell." Giving herself the afternoon off, not even a by-your-leave, Gloria headed off to the maid's room at the back of the house to change into her street clothes. A few minutes later, she let herself out the garden gate.

• • •

"That seems like a tough book for a young lady of such tender years."

"Excuse me?" Beatrice threw a defensive cutting glare at the older man. He'd caught her off guard, though she'd seen his eyes following her ever since she entered the bookstore. "You have something to say to me?" She curled the Gray's Anatomy possessively into the crook of her arm, price sticker hidden against her body. Two more months of saving before she could afford it.

He looked shyly at her. "Sorry if I offended, Miss," he said. "My name is Samuel."

Would be handsome, if he'd chill out a bit. Beatrice's wariness thawed a little. Middle of the sun-hot day, and he wearing black wool jacket and pants. His crisp white cotton shirt was buttoned right up, held in place by a tasteful, unimaginative tie. So proper, Jesus. He wasn't that much older than she.

"Is just… you're so pretty, and it's the only thing I could think of to say to get

you to speak to me."

Beatrice softened more at that, smiled for him and played with the collar of her blouse. He didn't seem too bad, if you could look beyond the stocious, starchy behaviour.

• • •

Beatrice doubtfully patted the slight swelling of her belly. Four months. She was shy to give Samuel her news, but she was starting to show. Silly to put it off, yes? Today she was going to make her husband very happy; break that thin shell of mourning that still insulated him from her. He never said so, but Beatrice knew that he still thought of the wife he'd lost, and tragically, the one before that. She wished she could make him warm up to life again.

Sunlight was flickering through the leaves of the guava tree in the front yard. Beatrice inhaled the sweet smell of the sun-warmed fruit. The tree's branches hung heavy with the pale yellow globes, smooth and round as eggs. The sun reflected off the two blue bottles suspended in the tree, sending cobalt light dancing through the leaves.

When Beatrice first came to Sammy's house, she'd been puzzled by the two bottles that were jammed onto branches of the guava tree.

"Is just my superstitiousness, darling," he'd told her. "You never heard the old people say that if someone dies, you must put a bottle in a tree to hold their spirit, otherwise it will come back as a duppy and haunt you? A blue bottle. To keep the duppy cool, so it won't come at you in hot anger for being dead."

Beatrice had heard something of the sort, but it was strange to think of her Sammy as a superstitious man. He was too controlled and logical for that. Well, grief makes somebody act in strange ways. Maybe the bottles gave him some comfort, made him feel that he'd kept some essence of his poor wives near him.

• • •

"That Samuel is nice. Respectable, hard-working. Not like all them other raga-muffins you always going out with." Mummy picked up the butcher knife and began expertly slicing the goat meat into cubes for the curry.

Beatrice watched the red lumps of flesh part under the knife. Crimson liquid leaked onto the cutting board. She sighed, "But, Mummy, Samuel so boring! Michael and Clifton know how to have fun. All Samuel want to do is go for country drives. Always taking me away from other people."

"You should be studying your books, not having fun," her mother replied crossly.

Beatrice pleaded, "You well know I could do both, Mummy." Her mother just grunted.

Is only truth Beatrice was talking. Plenty men were always courting her, they flocked to her like birds, eager to take her dancing or out for a drink. But some-how she kept her marks up, even though it often meant studying right through the night, her head pounding and belly queasy from hangover while some man snored in the bed beside her. Mummy would kill her if she didn't get straight A's for medical school. "You going have to look after yourself, Beatrice. Man not going do it for you. Them get their little piece of sweetness and then them bruk away."

"Two patty and a King Cola, please." The guy who'd given the order had a broad chest that tapered to a slim waist. Good face to look at, too. Beatrice smiled sweetly at him, made shift to gently brush his palm with her fingertips as she handed him the change.

• • •

A bird screeched from the guava tree, a tiny kiskedee, crying angrily, "Dit, dit, qu'est-ce qu'il dit!" A small snake was coiled around one of the upper branches, just withdrawing its head from the bird's nest. Its jaws were distended with the egg it had stolen. It swallowed the egg whole, throat bulging hugely with its meal. The bird hovered around the snake's head, giving its pitiful wail of, "Say, say, what's he saying!"

"Get away!" Beatrice shouted at the snake. It looked in the direction of the sound, but didn't back off. The gulping motion of its body as it forced the egg farther down its own throat made Beatrice shudder. Then, oblivious to the fluttering of the parent bird, it arched its head over the nest again. Beatrice pushed herself to her feet and ran into the yard. "Hsst! Shoo! Come away from there!" But the snake took a second egg.

Sammy kept a long pole with a hook at one end leaned against the guava tree for pulling down the fruit. Beatrice grabbed up the pole, started jooking it at the branches as close to the bird and nest as she dared.

"Leave them, you brute! Leave!" The pole connected with some of the boughs. The two bottles in the tree fell to the ground and shattered with a crash. A hot breeze sprang up. The snake slithered away quickly, two eggs bulging in its throat. The bird flew off, sobbing to itself.

Nothing she could do now. When Samuel came home, he would hunt the nasty snake down for her and kill it. She leaned the pole back against the tree.

The light breeze should have brought some coolness, but really it only made the day warmer. Two little dust devils danced briefly around Beatrice. They swirled across the yard, swung up into the air, and dashed themselves to powder against the shuttered window of the third bedroom.

Beatrice got her sandals from the verandah. Sammy wouldn't like it if she stepped on broken glass. She picked up the broom that was leaned against the house and began to sweep up the shards of bottle. She hoped Samuel wouldn't be too angry with her. He wasn't a man to cross, could be as stern as a father if he had a mind to.

That was mostly what she remembered about Daddy, his temper—quick to show and just as quick to go. So was he; had left his family before Beatrice turned five. The one cherished memory she had of him was of being swung back and forth through the air, her two small hands clasped in one big hand of his, her feet held tight in another. Safe. And as he swung her through the air, her daddy had been chanting words from an old-time story:

> Yung-Kyung-Pyung, what a pretty basket!
> Margaret Powell Alone, what a pretty basket!
> Eggie-law, what a pretty basket!

Then he had held her tight to his chest, forcing the air from her lungs in a breathless giggle. The dressing-down Mummy had given him for that game! "You want to drop the child and crack her head open on the hard ground? Ee? Why you can't be more responsible?"

"Responsible?" he'd snapped. "Is who working like dog sunup to sundown to put food in oonuh belly?" He'd set Beatrice down, her feet hitting the ground with a jar. She'd started to cry, but he'd just pushed her towards her mother and stormed out of the room. One more volley in the constant battle between them. After he'd left them Mummy had opened the little food shop in town to make ends meet. In the evenings, Beatrice would rub lotion into her mother's chapped, work-wrinkled hands. "See how that man make us come down in the world?" Mummy would grumble. "Look at what I come to."

Privately, Beatrice thought that maybe all Daddy had needed was a little patience. Mummy was too harsh, much as Beatrice loved her. To please her, Beatrice had studied hard all through high school: physics, chemistry, biology, describing the results of her lab experiments in her copybook in her cramped, resigned handwriting. Her mother greeted every A with a non-committal grunt and anything less with a lecture. Beatrice would smile airily, seal the hurt away, pretend the approval meant nothing to her. She still worked hard, but she kept some time for play of her own. Rounders, netball, and later, boys. All those boys, wanting a chance for a little sweetness with a light-skin browning like her. Beatrice had discovered her appeal quickly.

• • •

"Leggo beast..." Loose woman. The hissed words came from a knot of girls that slouched past Beatrice as she sat on the library steps, waiting for Clifton to come and pick her up. She willed her ears shut, smothered the sting of the words. But

she knew some of those girls. Marguerita, Deborah. They used to be friends of hers. Though she sat up proudly, she found her fingers tugging self-consciously at the hem of her short white skirt. She put the big physics textbook in her lap, where it gave her thighs a little more coverage.

The farting vroom of Clifton's motorcycle interrupted her thoughts. Grinning, he stewed the bike to a dramatic halt in front of her. "Study time done now, darling. Time to play."

He looked good this evening, as he always did. Tight white shirt, jeans that showed off the bulges of his thighs. The crinkle of the thin gold chain at his neck set off his dark brown skin. Beatrice stood, tucked the physics text under her arm, smoothed the skirt over her hips. Clifton's eyes followed the movement of her hands. See, it didn't take much to make people treat you nice. She smiled at him.

• • •

Samuel would still show up hopefully every so often to ask her to accompany him on a drive through the country. He was so much older than all her other suitors. And dry? Country drives, Lord! She went out with him a few times; he was so persistent and she couldn't figure out how to tell him no. He didn't seem to get her hints that really she should be studying. Truth to tell, though, she started to find his quiet, undemanding presence soothing. His eggshell-white BMW took the graveled country roads so quietly that she could hear the kiskedee birds in the mango trees, chanting their query: "Dit, dit, qu'est-ce qu'il dit?"

One day, Samuel brought her a gift.

"These are for you and your family," he said shyly, handing her a wrinkled paper bag. "I know your mother likes them." Inside were three plump eggplants from his kitchen garden, raised by his own hands. Beatrice took the humble gift out of the bag. The skins of the eggplants had a taut, blue sheen to them. Later she would realise that that was when she'd begun to love Samuel. He was stable, solid, responsible. He would make Mummy and her happy.

Beatrice gave in more to Samuel's diffident wooing. He was cultured and well-spoken. He had been abroad, talked of exotic sports: ice hockey, downhill skiing. He took her to fancy restaurants she'd only heard of, that her other, young, unestablished boyfriends would never have been able to afford, and would probably only have embarrassed her if they had taken her. Samuel had polish. But he was humble, too, like the way he grew his own vegetables, or the self-deprecating tone in which he spoke of himself. He was always punctual, always courteous to her and her mother. Beatrice could count on him for little things, like picking her up after class, or driving her mother to the hairdresser's. With the other men, she always had to be on guard: pouting until they took her somewhere else for dinner, not another free meal in her mother's restaurant, wheedling them into using the condoms. She always had to hold some thing of herself shut away. With Samuel, Beatrice relaxed into trust.

• • •

"Beatrice, come! Come quick, nuh!"

Beatrice ran in from the backyard at the sound of her mother's voice. Had something happened to Mummy?

Her mother was sitting at the kitchen table, knife still poised to crack an egg into the bowl for the pound cake she was making to take to the shop. She was staring in open-mouthed delight at Samuel, who was fretfully twisting the long stems on a bouquet of blood-red roses. "Lord, Beatrice; Samuel say he want to marry you!"

Beatrice looked to Sammy for verification. "Samuel," she asked unbelievingly, "what you saying? Is true?"

He nodded yes. "True, Beatrice."

Something gave way in Beatrice's chest, gently as a long-held breath. Her heart had been trapped in glass, and he'd freed it.

• • •

They'd been married two months later. Mummy was retired now; Samuel had bought her a little house in the suburbs, and he paid for the maid to come in three times a week. In the excitement of planning for the wedding, Beatrice had let her studying slip. To her dismay she finished her final year of university with barely a C average.

"Never mind, sweetness," Samuel told her. "I didn't like the idea of you studying, anyway. Is for children. You're a big woman now." Mummy had agreed with him too, said she didn't need all that now. She tried to argue with them, but Samuel was very clear about his wishes, and she'd stopped, not wanting anything to cause friction between them just yet. Despite his genteel manner, Samuel had just a bit of a temper. No point in crossing him, it took so little to make him happy, and he was her love, the one man she'd found in whom she could have faith.

Too besides, she was learning how to be the lady of the house, trying to use the right mix of authority and jocularity with Gloria, the maid, and Cleitis, the yardboy who came twice a month to do the mowing and the weeding. Odd to be giving orders to people when she was used to being the one taking orders, in Mummy's shop. It made her feel uncomfortable to tell people to do her work for her. Mummy said she should get used to it, it was her right now.

The sky rumbled with thunder. Still no rain. The warmth of the day was nice, but you could have too much of a good thing. Beatrice opened her mouth, gasping a little, trying to pull more air into her lungs. She was a little short of breath nowadays as the baby pressed on her diaphragm. She knew she could go inside for relief from the heat, but Samuel kept the air-conditioning on high, so cold that they could keep the butter in its dish on the kitchen counter. It never went rancid. Even insects refused to come inside. Sometimes Beatrice felt as though the house were really somewhere else, not the tropics. She had been used to waging constant war against ants and cockroaches, but not in Samuel's house. The cold in it made Beatrice shiver, dried her eyes out until they felt like boiled eggs sitting in their sockets. She went outside as often as possible, even though Samuel didn't like her to spend too much time in the sun. He said he feared that cancer would mar her soft skin, that he didn't want to lose another wife. But Beatrice knew he just didn't want her to get too brown. When the sun touched her, it brought out the sepia and cinnamon in her blood, overpowered the milk and honey, and he could no longer pretend she was white. He loved her skin pale. "Look how you gleam in the moonlight," he'd say to her when he made gentle, almost supplicating love to her at night in the four-poster bed. His hand would slide over her flesh, cup her breasts with an air of reverence. The look in his eyes was so close to worship that it sometimes frightened her. To be loved so much! He would whisper to her, "Beauty. Pale Beauty, to my Beast," then blow a cool breath over the delicate membranes of her ear, making her shiver in delight. For her part, she loved to look at him, his molasses-dark skin, his broad chest, the way the planes of flat muscle slid across it. She imagined tectonic plates shifting in the earth. She loved the bluish-black cast the moonlight lent him. Once, gazing up at him as he loomed above her, body working against and in hers, she had seen the moonlight playing glints of deepest blue in his trim beard.

"Black Beauty," she had joked softly, reaching to pull his face closer for a kiss. At the words, he had lurched up off her to sit on the edge of the bed, pulling a sheet over him to hide his nakedness. Beatrice watched him, confused, feeling their blended sweat cooling along her body.

"Never call me that, please, Beatrice," he said softly. "You don't have to draw attention to my colour. I'm not a handsome man, and I know it. Black and ugly as my mother made me."

"But, Samuel... !"

"No."

Shadows lay between them on the bed. He wouldn't touch her again that night.

Beatrice sometimes wondered why Samuel hadn't married a white woman. She thought she knew the reason, though. She had seen the way that Samuel behaved around white people. He smiled too broadly, he simpered, he made silly jokes. It pained her to see it, and she could tell from the desperate look in his eyes that it hurt him too. For all his love of creamy white skin, Samuel probably couldn't have brought himself to approach a white woman the way he'd courted her.

The broken glass was in a neat pile under the guava tree. Time to make Samuel's dinner now. She went up the verandah stairs to the front door, stopping to wipe her sandals on the coir mat just outside the door. Samuel hated dust. As she opened the door, she felt another gust of warm wind at her back, blowing past her into the cool house. Quickly, she stepped inside and closed the door, so that the interior would stay as cool as Sammy liked it. The insulated door shut behind her with a hollow sound. It was air-tight. None of the windows in the house could be opened. She had asked Samuel, "Why you want to live in a box like this, sweetheart? The fresh air good for you."

"I don't like the heat, Beatrice. I don't like baking like meat in the sun. The sealed windows keep the conditioned air in." She hadn't argued.

She walked through the elegant, formal living room to the kitchen. She found the heavy imported furnishings cold and stuffy, but Samuel liked them.

In the kitchen she set water to boil and hunted a bit—where did Gloria keep it?—until she found the Dutch pot. She put it on the burner to toast the fragrant coriander seeds that would flavour the curry. She put on water to boil, stood staring at the steam rising from the pots. Dinner was going to be special tonight. Curried eggs, Samuel's favourite. The eggs in their cardboard case put Beatrice in mind of a trick she'd learned in physics class, for getting an egg unbroken into a narrow-mouthed bottle. You had to boil the egg hard and peel it, then stand a lit candle in the bottle. If you put the narrow end of the egg into the mouth of the bottle, it made a seal, and when the candle had burnt up all the air in the bottle, the vacuum it created would suck the egg in, whole. Beatrice had been the only one in her class patient enough to make the trick work. Patience was all her husband needed. Poor, mysterious Samuel had lost two wives in this isolated country home. He'd been rattling about in the airless house like the egg in the bottle. He kept to himself. The closest neighbours were miles away, and he didn't even know their names.

She was going to change all that, though. Invite her mother to stay for a while, maybe have a dinner party for the distant neighbours. Before her pregnancy made her too lethargic to do much.

A baby would complete their family. Samuel would be pleased, he would. She remembered him joking that no woman should have to give birth to his ugly black babies, but she would show him how beautiful their children would be, little brown bodies new as the earth after the rain. She would show him how to love himself in them.

It was hot in the kitchen. Perhaps the heat from the stove? Beatrice went out into the living room, wandered through the guest bedroom, the master bedroom, both bathrooms. The whole house was warmer than she'd ever felt it. Then she realised she could hear sounds coming from the outside, the cicadas singing loudly for rain. There was no whisper of cool air through the vents in the house. The air conditioner wasn't running.

Beatrice began to feel worried. Samuel liked it cold. She had planned tonight to be a special night for the two of them, but he wouldn't react well if everything wasn't to his liking. He'd raised his voice at her a few times. Once or twice he had stopped in the middle of an argument, one hand pulled back as if to strike, to take deep breaths, battling for self-control. His dark face would flush almost blue-black as he fought his rage down. Those times she'd stayed out of his way until he was calm again.

What could be wrong with the air conditioner? Maybe it had just come unplugged? Beatrice wasn't even sure where the controls were. Gloria and Samuel took care of everything around the house. She made another circuit through her home, looking for the main controls. Nothing. Puzzled, she went back into the living room. It was becoming thick and close as a womb inside their closed-up home.

There was only one room left to search. The locked third bedroom. Samuel had told her that both his wives had died in there, first one, then the other. He had given her the keys to every room in the house, but requested that she never open that particular door.

"I feel like it's bad luck, love. I know I'm just being superstitious, but I hope I can trust you to honour my wishes in this." She had, not wanting to cause him any anguish. But where else could the control panel be? It was getting so hot!

As she reached into her pocket for the keys she always carried with her, she realised she was still holding a raw egg in her hand. She'd forgotten to put it into the pot when the heat in the house had made her curious. She managed a little smile. The hormones flushing her body were making her so absent-minded Samuel would tease her, until she told him why. Every thing would be all right.

Beatrice put the egg into her other hand, got the keys out of her pocket, opened the door.

A wall of icy, dead air hit her body. It was freezing cold in the room. Her exhaled breath floated away from her in a long, misty curl. Frowning, she took a step inside and her eyes saw before her brain could understand, and when it did, the egg fell from her hands to smash open on the floor at her feet. Two women's bodies lay side by side on the double bed. Frozen mouths gaped open; frozen, gutted bellies, too. A fine sheen of ice crystals glazed their skin, which like her was barely brown, but laved in gelid, rime-covered blood that had solidified ruby red. Beatrice whimpered.

• • •

"But Miss," Beatrice asked her teacher, "how the egg going to come back out the bottle again?"

"How do you think, Beatrice? There's only one way; you have to break the bottle."

• • •

This was how Samuel punished the ones who had tried to bring his babies into the world, his beautiful black babies. For each woman had had the muscled sac of her womb removed and placed on her belly, hacked open to reveal the purplish mass of her placenta. Beatrice knew that if she were to dissect the thawing tissue, she'd find a tiny foetus in each one. The dead women had been pregnant too.

A movement at her feet caught her eyes. She tore her gaze away from the bodies long enough to glance down. Writhing in the fast congealing yolk was a pin-feathered embryo. A rooster must have been at Mister Herbert's hens. She put her hands on her belly to still the sympathetic twitching of her womb. Her eyes were drawn back to the horror on the beds. Another whimper escaped her lips.

A sound like a sigh whispered in through the door she'd left open. A current of hot air seared past her cheek, making a plume of fog as it entered the room. The fog split into two, settled over the heads of each woman, began to take on definition. Each misty column had a face, contorted in rage. The faces were those of the bodies on the bed. One of the duppy women leaned over her own corpse. She lapped like a cat at the blood thawing on its breast. She became a little more solid for having drunk of her own life blood. The other duppy stooped to do the same. The two duppy women each had a belly slightly swollen with the pregnancies for which Samuel had killed them. Beatrice had broken the bottles that had confined the duppy wives, their bodies held in stasis because their spirits were trapped. She'd freed them. She'd let them into the house. Now there was nothing to cool their fury. The heat of it was warming the room up quickly.

The duppy wives held their bellies and glared at her, anger flaring hot behind their eyes. Beatrice backed away from the beds. "I didn't know," she said to the wives. "Don't vex with me. I didn't know what it is Samuel do to you."

Was that understanding on their faces, or were they beyond compassion?

"I making baby for him too. Have mercy on the baby, at least?"

Beatrice heard the snik of the front door opening. Samuel was home. He would have seen the broken bottles, would feel the warmth of the house. Beatrice felt that initial calm of the prey that realises it has no choice but to turn and face the beast that is pursuing it. She wondered if Samuel would be able to read the truth hidden in her body, like the egg in the bottle.

"Is not me you should be vex with," she pleaded with the duppy wives. She took a deep breath and spoke the words that broke her heart. "Is… is Samuel who do this."

She could hear Samuel moving around in the house, the angry rumbling of his voice like the thunder before the storm. The words were muffled, but she could hear the anger in his tone. She called out, "What you saying, Samuel?"

She stepped out of the meat locker and quietly pulled the door in, but left it open slightly so the duppy wives could come out when they were ready.

Then with a welcoming smile, she went to greet her husband. She would stall him as long as she could from entering the third bedroom. Most of the blood in the wives' bodies would be clotted, but maybe it was only important that it be warm. She hoped that enough of it would thaw soon for the duppies to drink until they were fully real.

When they had fed, would they come and save her, or would they take revenge on her, their usurper, as well as on Samuel?

Eggie-Law, what a pretty basket.

⌒

Nalo Hopkinson was born in Jamaica, and grew up in Guyana, Trinidad, and Canada. Her debut novel, *Brown Girl in the Ring* was the winning entry in the Warner Aspect First Novel contest, and led to her winning the Campbell Award for Best New Writer. She has since published many acclaimed novels and short stories as well as numerous essays. She currently teaches writing at the University of California, Riverside. Her latest novel is *Sister Mine*.

SILVERBLIND

A NOVEL EXCERPT

PRESENTED BY TOR BOOKS

TINA CONNOLLY

Please enjoy the following excerpt of the novel **Silverblind** *by Tina Connolly, coming this month from Tor Books:*

> *Dorie Rochart has been hiding her fey side for a long time. Now, finished with University, she plans to study magical creatures and plants in the wild, bringing long-forgotten cures to those in need. But when no one will hire a girl to fight basilisks, she releases her shape-changing fey powers—to disguise herself as a boy.*
>
> *While hunting for wyvern eggs, she saves a young scientist who's about to get steamed by a silvertail—and finds her childhood friend Tam Grimsby, to whom she hasn't spoken in seven years. Not since she traded him to the fey. She can't bear to tell him who she really is, but every day grows harder as he comes to trust her.*
>
> *The wyverns are being hunted to extinction for the powerful compounds in their eggs. The fey are dying out as humans grow in power. Now Tam and Dorie will have to decide which side they will fight for. And if they end up on opposite sides, can their returning friendship survive?*

CHAPTER ONE

INTERVIEW

Adora Rochart had not called on her fey side for nearly a decade, except for the merest gloss of power that helped keep her unnoticeable: allowed her to slip onto trolleys without paying, to slip under the radar, and incidentally to keep breathing. When the fey had showed her how to extract the blue from her system, they advised her to keep the tiniest film of fey dust about her. There was no other creature such as she: no other half-human, half-fey, and on many things the fey could not advise her.

But the Monday morning she went to her job interviews—that morning, for the first time in seven years, she unlocked the copper box of concentrated blue, and dipped her fingers in it. More than the dusting she had had. Far, far less than her whole self.

The blue must have sparkled on her fingers before being absorbed. Surely it must have tingled. But mostly, we may never know—why that particular morning, did she decide to bring the fey back into her life? Was it for luck? Was there fey intuition at stake, telling her she was about to need it? Or was it somehow the fey themselves, desperate about all that was to come, slipping their blue poison in her ear, telling her that she must side with them in the final war?

—Thomas Lane Grimsby,
Silverblind: The Story of Adora Rochart

• • •

Dorie sat neatly on one side of the desk, hands folded on top of the dirt smudge on her best skirt, heart in her throat. This was the last of the three interviews she'd managed to obtain—and the most important.

The desk was sleek and silver—like the whole building, shiny and new with the funds suddenly pouring into the Queen's Lab. The ultra-modern concrete-and-steel space had opened a scant year ago, but the small office was already crammed with the books, papers, and randomnesses of some overworked underling. On a well-thumbed book she could make out the chapter heading: "Wyverns and Basilisks: A Paralyzing Paradox." A narrow, barred window was half-covered by a towering stack of papers, but there was some blue summer sky beyond it. Perhaps if you stood on that chair and peered around it you could see the nurses marching at the City Hospital. Not that she was going to do anything so improper as stand on chairs today. This was her last chance.

The door buzzed as the underling scanned his ID medallion and walked in. Late, of course. He was probably a grad student from the University, thin and already stooped, in a rumpled blue suit, with a brown tie that had seen better days. Dorie refused to let her heart sink to her feet. There was always the chance that this boy was better than the two men she'd interviewed with that day, even if they had been higher on the ladder.

The underling sat down in his chair and moved stacks of papers with a dramatic groan for his overworkedness. Took out a pencil and began adding up a column of figures on a small notebook he carried. He didn't even bother to look up at her. "Let's get this farce over with, shall we?"

No. It was not going to go better at all.

Dorie pulled her papers from her satchel and passed them over. "I'm Dorie Rochart," she said, "and I'm interviewing for the field work position."

He dropped the papers on top of another stack without a glance and continued adding. "Look," he said to the notebook, "it's none of my doing. I'm sure you had very good marks and all."

"I did," Dorie interjected. She found his name on a placard half-buried in the remains of lunch. "Mr.... John Simons, is it? Pleased to meet you. Yes, I was top of the class." She had worked hard for that, after all. Firmly squashed all her differences and really buckled down. "I have a lot of fantastic ideas for ways this lab could help people that I'd really like to share with you."

"I'm sure, I'm sure," said Simons. "But be sensible, miss. You must realize they're never going to hire a girl for a field work position."

And there it was. He was willing to say what the first two men this morning had only danced around, mindful of keeping up the appearance that their labs were modern and forward-thinking and sensitive to the current picketings going on around Parliament. She could almost like him for being so blunt.

"I'm very qualified," Dorie said evenly. Of course she could not tell him exactly why she was so qualified. Being half-fey was the sort of thing for which they might just throw you in an iron box for the rest of your life. If they didn't hang you first. "I grew up in the country, and I—"

"I know, I know. You always dreamed of hunting copperhead hydras and silvertail wyverns like your brothers."

"I don't have any—"

"Or cousins, or whatnot." Simons sighed and finally put his pencil down. "Look, I don't want to be rude, but can we call it a day? I still have all this data to sort through." Finally, finally he deigned to look up at her, and his mouth hung open on whatever he was going to say.

This was the look Dorie knew.

This is what she had encountered twice before today—and more to the point, in general, always. The curse of her fey mother: beauty.

He stammered through something incoherent, in which she caught the words "girl" and "blonde." Finally he settled on, "I am very sorry. Terrible policy, terrible policy. Should be hiring girls right and left. You're not going to cry, are you?"

"Of course not," she said flatly. Dorie Rochart did not cry. She might, however, cause all those papers behind Simons to dump themselves on his head. It would be very satisfying. The fey in her fingertips tingled with mischief. She tucked her hands under her legs and sat on them.

He brightened. "Oh, good. I wouldn't know what to do." The mental wheels behind his eyes turned and Dorie braced herself, for now was the moment when they all propositioned her, and she didn't know what she would do then. The other two men that morning had done that… and her fey side had reacted.

Dorie had locked away her fey half for seven years. She couldn't trust herself with it. This morning, for the first time, she had retrieved just a trace. Just a smidge. It had felt so good, so *real*. Like she could face the day. Like she could sail through these interviews. A drop of blue, just to bring her luck.

But in seven years she had forgotten all her habits to control that part of her.

Her fingers had twitched, flicked, and had made a hot cup of tea "accidentally" spill on the first interviewer's lap. The second one, she had dropped a nearby spider down his collar. Simons had the misfortune to be third in line, and papers dumped on his head would be just the tip of the iceberg.

But to her surprise, he said, "Look, are you good at sums? There aren't any indoors research jobs right now, but I believe they're hiring more ladies to work the calculating machines. There's some girls in the physics wing crunching data."

Her fingers relaxed with this minor reprieve as she stood. He was safe for the moment. "I'm afraid not. Thank you for your—"

The door buzzed again. It swung open and a young eager face poked his head in. "Wyvern's hatching! Wyvern's hatching! Ooh, girl!" He blushed and left.

Perhaps Simons saw the light on her face, for he bended enough to say, "Look, I know you're disappointed, miss, uh, Miss Dorie." He blushed as he said her name. "I could… I could sneak you in to see the hatching before you go? As a, uh, personal favor?"

Dorie nodded eagerly. This was by far the most tolerable suggestive remark of the day, since it had the decency to come with a wyvern hatching.

"Stay behind me, then, and keep a low profile." His thin chest puffed out. "Top secret, you know? But they won't get too fussed about a girl if they see you—Pearcey brings in his latest bird all the time. I'll show you out when it's over."

Dorie followed Simons down the concrete hall to a lab room crammed with all the boys and men of the lab. He scanned his medallion and pulled her through behind him as the door opened. She caught a glimpse of the copper circle and saw a thin oval design there, its lines a faint silver glow. The same symbol was visible hanging on the lanyards of a few other men as well—some sort of new technology. Using electricity, she supposed. And a magnet, in that lock? She had not seen this sort of security before, but then she had been consumed with finishing her University studies this year.

She stood behind him, out of the way. She did not need to be told to stay to the back, as she felt conspicuous enough being the only girl. It was a clean, cold room, with metal tables and more rows of those narrow barred windows. The overhead lights were faintly tinged blue, and a smell of disinfectant hung in the air.

There was a small incubator in the middle of the room, made of glass and copper and lined with straw on the bottom. Inside was a grey egg speckled in silver. The top was thoroughly cracked and it was rocking back and forth. More chips from the egg tooth and a large piece broke off .

A man in a lab coat was making sure everyone was at their assigned sta-tion—from that and the murmurs she pieced bits together: one man was fetching a mouse for the new hatchling, another man was readying to seize the eggshell at the precise moment the wyvern was done with it and rush it to something called the extraction machine.

What was so important about the eggshell? Dorie wondered. In her child-hood, she had made note of the elusive wyverns whenever she stumbled across a pair, crept in day after day in half-fey state to that bit of the forest and stared in awe. No one had been interested in them then, or their eggshells. But she was not supposed to call attention to the fact that she was here, and she did not want to be thrown out, so she did not ask.

Across the concrete room she saw someone in a canvas field hat and her heart suddenly skipped a beat. Tam had always worn a hat like that—he called it his explorer hat. She hadn't seen her cousin for seven years, not since they were both fifteen and in the fey-ridden forest and—well. She wouldn't think about that now. Dorie peered around shoulders, wondering if it could pos-sibly be Tam. He would have liked this job, she thought. But the man turned toward her and she could see that it definitely wasn't Tam, not even Tam-a-decade-later. Of course, Tam had too much class to be wearing a hat inside.

Another crack, and the wyvern's wet triangular head came poking out. She heard an audible "awww" from someone. The man assigned to the task stood waiting, gloved hands out and ready to scoop up the apparently precious pieces of eggshell.

The egg broke all the way open and the little wyvern chick came wiggling out. Dorie barely noticed the process with the eggshell, as her attention was taken with the wriggly wet chick. They were bright silver at this age, and the sheen of liquid left from its hatching made it shine like a mirror under the laboratory lights. It stalked along, screeching for food. A short man swung a cage up onto the table, reached in with gloved hands to grab a white mouse by the tail. Dropped it into the incubator.

The little wyvern stalked along, its tiny claws clicking on the metal, its feet splaying out as it tried to learn balance. A man moved in front of her and by the time Dorie could see again the wyvern was comfortably gnawing on the mouse.

"Bloody-minded, aren't they?" said someone.

The short man brought a shallow bowl of water to set on the table and the wyvern chick stopped eating long enough to flap its wings and hiss, causing much laughter as the short man jumped back, spilling the water. A tall man in a finely cut suit said, "Doesn't like you much, does it?"

"Nasty little things don't like anyone," retorted the short man.

"And here I thought it was showing good taste," said the tall man in a pretend-nice way. The other scientists laughed sycophantically and Dorie thought this must be someone with power. She dropped her eyes as she realized he was looking back at her, and turned to Simons.

"What now?" Dorie whispered to her interviewer. "Will they return the chick to its parents?"

"Oh, no," Simons said. "We sell the hissy little things—to zoos and other research facilities, mostly. We're only interested in the eggs here, and they don't breed in captivity. Every so often someone makes arrangements with Pearce to purchase one as a pet—don't ask me why people want them. They don't like anybody. All they do is spit and scream at you, and when they're older, steam, too."

"Who's that man?" said Dorie, for Simons seemed to be in a question-answering mood. "The one looking at us."

Simons stiffened. Hurriedly he stepped in front of her as if to block the man's view. "Come on, come on, let me show you out," he said. "That's the lab director, and if he's cross about me showing you this I just don't even know. Hurry, miss."

Dorie started to the door, but stopped, Simons running into her. That boy, all the way in the corner, getting the wyvern chick more water. Wasn't that Tam after all? Or was her mind playing tricks on her now? She had not seen him for seven years, but surely—

"Dr. Pearce," said Simons, swallowing.

"Yes, this must be the one o'clock, correct?" The tall man was there, beaming down upon them in more of that faux-friendly way. "Showing her around a little bit?"

"Well, I—"

"Good, good. Miss Rochart, isn't it? If you'll come this way? I'd like to continue your interview in more comfortable quarters."

Simons looked as startled as Dorie felt, as the lab director escorted her to his office.

In stark contrast to the underling's office, this office was expansive and tidy. You could make seven or eight of Simons's office from it, and everyone knew that guys like Simons were the ones who did the real work. The omnipresent barred windows were replaced with a large plate-glass window. The new security building was across the street—a twin of this one, in blocky concrete and steel. And here was that clear view of the old hospital—and yes, the women with their placards attempting to unionize: Fair pay for fair work. A victory for one is a victory for all. Dorie strained to see if she could see her stepmother, Jane, who was not a nurse, but liked a good lost cause when she saw one.

The other significant object in the room was a large glass terrarium. Its sides were made of several glass panels set into copper, including a pair of doors fastened with a copper bolt. The top was vented with mesh, and the ceiling above the whole shebang was reinforced with anti-flammable panels of aluminum. Inside this massive display was an adolescent wyvern chick, about the size of a young cat. It was curled up in a silver ball on a nest of wool scraps and looked very comfortable.

Dorie wondered how secure the copper bolt was.

Dr. Pearce pulled out the chair for her, and leaned down to shake her hand. She realized now who he was—she had heard all the stories of his tailored suits, suave manner, and ice-chip eyes. Her hope bounded upward—talking to the lab director himself was an excellent sign. She had not gotten this far with the other two interviews.

Dr. Pearce had her sheaf of papers with him—her stellar academic record, her carefully acquired letters of recommendation. He smiled at Dorie—they always did—and sat down across from her. "The lovely Miss Rochart, I presume? So pleased to finally meet you."

Dorie tightened her fingers together at the mention of her looks, but she did not stop smiling. *The Queen's Lab. Focus on the goal. With this position you could really start to make a difference. Don't drop spiders on the lab director.*

She knew what she looked like—the curse of her beauty-obsessed fey mother. Blond ringlets, even, delicate features, rosebud lips. She could put the ringlets in a bun—which she had—and put on severe black spectacles—which she hadn't; she couldn't afford such nonsense—and still she would look like a porcelain doll. She had several times tried to tease the ringlets apart in hopes they would turn into a wild mop, which she always thought would suit her better. But no matter what she tried, she woke up every morning with her hair in careful, silken curls. Even now they were intent on escaping the bun, falling down to form softening ringlets around her face.

"And I you," said Dorie. Her normal voice was high and dulcet, but through long practice she had trained herself to speak an octave lower than she should.

He steepled his fingers. "Let's cut right to the chase, Miss Rochart—Adora. May I call you Adora? Such a lovely name."

"I go by Dorie or Ms. Rochart," she said, still smiling.

"Ah yes, the diminutive. I understand—after all, I don't make my friends call me *Dr.* Pearce *all* the time." He smiled at his joke. "Well, then, Dorie, let's have at it. I understand this is your third interview today?"

"Yes," she said. The laced fingers weren't working as well as she had hoped. She sat firmly on one hand and gripped the leg of her chair with the other. It would be terribly bad form to make that porcelain cup of tea with the gold rim levitate off the desk and dump itself down his front. "I understood that information to be private?"

"Oh, there are so few of us in this business, you understand. We are all old friends, all interested in what the new crop of graduates is doing." He smiled paternally at her. "And your name came up several times over lunch today."

"Yes?"

"Again, Adora—Dorie—let's cut to the chase. My colleagues were most amused to tell me of the pretty young girl who thought she could slay basilisks."

"I see," said Dorie. "Thank you for your time, then." She began to rise before her hands would do something that would betray her fey heritage and have her thrown in jail—or worse.

"No no, you misunderstand," he said, and he came to take her shoulders and gently guide her back to the chair. "My colleagues are living in the past. They didn't understand what an opportunity they had in front of them. But I understand."

"Yes?" Her heartbeat quickened. Was he on her side after all? A rosy future opened up once more. The Queen's Lab—a stepping-stone to really do some good. So much knowledge had been lost since the Great War two decades ago, since people started staying away from the forest. Simple things like what to do with feywort and goldmoths and yellowbonnet. She could continue her research into the wild, fey-touched plants and animals of the forest—species were disappearing at an alarming rate, and that couldn't be good for the fey *or* humans. And then, the last several times she'd been home, she'd hardly been able to *find* the fey in the woods behind her home. When she did, they were only thin drifts of blue.

But Dorie could help the humans. She could help the fey.

She was the perfect person to be the synthesis—and this was the perfect spot to do it. The Queen's Lab was the most prominent research facility in the city. If she could get in here, she could solve things from the inside.

Surely even Jane would approve of that.

Dr. Pearce smiled, one hand still on her shoulder. "If you've met any of the young men who do field work for us, you know they grew up dreaming of facing down mythical monsters."

He gestured expansively, illustrating the young boys' fervent imaginations. "Squaring off against the legendary basilisk, armed with only a mirror! Luring a copperhead hydra out of its lair, seizing it by the tail before it can twist around to bite you with its seven heads! Sneaking past a pair of steam-blowing silvertail wyverns, capturing their eggs and returning to tell the tale!"

"Yes," breathed Dorie. She put her hands firmly in her pockets.

"Those boys grow up," Dr. Pearce said. "Some of them still want to fight basilisks. But many of them settle down and realize that the work we do right here in the lab is just as important as risking your neck in the field." He perched on his desk and looked right at her. "Our country is mired in the dark ages of myth and superstition, Dorie. When we lost our fey trade three decades ago, we lost all of our easy, clean energy—all of our pride. We've been clawing our way back to bring our country in line with the technology of the rest of the world. We need some bold strokes to align us once more among the great nations of the world. And we can only do that with smart men—and women—like you."

She heard the ringing echo of a well-rehearsed speech, and still, she was carried away, for this *was* what she wanted, and more. "And think of all the good we could do with the knowledge we acquire in the field!" she jumped in, even though she had not planned to tip her hand till she was hired. "Sharing the benefits of all we achieve with everyone who truly needs them. Why, the good that can be accomplished from one pair of goldmoth wings! From a tincture of copperhead hydra venom! Do you remember the outbreak of spotted hallucinations last summer? My stepmother was the one who realized that the city hospitals no longer knew the country remedy of a mash of gold-moths and yellowbonnet. We worked together—she educating hospital staff, me in the field collecting. With the backing of someone like the Queen's Lab,

I could continue this kind of work. We could make a difference. Together." She was ordinarily not good with words, but she had recited her plans to her roommate over and over, waiting for the key moment to tell someone who could really help her.

"Ah, a social redeemer," Dr. Pearce said, and a fatherly smile smeared his face at her youthful enthusiasms.

This was not the key moment.

"But more seriously, Dorie," he went on, and his voice deepened. "I would like to create a special position in the Queen's Lab, just for you. A smart, clever, lady scientist like you is an asset that my colleagues were foolish enough to overlook." He fanned out her credentials. "Your grades and letters of recommendation are exemplary." He wagged a finger at her. "You know, if you had been born a boy we would never have had this meeting. You would have been snapped up this morning at your very first interview."

"The Queen's Lab has always been my first choice," said Dorie, because it seemed to be expected, and because it was true.

He smiled kindly, secure in his position as leader of the foremost biological research institution in the country. "Dorie, I would like you to be our special liaison to our donors. It is not false praise to assert how important you would be to our cause. The lab cannot exist without funding. Science cannot prosper. We need people like you, people who can stand on the bridge between the bookish boy scientist with a pencil behind his ear and the wealthy citizens that can be convinced to part with their family money; someone, in fact, exactly like you."

Her hands rose up, went back down. A profusion of thoughts pressed on her throat—with effort she focused to make a clear sentence come out. "And I would be doing what, exactly? Attending luncheons, giving teas?" He nodded. "Greasing palms at special late-night functions for very *select* donors?"

"You have it exactly."

"A figurehead, of sorts," said Dorie. Figurehead was a substitute for the real word she felt.

"If you like."

"*Not* doing field work," she said flatly.

"You must see that we couldn't risk you. I am perfectly serious when I say the work done here in the lab is as important—*more* important—than the work done by the hotheads out gathering hydras. You would be a key member of the team right here, away from the dust and mud and silvertail burns."

"I applied for the field work position," said Dorie, even though her hopes were fading fast. In the terrarium behind him, the adolescent wyvern was awake now, pacing back and forth and warbling. The large terrarium was overkill—their steam was more like mist at this age. It could as easily be pacing around Dr. Pearce's desk, or enjoying the windowsill. All it would take was a little flicker of the fingers, a little mental nudge on that bolt. . . .

Dr. Pearce brought his chair right next to hers and put a fatherly arm on her shoulder. She watched the wyvern and did not shove the arm away, still hoping against hope that the position she wanted was in her grasp. "Let me tell you about Wilberforce Browne," Dr. Pearce said. "Big strapping guy, big as three of you probably—one of our top field scientists. He was out last week trying to bring in a wyvern egg—very important to the Crown, wyvern eggs."

Dorie looked up at that. "Wyvern eggs?" she said, trying to look innocent. This is what she had just seen. But she could not think what would be so important about the eggs—except to the wyvern chick itself, of course.

Dr. Pearce wagged a finger at her. "You see what secrets you would be privy to if you came to work for us. Well, Wilberforce. He stumbled into a nest of the fey."

"But the fey don't attack unless provoked—"

"I wish I had your misplaced confidence," Dr. Pearce said. "The fey attacked, and in his escape Wilberforce stumbled into the clearing where his target nest lay. Alerted, the mated pair of wyverns attacked with steam and claws. He lost a significant amount of blood, part of his ear—and one eye."

"Goodness," murmured Dorie, because it seemed to be expected. "He must have been an idiot," which was not.

Dr. Pearce harrumphed and carried on. "So you see, your pretty blue eyes are far too valuable to risk in the field. Not that one cares to mention something as sordid as money"—and he took a piece of paper from his breast pocket and laid it on the desk so he could slide it over to her—"but as it happens, I think that you'll find that sum to be very adequate, and in fact, well more than the field work position would have paid."

Dorie barely glanced at the paper. Her tongue could not find any more pretty words; she could stare at him mutely or say the ones that beat against her lips. "*As it happens*, I have personal information on what your male field scientists get paid, and it is *more* than that number." It was a lie—but one she was certain was true.

Shock crossed his face—either that she would dare to question him, or that she would dare talk about money, she didn't know which.

Dorie stood, the violent movement knocking her chair backward. Her fey-infused hands were out and moving, helping the words, the wrong words, come pouring out of her mouth. "*As it happens*, I do not care to have my time wasted in this fashion. Look, if you did give me the field job and it didn't work out, you could always fire me. And what would you have wasted? A couple weeks."

Dr. Pearce stood, too, retrieving her chair. "And our reputation, for risking the safety of the fairer sex in such dangerous operations. No, I could not think of such a thing. You would need a guard with you wherever you went, and that would double the cost. Besides, I couldn't possibly ask one of our male scientists to be with you in the field, unchaperoned. . . ." His eyebrows rose significantly. "The Queen's Lab is above such scandal."

"Is that your final word on the subject?" Her long fingers made delicate turning motions; behind him the copper bolt on the glass cage wiggled free. The silver wyvern put one foot toward the door, then another.

"It is, sweetheart."

The triangular head poked through the opening as the glass door swung wide. Step by step . . .

"Thank you for your time then," Dorie said crisply. "Oh, and you might want to look into the safety equipment on your cages." She pointed behind him.

The expression on his face as he turned was priceless. Paternal condescension melted into shock as a yodeling teenage wyvern launched itself at his head. Dorie was not worried for his safety—the worst that could happen was a complete loss of dignity, and that was happening now.

"I'll see myself out, shall I?" said Dorie. She strolled to the office door and through, leaving it wide open for all to see Dr. Pearce squealing and batting at his hair as he ran around the wide, beautiful office.

～

Tina Connolly lives with her family in Portland, Oregon. Her stories have appeared in *Lightspeed, Tor.com, Strange Horizons,* and *Beneath Ceaseless Skies.* Her first fantasy novel, *Ironskin* (Tor 2012), was nominated for a Nebula, and the sequel *Copperhead* is now out from Tor. She narrates for *Podcastle* and *Beneath Ceaseless Skies,* runs the Parsec-winning flash fiction podcast *Toasted Cake,* and her website is tinaconnolly.com.

Language and Imaginative Resistance in Epic Fantasy

Kameron Hurley

I couldn't tell you the first word I learned. "Cheese," maybe. That delicious cream cheese my mother rolled in pea sprouts and fed to me on a plastic tray. Cheese was fucking delicious. To this day, I can't shake my cheese habit—it's the stuff of the gods, cheese is.

When we learn language as children, we often come to associate particular images with each word we learn. "What's that?" we'll say, pointing to the pale male figure in the blue uniform in a children's picture book, and we're told, "That's a police officer." Then someone will point to a pale female figure in white and say, "That's a nurse."

None of those professions is as great as cheese, but you get the idea.

The images we associate with these words are not only formative, but reinforced in much of the media we consume. "Police officer" conjures the image of that white man. "Nurse" delivers unto us that pale woman in the white hat, though really, outside a picture book or historical drama, who sees a nurse in that folded hat anymore? On occasion, yes, we'll see representative examples that contradict these early images, but no matter how many times we encounter policewomen, or male nurses, many of us find ourselves conjuring the same old imagery we learned to associate with the words as children whenever someone brings them up.

And writer? When I think the word "writer," my formative image is a pale man with a long white beard, like Walt Whitman, followed by Shakespeare, Thoreau, and maybe, if I'm lucky, Virginia Woolf, somewhere there in the unfolding kaleidoscope of images. My formative experience of the word "writer" was not me pointing to an image of Toni Morrison in a book and having my mom tell me "writer." In truth, it would not be until grade school when I learned of writers who were something other than the pale like me. Oh, sure, logically, you hear that "anyone" can be a writer, or "anyone" can be a nurse, but just like "cheese" initially elicited images of those cream cheese blobs slathered in pea sprouts to me—no matter how many goudas or manchegos I ate—so "writer" has always been, first and foremost, some old Walt Whitman-looking dude.

This is what I mean when I tell people that our view of the world, and reality, is a constructed one. Our brains—in their unending quest to be more efficient—often pull on early images and memories to construct our view of the real world. After all, what other information do we have to achieve this but those early stories about how the world is, how it works? When one is building an entire world from scratch—which is literally what our brains are doing in our early years—our first exposure to media is going to be the foundational media. Everything we encounter after that will be used to readjust that first framework for our world.

So when someone told me what epic fantasy was, sometime in my early years, and they pointed to Tolkien and his medieval castles and orcs and wizards… well. That was epic fantasy, defined. Anything else that came after that—any other type of author, in any type of other setting, either needed to be put outside that frame or somehow be mangled to fit within it.

Epic fantasy was defined. It made it harder to make other things fit into it.

What I soon realized is that it wasn't just me who struggled with that frame.

When I see the bestsellers in epic fantasy today, I can't help but see the same genre-framing contortions I did as a child played out on the shelves. I see what folks line up next to Tolkien, and Terry Brooks, and George R.R. Martin—them and their imitators and the not-so-imitation-but-what-publishers-would-like-to-market-as-such in nice neat rows, and there is a startling sameness to these writers and their milieus that is heartbreaking. Every epic is grand, the first time: the first Dragonlance novel, the first Joe Abercrombie book, but after those come the waves of imitators, the ones pushed on the reading public by publishers frantically scrambling to find more of the same—but just a little bit different, like, instead of a stable boy who's really a prince, can we have a courier boy who's really a prince?—before we weary of the latest iteration.

I see an entire "genre of the epic fantastic" that's been defined in the most narrow way imaginable. I want to see the weird cities of K.J. Bishop and

Steph Swainston up there next to the dudes with the swords and fiefdoms on the bestseller lists. These days, Adrian Tchaikovsky has pushed into the fray with an uncommon setting, as well as David Anthony Durham, and Brian McClellan replaces feudal swords with flintlocks . . .

But what's missing here, in my list of names? What am I writing out?

Where have all the women in epic fantasy gone?

Or, when we say "epic fantasy," does that just prompt us, immediately, to forget about everything outside the frame, to remember only, at best, the pseudonyms—the Hobbs or the K.J. Parkers?

I've seen a lot of women writers struggle in the epic fantasy field, facing reader and publisher expectations that assume their work must be something else, anything else, besides epic fantasy. Epic fantasy is Tolkien. Epic fantasy is *men*.

Kate Elliott, who has been writing epic fantasy for decades, has had recent work reviewed as solidly YA, and if one were to ask, today, what Elliott writes, many reviewers would answer "YA" or the more generic "fantasy." Author Delilah Dawson has related on Twitter that her original Blud series was, to her mind, a fantasy novel, but she was encouraged to play up the romantic elements and pitch it as a romance. Ann Aguirre writes books across a bunch of genres, but ask folks what she writes and you're likely to hear "YA" or "romance," not "science fiction" or even "fantasy." Women are often told, time after time, that they have a better shot at making it as novelist if they position themselves as romance writers than epic fantasy writers. Even when writers like N.K. Jemisin and Jaqueline Carey are positioned as epic fantasy, I still encounter readers who make faces and say, "Oh, that's not fantasy, really. Too much romance." Yet all the sex in the dude books? Totally fantasy!

It's hard for us to change our frame.

Romance and YA are not, for marketing reasons, bad places to be, but why do readers and reviewers continually place epic work by women, in particular, into another category, all but ensuring what we view as "epic fantasy" today becomes a clutter of male writers and women writing under male or gender-neutral pseudonyms like Mazarkis Williams, Robin Hobb, and (likely) K.J. Parker?

I'd argue this has little to do with content, as the three pseudonymous authors above write in a cozily epic and somewhat dark tradition reminiscent of the rest. Instead, it has to do with how we're taught to view and categorize artistic work.

Epic fantasy seems to have drifted into a prescriptive mode characterized by gritty descriptions, multiple POVs, abuse and maiming, medieval milieus, and, oddest of all (!), work that does this as written by male authors. Karen

Miller and Anne Bishop need not apply (Anne Bishop's pain-dealing cock rings, one imagines, may be too much for many grimdark epic fantasy readers to stomach).

When one holds up as examples of a type of fiction only work written by men, and only dark, pseudo-medieval work by men, it's an effective way of shutting out all other types of work. The strange thing is to watch people try and keep out what they don't believe fits into the frame. I've had people push my own work out of the "grimdark" mode of fantasy for having spaceships, and Karen Miller for not being "epic" enough, and Anne Bishop, naturally, for skirting that "romance" line too closely (too many cock rings!).

Once one has constructed a frame, one has to work very hard to maintain its borders, even when those borders can clearly be far broader. This was the frame they were shown. This is what fits. Everything else must be put in different boxes.

What we fail to understand when we critique the reading habits and choices and shoring up of the frames that people have made when called out about this—this lack of memory and categorization of women authors, this constant pushing out—is that though these are things done by individuals, the actions themselves are part of a broader system of dismissal and un-seeing that we've been internalizing—all of us—from the time we were children. We grew up in a system that wanted us to see and remember and prioritize particular voices and worldviews, and we perpetuate them whether we're aware of them or not.

If we're told that the only cheese is blue cheese, it's the first cheese we'll think of, and the cheese by which all others are measured. For those who don't care much for blue cheese, it may even lead one to think that all cheese is horrible, because they don't have an inclusive frame that can hold all the rest.

One of the greatest lies we've ever been told in the United States is that we are free and independent individuals. Most people will tell you marketing messages don't work on them, and they aren't sexist or racist at all—everyone is equal, everyone is the same. But the frame we've built for the world is not built on those ideas. The frame tells you these people do things, and these people have things done to them. These are assumptions and preconceptions built into our very language. It's no wonder it becomes an epic undertaking to try and dismantle them.

When I tell other writers these sorts of stories, about the inherent resistance of readers to including them in genres they actively want to write in, I get a lot of sour, grim faces. For good reason. Who the fuck wants to deal with all that? Who wants to fight all that? How can we kick down and help somebody re-build a frame of reference that's reinforced from every media message?

The answer is: We have to be part of rebuilding the landscape. The truth is we must be part of building new stories. But first we must pull down our own preconceptions of what we can and should and ought to write. We need to tear down the internalized despair over the long slog we've got ahead, and get to work.

I'm not saying that's easy. In truth, it's really, really hard. But the more I work at it, the more I've reimagined cheese not as some pale lumps covered in pea sprouts but a full-on Spanish cheese sampler, and you know? My life is richer for it. I'm branching out. There's hope.

Will any of this change the world? Will a single act change the narrative, and reimagine our language? No. But I can tell you that every great act starts with someone saying, "This isn't okay. This isn't truth." Where the real shift comes is when a small, passionate group of people sees it too, and takes on the task of reimagining the world with you.

I don't just write stories. I don't just sell book widgets. I create new narratives of the way *we* can be, of the way the *world* can be.

Are you with me?

∼

Kameron Hurley is the author of the subversive epic fantasy novel *The Mirror Empire* and the science-fantasy noir God's War trilogy. Her work earned her the Sydney J. Bounds Award for Best Newcomer and Kitschy Award for Best Debut Novel. Hurley has been a finalist for the Arthur C. Clarke Award, Hugo Award, Nebula Award, Locus Award, and BFS Award for non-fiction. She pens a bi-monthly column with *Locus Magazine* on writing-related topics and blogs regularly at KameronHurley.com.

WOMEN IN FANTASY ILLUSTRATION ROUNDTABLE

GALEN DARA

At this year's Illustration Masters Class, I took the opportunity to sit down and have a conversation with Julie Bell, Irene Gallo, Rebecca Guay, Lauren Panepinto, and Zoë Robinson. It was an incredible chance to talk to three very influential art directors and two internationally renowned artists about their personal journeys, their careers in the speculative fiction industry, and the state of women today working as illustrators.

Later I had the chance to loop two more artists into the conversation: Award-winning illustrator Julie Dillon and Women Destroy Fantasy! cover artist Elizabeth Leggett generously shared their own experiences and advice. I deeply appreciate each of these fantastic women for being so open with their insight and knowledge. It was a humbling and inspiring opportunity for me personally.

First off, what led you to work in the speculative fiction field? Was this always your intended career plan?

Irene Gallo: I think "plan" is overstating it. I grew up on *Close Encounters [of the Third Kind]* and then *Raiders of the Lost Ark*. I was obsessed with those two movies, especially *Raiders of the Lost Ark*. And then I literally stumbled into a Harlan Ellison book and went to hear him speak a few times. It was like junior high school or whatever. But then I did phase out of it, not so much out of a "plan" either. I went to college and was busy with college things, and when I got out, I got a job with Tor. I really came full circle, and really recognized everything around me. I was very lucky.

Julie Bell: I definitely didn't have it as a plan, either. I can look back and see a lot of the things I really liked when I was a kid, like Dulac and fairy tale art, things like that. I always thought that I was going to be an artist, and I wanted to do children's books. I had this idea of making my own fairy tale a long time ago, which I never did. I can see where what I'm doing definitely goes to that, it's just that I never actually put it into a plan of action. My life just, in this really magical kind of way, fell into it.

Lauren Panepinto: I'm the same. I'm an only child, and I was a tomboy, and I was kind of my dad's buddy. He was into baseball cards, and we always went to these baseball card shows. I always went straight to the comics section. You know, when you're a little girl, you can get advice: "What is a good comic book for a girl?" "Oh, *X-Men!*" And since I was hanging out there all the time, eventually I worked at the comic book store near my high school in Staten Island (Jim Hanley's Universe). I worked there through high school and summer vacations in college—I went to the School of Visual Arts for Graphic Design.

After graduation I got into books and worked for a couple different publishers. I was the art director in charge of paperbacks for Broadway/Doubleday when Orbit came to the US from the UK. That year there was a big shakeup in publishing; it had decimated my division, ending up with me getting laid off literally the week that Orbit was looking for a creative director to take over and dedicate themselves to only geek books. A friend called me and was like, "I heard you got laid off. I have a job for you!" It was just the most amazing luck. I met the publisher, Tim Holman. We talked about books and we talked about geekdom, and he even grilled me on my geek cred, "Have you really read *Chapterhouse: Dune*? Have you really read *The Simarillion*?" I finally had to show my elvish tattoo. So, the answer is, I ended up doing this by total luck and chance.

Zoë Robinson: Mine is very much similar—right place, right time. Except sort of the opposite in the childhood. I was a pretty isolated kid who lived very much in my head, so I read everything I could get my hands on. My books were my friends, and they were very much more real to me than everything else around me. I would draw a lot, partially to put flesh on that, and partially because it gave me something to do with my hands that adults wouldn't make me stop doing. It split my attention. I was constantly, constantly drawing. I ended up accidentally getting an art degree from a Liberal Arts school and wandering through weird jobs. Finally, a friend was like, "So, this place needs an art director… I hope they get somebody good… You should do it!" So I ended up getting hired at Fantasy Flight Games.

Rebecca Guay: I always wanted to be an artist, and I fell in love with *The X-Men* in seventh grade. I saw an issue of *The X-Men* in a newspaper stand, and was like, "What is this wonderful world?" and immediately was sold. I was also super into *The Raiders of the Lost Ark*. Oh my God. And *Star Wars*, but *Raiders*! I still have my twelve-inch Indiana Jones clock. It's in the guest room right now, waiting for the new studio. I was copying comics constantly through junior high and high school. My mom made a bet that by the time I was in college, I wouldn't want to go into comics. I was like, "I'll take that bet!" She was sure I'd grow up and be "serious" about art.

I got to college and I somewhat got sidetracked. I thought I'd go into kids' books, children's book illustration. In fact, I had a nice children's book portfolio when I graduated from Pratt, but I started dating George Pratt, who had just done *Enemy Ace*, which is this beautiful graphic novel. He started introducing me at parties and different get-togethers to the comic book world. I met Mike Mignola and Mike Kaluta and all these amazing people. I sort of met Frank Miller: I spilled a drink on him and ran away.

I started putting together my sample pages when I was working my day job as an assistant at Marvel Comics. My friend was in the art department at Marvel, and I was his assistant for sixty dollars a day, just getting anything anyone needed. Every night, I'd go home to my sample pages. I got my first ten-page story for Marvel, and that got me into an issue of *Swamp Thing*, which got me a full-time penciling gig for *Black Orchid*. That lasted two years, and on the side I was getting into kids' magazines, and also trading card work.

I didn't really intend to go into comics and science fiction/fantasy; I thought I'd go into kids' books, but ended up in comics, and then segued into *Magic: [The Gathering]* through comics, and graphic novels through *Magic*, and segued into fantasy, and then children's books came around, and it all grew from there.

Julie Dillon: I've always leaned towards fantasy and science fiction, even as a child. I've been drawing and painting my whole life, but I didn't start taking it more seriously until early high school, when I started wanting to draw pictures of scenes from books or characters I'd made up, and got frustrated with how bad I was at it. I particularly loved the artwork on the early *Magic: The Gathering* cards, so I'd copy the art from my favorite cards to help me practice. For a while, I got really into anime, and that dominated what I did for a few years. At that point I had improved enough that I would get occasional commissions from people online, but I still didn't consider art as a viable career, so I spent the next several years plugging away at a computer science degree. It wasn't until my mid-twenties that I started thinking maybe I should pursue art, since that's what I was doing in every bit of free time I had available. I enjoyed drawing and creating too much to keep it as a side-gig or hobby.

I enjoy the freedom of expression and potential for storytelling inherent in SF and fantasy illustration. There's so much room for experimentation and new ideas. Sometimes it's hard to explain to other people what it is I do for a living, though, since drawing dragons and warrior ladies and robots isn't necessarily the first thing that comes to mind when people think "artist."

Elizabeth Leggett: I have been a tabletop gamer since I was in elementary school. The art in the books sparked my imagination and matched the art I found myself trying to draw. It was like discovering friends rather than a career path. It was many years later when I finally accepted the constant yearning to illustrate full time as a "Life Goal." It became more than a dream. It became something worth planning a life around achieving.

There's been a lot of talk about gender parity in the SF illustrating field, about how few women, percentage-wise, are working as illustrators—especially since at least half of art students are female. Did your gender ever come into play in your careers? What are your thoughts about what causes this attrition?

Panepinto: These are definitely conversations Irene and I have had before, trying to think of all the female names, who's working and who's not, and it seems like there are so many female students that are into it right now, but then where are the working artists?

Robinson: I think it's just recently that it hasn't been just the hardheaded girls toughing it out. It's been very recently that generally, girls are aware that this is something that they're invited and allowed to do.

Panepinto: I think that it also comes out of the YA fiction. Harry Potter's got such strong characters—Hermione's such a great female character—and The Hunger Games.

Dillon: I've done most of my work online, working by myself at home, so it's difficult to gauge sometimes if gender has come into play in terms of my career path. Early on, it felt pretty isolating not seeing many other women in the big art forums at the time, but there have been more and more women becoming more visible in the field over the years.

Leggett: If my gender came into play in any negative way that kept me from illustration contracts, I am not aware of it. I think male and female illustrators face the same challenges. This is a frighteningly competitive business and that might be the crux of the matter. Males, generally speaking, accept competition as part of the process and some thrive on it. More and more women are stepping into this fray and discovering they thrive as well, but are having to catch up in the race.

Guay: It's still a confidence issue with girls. Believing that their art has weight, has gravity, is worth something. And it's not because the industry says it's not. I have never, ever encountered sexism.

Bell: Me neither. I've never had anybody even care if I was male or female.

Guay: It's always been about my work, and if anything, it's been a benefit, honestly. They're just happy to see a girl. It's benefited me on the reverse side.

Pinepinto: When I'm showing art samples to editors, they don't even know names.

Gallo: I think confidence is the issue. I remember seeing an awards ceremony where a woman had won, and she was delighted. Her acceptance speech was, "Oh my God, so many other people deserve to be here, thank you so much." My heart just sank the minute she said that, because a Dan Dos Santos or Donato would never get up there—they would be humble and say "amongst these amazing people, thank you"—but they would never say "I don't deserve this." So I do think there's a confidence issue.

But I also think there are stylistic issues, which are difficult to talk about. The default for a science fiction/fantasy book cover is a very male aesthetic, and when I get these beautiful portfolios of more feminine styles or more feminine themes, I can think of many fewer places that I could use that on.

Panepinto: I've been using a lot of female artists in the urban fantasy genre. I think Mélanie Delon's art is very "feminine," beautiful, and floral, and it's perfect for these books and I was super excited to be able to use her. I feel like this conversation isn't done. It lulls a bit and spikes a bit, but this "women in fantasy" conversation has been loudly advocated for at least a year.

Dillon: I feel like, while things are slowly evening out, there is still a degree of institutional bias that makes art seem like a more tangible career possibility for men than women. There are a lot of women working as illustrators, but they don't often hold as many visible higher-up positions. Some people have a tendency to be more dismissive of women illustrators, because there's this vague assumption that women only do decorative, quiet, or frivolous work: greeting cards, children's books, et cetera (dismissing this type of work is an issue in itself); while men are considered to be the ones doing the "real" work of fine art, concept art, and animation for films and games. This is flat-out untrue; all genders have much to offer in all areas of art, and one style of art isn't inherently more worthy or legitimate than other styles. But even when these assumptions are proven wrong, women working in concepting and animation and other typically male-dominated fields face an uphill battle to gain the same level of respect and recognition that men do, while men doing more decorative and introspective work tend to garner more legitimacy than their female counterparts.

Gallo: And certainly at Tor.com I could use a lot more of everything! The whole breadth of artistic styles more than anything else. That's been great, because I have been able to push that into the book covers more and more. There's more acceptance of all kinds of styles, regardless of who it's coming from.

Leggett: We are outnumbered at the moment, but that will change. There are so many creative, professionally focused, driven women finding better and better opportunities in this field every day. We are in the call lists. We are in the convention guest lists. We are mentoring and studying and working so beautifully that the male illustrators are taking notice. They are challenging themselves more as well. This is good for the science fiction and fantasy genres as a whole.

Dillon: One thing I have noticed is that I sometimes get contacted for work specifically because I am a woman artist; it doesn't happen too often, and while I'm happy for any work I get, the self-doubting part of my brain worries sometimes if tokenism is playing a part.

Robinson: Now, in gaming, sexism is a lot more salient, because it's a different kind of projective escapism. In gaming, the art shows who's invited to the table, and, until very recently, there was no diversity. It was all Caucasian males. In fact, if I don't specify race and gender in the art brief, I will get a 6'1", thirty-year-old Caucasian man with short dark hair, clean-shaven, and with dark eyes. I've noticed it in my office culture; at first, it took the interrupt of going in and saying, "This is old. Can we at least do X?" Now the culture is they do it by verbatim. They do the hundred twenty cards and then go through and make sure there's representation. They're excited about the diversity.

Guay: I've noticed less and less stylistic diversity since the '90's. More and more computer-generated, glossy, slick, high-tech look in a lot of stuff.

Dillon: When I get art assignments, I have been making more of a conscious effort to have more variety in the characters' appearances, to include more women and make sure that the women I do include are not all helpless waifish blondes. Most of the time it goes over well (or at least, I don't get complaints), but every now and then I'll receive feedback from an art director complaining that a female character was "too fat" or "too ethnic" or "not pretty enough," which just makes me all the more determined to try to be even more inclusive and diverse when I have the freedom to do so.

Robinson: I think, too, when it comes to sexism, that this new generation of artists is feeling it a lot more keenly, because of, I heard an artist describe it as "bro wolf-packing." With internet culture, it becomes much more apparent who's doing what and anyone can comment. In face-to-face physical meetings where you're going around, everyone's very polite and accepting, but you get on the internet and you have trolls. Everyone is much more loud.

Gallo: On the other hand, though, it does open up the conversation. I think these are conversations that I've been hearing about for years on the writer side and in conventions. They would happen in a room this big with twenty people in it, and it would just go away, and now that these conversations are online, sure, you get the trolling, and it's annoying when you get so many negative responses. But what's funny is, so many people are very surprised at how well formed the argument is, because it's new to them. They're like, "Whoa! Why am I being blindsided by this?" And we're like, "No, we've been talking about it for ten years. You just didn't hear it."

Panepinto: We've been practicing this conversation for years!

Robinson: I know a lot of women artists who have experienced very painful interactions because they are women, but it's an internet thing. I was having a conversation on Facebook the other day with artist Hannah Christenson about where did all the women illustrators go? And a bunch of guys got on the thread and were talking about how it was all biological that men are just better illustrators. On her Facebook page! It was her Facebook page, this female art director and female artist, talking about this thing, kind of in a quiet conversation, and these random strangers popped on and took over the conversation.

Then she and I started IMing. The conversation was like, "I wish that some of these young female artists would have this conversation that we're having!" So I made the Women in Fantastical Illustration Facebook group just for that reason. Overwhelmingly, the majority of illustrators have had the same experience. It's something very common, but I think that's sort of the new online post-feminist backlash, kind of a men's rights chamber on the internet.

Guay: I think we have to take that with a grain of salt, because there's always the occasional total bonehead who loves to just make something about you public. They do it just to be annoying. But I don't think it's a pervasive attitude. I stay away from those dialogues as often as possible because they deflect the attention from the places where I most want to send it. Because of course my ire goes up when someone's an asshole, and it's so frequent that people are assholes on the internet that you have to pick your moment. So I step away from those because the power is in the example I set. It's there that you inspire the up-and-coming artists. That's where I want my energy and voice to go.

Gallo: That is where the most power lies, definitely. Although there is a reason why when anybody says, "Who are the women in fantasy illustration?" you can name the same five people for the last fifteen years. And two of them are here! [Rebecca Guay and Julie Bell]. The other one is Kinuko Craft and the other one is Terese Nielsen. It becomes difficult. In the past ten years, it's difficult to name anybody beyond that, right? Who is it beyond that? Rowena Morrill, Diane Dillon of Leo and Diane Dillon...

Julie Dillon, that was an issue you addressed after your nomination for the Hugo Award last year, correct? The fact that's it's so hard to name off women in fantasy illustration?

Dillon: Honestly, while I was hugely honored and humbled by the nomination, it also felt a little strange, because there are so many other amazing women who have been working the field much longer than I have, who have not been nominated for that award yet. I really felt like they should have been recognized before me. The male artists who have been nominated over the years are well deserving and wonderful people, but there are so many amazing women out there who just don't seem to make it into the circles of award nominees with the same frequency that men do. I made that tumblr post (juliedillon.tumblr.com/post/66217741265/big-huge-list-of-some-amazing-women-artists) listing all the women artists I could find, because oftentimes people seem to have a hard time naming more than a handful of women artists. I wanted to have a big compilation that I could point to whenever someone claimed that there just weren't that many women artists out there.

Gallo: There are many up-and-coming women and hopefully it sticks, but I think there's always been the up-and-coming and there's always been attrition amongst women illustrators. And if you want to talk about women, talk about people of color... That is a much bigger, harder question.

Guay: At this year's Illustration Masters Class, there were no African-American students. And usually there is only one, maybe two. It's a catch-22. I find it easier to paint Caucasian skin, so I tend to paint that. Because there aren't as many African-American artists in the field, there's fewer paintings of African-Americans in the art. And so it's a terrible circle.

Robinson: I think that comes down to [the way] that art shows who is invited to the table. In college, I had just gotten a job as an art director at Fantasy Flight, and I was visiting my college roommate, who was black, and her family. Her little cousin, who was like eight, looked at me with tears in her eyes, and asked me if I could do some black heroes, because she loved fantasy, but she just didn't have any black heroines, and she wanted stuff that was like her. It's been surprisingly difficult to get that to happen. There's this board game I played that was cyberpunk, and one of the characters is an Indian woman. The marketing guy played with his wife and his wife's best friend, who happens to be Indian. She saw the character and just, her eyes lit up. She grabbed it and it's become her favorite game. She connected with that visual of her ideal self.

Bell: It has to do with who's buying it. Honestly, in my experience, most of the people buying my work are men. I've definitely had a few people who were collectors of mine who were different races than white, but most of them have been white men.

Gallo: People with money. People with access.

Panepinto: I think it's an interesting marketing question. Decisions are being made to market to the people who are buying these things, but you are also always talking about expanding markets. We run into that in publishing all the time. We had to deal with the Joe Abercrombie cover with *Best Served Cold*. The main character is a girl so I put a girl on the cover and everyone freaked out "Why is there a girl on the cover?" And I wanted to say "Talk to the author! He wrote the book!" A lot of the fan base was like, "There should be a guy on the cover because it's a 'guy' book even if it is a girl character." I wonder, again, how much of it is that that reaction is on the internet, right? I wonder how much of marketing is bound by precedent and how much of it is bound by the vocal minority.

Dillon: My hope for publishers (and people deciding on award nominations) is for them to be more open-minded when it comes to style and approach. When something is published, it helps gives artists and art styles more legitimacy, opening the door for more viewpoints and perspectives. All people have a lot to offer, and when we pigeonhole one group as the only way to be good at one thing, it cuts off the possibility of a broader range of viewpoints and fresh ideas and approaches, which further locks us into the same patterns.

Something that is often brought up when discussing attrition rates of women artists is the effect of motherhood upon a woman's career. Rebecca Guay and Julie Bell both raised children in addition to having successful illustration and art careers. Can you talk about that?

Guay: I remember when I was pregnant, another woman said, "I wonder what you are going to do when you have your baby because you won't have as much time to work on your art," and my head almost exploded under the concept that somebody thinks in a practical way that I can give up the art. First of all, I couldn't. Second of all, give up my paying job? Because I'm going to have a baby? So, there's a weird thing about having a baby and being an artist. Being a mom is wonderful, but being an artist is what I am. I remember nursing Vivian and working on *Magic* cards while holding her in my lap. I was back to painting when she was just a few days old.

Bell: I wasn't working professionally as an artist when my children were born; if I had been getting money for my art, it might have been a different thing, I don't know. It was a struggle. It was a matter of knowing I needed to do art and making time to work on it in spite of the fact that it wasn't a career yet.

Panepinto: And a whole other conversation is that none of the three art directors present have children. And my joke answer, which is not always a joke answer, is, "I have fifty cover babies every month!" which is not really an answer, I know. But you see on Facebook these two women artists who just had babies in the last month and are working on their freelance jobs. Women are figuring it out.

Leggett: Sometimes paying the rent wins. Sometimes having better insurance wins. This is especially true for parents. We are not losing our female illustrators fresh out of art school because they are female and being discriminated against. We are losing them because what we do is viewed by most of society as a luxury and not a necessity. Luxuries are the first things to go when the cash gets sluggish. Illustration is a dream job. It is a calling. It is a chance to get paid for getting all of the images swimming around in your skull out into the world. It is not, however, necessarily financially wise. The competition, as I mentioned before, is fierce. An illustrator has to find gigs, keep up with the sales and the business end, attend conferences to make the connections, make deadlines no matter what, and, in their copious spare time, create art.

Guay: And it's just logistics that you're exhausted as a mom, and if you happen to have a husband who is working a full-time job and you were working as a full-time illustrator and you have a baby, and there's any other way that money might come in the door, it's easy to slowly slip away and slowly do less and less. But my income was the primary income in our family. It was hard, but in some ways it was lucky, because I had to keep working. And you know you are never going to stop… but maybe if I hadn't had as solid a career prior to having a baby, if I had had a baby when I was twenty-five or twenty-six and I was still on unsure footing in terms of myself as an artist, and I hadn't solidified my career, maybe I could have drifted. I think that could happen to a lot of women and maybe that is why some potential up-and-comers just at the point that they are starting to get traction have a baby. Women still do carry most of the weight of caregiving for small children.

Bell: I remember when my kids were still babies, and I had a moment when I felt my head was going to split because I wanted to be doing my art now but I knew that five minutes from now I'm going to have to do something with the baby. I remember thinking to myself, "wait, does this mean I can't do this art or what?" and I told myself, "no, you have a brain and you can teach yourself to shift back and forth." I just had to teach my brain to be a lot more flexible than it had been, had to really consciously train myself. And then it wasn't until my kids were eight and ten when I started making a name for myself with my art. And by that time it was easier. When they are babies, you are so exhausted, and you just need to realize that will pass and you'll get your feet under you again.

Guay: I have heard this so often from women coming to the Illustration Masters Class: "I was starting to get work, I was starting to get traction, but then I had my baby." I hear that so often. And it's just what it is, and it's hard, and you just need the fortitude to come back to it if you have gotten derailed. And some people might not have the energy for that uphill climb, because it *is* an uphill climb to establish yourself in this field.

Panepinto: Last year during the Women in Fantasy panel at Spectrum, when Tara McPherson was there and she had brought their young child—I forget how old Tara was but I think she's in her early thirties—and she said she very consciously made the decision that she wasn't going to have a child until her career had gotten to that point that she could survive. She knew she was going to have to coast for a year, so she waited until she would be okay. People wouldn't forget about her in the year she was focusing more on taking care of an infant.

Guay: Being a mom shakes your brain up. There's crazy brain chemistry that happens. You are just a different person after. And for some people, the need to make art might not be there afterwards. And there's nothing wrong with that.

Bell: And having a baby is a great thing! It's very fulfilling! And it's totally fine if someone could feel very satisfied and happy in that role and puts other stuff on the back shelf.

Guay: There's a lot of women who come to the Illustration Masters Class who fit this description. There's Kim Kincaid: She's a great example of coming back to an art career late and experiencing great growth. Teresa N. Fischer is another example of someone who came back to painting seriously after her child was older.

Gallo: She's doing so phenomenal right now.

Guay: So you can come back, it just takes a few years. I think that a lot of people just get lost along the way.

Bell: These two artists had their kids and then they got a little older and felt more of the confidence and the power in themselves and believed in themselves enough so that they could do this thing.

Gallo: As you talk about community, hopefully the internet (for whatever it's worth with all the trolls and jerks there are) and with the question of whether attrition will happen in this generation, having groups like the Facebook group Zoë started and being able to talk online and talk about these issues will keep people moving and not so isolated.

Panepinto: I was shocked! Zoë started that Facebook group and within three days there was over a hundred and fifty women having enthusiastic twenty-four-hour conversations! I couldn't keep up with it! They were so thoughtful and amazing and great, and so excited to just to hear that other people were thinking similar things.

Robinson: Yeah, those people were really hungry to talk in a safe space.

Any final words of advice that you would give to other women seeking a career as an SF illustrator?

Robinson: Do good work!

Dillon: Do what *you* want to do. Don't worry about what is expected of you, or what style or field you think will command the most respect, or whether or not it feels like you belong, and just do what feels most genuine to you. Do what you love with your whole heart, and things will work out, even if it's not in the way you first imagined when you started out.

Gallo: Keep at it. There's a lot of setbacks for everybody, so make sure you keep working.

Guay: It wouldn't be any different than advice I'd give to any artist.

Bell: Be intelligent, work hard, work smart.

Leggett: Know yourself and know what really are your dreams. Know the difference between wishes and needs in yourself. Give time and make financial and emotional decisions that support those needs. Network with others dealing with these decisions. Feed your creative need every chance you can, even if it is after two days of double shifts. If you have children, share your joy of art with them. If you decide to pursue it, be courageous! This is a very tough gig, but so worth it!

Panepinto: Make sure you keep in mind that you deserve it as much as the other guy, to speak to the confidence problem. It seems so cheesy, but just believe that you have the right to be there. Don't doubt it.

Dillon: Everyone has an important viewpoint to offer the world. And if your chosen field doesn't tend to have many voices like yours, your unique viewpoint is all the more valuable (even if everyone doesn't see it that way right away).

—With thanks to Zoe Kaplan for doing the lion's share
of transcribing the audio portion of this interview.

~

Julie Bell's credits include creating advertising illustrations for the elite of the corporate world, such as Nike, Coca-Cola, and The Ford Motor Company, painting book covers for the major publishing houses in NYC, or doing album covers for artists such as Meat Loaf. She was the first woman ever to paint Conan for Marvel Comics, which paved the way for many other commissions from Marvel, DC, and Image Comics to illustrate superheroes in fully rendered paintings. In 2000, she was given an assignment to do the covers of Jane Lindskold's Firekeeper saga, a series of fantasy novels that starred a large wolf with magic powers. The success of that first wolf painting brought more animal assignments as well as private commissions, which included horses. Now she is finding a new sense of herself in painting the animals just as they are, without supernatural powers.

Julie Dillon is a Hugo and Chesley Award-winning, World Fantasy Award-nominated science fiction and fantasy artist, with clients such as Penguin Books, Simon & Schuster, Tor Books, and Wizards of the Coast.

Irene Gallo is the Chesley Award-winning and World Fantasy Award-nominated art director of Tor Books and the Associate Publisher of *Tor.com*. She's been on the board of Directors of the Society of Illustrators and Spectrum Fantastic Art, and has helped curate the Spectrum exhibitions at the Museum of American Illustration. She also helps organize MicroVisions, a charity auction of mini paintings by top illustrators. By far, the most exciting part of her job is working with all the wonderful artists and becoming good friends with many of them.

Rebecca Guay has been painting professionally for twenty years, during which time she built a formidable reputation in contemporary and pop culture art and illustration. She has exhibited in both solo and group shows at renowned galleries and museums including the R. Michelson Galleries and The Allentown Museum of Art, as well as the Eric Carle Museum, and has been acquired into the permanent collection of the American Museum of Illustration at the Society of Illustrators in NYC. An ARC 2013 and 2014 finalist, Rebecca has also been the recipient of many significant awards and honors, including numerous gold medal awards from the Spectrum Annual and several Gold and Bronze Medals from the Society of Illustrators West Annual for Best in the Original Works/Gallery category, and she is currently nominated for a Chesley Award. In addition to her career as an artist, she is also the creator of The Illustration Master Class (illustrationmasterclass.com) and SmArt School (smarterartschool.com).

Elizabeth Leggett is a twenty-year veteran freelance illustrator. Her artistic influences include Michael Kaluta, Donato Giancola, John Jude Palencar, and Jeremy Geddes. She completed a seventy-eight-card tarot in a single year and launched it into a successful Kickstarter (Portico Tarot and Art Prints). In December, she won two places in Jon Schindehette's ArtOrder Inspiration, and she provided internal art for the Women Destroy Science Fiction! issue of *Lightspeed* and is the Women Destroy Fantasy! cover artist and art director.

Lauren Panepinto has worked in every publishing genre and collaborated with artists as varied as Shepard Fairey and John Harris. As the Creative Director of Orbit Books and Yen Press for the past five years, she has been trying to merge the worlds of genre and commercial publishing and figure out what SFF publishing looks like in the present world of mainstream "geek" media.

Zoë Robinson is the Senior Art Coordinator and founding member of the Art Direction Team at Fantasy Flight Games.

Galen Dara sits in a dark corner listening to the voices in her head. She has a love affair with the absurd and twisted, and an affinity for monsters, mystics, and dead things. She has illustrated for 47North, Edge Publishing, *Lightspeed, Fireside Magazine,* Apex Publications, *Lackington's,* and *Goblin Fruit.* Recent book covers include *War Stories, Glitter & Mayhem,* and *Oz Reimagined.* She won the 2013 Hugo for Best Fan Artist and is nominated for the 2014 Hugo for Best Professional Artist. Her website is galendara.com, and you can follow her on Twitter @galendara.

Artist Gallery

Julie Bell, Julie Dillon, Rebecca Guay, and Elizabeth Leggett

Julie Bell's credits include creating advertising illustrations for the elite of the corporate world, such as Nike, Coca-Cola, and The Ford Motor Company, painting book covers for the major publishing houses in NYC, or doing album covers for artists such as Meat Loaf. She was the first woman ever to paint Conan for Marvel Comics, which paved the way for many other commissions

from Marvel, DC, and Image Comics to illustrate superheroes in fully rendered paintings. In 2000, she was given an assignment to do the covers of Jane Lindskold's Firekeeper saga, a series of fantasy novels that starred a large wolf with magic powers. The success of that first wolf painting brought more animal assignments as well as private commissions, which included horses. Now she is finding a new sense of herself in painting the animals just as they are, without supernatural powers.

Julie Dillon is a Hugo and Chesley Award-winning, World Fantasy Award-nominated science fiction and fantasy artist, with clients such as Penguin Books, Simon & Schuster, Tor Books, and Wizards of the Coast.

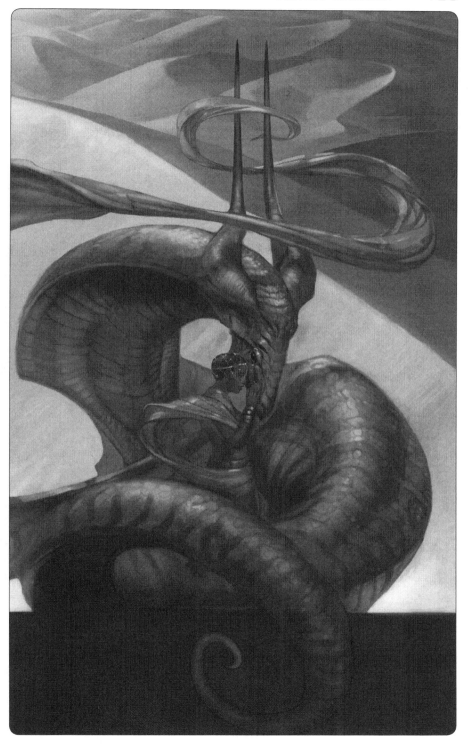

Rebecca Guay has been painting professionally for twenty years, during which time she built a formidable reputation in contemporary and pop culture art and illustration. She has exhibited in both solo and group shows at renowned galleries and museums including the R. Michelson Galleries and The Allentown Museum of Art, as well as the Eric Carle Museum, and has been acquired into the permanent collection of the American Museum of Illustration at the Society of Illustrators in NYC. An ARC 2013 and 2014 finalist, Rebecca has also been the recipient of many significant awards and honors, including numerous gold medal awards from the Spectrum Annual and several Gold and Bronze Medals from the Society of Illustrators West Annual for Best in the Original Works/Gallery category, and she is currently nominated for a

Chesley Award. In addition to her career as an artist, she is also the creator of The Illustration Master Class (illustrationmasterclass.com) and SmArt School (smarterartschool.com).

Elizabeth Leggett is a twenty-year veteran freelance illustrator. Her artistic influences include Michael Kaluta, Donato Giancola, John Jude Palencar, and Jeremy Geddes. She completed a seventy-eight-card tarot in a single year and

launched it into a successful Kickstarter (Portico Tarot and Art Prints). In December, she won two places in Jon Schindehette's ArtOrder Inspiration, and she provided internal art for the Women Destroy Science Fiction! issue of *Lightspeed* and is the Women Destroy Fantasy! cover artist and art director.

Women Destroy Urban Fantasy:

An Interview with Carrie Vaughn and Kelley Armstrong

Sandra Wickham

I'm a big fan of Urban Fantasy. I read it, I write it, and I admire many of the authors in the genre. Urban Fantasy has been around for a long time, under different names, with varying surges and dips in popularity. I wondered if women writing in this sub-genre felt targeted by those who would say women are destroying fantasy. To find out, I thought I would go straight to the source.

It's my pleasure to bring you a conversation with two of the top authors in Urban Fantasy, Carrie Vaughn and Kelley Armstrong, with their take on the genre. These two women have been highly influential in my own writing career, both as *New York Times* Best Selling Authors, mentors, and examples of prolific, successful, and professional women.

What reaction do you have when you hear people say that female authors are destroying science fiction and fantasy?

Vaughn: Well, I kind of want to laugh. Women have been part of science fiction and fantasy all along, and that we're even still having this conversation speaks to the way that women's work is constantly marginalized. It's so ironic that you'll hear people talk in one breath about how women are better at writing fantasy and men are better at science fiction, and in the next breath talk about how of course men write better epic fantasy, and women really only write that "girly" fantasy. There are some folks who'd squeeze us out entirely if they could. As I said, we've been doing it all, all along, and it's annoying that we have to keep pointing that out.

Armstrong: How exactly does anyone "destroy" a genre? The categories exist because readers say "I like this sort of book," and a genre emerges or shifts to satisfy that market interest. There will be fluctuations within it, as interests change and the audience changes. That's what keeps a genre alive, not what destroys it. It is destroyed when people stop reading it, and somehow I don't think female authors are out there campaigning for people to stop reading fantasy and science fiction.

What stereotypes do you encounter in regards to Urban Fantasy as a genre? How do you respond?

Vaughn: I once did an interview where the first question I was asked was "How do you handle writing explicit sex scenes?" I responded with, "Ask me how I know you don't read my books." Because I don't *have* explicit sex scenes in my books. I was also at signing once when someone walked up, looked at my books, and asked me if I wrote "that porn stuff." So, yeah: People take one look at those hot covers with the sexy babes, and immediately think it's all sex. These days, I just kind of sigh and shake my head.

Armstrong: I think it's like any other genre—people who don't read it are certain they know what it is and often have a very narrow definition. The stereotype I usually encounter is that UF is all overpowered, kick-ass chicks who are supposed to be saving the world but spend more time trying to pick a mate from the dozen guys pursuing them. I have never written that plot. I have never read that plot. It's more common to see paranormal thrillers with capable women—sometimes fighters but often not—and long-term romantic relationships, with those relationships taking a backseat to the action and mystery.

Why do you think UF seems to be a female-dominated genre? Or is a statement like that perpetuating more stereotypes? Does the genre need more male authors?

Vaughn: The statement is perpetuating stereotypes, because it is a myth.

(Like so many statements about women's writing and women's genres.) I'd guess something like forty to forty-five percent of my readership is male—this surprises people, but come to one of my signings or book events and you'll see. Look at the comments on my Facebook page. Or any UF author's page. Lots of men read this, and lots of men write this—if you see a UF book whose author uses initials, it's often a male author trying to hide his gender. Just like so many female authors have done when publishing science fiction.

The other thing that happens is if the author is a man, it may not be classified as UF, even if it has all the hallmarks of the genre. And if I had a nickel for every time I've heard the statement—"Well, I don't really like urban fantasy—except for Jim Butcher's books, of course."—I would have a lot of nickels. We're in Joanna Russ territory, here, in her analysis of the ways women's writing gets classified as different or lesser, even when it looks just the same as men's writing in the same category.

So yeah, I'd really like to stop with the "UF is female-dominated," because in my experience it simply isn't true. The perception has clouded the reality.

Armstrong: I've been around since the current flavor of UF began, back when these books were called paranormal suspense. Laurell K. Hamilton had been writing them for a few years. Then Jim Butcher started his Dresden Files. Charlaine Harris started the Southern Vampire series a year later, at the same time I started the Otherworld. So of the four, three were women, and not everyone included Butcher's books in the same category. Those three also wrote female protagonists. The audience then was largely female—guys being less likely to read female protagonists, especially in first-person narration. When publishers went looking for more books "like these," they actively sought out female authors. Women who already wrote fantasy were pointed in this direction, and that's where many of the "next batch" of UF writers came from. It's not surprising then that it became a female-dominated genre. And, yes, it would be great to see more guys writing it, of course!

What do you think the future holds for Urban Fantasy and its authors? Is Urban Fantasy on its way out as the rumors profess, or will women continue to "destroy" this genre?

Vaughn: You know, I've been predicting the end of urban fantasy for something like six years now, and I've been wrong all this time. That said, all the major series seem to be wrapping up, and there does seem to be a slowdown—I get the feeling it's a lot harder to break in with UF than it used to be. But as with anything, a really great idea, a really new take on it all, will find an audience.

Armstrong: The form of UF that arose in the last decade is fading. Charlaine Harris has ended her series. I've ended mine. Kim Harrison is on her last couple of books. The list goes on. So far, though, the authors who are ending their series aren't getting out of fantasy altogether. They're just taking a slightly different approach. My new series is more mystery, less paranormal—incorporating folklore and superstition rather than werewolves and witches. I think this is how the genre will continue, evolving rather than dying out.

What advice would you have for other female authors of urban fantasy, paranormal fantasy, or fantasy that may be facing challenges based on their gender or their chosen genre?

Carrie: From a writing/craft standpoint, I have to get this off my chest: Be aware of the tropes you're working with, and be very aware of stereotypes and pitfalls you might be falling into. It makes me sad that a genre that is supposed to celebrate powerful women so often perpetuates patriarchal patterns/clichés, and doesn't pass the Bechdel Test.

And then, stick to your guns. UF has a huge, devoted audience, and cling to that to keep you going when the rest of the genre community seems to be sneering at you.

Armstrong: Ignore it and focus on your own path. That may not be a popular answer, but I was a computer programmer in the days when it was a rare career choice for women. I got used to being the only woman in the office other than the receptionist. I got used to being treated like an interloper or, worse, the product of affirmative action. I knew that wasn't the case—I graduated at the top of my class—so I said "screw it" and focused on the work, and let the results prove that I'd earned my position. That's what I do as an author. I write whatever I want and I ignore the noise. If I get snark from a male author, a look at his Bookscan figures kills the sting, because it's the same thing I encountered in programming—the guys who outperform me aren't the ones taking those shots, so I can chalk it up to sour grapes and move on.

~

Carrie Vaughn is the bestselling author of the Kitty Norville series, the most recent of which is the twelfth installment, *Kitty in the Underworld*. Her superhero novel *Dreams of the Golden Age* was released in January 2014. She has also written the young adult novels *Voices of Dragons* and *Steel*, and the fantasy novels *Discord's Apple* and *After the Golden Age*. Her short fiction has appeared in many magazines and anthologies, from *Lightspeed* to *Tor.com* and George R.R. Martin's Wild

Cards series. She lives in Colorado with a fluffy attack dog. Learn more at carrievaughn.com.

Kelley Armstrong has been telling stories since before she could write. Her earliest written efforts were disastrous. If asked for a story about girls and dolls, hers would invariably feature undead girls and evil dolls, much to her teachers' dismay. Today, she continues to spin tales of ghosts and demons and werewolves, while safely locked away in her basement writing dungeon. She lives in southwestern Ontario with her husband, kids, and far too many pets. Learn more at KelleyArmstrong.com.

Sandra Wickham lives in Vancouver, Canada, with her husband and two cats. Her friends call her a needle-crafting aficionado, health guru, and ninja-in-training. Sandra's short stories have appeared in *Evolve, Vampires of the New Undead*; *Evolve, Vampires of the Future Undead*; *Chronicles of the Order*; *Crossed Genres*; *LocoThology: Tales of Fantasy & Science Fiction*; and *The Urban Green Man*. She blogs about writing with the Inkpunks, is the Fitness Nerd columnist for *The Functional Nerds,* and slush reads for *Lightspeed Magazine.*

In Other Worlds: The Female Stars of Tie-in Fiction

Shanna Germain

Tie-in fiction—books and stories set in shared worlds—has a long history of providing fans with new dimensions and elements of their favorite games, shows, and movies. As tie-in fiction continues to grow in popularity, the field of talented, passionate authors also continues to grow. Here, we talk to four of them, delving into their career origins, the role that gender plays (or doesn't) in their success, and the effects of constraints on creativity.

Please introduce yourselves, in case there are any readers out there who aren't yet familiar with your work.

Erin M. Evans: I write the Farideh/ Brimstone Angels series, set in the world of the Forgotten Realms. My second book, *Lesser Evils*, won the 2012 Scribe Award for Best Speculative Original Novel, and my most recent title, *The Adversary*, was the third book of the Sundering series.

Elaine Cunningham: I started writing tie-in fiction way back in the Jurassic Era (aka "D&D Second Edition.") My first novel was *Elfshadow*, a mystery in a fantasy setting. Since then I've written over twenty novels, about three dozen short stories, and a graphic novel. I've worked in a number of licensed settings: Star Wars, Forgotten Realms, EverQuest, Pathfinder Tales, and several small settings.

Margaret Weis: Thirty years ago, my co-author, Tracy Hickman, and I wrote

Dragons of Autumn Twilight, the first volume of the Dragonlance Chronicles based on the Dungeons & Dragons Dragonlance RPG for TSR, Inc. That book and the sequels that followed were on the *New York Times* bestseller list and have been in continuous publication ever since.

Marsheila (Marcy) Rockwell: I'm the only author who has written official tie-in novels for the popular MMORPG, *Dungeons & Dragons Online* (*The Shard Axe* and *Skein of Shadows*, both of which were nominated for the IAMTW's Scribe Award), so I'm pretty proud of that. I'm also currently working on the second book in a trilogy based on the *Neil Gaiman's Lady Justice* comic books, and when they come out, they'll have both my name and Neil's on the cover, so that's pretty exciting. I also have two original collections out, *Tales of Sand and Sorcery* and *Bridges of Longing and Other Strange Passageways*, and my agent is currently shopping an original series about a paranormal profiler that I think will be a lot of fun.

Writing tie-in fiction isn't the kind of thing where you went to your guidance counselor in high school and said, "What should my career choice be?" and she said, "Hey, I know—you should write fiction set in someone else's universe for a living." When and how did you first learn that writing tie-in fiction was an actual job option, and how did you get started down that career path?

Evans: My first job in publishing was with Per Aspera Press. The editor, Jak Koke, was the first author I'd met in real life who'd written tie-in novels. At the time, I didn't really see the allure, but I can remember talking to him about what writing for a shared world was like. After that, I worked at Wizards of the Coast as an editor for their novel department, so I got immersed in shared worlds. One day, Susan J. Morris, the main line editor for Forgotten Realms, asked me if I wanted to audition for a Realms novel. It was for Ed Greenwood Presents Waterdeep, and it turned out that Susan and Ed loved my pitch for *The God Catcher*!

Cunningham: Back in 1990, *Writer's Digest* magazine advertised an open call for a new fantasy line. I'd never heard of TSR or the Forgotten Realms, and at the time I had zero knowledge of D&D. But I bought the old gray boxed set, a couple of gaming modules, and all the novels written up to that point—I think there were four—and plunged in. Something clicked, and I knew this was a place I could happily inhabit.

Weis: I was hired by Jean Black, head of the TSR book department, in 1983. Part of my job was to work on the new Dragonlance game product created by game designer Tracy Hickman. The RPG was to feature twelve adventure modules with three tie-in novels. At the time, there had never been a novel tie-in for a game adventure. Since the plotline was quite extensive (covering twelve modules), my job was to provide background for the characters (all we had were the game stats and what they looked like!) and the plot for the novels. TSR planned to hire an experienced author to write the books.

The author they hired didn't work out. By that time, Tracy and I were in love with this world and the characters and we didn't like what was being done with them. We knew them better than anyone because we had been spending months working with them. Tracy and I decided to go for it. In one weekend, we wrote the prologue and the first five chapters and gave them to Jean Black, asking her to read them and, if she liked them, to let us write the books. Jean spent an hour with the chapters, then came to us and said, "Wow! This is what we've been looking for!"

She fired the other author and hired us. So, in a way, I didn't decide to write tie-in novels so much as the tie-in novel decided I should write it.

Rockwell: I've been playing D&D since third grade, and writing my own fantasy stories since sixth. When I discovered that there was a medium that combined those two loves? That's what I wanted to do. No Great American Novel for this wannabe—I really just wanted to write D&D books. So when Wizards of the Coast held an open call for *Maiden of Pain* (a Forgotten Realms novel in The Priests series) back in 2003, I jumped at the opportunity. My proposal didn't win, but it did bring me to the attention of WotC's editors, and I got the opportunity to submit to several more calls until I finally hit with one for the Eberron Campaign Setting (which eventually became the novel *Legacy of Wolves*).

Working inside someone else's world has some constraints because you have to stick to the canon. Do the parameters feel freeing or do you find it constraining?

Evans: For me, the constraints are inspiring. I've had elements handed to me at the start. I've wound up where another creator has contradicted my story in some way. I've found places where the "lore" here doesn't match the lore there, or the lore is just confusing or goofy. At first, it's maddening. But having those pieces that can't move defines the space around them. What fits here? What can you do to shape the story the way you want, while accommodating this detail? What can you do to join this detail and that? I love that sort of problem solving and I think you get a whole other level of it when writing shared world.

Cunningham: Writing for a licensed setting is very much like writing historical fiction. You need to know the politics, the players, science and technology (which in fantasy includes magic), geography, belief systems, and social mores and customs. You have to know how people talked, how they made a living, and how they viewed the world. In short, you need to do a lot of research if you're going to capture a sense of time and place. The process is very similar; the only real difference is that in fantasy, the "history" is fictitious. Maybe you can't blow up a city or kill off a NPC, but there's a great deal of room for creativity. Most of the time, you'll be writing about characters you created. If you do write about existing characters, such as in the Star Wars Extended Universe, you get to create that story's plot. Sure, there are several layers of review and approval, but I seldom felt constrained by a setting's parameters.

Weis: After Tracy and I left TSR to write novels set in our own worlds, the company continued to publish DL novels. The editorial department was focused on the books and getting them out on the market and didn't spend much time worrying about canon. To give them credit, no one at the time really thought consistency in the setting would matter much to the readers. Authors were given free reign to do what they wanted in the early days, so long as they remained true to the D&D setting.

That changed later, which meant that those of us who returned to the world had to try to decide what was canon and what wasn't. I've always felt that writing tie-in novels requires a *lot* more creativity than working in an author's own world, simply because you have to perform creative gymnastics in order to remain true to the world and true to yourself as an author.

Rockwell: I've been lucky in that I've been given a lot of free rein in writing my tie-in stories, from creating my own characters to fleshing out areas that haven't seen a lot of use in other books. In a shared world, you have to make sure what you write doesn't contradict what has gone before or what the editors may have planned for the future, and while you can play with certain iconic characters and places, you have to return them to the shelf unchanged when you're done, which can be challenging. But on the other hand, you also have a vast array of resources at your fingertips, from source books to other authors to fans of the setting (who *always* know more about it than you ever will). I personally think the sheer joy of getting to contribute to a property you love far outweighs any editorial or bureaucratic constraints.

This issue focuses specifically on women in fantasy, so let's talk about gender for a bit. There are a lot of great conversations happening about the ways in which being a woman in the industry has changed throughout time, but there's another correlating factor that I'm interested in—the experience of being a woman as it relates to success. What are the ways that gender did (or didn't) matter at the beginning of your career, and has that changed now that you are more established in your field?

Evans: Less my gender, but my character's: When I started, there was a lot of pressure to shy away from feminine things, lest you scare the boys off. But I really didn't want to—my main characters, Farideh and Havilar, start out as teenaged girls, and even if they're screaming badasses in a sword & sorcery epic, they're still living the experiences of young women. That's what I wanted to write about, alongside all the battle and magic and monsters. As the series has gone on, those kinds of concerns—romance, body image, trying to grab at some sort of agency—inevitably become more pronounced. But contrary to the fears that the boys would run from it, the Brimstone Angels series has done really well with the existing Forgotten Realms audience, as well as pulling in readers who feel like it speaks to them better. And my publisher has seen that and let me tell the story the way I want to.

Weis: To be honest, gender simply never occurred to me. I majored in creative writing and literature in college in the '60s. I wrote because I love to write. It never occurred to me that I couldn't because I was a woman.

In my experience, the RPG industry was extremely opening and accepting of women. The problem the industry faced was that according to a survey done at the time, ninety percent of RPG players were male. One of our objectives in writing Dragonlance was to provide strong female characters in the novels to encourage women to try the game.

Rockwell: I sold my first short story to *Marion Zimmer Bradley's Fantasy Magazine* back in 1994, and I always thought that my gender was probably a plus in that case, but generally, I haven't felt like it's been too much of a factor in my writing career.

I do remember when Wizards of the Coast was first marketing *Legacy of Wolves*, some of the copy I saw talked about me being the only woman writing in the Eberron setting, and I didn't really know what to make of that. Why should it matter what my gender was, as long as I was telling a good story?

But I never felt like I was "the token female" or anything like that.

When we look at the gender numbers—from awards to publication credits to sales—it's easy to say that there's a long way to go in terms of gender equality in the fantasy field. However, it seems to me that the numbers don't always tell the whole tale. What's happening under the radar that's making a difference?

Evans: I think most game companies have started to realize that women and girls are their audience, that we're not some alien force that's going to ruin the experience of their base. For Wizards of the Coast in particular, with the Sundering project we were encouraged to think about the makeup of our casts—gender expression, race, sexual orientation. There's an awareness there that I don't think you would have seen five years ago.

Now, that said, I'm the only female author writing for them, and Farideh is the only female main character. So I do think there's still a long way to go. But the intention is there.

Weis: We are seeing so many more women involved in the RPG industry these days. In my case, I own my own company. My lead designer and project manager is a woman. In addition, we hire women artists and writers. Mind you, we don't hire because they are women, but because they do damn good work!

Rockwell: I have the sense that there are more female creators in the gaming field especially, and that they are starting to receive more recognition for their work as individuals, not just as names in a list of credits. And in terms of both gaming and publishing, I think there is definitely more of an interest in hearing from diverse voices. Like anything else, though, there's a supply-and-demand dynamic; we're seeing more diverse voices, especially in publishing, because the reading public is demanding them. And if we want to see even more, readers have to show publishers that by supporting the voices that are out there now, so they'll be more willing to take chances on new ones in the future.

~

Shanna Germain claims the title of leximaven, Schrödinger's brat, vorpal blonde, and Midas's touch. Her stories, essays, articles, and novellas have found their forever homes in hundreds of magazines, newspapers, books, and websites. Her most recent publications include the horror-fantasy short story collection *The Lure of Dangerous Women* and the erotic novel *Leather Bound*. She is the co-owner of Monte Cook Games, LLC, and the lead editor of *Numenera* and *The Strange*.

THE FROG SISTER

SOFIA SAMATAR

Now, as mentioned earlier, the vizier, who put the girls to death, had an older daughter called Shahrazad and a younger one called Dinarzad. The older daughter, Shahrazad, had read the books of literature, philosophy, and medicine. She knew poetry by heart, had studied historical reports, and was acquainted with the sayings of men and the maxims of sages and kings. She was intelligent, knowledgeable, wise, and refined. She had read and learned. One day she said to her father . . . "I would like you to marry me to King Shahrayar, so that I may either succeed in saving the people or perish and die like the rest."

With these words, the world's most famous storyteller makes her appearance. Shahrazad (sometimes spelled Scheherazade), heroine of that fabulous compendium of poetry and fantasy, *A Thousand and One Nights*, has been a powerful catalyst for discussions of women and storytelling, of rhetoric and political strategy, of feminism, of narrative structure, and of fantasy. I love Shahrazad. In one of my poems about her, she can't even spoil the coffee without creating a tiny and furious drama. If she were a writer, she'd never get writer's block (partly, of course, because the stakes are too high). But Shahrazad isn't a writer, which is one of the things I find interesting about her. She's a reader, but in a culture that privileges speech and memory. She reads, remembers, and speaks. I believe that we can, without detaching Shahrazad from the context in which she arose, see her as a figure for women fantasists all over the world, whether they write their stories or tell them.

In 1967, Nongenile Masithathu Zenani, an artist of iintsomi, the Xhosa genre of oral fantasy stories, told a story about a girl and a frog. The girl and the frog were twins, but the mother, horrified at having given birth to a frog, sent it away to be buried in ashes. As for the girl, she couldn't work. *She was just that round thing.* She lay on the floor, inert, until one day, when her mother was away in the fields, a frog knocked at the door. When the frog was with her, the girl could get up and work. *Oh, Child of my mother, you've helped me!* But the frog, frightened of their mother, ran away before she came home, leaving the girl as helpless as before.

The drama of the story springs from the community's confusion and efforts to solve the mystery. They know the girl can't work; who, then, is cooking and sweeping the yard? The girl refuses to tell. Eventually, though, the truth comes out: *I was born with this frog. My mother gave birth to both of us.* The girl reveals that her secret power is in fact her rejected sibling. *This is the one that was taken and put in the ashes.* The small, the inadequately human, the scorned, the repulsive, the trash: this is the source of productivity.

She is my sister. We were born on the same day.

It seems to me that the roots of fantasy are oral, while the roots of science fiction are written. (If this is true, then perhaps their meeting point is Mary Shelley's *Frankenstein*: a novel born of evenings sharing ghost stories around the fire.) Writing, of course, is a mere blip in human history: As the critic Christopher Prendergast puts it, "if we think of history on the model of a calendar, writing emerges only on the last stroke of midnight, 31 December." In addition, writing does not emerge equally everywhere. This is true of science fiction as well. Fantasy, on the other hand, in the form of fairy tales, ballads, ghost stories, nursery rhymes, and the epic poetry of bards and griots—fantasy is far older, and universal. Like the girl and the frog, fantasy and humanity were born on the same day.

That said, it's true that some forms of fantastic narrative have been practiced more commonly by men, such as various epic poetry traditions, while others are more closely associated with women, such as fairy tales and iintsomi. Predictably, scholars inform us that men tell the long stories and women tell the short ones. This continues to be said even when it isn't true, the implication being that men's work is major and women's minor—a pattern that gets repeated in all sorts of contexts. Our conversations, criticism, and media reinforce this untruth. Think about contemporary genre fantasy in English: despite the contributions of Ursula K. Le Guin, N. K. Jemisin, Robin Hobb, and others, the fantasy writer who leaps to mind for most people is male, and his middle initials are probably R. R.

It's important to struggle against the marginalization of women (and others outside the dominant category of straight white men), in genre fantasy as elsewhere. It's also important not to reduce women's fantasy narratives to those that are written (even worse, to those that are written in English). Where would we be without fairy tales, without sad romances sung over a sink full of dishes, without stories told, and sometimes believed or half-believed, about angels, haints, and the evil eye? Like the girl in the iintsomi, we make our lives poorer, and our work impossible, if we ignore that part of our heritage the literary world tends to bury in ashes: the amazing richness of women's oral culture.

This is not to say that only women are connected to this oral culture, but they have been, and are, more likely to be restricted to it, and for that reason they make particular contributions to it. In the light of this fact, it's clear that women who write fantasy are not newcomers or fringe-dwellers, but inhabitants of multiple grand traditions of the fantastic. I want to see us celebrate these traditions, because oral culture is vaster and more diverse than written culture. Writing is such a small part of storytelling. You can tell a tale with a word, a gesture, a sigh. Storytellers know this. *The body is poetry's door.*

Like the girl in the iintsomi, Shahrazad has a sibling: Dinarzad, or Dunyazad. She is the minor voice to Shahrazad's major one, the frog sister. Her role is to lie underneath the bed and, after the king has had sex with Shahrazad, ask for the story that will save their lives. *Sister, if you are not sleepy, tell us one of your lovely little tales to while away the night, before I bid you good-bye at daybreak.* The younger sister is not a hero: Her voice is a whisper, her space as confined and domestic as possible. Yet Shahrazad couldn't speak without her—without the intimate murmur that, to me, stands in for women's community, shared history, and traditions of tale-telling and song.

I've always found it moving that the name *Shahrazad*, according to one interpretation, means "The One Who Frees the City," while *Dunyazad* means "The One Who Frees the World."

Sources

The Arabian Nights, translated by Husain Haddawy, 2008.

The World and the Word: Tales and Observations from the Xhosa Oral Tradition, by Nongenile Masithathu Zenani and Harold Scheub, 1992.

Debating World Literature, by Christopher Prendergast and Benedict Anderson, 2004.

The line "The body is poetry's door" was said by a Zulu woman storyteller, unfortunately unnamed, quoted in *The Tongue is Fire: South African Storytellers and Apartheid,* by Harold Scheub, 1996.

Sofia Samatar is the author of the novel *A Stranger in Olondria*, winner of the 2014 Crawford Award, as well as several short stories, essays, and poems. Her work has been nominated for multiple awards. She is a co-editor for *Interfictions: A Journal of Interstitial Arts*, and teaches literature and writing at California State University Channel Islands.

THE PRINCESS AND THE WITCH

KAT HOWARD

Once upon a time, there was a woman who told stories. Stories of witches and of princesses and of choosing true love. Stories that began once upon a time, and ended in happily ever after. You think you know what these stories are, and oh, perhaps you do. But until this woman, until Marie-Catherine d'Aulnoy, the stories were not yet called what they are now. But she wrote these stories, and she gave them their name—contes des fées. Fairy tales.

To name a thing is to have power over that thing. We learn that in fairy tales.

I grew up on fairy tales, like many of us do. Cinderella at the ball; Red Riding Hood trusting a wolf and walking too deep in the woods; Beauty, handed over to a Beast for the price of a rose. And then, midnight struck. I turned away from them. I was too grown up for such things, and I knew I would never be a princess.

Women and stories and power are deeply entwined with the literary fairy tale (and by literary, please know that I am not opining about quality, or where the collected volumes ought to be shelved, but rather borrowing a term of art from the scholar Jack Zipes, who uses the term to distinguish the written-down versions of fairy tales from their oral and folkloric roots). There is a power in taking a story and making it your own, whether by naming it, or by taking its elements and subverting them, turning them inside out so that the seams—and the seems—of the story show, and then putting them back together. Maybe the pieces don't fit, not exactly. Maybe the princess is now a witch.

Maybe that's exactly how things should be.

I can tell you how I came back to fairy tales. I read Jane Yolen's retelling of Sleeping Beauty, *Briar Rose*, and it broke my heart, and it cracked open my head. There was a list, somewhere in the book, of other books I should read.

And so I set about devouring the anthologies edited by Ellen Datlow and Terri Windling. I wish I could remember which one I read first, but I suppose it doesn't matter, because eventually I read them all. I am still reading them.

The literary fairy tale, which arose as a distinct genre in the salons of d'Aulnoy and her compatriots in France at the end of the seventeenth century, has always been part of the literature of subversion, a genre of protest. The writers of these stories were generally people on the edge of the court, who were writing as a way to seek social advancement—Cinderellas, each attempting to be their own fairy godmothers. The Comtesse de Murat was denounced by her family for unruly behavior and lesbianism, and was exiled by King Louis XIV for satirizing his relationship with his mistress, Madame de Maintenon. Madame d'Aulnoy was married by abduction (with the consent of her father, who sold her to her kidnapper), and then fled France due to scandal. She turned to writing (and possibly espionage) to support herself, and continued writing even after she was able to return to France. Even Marie-Jeanne L'Héritier, who was a salonierre by inheritance, was not in a privileged position. Like all these women who wrote and shared their fairy tales in the salons, she was watched by the court at Versailles, tabs kept on her activities and especially on her words. And the salon conversation itself—with its ideals of gender equality in conversation and intellect—was by its nature socially subversive.

Even the aspect of fairy tales that might now seem conventional, too heteronormative, and too problematic for women who have no desire to be saved by a prince and then set up in his castle—the happy ever after, the romantic ending of true love's kiss and the subsequent marriage—was its own kind of subversion. Love freely chosen, rather than love decreed by a forced marriage.

When I was a little girl, I wanted to be the princess in the fairy tale. Not because I necessarily wanted the prince—he was secondary at best. Even then, I stopped being interested in the Beast when he turned from the gorgeous leonine roar of a beast into the pale, blond, ordinary prince. I wasn't interested in ordinary. What I wanted was to be the foot that fit the glass slipper, the girl who would wake, still living, and rise out of her coffin of glass. The girl at the heart of the story.

Though men were active in this salon culture as well, the movement, and the genre, was led by women, and it was a movement that shared many of the ideals of modern feminism, including the idea that women's writing was equal to men's. Fairy tales were ways for women to write their own stories—to be the princess, yes. But to also be the fairy godmother, to be the witch, to be the old woman in the forest who would get you safely out of the story for the price of a kindness.

Now that I am grown up, I want to be the woman who writes the fairy tales.

Because, like the women in those French literary salons, like Margaret Atwood and Angela Carter and Catherynne M. Valente, I have learned that behind the pen is where the power is. That power is with the witch, with her life hidden outside herself, to be the wise woman who knows what cup not to drink from, and who will tell you, but only if you deserve to know. That power is with the woman who tells the story, who changes the shape of things. Magic words.

I do not want to be the princess anymore. I want to be the witch.

Even in the modern day, women writers have continued to engage with the literary fairy tale, have continued to pick up these stories, and pull them apart. To use them in the same way as their earlier writers did—to observe society from its edges and use magic and wonder and strangeness to critique the pieces of it that try to define what happily ever after is, and who deserves the chance at one.

Perhaps because subversion has been built into the literary fairy tale from the beginning, it is a pattern that has been born into the fairy tale again and again. Women writers in particular take the stories and say, if you make us a princess, you will discover that we are witches. We can dance in glass slippers, true, but we can also wear out iron shoes walking to get what we want. We may well wear red, but we do so to show the wolves that they should be afraid to walk into the woods with us.

We remember that happily ever after is where the story begins.

And we are still writing.

Sources

Warner, Marina. *From the Beast to the Blonde: On Fairy Tales and Their Tellers*. New York: Noonday, 1994.

Wonder Tales: Six Stories of Enchantment. Marina Warner, ed. Gilbert Adair, John Ashbery, Ranjit Bolt, A.S. Byatt, and Terence Cave, trans. New York: Farrar, Straus and Giroux, 1994.

Zipes, Jack. *The Irresistible Fairy Tale: The Cultural and Social History of a Genre*. Princeton: Princeton UP, 2012.

Zipes, Jack. *When Dreams Came True: Classical Fairy Tales and Their Tradition*. New York: Routledge, 1999.

~

Kat Howard is the World Fantasy Award-nominated author of over twenty pieces of short fiction. Her work has been performed on NPR as part of *Selected Shorts,* and has appeared in *Lightspeed*, *Subterranean*, and *Apex*, among other venues. Her novella, *The End of the Sentence*, written with Maria Dahvana Headley, was recently released by Subterranean Press. You can find her on twitter as @KatWithSword and she blogs at strangeink.blogspot.com.

Read the Destruction:

WDF's Handy Guide and Recommended Reading List

Wendy N. Wagner

Reading a book is a strangely intimate experience. The words seep beneath the skin and touch one's very character, not to mention one's ideas of the world and how it works. Books can kindle passion, start a revolution, change a life.

I think it is fair to say that our human world is made of texts: stories, informative books, movies, comic books, instruction manuals. Some, like the manual that came with your blender, will barely affect your mood, let alone change the way you engage in society. Other texts, like the books you were forced to read in school, become the underpinnings of our culture. When we look at those books, that canon, we see our society reflected in the mirror of their words. Recommending a book to another person not only reflects on your taste in literature, it sheds light on your own self and your relationship to the world.

When we look at the recommended reading lists of our SF/F genre communities, we tend to see a very particular reflection, a reflection that, as author Julie McKenna so cleverly puts it on her blog, is "male and pale" (bit.ly/male-andpale). If you look at NPR Books' 2011 Top 100 Science Fiction and Fantasy Books, as selected by its readers (bit.ly/npr100), you'll see that only fifteen books on the list were written by women, and that the top nineteen were all the product of white men.

Why is SF/F so dominated by men when there are so many women putting out great works of fiction?

It's a massive issue that is bigger than any single article could ever hope to address—but perhaps one tiny component is that not enough books by women and minority writers get recommended to other readers.

For example, in 2011 (a good year for reader polls, apparently), *The Guardian* asked readers to recommend their favorite science fiction and fantasy works. The award-winning genre author Nicola Griffith decided to crunch those numbers and came up with an astonishing figure: "I scanned the *Guardian* comments—yes, all of them—and counted only eighteen women's names. Eighteen. Out of more than five hundred," (bit.ly/nicolag). That's right. *The Guardian's* readers were happy to shout out book recommendations—but like NPR's readers, their shouts were overwhelmingly for male writers.

Perhaps England is not a good representation of the state of the genre. Its lack of friendliness to women writers has been well discussed. On Foz Meadows' Tumblr, there's an excellent discussion and analysis of one large English bookseller's pamphlet of genre book recommendations (bit.ly/fozmeadows), where number crunching showed "of the *one hundred and thirteen* authors listed in the genre-specific sections, there are a grand total of *nine women* and, as far as I can tell, *zero POC.*" Moreover, it should be noted that since 1972, when the British Fantasy Society began giving out the August Derleth Award for Best Novel, the award has only gone to a woman twice, to Tanith Lee in 1980, and to Sam Stone in 2011 (who returned the award as a response to furor over the award's administration).

The giving of awards is the first step in forming canon—that list of works by which our community defines itself, and which sets the standards for new writers entering the field. The Great Books of the fantasy genre form our very understanding of what the genre even means. Fantasy is more than just a hodge-podge of tropes and settings; it is a series of interconnected discussions of the imagination and human nature, built from a common language of Great Books. When the works of PoC and women writers get forgotten, get left out of the canon, then we lose important ideas about what it means to dream and what it means to be human. (For more on this topic, read my blog post "Read the Destruction: Award Winning Novels by Women" at bit.ly/destroy-winners.)

But beyond the safe harbor of award-winning books, the work of female fantasists can be unexplored territory—so I turned to our contributors for advice. Some of the works on this list have been mostly forgotten. Some of them are ones you may have read before. Some are by white women. Some are by women of color. Some are controversial. Some are just plain fun. And maybe—just maybe—some of them will show you a new way to be a thinking, dreaming human being.

THE PRINT-AND-READ HANDY GUIDE
—AN INTRODUCTION

This guide is the perfect size to print out, stuff in your wallet, and take with you to your local bookstore or library. It's a great way to start picking up books by authors that are unfamiliar to you.

Read the Destruction: a Print-and-Read Handy Guide				
If you like ...	GEORGE R. R. MARTIN	J. R. R. TOLKIEN	NEIL GAIMAN	JIM BUTCHER
for the ...	*gritty medieval atmosphere and epic drama*	*human heroism steeped in myth*	*mythical elements affecting human-scaled problems*	*magic and mystery in a contemporary setting*
Then you should read:	C. S. Friedman Kate Elliott Kameron Hurley Katherine Addison Aliette de Bodard	Patricia McKillip Robin Hobb Robin McKinley Barbara Hambly Sofia Samatar	Terri Windling Karen Lord Jane Yolen Nnedi Okorafor Theodora Goss	Kelley Armstrong Carrie Vaughn Kim Harrison Patricia Briggs Seanan McGuire L. A. Banks

Download at DestroySF.com/WDF-Guide

Obviously, not every book by each author is going to be a perfect match for the column I've placed it in. After all, Seanan McGuire writes science fictional zombie horror novels as well as urban fantasy ones. But at least this chart will give you a starting point.

WDF'S FRIEND, CONTRIBUTOR, AND STAFF RECOMMENDATIONS: NOVELS & SERIES

Here's where a bunch of awesome women go into detail about the books they love and think you should read. It's like getting a bunch of book recommendations from your friends, if your friends were all in the business of writing and publishing genre fiction.

Jane Yolen
Winner of the World Fantasy Award for Life Achievement

The Earthsea Cycle by Ursula K. Le Guin: Deep, beautiful, full of new meanings every time you read them.

Beauty **by Robin McKinley:** Stunning first novel reworking of "Beauty and the Beast."

Archer's Goon by **Diana Wynne Jones:** Funny, anarchic, surprising, and with the greatest line in fantasy novels for kids, "Power corrupts, but we need the electricity." I want the T-shirt!

Elizabeth Bear
Winner of the John W. Campbell Award for Best New Writer

The Salt Roads by **Nalo Hopkinson:** A challenging, beautifully written narrative following the lives of several fascinating women alive at different points in history but spiritually linked to one another.

The Drowning Girl by **Caitlín R. Kiernan:** Her masterpiece to date, the compelling story of a woman struggling to reconcile treatment for her mental illness with her glimpses of magical creatures.

Redemption in Indigo by **Karen Lord:** A fable about love, betrayal, forgiveness, and food.

The Goblin Emperor by **Katherine Addison:** Political intrigue and steampunk elves.

T. Kingfisher
Women Destroy Fantasy! Fiction Contributor

Everybody and their brother has probably already recommended *The Goblin Emperor* by **Katherine Addison** (but if they haven't, that one!) Otherwise, I'm fond of:

Jinian Footseer by **Sheri S. Tepper:** To this day, I'm still not sure why this book works so well for me. The elements—a world where people have various magical talents and fight battles with them—have been done to death and back. But with an utterly sympathetic heroine and a self-aware planet, it rapidly transcends anything similar in the genre. (First of a trilogy.)

Rose Daughter by **Robin McKinley:** It's a Beauty and the Beast story, beautifully retold, with a sympathetic Beast and a practical Beauty, and it rapidly became the version that replaced all others in my head. (Plus, there are roses fertilized with unicorn manure, so, y'know, what's not to love?)

The Wood Wife by **Terri Windling:** There are not enough fantasy novels set in the American Southwest. This was the book that, around eighteen or so, I wanted to be my life. (Which might have been fairly uncomfortable, all things considered.) It evokes the desert better than any other fantasy I have read and I cannot recommend it highly enough.

H. E. Roulo
Women Destroy Fantasy! Fiction Contributor

The Cold Fire trilogy by C. S. Friedman: A dark and beautiful series. She presents a well-wrought world inhabited by creatures pulled from the darkest reaches of the human mind. She writes with strength of purpose and the characters' decisions have consequences. The reader is introduced to an amazing anti-hero. The first book is *Black Sun Rising*.

The Liveship Traders trilogy by Robin Hobb: Her world is well built, and her characters strongly motivated. She balances a large cast of characters and continually introduces new and exciting elements. Though sometimes dark and violent, there is also delight in the worlds she creates. The first book in the Liveship Traders is *Ship of Magic*. (Note: If you only have time for a short story, read her SF short story "A Touch of Lavender," a Nebula and Hugo finalist.)

Julia August
Women Destroy Fantasy! Fiction Contributor

The Darwath series by Barbara Hambly; The Deverry Cycle by Katherine Kerr; The Crown of Stars series by Kate Elliott: What can I say to sell these books? (And there are a lot of books here.) Well, to begin with, there is rich and historically inspired worldbuilding on a truly epic scale. Can I tell you how much I love the names of Katherine Kerr's young dragons? I love those names and in general Kerr's complex and layered use of history in the Deverry Cycle. I love how Kate Elliott's world diverges from its medieval template in fascinating and perfectly logical ways. I love the bitter Mythos flavour of Barbara Hambly's Darwath, among other allusions spotted only years after I first discovered the original trilogy on someone else's bookshelf. And maybe most importantly, I love so many characters across all three series. Off the top of my head, indiscriminately and not at all exclusively, Gil, Ingold Inglorion, Rhodry, Jill, and Alain are all inscribed on my memory—and I definitely think the right sibling ended up on the throne in *Crown of Stars*.

Kameron Hurley
Women Destroy Fantasy! Nonfiction Contributor

Ascension **by Jacqueline Koyanagi:** I blurbed this book thusly, "There are badass women running around doing badass things and falling in love with each other and with starships, and I'm totally down with that." I rest my case.

Black Wine **by Candas Jane Dorsey:** This book opens with: "There is a scarred, twisted old madwoman in a cage in the courtyard." And just gets better from there. Folks who read [my story] "Enyo-Enyo" will see some similarities in theme here. Weird time displacement, meetings-of-oneselves, despair, loss, madness.

The Etched City **by K.J. Bishop:** It's about two old war veterans—a roguish man and jaded woman doctor—who try to carve out a life for themselves after being on the losing side of a great war.

Sandra Wickham
Women Destroy Fantasy! Nonfiction Contributor

- **Kim Harrison**: The Hollows series

- **Patricia Briggs**: The Mercy Thompson series & the Alpha and Omega series

- **Richelle Mead**: Dark Swan series

- **Devon Monk**: Allie Beckstrom series

- **Kat Richardson**: Greywalker series

- **Kelley Armstrong:** Women of the Otherworld series

- **Diana Rowland:** The Kara Gillian series & the White Trash Zombie series

Kat Howard
Women Destroy Fantasy! Nonfiction Contributor

Jonathan Strange & Mr Norrell **by Susanna Clarke:** This book is in my top five books of all time. It is an enormous doorstop of a book, complete with footnotes (which you must read, because some of the most gorgeous and eerie bits of the story are tucked into the footnotes.) I reread it every year. Reading this book is the closest I have ever come to feeling like the world is magic, that it is tucked away, waiting for us to wake it up.

Mortal Love by **Elizabeth Hand:** Really, it would be hard to go wrong with reading anything that Elizabeth Hand has written, and so I recommend you do. But *Mortal Love* has so many of my favorite things—art and poets and rock stars and mythology. Reading it feels like drinking absinthe. Pair it with A. S. Byatt's *Possession*.

All Our Pretty Songs by **Sarah McCarry:** A punk version of the Orpheus myth, set in a city that may well be early '90s Seattle. Lush language, and one of the best and strongest female friendships I have ever read. If I had found this book when I was younger, I'd have bits of it tattooed on my body. And it's the first of a trilogy, so you have even more gorgeous heartbreak waiting for you.

Shanna Germain
Women Destroy Fantasy! Nonfiction Contributor

All the Wind-Wracked Stars by **Elizabeth Bear:** The language breaks my writer heart, because I know that in a million years, I will never write anything so dangerously beautiful, and because I fall in love with the characters. They delight me and inspire me, and then break my heart into a thousand glittering shards, every time.

The Handmaid's Tale by **Margaret Atwood:** I used to think that I loved this book purely for nostalgic reasons—it was one of the first books that I read where I remember feeling so connected to a female character, especially because I understood, perhaps for the first time, that there was a possible future, a possible world, where I could be treated in a certain way because of my gender. But when I went back and re-read it recently, I discovered that it wasn't all nostalgia. This book still burns with a brilliantly drawn protagonist, deft turns of phrase, and a scary view of a future that continues to resonate with me.

Who Fears Death by **Nnedi Okorafor:** The non-linear, punch-in-the-gut ride that this futuristic novel takes you on is so brave and fierce and complex that I feel like I could return to it again and again and find something new and wondrous inside it. This novel is beautiful and terrifying in that beauty.

Sofia Samatar
Women Destroy Fantasy! Nonfiction Contributor

Kalpa Imperial **by Angélica Gorodischer:** Translated by Ursula K. Le Guin, this is the first work by the prolific Gorodischer to appear in English. A collection of linked stories on the rise and fall of empires and the lives of ordinary people caught up in history.

Cloud & Ashes **by Greer Gilman:** A trilogy in one volume, set in Gilman's astonishingly rich Cloud mythos. Gilman is the heir of Shakespeare; don't miss this intoxicating blend of folklore, symbolism, and magic.

Redemption in Indigo **by Karen Lord:** This is Lord's debut novel. Inspired by a Senegalese folktale, it's a beautifully told and very funny adventure of love and chaos.

Dana Watson
Women Destroy Fantasy! Staff

I have several female authors that I will read absolutely anything by: **Tanya Huff**, **Elizabeth Bear**, and **Seanan McGuire**. All three of them write heedless of genre lines pretty widely, but I started all of them through fantasy. (Also **Ilona Andrews**, but that's technically a husband & wife team writing under one name.)

Other authors whose fantasy I've loved over the years include: **Melanie Rawn**, **Kate Elliott**, **Mercedes Lackey**, and **Jennifer Roberson**. **Tamora Pierce's YA**, of course. And I'm not sure any list is complete without **Robin McKinley's** *The Blue Sword*.

Jude Griffin
Women Destroy Fantasy! Staff

The Fifth Sacred Thing **by Starhawk** is the only book to ever make me feel homesick for a world that didn't exist, but was surely mine. Also:

- **The Hollows Series by Kim Harrison**

- *Ship of Magic* **by Robin Hobb**

- *The Hero and the Crown* **by Robin McKinley**

- *The Sevenwater trilogy* by **Juliet Marillier**

- *Kushiel's Dart* by **Jacqueline Carey**

- *Graceling* by **Kristin Cashore**

- *Poison Study* by **Maria V. Snyder**

- *Wild Magic* by **Tamora Pierce**

- *Son of Avonar* by **Carol Berg**

Laurel Amberdine
Women Destroy Fantasy! Staff

The Golden City and **The Seat of Magic** by **J. Kathleen Cheney:** Alternate 1905 Portugal with cool magical sea people.

The Cassie Scot series by **Christine Amsden:** Fun, romantic urban fantasy series about a young woman with no magic ability trying to make a name for herself in a town full of powerful sorcerers. Small press release.

Rachael Jones
Women Destroy Fantasy! Staff

The Hero and the Crown by **Robin McKinley:** I read a lot of fantasy as child, and this was the first one I remember really seeing myself in, after a long parade of Arthurian-type fantasy where women are doled out as prizes or are treated to the typical madonna/whore roles. In many ways, it was my introduction to feminist lit, and it's always stayed with me.

The Earthsea Cycle by **Ursula K. Le Guin:** Probably needs no explanation, and I'm sure I'm not the only one recommending it.

Jonathan Strange and Mr. Norrell by **Susanna Clarke:** Because it's over 1,000 pages long and I still got mad when it ended because it was too dang short! It's a story with a lot of moving parts—historical components mixed with folklore, tackling a lot of complex interpersonal relationships. I also loved how it tackled the theme of racial identity and the very real problems of race relations and slavery in the period, all tied into the novel's climax and resolution. Amazing stuff.

Author Spotlight: Kate Hall

Laurel Amberdine

What were some of the events or ideas that inspired this story?

This is a story about anger as much as art: about anger's power to trap and destroy, as well as its power to liberate. The scream is the anger that lives in every person who is forced to be someone/something they don't want to be, and it can either set you free or doom you. For the people in Felicity's society, anger ignored results either in the smothering of their true selves, and a life watching mirrors for the telltale return of feathers (for who you really are can never be entirely killed no matter how much you try) or—if you aren't successful at stifling yourself—turning into a bird outright. This is an idea that has been with me for some time, one that sharpened every time I saw society point a stern finger at an individual or group of people and say "If you want to be welcome, you have to abide by our rules," and then watched those people bend and break themselves into unrecognizable shapes to try and obey those limiting (and often arbitrary) rules.

Women in speculative fiction have heard for years about how they must write, act, sound or look in order to keep "their place" at the speculative fiction table, and for years many have had to smother their distinctive voices in order to meet those "rules." Women writers of color are told that dialect in their narration or dialogue is "alienating," lesbian writers are told their characters "will be hard to connect with," women who are not conventionally beautiful are advised not to attach author photos to the jackets of their novels. Our society tries to tell us, "Contort yourself into our box of 'acceptable lady writer' and maybe then we'll take you seriously." This made me angry. It continues to make me angry now. So, rather than smother said anger, I wrote about it.

A nightingale is the result of stifled music, and a seagull is the result of stifled scrimshaw carving. What other art/birds transformations might there be?

The transformation into a bird wasn't strictly due just to loss of art (though artists like Felicity and Claudette struggle more than others with turning or giving up their passion). The transformation could also be based on the qualities of the people themselves: Claudette loved music, Felicity loved the fierce beauty of the ocean and ships. In my notes for the original draft, Felicity's mother gave up dance, rather than turn into a swallow, a graceful bird that swoops and dances in flight. Other transformations in the story are related to the person's character: Mrs. von Moren, who loved and lost her only child, is turning into a cardinal, a bird known for being extremely protective of its young.

The only options available to Felicity and the others in her town seem to be to deny their art fully or to turn into birds. Felicity winds up as a seagull. Do you think that's a happier ending for her than how the others live?

That's a hard question. On the one hand, yes: as a bird, Felicity is free of the stifling society that tried to force her into a tidy box, one that denied her the thing she loved. On the other hand, no, because in becoming a bird, Felicity ceased to be Felicity. The woman she once was disappears entirely into the seagull. The tragedy of the story is that Felicity was shown a third way—the way of the woman in yellow, who didn't fear society and flouted the rules and norms that might have smothered her—but she didn't see it in time.

As a part of this special Women Destroy Fantasy! issue, can you share some of your favorite fantasy stories by women?

If I had to choose only a few, I would say the Nightrunner series by Lynn Flewelling, *The Night Circus* by Erin Morgenstern, "Phosphorous" by Veronica Schanos, and the Clockwork Century series by Cherie Priest. My one regret is that my list of favorites isn't more diverse, a situation I am in the process of rectifying.

What are you working on now?

Right now my major project is a YA novel I've been rewriting and revising for the last year, full of white crows, dimension-hopping shadows, and a pair of gutsy Dutch sisters! I've also been writing and critiquing short stories with my classmates from Odyssey Writing Workshop (class of '13), which has been a wonderful ongoing exercise in perseverance, craft development, and remembering to write every day.

Author Spotlight: H.E. Ruolo

Lee Hallison

What was the seed for this story?

The story began with the idea of a superhero whose power worked against her. From there, many ideas I'd been interested in exploring finally came together, and others were thrust upon me as the story developed.

Aisha, whose appearance is damaged, and the main character called Vixen, who has supreme control over her appearance, naturally feed into discussions of how women are presented, where they find their worth, and assumptions we make about ourselves that influence others who are different from us.

Aisha's skill with needle and thread are unusual for a superhero. Are you a seamstress, or do you like working with your hands?

I know only the basics of sewing. I gave Aisha the ability because it's solitary, and something she might have done before the violence against her. The familiarity makes it easy for her to dismiss her own powers.

Pregnancy also is unusual in a superhero story. Why did you choose to have her pregnant and needing a replacement instead of, for instance, old and retiring?

The story already has dark elements. Although old age is sometimes treated reverently, I liked the hopefulness inherent in pregnancy, which has the possibility for both joy and anguish. Vixen goes from supreme power over her physicality, to begging someone else for help with a body that is betraying her. When superheroes are relatable they are more interesting; there are aspects of life, no matter who you are, that can derail all plans.

The main character realizes she set things up so that other women would not want to be superheroes, but cannot find even a male superhero or a child to take her place. She did not change the cards or messaging before she returns to Aisha—will she learn her lesson and make changes to the images projected to the world?

Aisha isn't the only person to change during the course of this story. Vixen is shaken from complacency in her world view. She hasn't had to question her self-worth the way Aisha has.

She is confident in part because she is able to control every aspect of herself. When she loses that ability, she can relate better to Aisha despite all their differences. Few of us question how our assumptions influence the world around us. She has a chance to see what she's built, and I do believe her regret is real and will lead to action. She was always concerned about being a good role model. She's a superhero, after all, and a parent now.

What's next? You recently signed with a publisher for a book series—are you going to focus solely on that or continue writing short stories on the side?

Yes, I signed a three book deal with Permuted Press, and my first book is expected to come out in 2015. Even though I'm committed to writing the sequels, I'll still find time for short stories. Some ideas refuse to be ignored, and I find the restraints of a shorter medium inspires my creativity.

Author Spotlight:
T. Kingfisher

Liz Argall

I find that writers often re-imagine the fairytales they love the most or hate the most. I hated Cinderella with a burning passion as a kid, and so I loved your re-imagining. What is your relationship with the Cinderella fairytale and has your relationship changed over time?

I am right there with you—Cinderella was never one of my favorites! I have a vague memory of watching the Disney cartoon as a small child and finding the "Bippity-Boppity-Boo" song sort of embarrassing. Many fairy tales have their own sort of logic and don't hold up very well to scrutiny, but Cinderella's particularly bad in that regard—can you imagine what that slipper would be like after it had made the rounds of the kingdom? Particularly if you have people hacking their heels and toes off to fit into it! (I know, I know, it's supposed to be enchanted. Still.) And it also assumes that you can come in out of the scullery and walk right into a ballroom, and those are two entirely different skillsets. When would she have learned ballroom dancing in the first place?

I also felt the stepsisters got the short end of the stick. I had two stepsisters growing up, and they were both perfectly nice girls and we all just sort of lumped together and made the best of things.

I think you've written the best re-imagined selkie story I've ever read ("The Jackalope Wives") and with Hannah we have a Cinderella who's absolutely my Cinderella. Are there other fairytales you'd like to re-imagine?

Aw, thank you! Actually, there's a lot of fairy tales I'd like to re-imagine—it's one of my great joys. As much as I may grumble about some of the logic holes in fairy tales, there's a real weight and mythic quality that makes them a lot of fun to work with. I'm currently working on a novel-length retelling of Bluebeard and I have a comic for kids coming out next year that's about a hamster princess who is nominally Sleeping Beauty… except it's a hamster wheel instead of a spinning wheel.

Did you pick tufted titmouse as the species of bird because it's a terrific name? Or do you and tufted titmice share a more elaborate history together? Please say you have an elaborate back story!

Oh wow, now I wish I had a better one! "There I was, on fire, and the tufted titmouse pulled the fire alarm . . ." But no, they're actually one of my common garden birds that show up on the bird feeder. They're a really cute little bird, like a tiny gray and white cardinal, and a fairly brave one. There's a park up in Cape Cod where the titmice and the chickadees are so used to being fed that they'll land on your hand, and I've had one perch on my thumb for a few seconds. They weigh absolutely nothing. You can feel a little bit of scratchiness from the claws, but that's all.

Plus, it *is* a great name.

Do you think Hannah ever gets an orangery?

It's possible, but I think the Gardener is right—they're a lot of trouble in a cold climate! The lengths to which people went to, growing citrus back in the day… even as recently as the Regency, people are pouring vast amounts of money into maintaining hothouses, and I don't know if Hannah would think it worth the effort. Many of them were symbols of wealth as much as useful gardening.

That said, with a properly facing brick wall and some ingenuity, Hannah could probably grow some pretty exotic things. Gardeners have been keeping tropical plants going in less than tropical climates for centuries. I like to think she figures out how to grow oranges and pomegranates, at least!

Why nasturtium seeds?… I mean I know nasturtiums are beautiful and delicious, you have great taste in food and agriculture throughout this story. In my experience nasturtium seeds is a great hardy annual that enjoys poor soil that often self seeds, so it might not be too hard to get seeds once the plant is present in the region. Does the Duke control access to this exotic seed?

Well, nasturtiums are originally from Peru, and there are two varieties. The first one has an almost vine-like habit, and it's actually pretty picky—the Spanish imported it, but it was apparently not that easy to grow. Then the classic round-leaf version we all know and love got introduced somewhere around the 17th century, and it's a much sturdier plant. So there's about a century-long window where nasturtiums would probably have been known as a rare ornamental, before the Dutch brought the other species over and those spread like wildfire. Most of what we grow today is a hybrid of the two species. (On a good year, they take over my garden. On a bad year, they take over my garden... and the deck... and try to come into the house . . .)

As a grubby gal who's spent a lot of time in the garden or in an orchard I love all the agricultural details in this story. What sort of mix of personal experience and research did you use? Do you have any amusing gardening or agricultural anecdotes to share with us?

Well, the sorts of things that gardeners find funny might be a little opaque to non-gardeners—I mean, I think it's funny when I have a cucumber grow into a lattice, so you find this gigantic bright-orange thing the size of a baseball bat embedded between the slats and you have to cut it out with a knife! (Do other people find that funny? I don't think other people find that funny . . . .) But yes, I'm an avid gardener, which mostly means I kill a lot of plants every year and get very excited over manure. And I spend a lot of time muttering to myself about sowing beets and whether it's worth putting down radishes or whether they'll just bolt in the heat.

The closest I think I come to a genuinely funny gardening anecdote... well, I'm pretty bad with spatial measurements. So the first time I went to buy mulch from a garden supplier, I thought I wanted four cubic yards, and they're used to doing really big bulk orders, so they said "Are you sure that's enough?" And I thought, "Oh, hmm, maybe that's not as much as I thought it was, that's only like three feet by twelve feet, right? Maybe I should get more... It's not like mulch goes bad, and you always lowball how much of something you need..." So I ordered seven cubic yards and went home feeling like I had been very responsible and proactive and completely forgetting that a cube has a third dimension.

And then the dump truck arrived. And I was left with Mt. Mulch in my driveway—it was nearly as tall as I was, and it was just me and a pitchfork and a wheelbarrow! It took me a good two months to get it all moved around. I mulched *everything*.

What needs destroying in fantasy?

Probably everything, at one time or another! But at the moment, I wouldn't mind seeing—oh, less unrelenting awful people, maybe. I get very tired of horrible people doing horrible things for no apparent reason beyond wallowing in horribleness. I'm not asking for an end to conflicts or villains—we need plots to make stories, after all!—but I look at so many fantasies and the only characters I recognize from real life are the minor spear-carriers and the comic relief.

Perhaps I am just lucky to be surrounded by basically decent people who don't kick puppies professionally. But it often strikes me that a lot of heroes in fantasy novels are people who, in real life, we would back away from going "Ooooookay, dude... I'm just gonna... go... over here now . . . ."

Maybe we've got enough dragonslayers for the moment, and it's time for some people who are out doing environmental assessments on dragon eggshell thickness and dissecting griffin pellets to see what percentage of their diet is fish or something.

Author Spotlight: Julia August

Sandra O'Dell

"Drowning in Sky" is filled with poetry and a wondrous blend of imagery. Many of the images are quite old, echoing the goddess cycle from long before pre-Dorian myths and stories. What inspired you to weave this particular retelling?

Oh, this might get long. The inspiration for this story was one part myth to two parts history: the myth is the story of Arachne, of course, but the historical details are the sinking of Helike and the statue of Nike Apteros. I threw various other bits and pieces into the mix, but I'll concentrate on the important ones here:

(1) Arachne is the obvious role model for a woman who works magic through her weaving and who sucks the life from her lovers: although Arakhnë in the story claims to be the weaver, not the spider, in actual fact she's both. Even the myth here is really about how Arakhnë interprets her cultural heritage and uses it as a prism for how she relates to the women who sent her into exile.

(2) Helike was a Greek city that was struck by an earthquake in 373 BC and vanished into a lagoon overnight; later visitors reported seeing the ruins, and also the complaints of fishermen who caught their nets on a submerged bronze statue of Poseidon. Some people put the earthquake down to Poseidon's anger at the Helikonians. I generally prefer to make my major sea deity female, but the luxury of adjusting details like that is one reason why I write historical fantasy rather than straight historical fiction.

(3) And the Athenian statue of Nike Apteros ("Wingless Victory") was

unusual: in general, the goddess Nike was represented with wings, and there was a story that this particular statue had been made without wings so that Nike (that is, Victory), could never fly away from Athens. I always thought that clipping the wings of a goddess sounded like a proposition that would attract the wrong sort of divine attention, so even after I looked it up and discovered Nike Apteros had probably originally been an Athena Nike ("Victorious Athena") who was later interpreted as plain Nike, I wasn't going to throw the idea away.

Ann's pain is deliberately remote which makes it all the more heartbreaking. There is her grief for the duke, for the city of Florens and the dead she returned to motion, for Arakhnë, even for herself. You also touch on a terrible, lonely anger. What is it about the appeal of such primal emotions that encouraged your exploration in this story?

Remoteness is one of Ann's key characteristics. She's seen and done a lot of damage in the past, and most of it hasn't touched her very much, because it happened and/or she did it to people she didn't care much about or, worse, didn't find at all interesting. Ann's usual approach to human society is summed up in the moment when she walks unseeing through a blur of people and hones in on the one person in this whole city who does interest her. At this point in Ann's life, though, she's dealing not just with loss but also with the fact that she cares about the people and things she's lost, which is all the more upsetting because it's such an unfamiliar experience for her. Everyone experiences grief and loss at some point, but I find it particularly interesting to write about how it affects characters who aren't psychologically prepared to deal with it at all.

Modern fantasy is often seen as the realm of "women" and science fiction "men." Do you feel your own explorations of stories have been influenced by these attitudes?

No, not really. I have always read fantasy written by women and men and I have always read (rather less, I admit) science fiction written by women and men. I suppose the short answer is that I generally lean towards historical-flavoured fantasy because I love history, rather than for any other reason.

As a young writer, were there any particular women authors who challenged you to explore deeper meaning in your fiction?

Lots! I feel I may have been scarred for life by the looooooooooong wait times between books by Katherine Kerr and Kate Elliott particularly, and should really have been more grateful to find all three books of Barbara Hambly's original Darwath trilogy on someone else's bookshelf than I was. But I was about twelve and pretty innocent in the ways of publication schedules then. And there are too many other beloved writers and characters to list here, but Patricia C. Wrede's Cimorene from the Enchanted Forest Chronicles will always have a place in my heart.

What can we expect from you in the future? Are there any other mythic retellings on the horizon?

Maybe! But mixed with quite a lot of history, too.

AUTHOR SPOTLIGHT: DELIA SHERMAN

SANDRA O'DELL

This wonderful story about communication and discovery has remarkably little dialog, and the lack only serves to enhance the telling. How did you approach the challenge of writing characters who did not share a common language, or even point of reference?

The true answer to this question has nothing to do with craft. "Miss Carstairs" was the second story I'd ever written—not in my life, but as a serious writer with a one sale under her belt. It was 1983 or 4, and I didn't really know what I was doing. I had never been to a writer's workshop, taken a course, or read a book on writing. I was simply trying to make my ideas and characters line up with my inspiration—a clay statue of a merman I bought in Provincetown in 1983 and put on the window of my beach cottage so it could look out to sea. I was also reading Darwin's *The Origin of Species*, and was fascinated by his chapters on animal communication. Also teaching Freshman Composition to students who seemed to come from a different planet and a difficult patch in a friendship with a woman I liked enormously but found hard to get along with. Not that I was thinking about that consciously—I couldn't have. Consciously, it was Darwin and the statue and the pros and cons of the solitary life. As for the communications, Darwin himself, in the first edition of *The Origin of Species*, hypothesizes about marine mammals evolving telepathy, which would have atrophied when they came to spend more time on land, but possibly not disappeared—kind of like a mental appendix. After reading that, how Miss Carstairs would communicate with her catch was pretty much set.

The narrative voice carries the story along, lending itself to the characters and setting, and harkening back to the fiction of the late 1800s and early 1900s. Why did you chose this particular setting and voice?

Well, what other voice would suit a story about Darwin and evolution and women who were educated and uninterested in marriage or charity work or even community (or at least the kind of communities open to them) and big, lonely houses above the sea? Seriously, though. At the time, I was reading a lot of 19th century fiction—mostly English, but some American. It was, as it were, the water I was swimming in and by far the easiest voice for me to write in. As for the setting, I was living on Cape Cod at the time—which has no cliffs, but hey. Gothic houses are set on cliffs. It's a thing.

Fantasy is often defined by its tropes—mermaids, sirens, dryads—yet your merman deliberately subverts the hyper-feminine magical creature trope. What made you decide to flip this particular stereotype and present a distinctly male character?

Well, my merman statue was male, so there's that. There's also the fact that long-haired sirens with big breasts have always struck me as, er, aerodynamically unsound. I mean, think of the drag. Think of the difficulty of maneuvering really fast burdened with pectoral bags of tissue instead of fins. Sure, arms make up for something, but that's more than balanced by the possibility of getting your hands tangled in all that hair. No, traditional mermaids would never have evolved. And this is a story about evolution, according to the best 19th century principles.

This story presents a merfolk species based more in the realm of science than one of magic. If you were to return to this world, what other magical species would you like to present in such a fashion?

When I wrote the story, I felt I was writing in this world, our world, one lacking any magic outside the ordinary miracles of scientific, observable fact. It might be interesting to look at some of the blended creatures from Greek mythology, like hippogriffs and centaurs, or from Pliny and Herodotus, like the headless Blemmeyae. It's always fun to see what happens when you rub magic and science together. After all, they are strongly allied.

Many of your novels and stories focus on the struggle for personal freedom as seen through the lens of history, *The Freedom Maze* **in particular. What spawned your interest in the history of such struggles?**

Until you asked this question, I had no idea that's what I was writing about, but of course you're right. The thing about writing is that while you're consciously researching and writing a story about, say, scientifically plausible mermen, asexual women, and the infinite varieties of human affection, your subconscious is busily weaving a different story entirely, about love that seeks to own, or plain, middle-aged, scientific spinsters trying to make a place for herself in a culture that doesn't believe such a creature could possibly exist. So I guess I must be interested in such struggles, although I wasn't consciously aware of it. Perhaps it comes from coming of age in the 60s. Perhaps it comes from having been something of a disappointment to my mother, who would have preferred a biddable social butterfly to the stubborn scholar she got. I did, however, get my love of history from her—or from the biographies of Eleanor of Aquitaine, Mary Tudor, and Elizabeth I on her bedside table. I always loved historical fiction, and when I started to write, that's what I wrote. At first it was because the past was so much more colorful than the rather colorless present that was my graduate school experience. But it grew into a strong sense that it's important to look at the past because our present grows out of it, both the positive and the negative. The past may be a foreign country where they do things differently, but it's also our ancestral home that has shaped who we are.

Also, putting things in the past allows me to write about myself without having to reveal anything specific. I like that. And the clothes. I wouldn't want to wear a corset, but I like writing about them.

What can we expect from Delia Sherman in the future?

More corsets. The book I'm going to start as soon as I hand in the one I'm currently revising is a clockwork-punk thriller-mystery-romance-ghost story-sub-Dickensian thing about a Welsh blacksmith's daughter who becomes an inventor, moves to London, and gets mixed up with a Great Detective. After that, I've got a Hansel and Gretel retelling set in New York in 1929 to research and write. Possibly more short stories, although I'm not a natural short story writer and writing one takes me a lot longer than I wish it would.

Author Spotlight: Nalo Hopkinson

Liz Argall

I love the multiple uses of eggs and bottles in this story. I was particularly struck by idea that the protagonist was the egg, slowly and perniciously sucked into this bottle of a relationship. I was so drawn to this aspect of the story that the Bluebeard element caught me by surprise and made me gasp out loud. When and how did the bottle and egg themes emerge when you were writing this story?

I wrote it so long ago that it's difficult to remember. I think I wanted to write about Bluebeard, so I probably searched my mental bank of fascinations to find associations. Bluebeard gives his wife an egg, and when she enters the forbidden room, she drops the egg in horror and gets blood on it. The bloodstain won't come out, and that's how Bluebeard knows she's been in the room. So right away, the folktale has associations with menstruation and a loss of both innocence and reproductive possibility (the latter in the sense that if you're trying to get pregnant, every month you menstruate is a month in which you didn't succeed). I've known the "Yung Kyung Pyung" snippet since I was a girl, though I don't remember from which folktale. Those three sisters have the most arresting names! Especially Eggie-Law. And I'd recently read the science experiment about creating a vacuum in order to suck a boiled egg into a bottle. Have yet to do that experiment. Plan to do so someday. Anyway, take all three of those eggy associations, sprinkle on the seasoning of knowing that the "Fitcher's Bird" version of the story includes the wife dressing up as an enormous bird, squish all together, and come up with a Bluebeardish story line that could make them all be part of the story. That's the closest I can explain how I did it.

The entrapment of the duppy wives adds a brilliant extra level to this re-imagining as well as uncertainty around the ending. I found myself wondering if there were other layers of Caribbean folk tales and folk lore that I might not have the depth of Caribbean literacy to see in the text? Are there any other interesting cookies or references you'd like to share with us?

There's the bottle tree. It's like a wasp trap for ghosts. It's a tree or section of a tree that has been trimmed of its leaves. You shove bottles over the trimmed ends of the branches. Blue glass bottles are best. You erect the bottle tree outside your home. The duppies go inside the bottles and can't figure out how to get out, because the bottles are upside-down. If they're trapped inside the bottle tree, they can't come into your house to trouble you.

The tragedy and visceral loss of human potential through colonial power structures and internalized racism is made flesh in this story. It makes a powerful statement. Bluebeard can be a hard character to care about, but I found my grief for Samuel shot through the roof as my dread of him grew. Samuel is so trapped in a cold world that he rages and kills things that might make him experience real warmth and human connection. The possibility that dark skin, especially his dark skin, could be beautiful is such a violent attack on the colonial values he has internalized that it will drive him to murder. Beatrice is a very likeable character in part because she resists colonial values and is able to see, enjoy and appreciate beauty—beauty in general, but particularly beauty in brown skin. I feel like her enjoyment and appreciation of the world around her is what helps her be strong. What role do you think beauty and pleasure serve when challenging & resisting invasive colonial constructs?

The thing about Beatrice is that she's also affected by the same colonialism. She knows full well that her lighter skin colour, less bushy hair, and less African features make her desirable to certain men, and she's not above preening so as to attract them. And of course she should be able to enjoy her own beauty, to show it off, to flirt. But it's not an uncomplicated pleasure. It's a pleasure that the world works very hard to deny dark-skinned women. It's easier for Beatrice to love all the shades of brown skin because she's allowed to love her own. (Most of the time. In that particular location. If she were to move to white-dominant North America, dominant culture values would effectively make her into a negro first and devalue her beauty. And she'd still have to deal with the exoticization from straight white and black men alike, with the resentment she already experiences from some darker-skinned women. No one of any race or combination of races escapes racism. We all just experience it differently, depending on our circumstances.) In addition to all that, Beatrice pretty much ignores other women—this story deliberately fails the Delany/Bechdel test—and has chosen to use her light-skin privilege to snag a mate who will support her rather than figuring out how to support herself. And yet she is a good soul. She truly loves Samuel; she wouldn't be with him if she didn't. She's compassionate and sensual. She seeks joy and tries to share it with others. She treats others with respect. She's supportive to her man. It should be enough. But the world is harsh, and often those things aren't enough. Beatrice has put herself into a situation of depending solely on Samuel. When he turns out to be murderously unhinged, the only beings she can reach to for help are the angry ghosts of his previous victims. That may be enough to save her, or it may not.

Gloria has been with the household for a long time. Do you think Gloria has a sense of what happened to Samuel's previous wives? I feel like she is sincere about a pickney being a blessing, but she certainly left the house swiftly when Beatrice announced she was going to tell him!

In my mind, Gloria doesn't know. She leaves quickly because it's Friday night and she wants to be about her own business. She's an employee, not a member of the household, and she wisely never forgets that.

What does it feel like knowing your short story is studied in universities and that people write papers about it?

I don't know whether this one is studied in universities, but others of mine certainly have been. It's the best. Feeling. Ever.

What needs destroying in fantasy?

The practice of representing non-Christian gods as demons that can be vanquished by chanting prayers at them in church Latin. The ubiquitous usage of invariably accurate books of prophecy as a short-cut around actual plot development. As a part of that, the faux-mystical assertion that unspecified "ancients" were able to see into the future. As a corollary to that, the implication that our fates are pre-determined. Because how boring is that?

Coming Attractions

This issue was a special one-off issue of *Fantasy*, so there *is* no next issue per se. But never fear! There will be plenty more fantasy in next month's issue of *Lightspeed*. Coming up in November…

We have original science fiction by Sunny Moraine ("What Glistens Back") and Annalee Newitz ("Drones Don't Kill People"), along with SF reprints by Susan C. Petrey ("Spidersong") and Roz Kaveney ("Instructions").

Plus, we have original fantasy by Kat Howard ("A Flock of Grief") and Matthew Hughes ("Enter Saunterance"), and fantasy reprints by Gheorghe Săsărman ("Sah-Hara") and Jennifer Stevenson ("Solstice").

All that, and of course we also have our usual assortment of author and artist spotlights, along with a pair of feature interviews. For our ebook readers, we also have our usual ebook-exclusive novella reprint and a pair of novel excerpts.

It's another great issue, so be sure to check it out.

• • •

Looking further ahead, there is, at least, the possibility of another issue of *Fantasy* down the line. When we did our Women Destroy Science Fiction Kickstarter campaign, we announced at the end of it that in 2015 we'd be doing a Queers Destroy Science Fiction! special issue. Well, as with the WDSF project, we'll have some stretch goals to unlock, one of which will be a Queers Destroy Fantasy! issue. So keep an eye out for news about the campaign. Stay tuned to our new website for the Destroy Projects at DestroySF.com.

Subscriptions
& Ebooks

If you enjoyed reading this issue, please consider subscribing to *Lightspeed* (which incorporates *Fantasy Magazine)* or *Nightmare.* Subscribing is a great way to support the magazines, and you'll get your issues in the convenient ebook format of your choice. You can subscribe directly from our website, via Weightless Books, or via Amazon.com. For more information, visit lightspeedmagazine.com/subscribe or nightmare-magazine.com/subscribe. We also have individual ebook issues available at a variety of ebook vendors, and we now have Ebook Bundles available in the *Fantasy, Lightspeed,* and *Nightmare* ebookstores, where you can buy in bulk and save! So if you need to catch up on the magazines that's a great way to do so. Visit fantasy-magazine.com/store, lightspeedmagazine.com/store, or nightmare-magazine.com/store for more information.

ABOUT THE EDITORS

CAT RAMBO
GUEST EDITOR & ORIGINAL FICTION EDITOR

Cat Rambo lives, writes, and teaches by the shores of an eagle-haunted lake in the Pacific Northwest. Her 150+ fiction publications include stories in *Asimov's, Clarkesworld Magazine,* and Tor.com. Her short story, "Five Ways to Fall in Love on Planet Porcelain," from her story collection *Near + Far* (Hydra House Books), was a 2012 Nebula nominee. Her editorship of *Fantasy Magazine* earned her a World Fantasy Award nomination in 2012. For more about her, as well as links to her fiction, see kittywumpus.net.

TERRI WINDLING
REPRINT EDITOR

Terri Windling is a writer, editor, and artist specializing in fantasy literature and mythic arts. She has published more than forty books, winning nine World Fantasy Awards, the Mythopoeic Award, the Bram Stoker Award, and placing on the short lists for the Tiptree and Shirley Jackson Awards. She received the S.F.W.A. Solstice Award in 2010 for "outstanding contributions to the speculative fiction field as a writer, editor, artist, educator, and mentor." Her work has been translated into French, German, Spanish, Italian, Czech, Russian, Turkish, Korean, and Japanese. She has served on the boards of the Interstitial Arts Foundation and the Mythic Imagination Institute (U.S.), and is currently a member of the advisory board for the Sussex Centre for Folklore, Fairy Tales, and Fantasy at the University of Chichester (U.K.).

WENDY N. WAGNER
NONFICTION & MANAGING EDITOR

Wendy N. Wagner's short fiction has appeared in magazines and anthologies including *Beneath Ceaseless Skies, The Lovecraft eZine, Armored, The Way of the Wizard,* and *Heiresses of Russ 2013: The Year's Best Lesbian Speculative Fiction.* Her first novel, *Skinwalkers,* is a Pathfinder Tales adventure. She served as the Assistant Editor of *Fantasy Magazine* and is currently the Managing/ Associate Editor of *Lightspeed* and *Nightmare.* An avid gamer and gardener, she lives in Portland, Oregon, with her very understanding family. Follow her on Twitter @wnwagner.

GABRIELLE DE CUIR
PODCAST PRODUCER

Gabrielle de Cuir has narrated over one hundred titles specializing in fantasy, humor, and titles requiring extensive foreign language and accent skills. Her "velvet touch" as an actors' director has earned her a special place in the audio-book world as the foremost choice for best-selling authors and celebrities. She is the writer and director of the Award winning short film *The Delivery,* which deals with an Alice-in-Wonderland version of audiobooks. Her own film credits include *Ghostbusters, American President,* and *Fright Night.* She spent her childhood in Rome growing up with her wildly artistic and cine-matic father, John de Cuir, four-time Academy Award winning Production Designer, an upbringing that taught her to be fluent in Romance languages and to have an unusual appetite for visual delights.

ELIZABETH LEGGETT
ART DIRECTOR

Elizabeth Leggett is a twenty-year veteran freelance illustrator. Her artistic influences include Michael Kaluta, Donato Giancola, John Jude Palencar, and Jeremy Geddes. She completed a seventy-eight-card tarot in a single year and launched it into a successful Kickstarter (Portico Tarot and Art Prints). In December, she won two places in Jon Schindehette's ArtOrder Inspiration, and she provided internal art for the Women Destroy Science Fiction! issue of *Lightspeed* and is the Women Destroy Fantasy! cover artist and art director.

JUDE GRIFFIN,
ASSISTANT & AUTHOR SPOTLIGHTS EDITOR

Jude Griffin is an envirogeek, writer, and photographer. She has trained llamas at the Bronx Zoo; was a volunteer EMT, firefighter, and HAZMAT responder; worked as a guide and translator for journalists covering combat in Central

America; lived in a haunted village in Thailand; ran an international frog monitoring network; and loves happy endings. Bonus points for frolicking dogs and kisses backlit by a shimmering full moon.

SANDRA ODELL,
AUTHOR SPOTLIGHT INTERVIEWER

Sandra Odell is an avid reader, compulsive writer, and rabid chocoholic. She attended Clarion West in 2010. Her first collection of short stories was released from Hydra House Books in 2012. She is currently hard at work avoiding her first novel.

LEE HALLISON,
AUTHOR SPOTLIGHT INTERVIEWER

Lee Hallison writes fiction in an old Seattle house where she lives with her patient spouse, an impatient teen, two lovable dogs, and the memories of several wonderful cats. She's held many jobs—among them a bartender, a pastry chef, a tropical plant-waterer, a CPA, and a university lecturer. An East Coast transplant, she simply cannot fathom cherry blossoms in March.

LAUREL AMBERDINE,
AUTHOR SPOTLIGHT INTERVIEWER & COPY EDITOR

Laurel Amberdine was raised by cats in the suburbs of Chicago. She's good at naps, begging for food, and turning ordinary objects into toys. She recently moved to San Francisco with her husband, and is enjoying its vastly superior weather. Between naps she's working on polishing up a few science fiction and fantasy novels, and hopes to send them out into the world soon.

LIZ ARGALL,
AUTHOR SPOTLIGHT INTERVIEWER

Liz Argall destroyed fantasy from an early age, as chewed on books smeared with crayon will attest. She writes fractured fairytales, literary SF and the occasional Jules Vernian ghost story set in space. Her work has been published in places like *Apex Magazine, Strange Horizons, Daily Science Fiction, and This is How You Die: Stories of the Inscrutable, Infallible, Inescapable Machine of Death.* Go read her web comic, *Things Without Arms and Without Legs,* a comic about creatures who are kind: thingswithout.com.

ADDITIONAL STAFF

Copy Editors
Dana Watson
Laurel Amberdine

Proofreaders
Debra Jess
Rachael Jones
Sarah Slatton
Amanda Mitchell

Art Director / Cover Artist
Elizabeth Leggett

Illustrators
Ashley Stewart
K. A. King
Sandra Buskirk
Tara Larsen Chang

Book Production / Layout
Michael Lee

Cover Design
Elizabeth Leggett & Michael Lee

Publisher
John Joseph Adams

First Readers
Alyc Helms
Amber Barkley
Andrea Johnson
Britt Gettys
Caren Gussoff
Christina Vasilevski
Deanna Knippling
Gail Marsella
Georgina Kamsika
Gwen Perkins
Jude Griffin
Kristi Charish
Laura Newsholme
Laurel Amberdine
Lianna Palkovick
Lisa Andrews
Louise Kane
Nicole Walters
Robyn Lupo
Sandra Wickham
Sarah Kirkpatrick
Stephanie Lorée
Stephanie Sursi
Sylvia Hiven

THE APOCALYPSE TRIPTYCH

EDITED BY JOHN JOSEPH ADAMS AND HUGH HOWEY

BEFORE THE APOCALYPSE	DURING THE APOCALYPSE	AFTER THE APOCALYPSE
MARCH 2014	SEPTEMBER 2014	MARCH 2015
Trade Paperback ($17.95)	Trade Paperback ($17.95)	Trade Paperback ($17.95)
Ebook ($4.99)	Ebook ($6.99)	Ebook ($6.99)
Audiobook ($24.95)	Audiobook ($24.95)	Audiobook ($24.95)
ISBN: 978-1495471179	ISBN: 978-1497484375	ISBN: 978-1497484405

FEATURING ALL-NEW, NEVER-BEFORE-PUBLISHED STORIES BY

Charlie Jane Anders	Tobias S. Buckell	Ken Liu	Scott Sigler
Megan Arkenberg	Tananarive Due	Jonathan Maberry	Carrie Vaughn
Paolo Bacigalupi	Jamie Ford	Matthew Mather	Robin Wasserman
Elizabeth Bear	Hugh Howey	Jack McDevitt	David Wellington
Annie Bellet	Jake Kerr	Seanan McGuire	Daniel H. Wilson
Desirina Boskovich	Nancy Kress	Will McIntosh	Ben H. Winters
	Sarah Langan	Leife Shallcross	

Made in the USA
San Bernardino, CA
20 March 2019